COLD
KILLERS

Lee Weeks was born in Devon. She left school at seventeen and, armed with a notebook and very little cash, spent seven years working her way around Europe and South East Asia. She returned to settle in London, marry and raise two children. She has worked as an English teacher and personal fitness trainer. Her books have been *Sunday Times* bestsellers. She now lives in Devon.

ALSO BY LEE WEEKS

Dead of Winter
Cold as Ice
Frozen Grave
Cold Justice

COLD
KILLERS

LEE WEEKS

**SIMON &
SCHUSTER**

London · New York · Sydney · Toronto · New Delhi

A CBS COMPANY

First published in Great Britain by Simon & Schuster UK Ltd, 2016
A CBS COMPANY

1 3 5 7 9 10 8 6 4 2

Simon & Schuster UK Ltd
1st Floor
222 Gray's Inn Road
London WC1X 8HB

www.simonandschuster.co.uk

Simon & Schuster Australia, Sydney
Simon & Schuster India, New Delhi

A CIP catalogue record for this book
is available from the British Library

Hardback ISBN: 978-1-4711-4756-2
eBook ISBN: 978-1-4711-5320-4

Typeset by M Rules
Printed and bound by CPI Group (UK) Ltd, Croydon, CR0 4YY

Simon & Schuster UK Ltd are committed to sourcing paper
that is made from wood grown in sustainable forests and support the Forest
Stewardship Council, the leading international forest certification organisation.
Our books displaying the FSC logo are printed on FSC certified paper.

For Roy Wallace
26/9/1952 – 21/9/2015
Thanks for all the love and laughter.

Prologue

18 December

'Do you know how it is done?'

The question was directed to a man, hog-tied and gagged, lying on the concrete floor. It was never meant to be answered. The man was coming round from a deep, knocked-out sleep. He was trying to focus through the blood in his eyes. 'No? Then I'll tell you.'

He tilted the woman's chair back, so it rested against his thighs, and leaned over her. Lifting her chin, he ran the blunt edge of the knife down her throat.

'Many people believe the right way is to slit across horizontally before dragging the tongue through, but this is not correct.' He looked over at the man on the floor who was screaming into his gag.

'Here, this is where you begin your cut, at the base of the throat, insert here and then carefully drag the knife upwards.' He paused and looked up. 'Say goodbye to your colleague, Inspector Carter.'

Chapter 1

Ten days earlier

'Christ, what a pantomime.' Detective Inspector Dan Carter scrutinised the footage coming to him live as he listened to the commentary from the broadcaster. 'We're taking a big risk here.' Carter crossed his arms over his chest defensively. 'We're fighting fire with fire. I have to justify this going ahead. We've already diverted the traffic. Will we get what we need? Will it lead us to the killer?' He looked across to Robbo, the crime analyst, for an answer. Robbo looked poised to reply, but didn't. Carter continued: 'Are they in the crowd? There are three more gang members in the morgue this morning. This has to work.'

Robbo looked up and over at Carter and gave a smile that didn't reach as far as his eyes. 'It was the right decision. It's going to be worth it,' he answered decisively and gave his reassuring look, which left Carter nodding slowly, uncrossing his arms and tapping his fingers impatiently on the desk as he eyed the screen.

'You don't drop the body of your victim at his mother's doorstep unless you understand the way these East End gangs work. He's a national treasure in the criminal fraternity: lowlife royalty.'

'It was the car park outside her block of flats. Not really at her doorstep. Anyway, Sandra doesn't live there any more: she's another of our prime exports to the Costa del Sol,' Robbo said, scrolling through the images of mugshot photos on his screen. He made notes as he studied the faces. 'Christ, there's a slice of British crime history in the East End today.'

'The apartment block is still family-owned, isn't it?' Carter wasn't letting the point go.

Robbo shrugged, nodded, conceded the point: 'That's a big risk, it's not a family you want to mess with.'

'Talking of risk, the church took a massive one, allowing it to go ahead,' said Carter. 'I wouldn't have been so generous, if I was them. Obviously they had no idea that we'd be using dead Eddie as bait.'

'True, and they probably felt they had no choice,' answered Robbo. 'This was the Butchers' family church. The old man had his funeral service there. Harold got married in it. Eddie was christened, even went to Sunday school here.'

'Tony didn't get married in it, though.' Carter kept his eyes on the screen. 'Too low-key for him: he had a big Essex wedding. And neither did Eddie: he ran off to Vegas when it was his turn.'

Photos of Marbella's Golden Mile popped up on the screen with sunny scenes of Golden Bentleys and infinity pools. There was a photo of Eddie and his wife Della relaxing on sun loungers. Behind them was a shot of their villa, majestic in the sunshine. Eddie Butcher was raising a glass of champagne to the photographer.

'And, what the hell does this commentator think he's doing?' Carter leaned forwards towards the screen, with his hands flat on the desk. 'Let's hear some home truths about Eddie Butcher and the damage he caused instead of treating him like a celebrity. Tell the folks how he got the money to build that Taj Mahal look-alike behind them. We really don't need to see photos of him enjoying a luxury lifestyle on stolen money.'

Robbo mumbled his agreement while crossing to grind some coffee beans and make fresh coffee, his favourite thing. He blended his own beans in his quest for caffeine perfection. He kept the tools necessary for it on top of the filing cabinet in the corner of the room. His office was too small to allow for any other luxuries. Three desks were laid out in a horseshoe shape; whiteboards were on the walls. A printer and filing cabinets took up the rest of the space. Fletcher House had been purpose-built to house three major investigation teams but it had not allowed for the ever-expanding need each team had for space.

Carter continued monitoring his screen as the funeral procession was making its way along the cobbled road leading to St Matthew's Church. As it passed the Old Jewish Bakery, the proprietor, Lev, a large man of Russian Jewish descent, born and raised in the East End, came to stand and pay his respects. He blocked the doorway of his bakery as he watched the cortège pass. He'd been busy all morning. He knew a lot about the life of East End criminals. He stood, head bowed, in deference to a family who had extorted protection money from his family for the last sixty years. He had gained security, stability in a volatile world, and it had allowed his business to survive even in the hard times – *mostly* in the hard times – but he had never been too ambitious, never got too big. He knew his place.

A voice came over the radio: 'A group of gang members approaching across the railway bridge, from the direction of the Catherine Booth allotments, sir, I count nine youths.'

Carter looked at the images coming from the surveillance camera. The graffiti artwork up the steps and across the railway bridge was as bold as the spikes meant to deter the artists. He studied the swagger of the pack: hoods up, eyes down, furtive and jittery, their hands pushed deep inside pockets.

They paused at the painted ballerina on the wall, at the bottom of the steps. She eyed the youths as they passed her and the first few reached the arches beneath the railway line and the mini-cab firms.

'Intercept now,' said Carter. 'Do not allow them to get any further.'

Carter pushed back his black, Italian-heritage hair. His temples were turning silver now that he was edging closer to forty. He'd joined the police force after leaving school. He had been in the major investigation team for the last eight years. 'Who are they, do we know?' he asked as Robbo scrutinised the footage and zoomed in on the group of hooded youths.

'The Blood Boys. They're rising stars in Whitechapel,' he said. 'One of their members was killed in the gang fight last week. They'll be here looking for revenge. They must have decided today was a great day to earn their colours.'

Carter didn't comment, his full attention was on the screen. He was watching plain-clothes officers moving past the ballerina on the steps. He watched them intercept the four youths; the others ran back over the railway bridge.

'Let them go,' Carter said into his radio. 'We have more to worry about. We need every officer to be on high alert now as the crowds converge. Whatever you do don't cause panic; don't disrupt the procession. We are here to watch and observe. If you do make an arrest, make it discreetly.'

Robbo came across to look at Carter's screen with him. Carter had switched the view back to see the horse-drawn carriage carrying the coffin. *Eddie* was spelled out in wreaths of red, white and blue flowers.

'You've got to hand it to them – they've done it in style,' said Robbo. 'The horses look great.'

'The only thing I'd like to hand to them is a grenade minus the pin and with two seconds already on the clock,' answered Carter.

Robbo didn't reply; he went back over to his desk. Behind him, on a whiteboard was written 'Operation Topaz'. It was the name given to the investigation into Eddie Butcher's murder. It was Robbo's job to piece together the timeline of Eddie's last days, hours.

'The cortège is nearly there,' Robbo said, as he watched his screen.

Carter nodded, but he was focused on a mixed-race woman standing opposite the church gates. Her face was partially hidden by a black hat, the baseball type with a large peak. Her black hair was caught back in a low pony-tail. Her hands were thrust into the pockets of her black puffa jacket. She was slim, taller than average, late twenties. She was watching the crowd, watching the church. She had the look of someone for whom life was a constant puzzle.

'Move them back,' Carter said into his radio. 'The crowd's getting too congested around the gates.'

His eyes went back to the woman in the hat. She was watching the mourners, watching the slow path of the cortège. She could pass for a downtrodden single parent with two kids in a double buggy. But there was no buggy. She looked like she was a gym user after a big night out. Her broad, strong shoulders were rounded a little as if she were trying to hide in the crowd. She wore no make-up. She didn't want attention.

He switched to a view facing the oncoming cortège and zoomed in. The camera was searching for faces in the crowd. It was looking for faces that matched records. Interpol had sent lists of known criminals who had been on the move the last two months. They had crawled out of their Mexican strongholds, their Floridian beachside palaces and their Bogotá brothels, some to come and pay respects, others to cash in on the aftermath.

Carter spoke into his radio: 'It's reaching crisis point around the church gate. Control the crowd. Move them back. Do not allow them to get too close to the cortège.'

'Shit,' said Carter as a voice cut in: 'Suspicious male, making his way in from left rear of cortège, possible concealed weapons. Jeezus Christ!' Carter took an involuntary step back from the screen as the sound of automatic gunshots ripped through the air. Panic ensued as the crowd tried to get away. The driver lost control of the horses.

The voice of the commander at the scene came over the radio: 'Stand down. Stand down. It's just a firework, a firework. Get those horses under control. Calm the crowd, people are getting crushed.'

'Something's going on at the railway bridge,' said Carter into his radio. 'I can see a person on the floor, someone's been stabbed.'

The firework whizzed and cracked into the air and the horses reared as the banger jumped around their legs.

The officer in charge appealed for calm over a loudhailer. But there was mayhem at the feet of the ballerina as the gangs took their chance to start fighting.

The carriage started rolling backwards. Three times the coffin thudded against the inside of the doors before it broke through and was ejected from the carriage, dropping with force onto the road. The carriage continued reversing, pushed backwards by six panicking horses – it backed over the coffin.

The volume of Sandra Butcher's anguished screams was matched by the shouts from bodyguards and the loudhailer appealing for calm.

The smoke from the firework fizzed and died as it left a sulphurous cloud and Eddie Butcher's body rolled out onto the road.

Chapter 2

The Marbella sun was strong, even in winter, but it was interrupted by the occasional storm, which brought clarity to the air. It was hot enough for an Englishman abroad. Tony Butcher had lived on the Golden Mile for over twenty years. And, over those years, he had grown to hate the sun. Where it used to warm his bones, now it scorched them. It shrivelled his skin and, when he looked into the mirror, he saw a parody of his former self. He saw the shape of his skeleton. He saw his skull pushing through his face.

He had been a smart man once, a 'man about town'. His wardrobe was still stocked with brightly coloured silk ruffled shirts and brocade waistcoats. He had a large collection of hats neatly stacked in a temperature-controlled closet. Nowadays, though, he preferred his uniform of baggy, washed-out combat shorts with a canvas belt and a vest from Ibiza.

Tony looked at his bare feet as he walked through the long cool room, which had a veranda on three of its sides. He watched each foot spread across the cold marble as his weight shifted from one to the other. This was his trophy room. He would recount how he shot most of the animals on the walls, but, at best, he told half-truths. The killer lion, whose head had pride of place between the two sets of French windows leading to the veranda facing the sea, was a man-eater, so he claimed, but he had not shot it. He'd bought it from a restaurant in Namibia, where it had been hung on the wall. He had shot a giraffe. There was one jutting out from the corner of the room. With its long thick neck and small head, it had taken Tony twelve attempts to shoot the giraffe that day. In the end, a real hunter had stepped in to end the animal's suffering. The giraffe was in such a mess that the giraffe on the wall wasn't even the one that Tony had tried to kill. This was one that had been bred in captivity, and was killed by an Italian tourist who couldn't be bothered to have it mounted and flown home and hadn't even bothered to get out of his car to shoot it.

Tony stopped before the television screen on the wall. Sky News was relaying live footage from the funeral in Bethnal Green. The broadcaster was fleshing out the slow progress with a criminal history of the Butchers. For the umpteenth time that day Tony Butcher heard his name linked with the Great Diamond Heist of '91. They talked about him and Eddie being sent down for their part in disposing of the diamonds.

'Say something we don't all fucking know. You didn't know how it was done then, and you don't know now.' Tony laughed at the image of him and Eddie being led away to Wandsworth Prison in '92.

'Handsome-looking devil!' he said about himself, and then turned away and sighed irritably. He went to stand by the open French windows and looked out to the sea beyond. The horizon was sparkling, the sea was a colder colour blue that you only saw in winter: deep, dark, sapphire. He could hear the noise of traffic coming from the Golden Mile. He heard the sound of horns beeping. The sparrows chattered in the garden below as they washed their feathers in the spray from the fountains. Years ago all these elements would have charmed him, made him feel relaxed and happy with his world, but not now. Tony ached to ride his motorboat on the sea; he wanted to drive one of his many cars at break-neck speed along the Golden Mile, beeping his horn all the way. He hated the noise of the sparrows. They seemed to say, *What you going to do, Tony? What you going to do?* Over and over again. He tried hard to ignore them but his senses were so highly tuned that he could not. It made his blood boil. He had bought a falcon six months ago; he was going to train it to pick them off one by one, but it had attacked him and escaped and sometimes he thought he saw it flying up in the sky. Sometimes he watched the vapour trails from planes and the brightness made his eyes water. It made him cry.

He turned his head to listen; his ears were too sensitive to every sound. Like a bat, he registered every small vibration in the house. Above the noise from the television and the sparrows, he heard the faint creaking of movement in the house. Somewhere, there were footsteps shuffling, someone was sliding, instead of walking properly. He felt instantly furious. If the maids didn't start picking up one foot in front of another, he muttered to himself, he'd cut their legs off and make them shuffle around on their arses. Tony laughed to himself as he remembered a child he knew on his street. Disabled from thalidomide, small stunted arms and legs, and they carried him around as if he were a prince. Tony had envied him and so had stolen the boy's pet rabbit and hung it from a tree in the woods. No one found the rabbit for days and Tony had been back many times to watch it decompose. Now the smell of that animal rotting was never far from his nose. The fizzy smell of decomposition both repelled and excited him.

Tony looked down at the hairs on his shins and felt each follicle open, breathe, and the hair grow, and he began scratching furiously until his legs were bleeding. He stood wide-eyed and panting from the exertion, skin and flesh beneath his nails. He felt his skull throb as it pushed against the skin on his face.

He knew he was beyond stir-crazy. He had become part of the dust that spun in the sunshine, part of the walls that closed in on him, one piece of the mosaic floor. He was one of the sparrows. He turned at the words from the commentator.

Tony can't leave his luxury villa.

He stamped his foot and swore at the television before crossing to the coffee table and tipping out cocaine from the packet he kept in a jewellery box. He tapped away angrily, chopping the cocaine up to a fine powder with a credit card, moving it around meticulously and scraping it into fine straight lines. He picked up a rolled note and hoovered up a long line. Then he sat back to allow it to settle down his throat.

'"Tony can't leave his luxury villa,"' he mimicked. 'Oh yes, he can, and he will, when he's ready. When I come out of this place the whole world will know about it. I haven't been sat here on my arse for nothing. I've been incubating and I'm about ready to hatch.' He grinned at the image of himself he had in his mind. A flying moth, bigger than an eagle, flying above the planes fighting with the falcon.

He turned sharply at the noise of the fireworks on the television and ran towards the screen. He began to roar: 'Don't you fucking dare!'

Chapter 3

'How are things now?'

In Fletcher House, DI Carter was still watching the scene from outside St Matthew's Church, when his colleague Detective Sergeant Willis walked in. She'd come straight from Bethnal Green.

'The paramedics had to perform CPR on one lad. He was lucky: the knife just missed his heart. No one from the crowd was hurt in the panic. Just the gangs causing trouble.'

Carter sighed, relieved. He knew that, even though the day hadn't gone as well as he had hoped, it could have been worse.

'Did they scrape Eddie Butcher back up okay?' he asked with a smile.

'Just about,' Willis replied. 'It would have been funny, except it wasn't.'

'Oh, believe me, it made us smile, didn't it, Robbo?'

'Absolutely not.' Robbo hid a grin behind a cough.

Pam, at the third desk in the room, peered from around the side of her monitor and scowled at Robbo and Carter in turn.

Carter held up his hands in the air.

'Apologies, Pam.'

Pam was a civilian who worked mainly on collating data from the Internet and monitoring social media groups for investigations. She and Robbo had worked together for twenty years, since back in the day when Robbo was a serving police officer before he was forced to take retirement and chose to retrain as a crime analyst.

Willis took off her jacket and threw it over the back of the chair then dropped the black peak cap onto the desk.

Carter looked at it in disgust.

'Where did you get that?' he asked. 'I couldn't work out what you looked like: tired single parent or drug dealer.'

'Lost property. I was going for a bit of both.'

'Well, put it in the bin, for Christ's sake.'

Willis moved it from on top of the desk to underneath it. She intended to keep it.

Carter swung round in his chair, stood and went across to help himself to a coffee from the cafetière on top of the filing cabinet.

Willis opened up the post-mortem report on Eddie Butcher.

She read out loud, 'No alcohol, no drugs. No food in his stomach. He hadn't eaten for twelve hours.' She stood and went across to pin up a photo of Eddie Butcher from the post-mortem. 'Cause of death – still awaiting results on the organs. He was reverse-hung,' she said, 'with his hands tied behind his back by the wrists; then he was suspended. It caused his shoulders to dislocate.'

'Strappado,' said Robbo. 'It's a recognised form of torture, normally accompanied by electric-shock treatment. The Colombians love it.'

Willis pinned up the photographs of small pairs of wounds around the genitalia of the victim.

'Two electrode points which caused fifty-eight injury sites of second-degree burns made by a Taser-type machine.' She added a close-up of Eddie Butcher's left hand. 'Nails were pulled, probably using point-edged pliers.'

'Nasty. So they came prepared?' Carter said, as he swivelled in his chair and watched her pin up the photos. 'Very professional. If this was done for fun, then they make a habit of it. If this was for information, pretty sure they would have found out what they needed to know.'

'That's if he knew the answers to their questions,' answered Robbo. 'For a man who builds houses for a living, he's died a pretty violent death. He must have pissed off some South American cartel to get his tongue dragged through his neck.'

'Builds houses using what kind of money?' asked Carter. 'Laundered? Stolen? I suppose that's the question. You can take the man out of the villainous East End, but can you take the East End villain out of the man? This isn't your average property developer who might get a loan from the bank, this is a man who kick-started his career by stealing from other people.'

Pam stopped her typing to look up over her reading glasses.

'Just found a photo of Eddie's corpse on the Internet,' she said. 'He was still in the car park when this was taken.'

Carter went across to look at her screen.

'Yeah, got to be one of the bin men; probably took a selfie, too. A photo was bound to be leaked to the press. It's been a month since he was murdered. I'm surprised they

waited this long,' said Carter, walking back to his desk.
'Sign of the times, I'm afraid.'

'The bin men must see a lot of death,' said Willis, as
she stood back to study the images she'd pinned up so far.
'Drug overdoses, homeless.'

'Not usually tortured, with a bullet between the eyes and
a tongue pulled through his neck.' Carter sat upright and
took a swig of coffee. He was watching the church on the
screen. 'Okay, here we go, they're coming out.'

Willis and Robbo came across to look at Carter's screen
together.

'There's Laurence Butcher with Sandra now,' said
Robbo. 'He's always been a mummy's boy. Not sure who's
supporting who. Sandra looks like she's carrying him.'
Robbo squinted at the screen. 'Those two women at the
back, with hats, are Sandra's sisters. Harold's ex-wife,
Lucinda, is there. Her kids: Harold's stepkids.'

The family were thanking mourners outside the church
as people passed them one by one. Della Butcher took her
place at the end of the line of family members. She turned
her head from the rain that was driving sideways, and the
net across her face lifted in the wind.

'Are any of Della Butcher's family there?' asked Willis.

'No,' answered Carter. 'We'll get a detailed list when
Intel has had time to look at all this footage.'

'His widow looks different from what I expected,' said
Willis. 'I thought she'd be more of a footballer's wife type,
but she's dressed a lot more discreetly than his mother
Sandra with her fur-trimmed coat and diamonds. Plus, she
looks young.' Willis looked at her notes. 'Eddie Butcher
was what, fifty-two?'

'She's thirty-eight,' answered Carter. 'She married Eddie

in 2004.' Willis glanced across to see if Carter was reading the information, but he wasn't.

They watched the coffin being loaded inside the hearse. It was now wrapped in a Union flag, to hide the damage done by the reversing wheels of the carriage.

'I thought the immediate mourners are supposed to leave together, in the same car,' said Willis. 'Della's gone in the one with Harold's ex-wife. Is that significant?'

'Yeah,' said Carter, 'that's what she is to them now, an ex-wife, back of the queue.'

Robbo glanced across at Pam. 'What's their itinerary?'

'From here, they're going for a private burial in Chingford Cemetery. They have a plot near the Krays. Then they're staying in the area for a wake in a country estate on the edge of Epping Forest. It's a place called Giddewell Park.'

'It's a pretty low-key affair,' said Willis. 'Only the immediate relatives and close friends are invited. The family are staying the night there.'

Robbo looked at Carter. 'Are you going out there?'

Carter shook his head. 'I have no intention of driving out there. Plus, we've spent enough taxpayers' money on policing the funeral. I don't care if someone wants to shoot the lot of them.'

'I think that's interesting,' said Willis. She had walked back across to the photos of Eddie Butcher's injuries. 'Someone killed him first then pulled the tongue through afterwards. It was as if they were slightly uncomfortable with killing him like that, so they dispatched him with a bullet.'

'They might have run out of time,' said Robbo as he walked across to join her.

'But they definitely wanted us to know this had to do with the cartels. Cartels on British soil. Or British cartels?'

Chapter 4

Tony was still shaking with rage. The television screen was frozen on the anguished face of his mother Sandra cradling his brother's corpse. Tony hadn't moved from the spot for thirty minutes, then he heard the sound of the main gates opening. He took long slow breaths as he forced himself calm. He turned the television off and walked out to greet the people he was expecting. Two men got out of the car. One was Marco, a tall, blond mix of Dutch and Colombian: big-boned and sallow-skinned, with a man-bun and low-slung pinstriped trousers, a big-buckled designer belt and a black, open-chested shirt. The other was a Spaniard and shorter, dressed in a dark-blue business suit and tie; he was carrying a briefcase. Tony was watching from the hallway, his bare feet on the mosaic sundial.

'Señor Francisco, thank you so much for coming.'

'Not at all, Mr Butcher. It is my pleasure,' the Spaniard answered Tony while staring at Tony's bare feet and his scratched legs.

'Marco?' Tony said, by way of greeting the tall, ashen-haired man whose body proportions were all wrong, massive shovel-like hands, and a neck that was too spindly-looking to support such a big head. He had been working for Tony for the last six months. He was fast becoming indispensable: a feeder for Tony's ambitions. No job was too dirty or too outrageous. No limits or boundaries that they couldn't cross over together.

'Drink, Señor Francisco?' Tony asked.

'We'll go into my study,' Tony said to Marco, who nodded his understanding.

'Just some water, please.'

They walked towards the trophy room but turned left and entered an office, which was made to be as close to the Don's office from the *Godfather* films as possible. Some of the props had been obtained straight from the set. Besides Tony's oversized desk, set at an angle in the corner opposite the door, there was another, smaller desk, a drinks trolley, cabinets and bookcases, a leather sofa and two armchairs. The second door in the Don's office, behind Tony's desk, led down to the basement of the villa.

Tony closed the door behind them and poured some water from a decanter and passed it to Francisco. Beads of sweat had begun to appear on Francisco's top lip and forehead.

'How can I help, Mr Butcher?' Francisco asked, sipping on the water and looking uneasy. 'This is about your brother's estate, I believe.'

Tony went behind his desk and sat down.

'I have to be honest with you, Señor Francisco.' Tony pointed to a seat and Francisco reluctantly accepted. Marco stayed where he was, standing between Francisco and the door. 'I have asked you here for two reasons. One is my brother's will and the other is a more delicate matter.'

Tony rested his forearms on the desk and breathed deeply as he smiled at Francisco.

'You work for the Mendez cartel, don't you?'

Francisco shook his head. Shocked, flustered, he turned to look for help Marco's way. Marco smirked.

'I don't know that name, I'm sorry. I am a lawyer.'

'You are also a bookkeeper for the Mendez cartel, here in Spain.'

'There must be some mistake.' He grinned nervously, looking for assistance again, but getting none.

'No, I don't think so,' said Tony. 'We pay into accounts at the banks here. Accounts ending in 563, 908 and 300. We pay in, you launder for the Mendez cartel, is that right?'

'Absolutely not. I am a legitimate member of the legal profession. I have all sorts of clients. I cannot be sure what you're asking me.'

'I'm asking you where my money has gone for the latest shipment. We paid it in. Isn't that so, Marco?'

'Absolutely.'

'Now, it has disappeared and we are in deep trouble, through no fault of our own.' Tony sat back and watched Francisco's panic level rise.

'Señor Butcher, I cannot help you with this.' Francisco's eyes were looking for a way out of the room that didn't involve getting past Marco. 'I would like to go now.'

Tony lifted his hands from the desk, palms open.

'No, no. Please sit back down.' Marco laid a hand on Francisco's shoulder. 'I apologise, unreservedly. My mistake.' Tony smiled. 'No hard feelings. *Lo siento, señor,* I was only joking, *hombre.*' He laughed and Marco chuckled. Francisco tried to join them but nothing came out of his mouth. He took a sip of water and sat nervously.

'I didn't bring you here for that. Your firm has been dealing with my brother Eddie's will?'

'Yes, he left me with that honour, and please accept my sincere condolences for your loss. Your brother was a great man.'

'He was an idiot.'

Marco giggled.

'Sorry. Pardon, Mr Butcher.'

'He was not right in the head when he made his will. I want you to look into my brother's estate again; I have drawn up a new will. I will make sure everything's fair and you'll get a million euros for your trouble. I want you to sign over every asset he has to me.'

'A new will?'

'Correct. He made a new will, who knew?' Tony picked up a bunch of papers from the top of his desk and fluttered them in the air. 'I just need you to sign it off.'

'With all due respect, Señor Butcher, that is not something I can do. There are procedures to follow. The will we made for Eddie is a legal document.'

'And we are going to make another legal document right here.'

'I cannot do that.'

'Okay, all right, I understand your reluctance.' Tony stood, smiled. 'Marco, we will show Señor Francisco out and, at the same time, show him what we found to help him understand how important this is to me. It is just a small thing I think we should bring to his attention.'

'This way,' Marco said as he waited for Francisco to get to his feet and then he ushered him forwards, towards the door behind Tony's desk. Tony led the way down a narrow passageway and to a flight of stairs and down into the garage beneath the house. As they walked through the forecourt, Francisco tried to make conversation: 'You have many cars, Señor Butcher?'

Tony didn't reply as he speeded up, weaving through the covered luxury cars, until he stopped at the back of the garage, at the control room.

He nodded to Marco who unlocked the door and stood back to show Francisco what was inside. A small girl was sitting on the floor, tied by her neck to a gas cylinder.

Francisco lunged forward with a scream of anguish.

'No, not my daughter!'

Chapter 5

'Eddie was found dumped in a car park in Old Street,'
Robbo said, 'at five in the morning on November the 6th.
He'd been dead for between two and three hours. He was
last seen by his brother Harold at ten the morning before.
In his statement he says they had breakfast together in the
Baramba Café on Shoreditch High Street. After that, at
ten minutes past ten, they separated. We know he didn't
drive anywhere because his hire car was still in the car
park.'

Robbo stood in front of the timeline.

'How did Harold seem when you interviewed him?'
Robbo asked Willis.

'Tired, hard-faced, a man used to flicking a switch. He
said Eddie left him to go and see a client.'

'Even if you're late building someone's extension, you
don't expect to get tortured and executed,' said Robbo.

'I suppose we have to remember what kind of clientele
he builds them for,' Carter said. He took a sip of his coffee.
'He builds villas for Mafia bosses, drug barons, wealthy
villains.'

'And, for huge money,' added Pam, 'although, according
to his tax returns in the last two years, he's not earning

the money he was.' She continued scrolling through data on her screen.

'What, millions instead of billions?' Robbo asked as he took his bag of Haribo sweets away from Willis, whose hand was wedged inside it. Willis and Robbo shared an addiction to sugar.

'Eight years ago his property company was worth three million, but it registered a loss last year. I've got a list of all the projects he's been working on,' said Pam. 'Not one of these villas is worth less than five million quid. And that's a cheapy. The outlay on them must be massive and, from the look of his books, he doesn't get a deposit,' added Pam. 'This is all done on trust. It's easy to go wrong.'

'It's also easy to hide a lot of expenses,' said Robbo. 'These are going to be people who turn up to buy a house with cash in suitcases.'

'We took a statement from his general manager, Billy Manson, two weeks ago,' said Willis. 'He said that business was as good as it had ever been, just that getting money from rich people was tricky sometimes and that they had always to pay for materials up front. Sometimes there was a lean period.'

'That's a lesson on how to become rich,' said Robbo. 'Hang on to every penny.' He slid his chair along the length of his desk to reach his cup of coffee. 'Or, alternatively, steal diamonds and then buy a business building villas for other people who steal diamonds, sell drugs, traffic people, et cetera, et cetera.'

'Presumably,' said Pam, 'Eddie's supplying legitimate products to fit out these villas, and they come from legit companies with bookkeepers and accountants to answer to. And, when you're putting in such high specs I guess it's possible to lose a lot of money very quickly. I mean a few solid platinum baths go missing and you're down a few hundred thousand.'

'Does Manson check out?' asked Carter, addressing Willis while keeping one eye on his screen.

'There is nothing on him,' answered Willis. 'He's worked for Paradise Villas for the last fifteen years, since it started. He seems to have got on well with Eddie. There's nothing written down to the contrary. He seemed really upset about Eddie's death. It was hard to get him to compose himself.'

'Eddie had made more visits to the UK in the last two months than he'd made in the previous two years. Did Manson have an answer for that?'

Willis shook her head. 'He said it could have been something to do with the family; it wasn't to do with work. Work was going well.'

A figure passed by the window overlooking the corridor outside Robbo's office and Chief Inspector Bowie walked in. He was not usually immaculate, but today his suit had been carefully chosen. Today he knew he would be under scrutiny. Carter was the SIO but he had the look on his face of a man beginning to feel the pressure. He would be the one to face the press. He had allowed the funeral of a notorious gangster to go ahead. The press were after some answers and he agreed to be interviewed on the evening news and explain what happened at the funeral.

'You better prepare me a statement to give to the hyenas,' he said. 'Did we get what we wanted?' he asked as Willis offered him a seat. He declined it. He was looking at Carter for an answer.

'It's too early to have a full list of people of interest yet, sir,' answered Carter. 'But I am confident it will all have been worth it, despite the scuffles at the end.'

'What was the reason for all that?'

'We think it was a revenge attack. The gang situation in this area is worrying. Eddie's death has spurred a whole lot of activity that we didn't expect.'

'Did the UCs come up with anything? I haven't seen such a gathering of old-time crooks since Reggie Kray's funeral.'

'Exactly!' Carter smiled ruefully. 'We've got plenty of undercover officers out working the pubs and clubs in the East End tonight, sir. I have a useful informant who's right in the middle of the local scene in Bethnal Green. I'm going to catch up with him in the next twenty-four hours and I'm pretty sure he'll have something for us.'

Bowie nodded thoughtfully and cleared his throat. It was a nervous habit that worsened when he was under pressure, as if something were slowly choking him. His long thin neck didn't fill out his collars or his shoulders his jackets. It seemed like only fabric kept him standing. He'd lost a lot of weight in the last year. Carter and Bowie had known one another since they had joined the force. Bowie wasn't liked by most of the officers who served under him. He had a reputation for setting others up to take the blame for his own mistakes. Carter was the only one who ever agreed to have a social drink with Bowie.

'Tonight should be a good night for picking up information in the pubs around the East End. We're confident, sir.'

'Good,' Bowie said, looking across at the timeline on the board behind Robbo's desk. 'We can't afford a blood bath on the UK streets. We don't want a drugs war played out over here. Whatever it is that Eddie got himself mixed up in we need to know fast. Are we watching who goes to the wake this evening?'

'Yes, it's covered,' answered Carter.

'I thought you were supposed to be on holiday this week.' Bowie frowned at Carter.

'Yeah, I was.'

Chapter 6

Tony and Marco watched as Tony's wife, Debbie, cleaned and tidied the trophy room around them. The house was full of tension. The maids were whispering. There had been tears. A local girl, who normally worked in the kitchen, and had been called in to lend a hand in the bedrooms, had been assaulted by Marco. Now, Debbie was trying to keep a lid on things and contain the damage. None of the servants wanted to come near either of the men.

Marco was sitting, stripped to the waist, on the sofa. His skin glistened across his toned chest and ripped abdominals. He had black chest hair in two tufts over his pink nipples. One of his nipples was pierced with a ring. He was as nervous as a fly, he smelled of stale sweat. His over-large features were ill-matched and his eyes as close as a gorilla's, his brows fair and Neanderthal-heavy. His teeth were large and even but yellowed at the gum. His skin had the look of cottage cheese. His back bore the scars of a flogging. The deep, open wounds had never been stitched together and remained as grooves in his pockmarked skin. The scars were old but they still caused him pain – he felt them tug and pull. As a thirteen-year-old he'd been caught with his pants down, and in the middle of raping one of the servant girls, Marco had been whipped by his father so badly that he'd lost consciousness and been woken by his father urinating on him. He had crawled away to lie on his bed and fester. He often reflected that it had made a man of him, but what kind of man?

Debbie was watching them from the far side of the room as she picked fluff from the antelope hide over the back of one of the sofas. Tony followed Marco's gaze, and saw that he was watching her. The room was growing dark now, the evening descending fast. Marco grinned at her. She turned and walked out, muttering as she went.

'Your woman doesn't like me.' Marco laughed.

Tony was chewing the inside of his cheek as he shook his head, distracted. He tapped away at the cocaine, hunched over the table.

'She'll get used to you. She'll have to, won't she? She thinks we're a bad influence on one another; she doesn't see the genius like I do. She also thinks you had something to do with Eddie's death,' he said, as he glanced across at Marco.

Marco didn't answer. He stood and went to look at the evening outside the doors. Debbie had closed them. He opened them again. The air was damp and colder than of late but the fog had cleared and the lights from ships on the horizon blinked at him.

Tony's eyes were bright as he watched Marco in the gloom, and he waited for a response.

'I tried to prevent it. Now Eddie has left us in the shit,' Marco finally said, as he closed the windows, but stayed where he was, looking out to sea.

'It didn't need to happen like that,' Tony said, lowering his voice.

'I agree. Absolutely. But it was an accident, an unavoid-able catastrophe. And . . . every tragedy has a silver lining. One man's misfortune is another's . . . opportunity,' Marco said, still staring out at the ships, before turning round and grinning at Tony. He began chopping furiously, animated, jiggling. Coke was flying off the glass top, into the air, covering the floor in a fine white powder. 'Eddie's going to make it up to us, from the grave. We take everything he owns and we build on it. We build ourselves a future.'

'Yes yes . . . yes. But I wish he had just done that small thing for us.'

'No good wishing your life away, wishing it down the pan, we need to gather all the funds we have together now. My family is not waiting around, the shipment is ready to be dispatched,' Marco said. 'We need to get the rest of the money now. We lose face on this? We lose our balls.'

'Yeah, I know, I know. When Harold gets here I'm going to put this on him to find it. Harold will know who to squeeze.'

Marco turned away. His contempt for Harold was clear.

'What about our friends in the basement?' he asked. 'And, what about the legal stuff? How do we know it's going to be okay? The Mendez cartel must be fooled into thinking it's not our fault their money is missing, at least until we have the rest of the funds in place. It's got to be believable. We need to buy time.'

'Of course it is going to look believable. It's going to be signed by their lawyer, for Christ's sake. He will sign it and then he will take a long holiday.'

Marco came away from the window. 'When we finish with the bookkeeper and his daughter, where did you have in mind to take them? It's too risky to hire a boat.'

'Eddie's property. There's an olive grove and wasteland at the back. We can get there without going by road.'

'We should do it now. I need to go back to the UK with something in writing. It has to be convincing.'

'Yes.'

Tony sprang to his feet and led the way through the office and down to the garage. Marching ahead of Marco, his cheesecloth shirt flapped in the breeze that always rose from the lower floors, up like a wind tunnel through the corridor.

They crossed over the forecourt and Tony stopped by the door to the control room and grinned at Marco. He opened the door and leaned his weight on it as he peered inside.

The bookkeeper, Señor Francisco, was naked and bound, feet and hands behind his back. But he had still managed to work his way across to his daughter, his head next to hers. The daughter was still tied by a rope around her neck. She looked to be unconscious.

Tony went inside. He squatted down froglike next to the young girl. He stroked her face. She didn't react. Marco spoke from his place at the door.

'She looks a funny colour. There's no air in here.'

'I know, I know.' Tony beckoned him forward. Marco stepped inside, closed and locked the door behind him.

Tony looked the girl over and touched her hair as he smiled at Francisco.

Marco was already sweating in the windowless, airless room, with its breezeblock walls and concrete floor. On the walls were the control panels for the garage and the climate control needed to keep the cars in tip-top condition. It pumped out heat from its blinking switchboard.

'Any water in here?' asked Marco.

Tony shook his head.

'But, there can be, when Señor Francisco here agrees to my terms.'

Marco hadn't meant for them, he was thirsty, but he nodded anyway.

Tony went across to the top of the control box and took down the documents he had put there.

'Sign these papers.'

Francisco looked at Marco, as if he might be the only hope of reason in the room. Marco stared, unblinking, back. Francisco hung his head. He looked like a man who was anticipating the fall from the cliff and the double devastation of seeing his daughter flung before him. He nodded. Tony removed his gag.

Francisco croaked, 'Free my daughter and I will sign it.'

Tony laughed. 'It doesn't work like that. You have nothing to bargain with, whereas I' – he reached out to stroke the little girl's leg – 'I will get someone else to do it and I will strangle you with your own daughter's intestines. You sign it, I give you my word, I will let her go.'

'Please,' Francisco begged Marco. Marco stared coldly back. Francisco nodded. 'I'll sign it. Please untie her. Get her some water. She is not well. Let her go.'

'When I say so.'

Tony turned the pages to the appropriate signatures needed. He motioned for Marco to come forward and free Francisco so that he could sign the forms.

'Here, here.' He gave him a pen and piece of card to lean on.

Francisco signed the papers and handed them back. 'You will need me if this goes to court. I can help you, Señor Butcher. I know all the right people for this.'

Tony looked at him incredulously.

'Of course you do.' He handed Francisco another set of papers. Francisco paused as he read them.

'They will not believe you gave me the money to deposit. They will not believe it. It is not as simple as this. I can help you move money to cover the shortfall. I can help you with this. I can move funds around to cover for the loss.'

'Sign.'

Tony checked the papers before putting them back above the control box.

Francisco looked from one man to another and tried to come between them and his daughter. Tony stepped forward and took a small, short-bladed knife from his pocket. As Francisco brought his arm up to try to protect himself, he stabbed Francisco repeatedly in his chest. The puncture wounds opened one by one.

'What the fuck? Why did you do that? We needed him. Shit, look at the floor, you should have protected the floor: the concrete is like a sponge,' said Marco as he edged across to look at the papers. 'He could have been more use to us. Maybe he was right. He could have helped us.'

'I didn't like him. Lawyers, judges, policemen, they're all ten a penny. You get a lot of corruption for your euro here. You go and get something to clean this up. Ask Sheena for everything you need. Package him up, we'll get rid of him later.'

'And her?'

'Leave the child for me to play with.'

'We could take her and dump her somewhere. She's sick,

anyway. She won't last the night. We can make it look like she wandered off.'

'Yeah, maybe.' Tony was waving Marco away as he went across to the child. His mind focused on one thing. There was an odd whining noise in the room, coming from the control box, and it kept stopping, whining, restarting, repeating just like the sparrows: *What you going to do, Tony? What you going to do?*

Chapter 7

Fletcher House was cold; the heating had broken down. A memo came round:

Now winter has hit hard and Christmas is coming. Will everyone please support the Christmas Giveaway in support of the refugees and give generously.

'Winter has hit pretty hard here too.' Carter stood. 'I'm starting my own collection for a heater for my office.'

Willis looked up from her screen at the shivering figure next to her.

'Your nose is like Rudolph's,' she said with a smile. 'Maybe you're getting a cold.'

Willis was sitting at her desk in the inquiry team office; it was the biggest office. Thirty-eight officers made up MIT 17, and it was one of twenty-four major investigation teams in London. The inquiry team office was where all the detectives who did the main bulk of work were. Visiting sergeants, DCs, they also were given a workspace at one of the six long desks that housed three workstations on each side. Carter shared an office with two other inspectors but he was rarely in it. He preferred to work surrounded by the team.

Carter groaned. 'That's all I bloody need.'

'If you had a fever you'd be too hot,' said Willis, 'not cold.'

'Something to look forward to then,' said Carter. 'I'm off, Eb.'

'Home?' She turned in her chair. 'Really?'

'Yes, really, *home*. I feel rough. I'm going to try and nip this in the bud.'

She looked at him incredulously. 'Are you okay? Has Cabrina been in touch?'

'No, she hasn't. I think she's still a bit sore with me for not going on holiday.'

'Really? Just a bit, you think?' Willis said, turning back to her monitor.

'She'll be okay in a few days,' he said as he walked out of the office, pulling his scarf up over his nose.

Willis spent the next two hours looking at the history of some of the faces who'd attended the funeral and then she went to see Robbo in his office. It was nearly eleven.

'Pam gone home?' Willis asked, glancing at the clock on the wall.

'Yes. Some people have got one, you know.' Robbo rolled his eyes and smiled wearily. He had intended to go home an hour ago but he had passed the point where his wife would be pleased to see him. Now she would be in bed and he told himself it didn't matter what time he crawled in beside her. It didn't matter that they had no contact with one another any more. He told himself many couples that stopped having sex still had great marriages.

'I need more background on the Butchers and their associates,' she said, picking up the empty cafetière and examining it. 'There were several people, identified in the crowds at the funeral that had made the trip over from abroad. Quite a few that had bought villas from Eddie in the last fifteen years since Eddie started his company in 2000. There were eighteen of them, at the last count. Of those, five were here at the time Eddie was killed.'

'We can't discount anyone. The job done on Eddie was bespoke. Someone paid someone else to do that.'

'Some of those who came were old criminal connections to the family who hadn't been seen in the UK for ten or more years.'

'I know, I was looking at that myself. The Butchers still command that much respect, I suppose,' said Robbo. 'Okay, go and rinse that out,' he said, pointing to the cafetière, 'and I'll make some fresh.'

When she returned Robbo made a pot of coffee as Willis drew up a chair.

'Here's the list.' Willis placed it on the desk before them.

He took it and scanned it with his eyes.

'I can see what you mean. There's a lot of criminal history here.'

'Yeah, I've cross-referenced as many as I can, but I need to know which to concentrate on,' said Willis.

'We are concentrating on those with the most recent direct contact with Eddie,' replied Robbo, 'starting present day and working backwards.'

'That's a lot of people. Eddie seems to maintain a service with his villas. He takes care of them afterwards. He lives near to a lot of them. I suppose it's easy for him to keep an eye on things.'

'Pam's getting in touch with any villa owners of interest. Where's Carter? Has he any thoughts on who to concentrate on from this list?'

'He's gone off sick tonight.'

'Really? He seemed to be pulling out all the stops for this case, now he's ill?'

'Yes, he does look rough. This case seems to be personal to him,' said Willis. 'He's even cancelled his annual leave. He's supposed to be on holiday right now.'

Robbo nodded. 'I know.' He stood. 'Coffee?'

'Please.'

Robbo came back over with the pot and tipped out the rest of the packet of Haribo onto his desk. Willis didn't wait to be asked. Robbo always left her the ones he knew she liked, even though he pretended he didn't do it on purpose.

'I feel like I'm missing something I should know,' said Willis as she ate the sweets, 'about this Eddie Butcher case. If we conclude that Eddie had got involved with some Colombian drug connections, which would explain the way he was killed, then we should hand this over to the NCA, Organised Crime Command, shouldn't we? They cover all areas of organised crime. They have more resources than us. Do we really care who killed Eddie?'

Robbo didn't answer straight away but then he nodded. 'We should stick with it. He died on our patch, but you're right: this is likely to have more to do with Tony than anyone else.'

'How come Tony is still free?' asked Willis.

'We've tried to get him many times. The Spanish police would love to close him down too but he's always clever enough to evade it, or at least his lawyers are. But you're right about this being personal to Carter, and not just him, for a few of us. We had a big operation in 2003 to try and get him.'

'Operation Argos?'

'Yes. Some of us were involved in that.'

'I started looking into it, but it doesn't really say a lot in the report. I can't get access to all of it. Can you get me in to study it? Can you fill in some gaps for me?'

'I'll do my best. Wait here. I'll go to the box-file store-room and see what I can find in there for you.'

Robbo returned with two files and handed them to her.

'Look after these. They aren't generally available. You can email me or text any questions you have. I'll be staying here this evening. Bring those back to me tomorrow, without fail.'

'I will.'

Willis left Robbo's office and checked her watch as she walked back down the corridor. It was twelve thirty. She tried Carter's phone. It went straight to answerphone. She turned round, picked up her coat from her desk and took the stairs down to the first floor, where there was a connecting door to Archway Police Station. She was going to check whether her friend from the canteen was still working or whether she needed a lift home as Willis had decided to head that way. She intended to grab a few hours' kip and have a shower, change her clothes.

As she opened the canteen door, the familiar smell of stale food hit her. She waited to catch the eye of the young man washing down the surfaces trying to relieve his boredom on the night shift.

'Is Teen still here?' she asked him.

He shook his head and went on smearing the dirt from his cloth across the stainless steel.

Willis went out past the front desk of the police station and doubled round to the car park. The road was bright with the rain. It was beginning to crystallise in places as the temperature had dipped to zero. She used the small runaround detective's car and drove home. After parking outside the terraced Victorian house off Newington Green that she shared with three others, she put her key in the front door and listened intently: no sound of the television, no music. She closed the door quietly behind her and crept upstairs to her room. She was relieved that the house was sleeping. She had a lot of work to get through and she knew Tina would want to have a quick catch-up chat, which would spill into a two-hour talk, easily. Along with her best friend Tina from the police canteen, Willis shared with two other women: a nurse and a teacher. The nurse was at work more than she was home, and the teacher was engaged to a social worker from Camden and hardly slept there any more.

The orange light from the street lamp outside meant there was always some light shining into her room. She never thought to buy thicker curtains. She never moved into a space and made it her own. She had lived a lot of her childhood in children's homes.

Willis didn't bother to undress. She'd give herself three hours' sleep, then up, shower and out of the door. First she checked her phone again for any message from Carter; there wasn't one. Then she lay back and closed her eyes. But she couldn't sleep. A half-hour later, she switched on the light and grabbed a coat. She wrapped it around her shoulders as she opened her laptop and lifted the files onto the bed, ready to read.

Just before one-thirty, Carter pulled up at the entrance to Giddewell Park. It was a one-time grand manor house and a hundred-acre estate, now turned into an events venue with a great golf course. It also boasted a two-Michelin-star restaurant.

'Any problems?' he asked one of the officers stationed at the entrance.

'One of the family has ordered a cab and asked to be taken to a hotel near the airport. Did you want us to provide security?'

'Which member of the family is it?'

'Eddie Butcher's widow, Della.'

'Where is she now?'

'She's waiting in the reception.'

'Okay. I'll take her where she wants to go. I'll make sure it's one of the hotels with twenty-four-hour security and then it should be okay to let her do what she wants. Radio up and tell the officer with her that I'm coming now.'

'Yes, sir.'

Carter drove along the tree-lined drive, decorated with white fairy lights for Christmas. He pulled up outside the main entrance and waited. Della Butcher was escorted out carrying her bag. The officer put her bag in the boot for her and she got into the passenger seat beside Carter.

She looked across at him: 'It's been a long time, Dan.'

Chapter 8

9 December

At half eleven the next morning Della Butcher walked through customs and out into the strong winter sunshine at Málaga Airport. She handed her bag to Marco.

Marco pulled his sunglasses down from his head. He had the air of a gangster on holiday. His blond hair was slicked back. His white shirt was open to reveal a massive gold crucifix, and he carried his jacket casually over one shoulder.

They headed across to the car park. He looked over and grinned.

'I saw you on the television. You looked hot, dressed in black.'

'That was my aim. To look hot at my husband's funeral. Marco, please keep your stupid fucking comments to yourself. Any of the family return yet?'

'Mrs Butcher is coming with Harold and Laurence – they're arriving late this afternoon. They're pissed with you.'

'Really? I don't give a shit.'

They walked across to the car, a new black Mercedes

G wagon that had been Eddie's pride and joy. Not seeing Eddie at the wheel hit Della hard in the sternum. The sorrow was mixed with rage at him and at everyone else. People's comments were still in her ears: it was inevitable, fitting almost, that he should die a violent death; they almost acted like she should have been proud of it. But she knew the softer side of Eddie. He'd always been gentle and sweet with her and, even though people said it was inevitable because Eddie had been a Butcher brother, he'd been straight for years. They had so many plans; so much they were going to do. Why had he let this happen?

She left Marco to load her bag in the car and climbed into the passenger seat. On the dashboard was Eddie's lighter. She picked it up and put it into the glove box. Marco glanced over at her.

'Tony wants to see you.'

'I'm going home first. I'm tired ...' Her voice trailed off as she sat back and stared out of the window. They drove out of the airport and hit the motorway and headed west to Marbella. She left the silence between them as she closed her eyes and her mind reran the events of the last twenty-four hours: the funeral, the faces. She was trying to recall the people she knew among them. They flashed into her head like strobe lights. When she opened her eyes, there was the sea. It dazzled her, electric blue. She never stopped feeling lucky to live there, to see the sea every day of her life and to understand that it was a luxury. But today its brilliance, clarity, sent needles of pain right into the back of her eyes. It hurt, everything hurt.

What kind of secrets? Other women? Was he travelling on the pretence of work just to screw his way around

Europe? She racked her brains to remember their last conversations. Eddie had been getting more wound up daily. He said he was thinking of leaving it all behind, of them starting afresh. Della had broached the subject of jetting off to the Caribbean to talk things through, to plan a new future. Eddie had agreed far too quickly.

'You book it, anywhere you like. Make it for Christmas. We'll spend it on our own in a villa in Barbados, how does that sound?'

'Too good to be true. What about your mum?'

'Mum's got Tony and Debbie. Harold will be over as usual. I want us to start moving away from the family. I wouldn't mind if we end up living up the coast a bit. Or maybe we head off to Cyprus to live for a year or two?'

'Is everything all right, Eddie?'

'Yes, princess. It's going to be okay. When I get home we'll start thinking about where we want to live, you and me.'

As she thought it she shook her head. No, their marriage was strong.

They pulled up at the gates of her home, Villa Adelphi. The security guard opened the gates. The immaculate lawn rose before them. They had designed it around the phases of the moon. The lawn was laid out as a series of crescents, differing heights, and palm trees planted in between. The irrigation system was working and sprinklers shot up across the lawn in a synchronised fountain display. The round full moon of Villa Adelphi loomed before them as they drove a circular route. White pillars and arches were designed to create a picture postcard of tranquillity. On a good day it looked like the gates of heaven with its domes and alabaster columns, its Moorish towers. On a bad day it looked like a sixties-inspired mosque. Whereas it used to seem breathtakingly beautiful, an oasis, now it seemed more like a mausoleum.

Inside the villa, Della went to shower and emerged, wrapped in a towelling robe. She walked back through the sitting room and picked up a cold glass of white from the kitchen as she went to sit on the veranda. There was a stillness with a fresh quality to the air before midday. She looked out at the mountains, their muted colours and lights always changing, always majestic. A rooster crowed. She looked down to the gardens that she and Eddie had designed together – even down to the six palms swaying in the breeze and casting reflections in the infinity pool. It should have been a heaven for them but there were always going to be complications.

Marco appeared on the veranda beside her. She adjusted her robe where it had fallen open. She was aware of Marco staring.

'Are you going to go and see Tony now?' he asked.

'In a minute. I'll walk.'

'He wants you to go now. I must drive you.' She didn't answer. She didn't look at him as he left. She stayed where she was and drank her wine and bit back the anger and the sorrow. Every time they ever got close to a perfect marriage something, someone, or just Eddie, spoiled it. When he'd built this villa for them they had created the perfect place to hide from the world, but then Tony built his further up the road. Always the family loomed over them.

She downed the rest of her wine and walked back inside to get changed.

Marco drove the few minutes up the road and down

the lane to Tony's villa. They pulled up outside the grand entrance to Villa Cassandra. Set in an acre and a half, it had been built in the style of an executive home in Essex but with the add-ons of a wraparound veranda on each of its three floors, which gave it the look of a ski-resort hotel. It could sleep fifty. It had three guest houses and a staff house, positioned around a central fountain, three pools and a beach house. The villa was accessed via a private lane, which made it easy to police and to secure.

As Della got out of the car and headed up the steps to the main house she looked up to see Debbie watching her approach from the veranda on the top floor. Marco left her. She walked between the alabaster columns and onto the mosaic floor in the hallway.

Tony was facing her as she walked into the trophy room. He was sitting side on to the views of the mountains and the sea. She knew why: he didn't want to look outside. He had grown sick of admiring nature. It had been ten years since he'd ventured into the town itself. Now he was a prisoner in his own Shangri-La. There were armed guards and there was razor wire on his fences. His dogs were trained to kill. Tony was scared of them.

Della walked towards him. The table in front of him was dusted in white, there were rings of wet from drinks spillage. He was turning a credit card around his fingers.

'I've been waiting for you,' he said, and pushed a line of coke her way.

She declined, repulsed, and sat down on the adjacent sofa.

He leaned in to vacuum up a fat line. She studied him. His shaven head had silver stubble. His face was stretched over prominent cheekbones. His lips were burned by the whisky. Cheeks flushed. He looked like an angry drag queen without her wig.

'Thought you might feel like letting go a bit – must have been difficult for you yesterday,' he said, sitting back and snorting loudly as he tilted his head back and his Adam's apple moved up and down as he swallowed.

He waited to see if she would speak. When she didn't, he sat up, took a few swigs of whisky and slammed the glass onto the table. He sat forward, resting his elbows on his knees as his head hung down. Della watched him. She listened to the hum and hiss of the water sprinklers outside the open doors and windows. A lizard had waddled in and was climbing the wall in bursts of activity. Somewhere in the house she heard movement. She knew Debbie would be hovering close by.

After a few minutes, Tony sat back on the sofa, with his arms outstretched on the sofa's spine. He looked up at the photo of Ronnie and Reggie Kray on the wall. He picked up his Scotch. 'The Krays, Eddie, all the good ones are gone. Hey? Aren't they, princess? Hey, you agree? You talking to me?'

'What do you want me to say?'

'They left his body dumped like it was rubbish,' Tony said as he shook his head mournfully. 'They left him muti-lated, like he was a joke. Like he was a fucking joke! And, I can't even go to his funeral. I can't even go to my little brother's funeral.' He glared at her for a few seconds before finishing his whisky just as Sheena, the maid, came in with a small tray and a glass of wine for Della. She placed it on a mat on the glass table. Della thanked her.

'Sheena?' Tony waved his glass in the air. 'Drinky?' He rattled the ice. 'Fresh drinky? Remember – your fucking job, Chinky . . .' He laughed and Sheena smiled back nervously. They heard the sound of Debbie talking to one of the servants in the hallway and then her feet shuffling their way.

'Debbie? Get the fuck in here,' he called out.

'Yeah, babes?' She arrived, and stood before him in a pair of lime-green towelling shorts, framing stick-thin, mahagony-coloured legs. He pushed a line of coke her way. She shook her head.

'Not now.'

'What the fuck? What is the matter with everyone?' Tony sat back annoyed and then looked at her with drunken, doleful eyes. Wet on his lips. His eyes flicked Della's way, and then he reached forward towards Debbie and slid his hand beneath her shorts.

She giggled, embarrassed, as she tried to push his hand away.

'I have to get on with things, Tony. We have everyone arriving here in a few hours.'

He tilted his head Della's way: 'She's back.'

'Yes, I know.' Debbie turned to her. 'I heard you left the wake early,' she said.

Della wasn't surprised. She knew the family, mother Sandra, Debbie, they always had it in for her.

'People started getting too drunk. I was exhausted. I'd done my duty.'

'Course you had. Course you bloody well had,' Tony said, waving Debbie away. 'And you can get on with your duties. I'm going to talk to Della here, our princess.' He slapped Debbie hard on the bottom as she turned to walk away. She rubbed her smarting backside and glared at Della, defying her to smirk.

Tony's jaw started sliding as he talked. His foot tapped incessantly. The sound of phlegm and cocaine chugged at the back of his nose and throat. 'I paid enough for it all – thousands that cost me. What the fuck went wrong, was this just a fucking joke?'

She shook her head. 'It went okay, Tony. It was always going to be risky putting on such a display.'

'Don't call it a display. Don't say that. It was the kind of funeral for statesmen. I'll fucking kill the kid who threw that firework.'

'It wasn't what Eddie would have wanted.'

'What wasn't?'

'He wanted to be buried here in Spain, in the olive grove, at the back of the villa. Something simple.'

Tony laughed, too loud, too long.

'Did he? Really?' Tony composed himself and grinned away as he went back to chopping coke. 'I think he said that just to keep you happy. He said that to make sure you opened your legs every day. Hey, princess?'

She stared at him. She couldn't help feeling that Tony was getting madder every day. She couldn't wait to leave, but, at the same time, there was something morbidly fascinating watching Tony. She wasn't going to be scared of him.

'I saw it was pissing with rain,' Tony continued, watching her closely. 'I thought, Can you fucking believe it? But you know what? Then, I thought it added something regal to the whole thing; what do you think, princess?'

He sidled to the edge of the sofa and reached over and laid his hand on her leg. She stared at it. It wasn't the first time, but certainly it was the most blatant. He never would have dared in front of Eddie. 'Hey, princess?' He patted her leg before removing his hand slowly. 'I want you to move into one of our houses on this estate.'

'Why would I do that? I'm all right where I am, in my own place. What did you want to see me about, Tony? I'm very tired right now.'

'We're all fucking tired,' he snapped. 'Okay. Okay.' He sat back in his chair. 'You're tired, I understand. But I want you to come to dinner tonight; Mum will be back. She's going to need us all around. After all, she had to bury her son yesterday, not something any parent should have to do. Laurence and Harold are bringing her over and I want us all to be together this evening. We need to talk, as a family. There are things to be discussed.'

'Like what?'

'Like the future and what Eddie would have wanted.' Tony took a gulp of his drink and wiped his mouth. 'Is Marco over at yours? Did he run you up here?'

'Where else would he be? You sent him over to spy on me.'

'Now, why would I do that? I put him over there to protect you. It's what Eddie would want me to do. Now, more than ever, you need to be careful.'

'Eddie was a legitimate businessman who was murdered. What has that got to do with me? The police will find who did it.'

'The British police? Really? Do you think they're not laughing themselves sick with all this that's happening to us? It's all their Christmases come at once. They must think it couldn't have happened to a nicer family. Eddie was tortured and executed. Now, I would say that was a little worrying, wouldn't you?'

She shook her head. 'I don't understand any of it. My

husband built villas for a living. He was a property developer. He was not a criminal. Eddie didn't need to make shady deals, he earned good money from the villas.'

'*Earned*, past tense. Not recently, princess. This lifestyle doesn't come cheap.' He shrugged and began splitting the cocaine into lines again. 'Eddie had a life you never knew about.'

'What do you mean?'

'I'm only saying Eddie put himself at risk by dealing with the wrong people. He should have known better. Life is cheap, princess. But, don't worry: we're going to make them pay for what they did to Eddie.'

'Who? Who did it? Why don't you tell me the truth?'

'Because I'm still working it all out in here.' He tapped the side of his skull with his forefinger. 'Lots of things need to come together, princess, then it will be crystal.'

Della got up and began walking away. He called after her.

'Wear something sexy tonight, in honour of Eddie.'

Chapter 9

Willis caught up with Carter at eleven that morning. He was heading into work.

She was about to head to Kent, to the Paradise Villas headquarters. She watched him lock his car. He looked distracted. She'd been waiting for him to get in touch since the previous evening. He returned to pick up something he'd forgotten. He caught sight of Willis. She walked across to him.

She reached him as he passed the police vans. 'I couldn't get hold of you last night.'

'Yes, sorry, I was dead on my feet.'

Willis was thinking that he looked as if he hadn't slept at all. He hadn't shaved. He had the same clothes on as the day before.

'I'm headed back to Kent to talk to Manson, the manager of Paradise Villas, again – I want to take more samples. Are you free to come with me?'

He nodded, a hanky over his nose. 'Let's do it.'

Carter drove out of the car park. Willis looked over.

'You all right, guv?'

'Yeah. Why?'

'You look like shit.'

'Thanks.' Carter took a look at himself in the driving mirror and rubbed the stubble on his chin that sounded like sandpaper. I have a cold, that's all, look in the glove compartment and hand me that electric razor, will you?'

Willis found it and switched it on as she passed it over. 'Do you want me to drive?'

'No way.' He glanced across, grinning. 'We need to get there today.'

'You come in late to work, and you still don't manage to shave?' Willis frowned.

'Yeah, let's leave this conversation, Eb, if you don't mind. Things on my mind. Besides, that's rich coming from you – you never make an effort and I meant to tell you to do something about your moustache months ago. Didn't have the heart.'

She thumped him on his arm.

'Jeezus, Eb, go easy.'

Willis and Carter had worked together for five years. Ever since she'd joined the MIT, he had been her partner. He had been a DS then, and she a detective constable. Carter was like family to her.

'Got a lot going on, that's all.'

He looked at his watch as he handed her the shaver back. 'Right now I'm supposed to be in Tenerife. I'd be having my first bottle of ice-cold beer of the day.'

'Why aren't you?'

He looked at her with a wounded expression.

'Christ knows, I didn't want to cancel it, Eb, but this case is important to me. Jeezus! I was looking forward to it.'

'We can handle this without you.'

'Yeah, cheers for that.'

'You know what I mean.'

'I know, I know, but, Cabrina doesn't really mind. She's gone off with Archie and taken a mate with her instead; it's still a couple of weeks in Tenerife. She'll have fun. There'll be plenty more opportunities to go on holiday.'

Willis looked at her phone. 'Shall I get the satnav working?'

'Don't worry, I know the way,' Carter said. 'We used to drive to Margate all the time when I was a kid. We'd all pile in the taxi and off we'd go. If we had time Dad used to take detours on the way back. Swanley was one of them. They had a great fish and chip shop there.'

'What about Ramsgate, do you know it well?'

'I know it, yeah. Been there many times, too. It's a bit more upmarket than Margate. It's got some great restaurants. There's an Italian there that I used to rate.'

'The one Della Butcher's family own? Della Cipriani?'

He shook his head as he cracked a smile.

'Christ, Eb, we've worked together too long and you must have done some serious digging to find that out.'

'I suppose I did. I also read the report from the officer on duty where the wake was held. Della Butcher left in your car last night. Who *was*, or is, she to you?

'I tried to find out about a family history for her but it says her parents live just outside Milan and then the trail ends. But she's mentioned in Operation Argos. They gave her maiden name as Vincetti, not Cipriani, and said that her last known address was in Ramsgate. Then I found out there are other family members there. What was she in Operation Argos? Was she a suspect then? Most of the information about her is blacked out.'

'I know, it's complicated. She chose to change her name. Probably because she was marrying a Butcher. Maybe she didn't want the Butchers to ever be able to interfere with her real family.'

'Again, how do you know all this? Who is she to you?'

'We had a relationship once, many years ago.'

'When?'

'Let me think ... I was in my mid-twenties. We met through our families, the Italian connection. My mum knew her dad's family, that kind of thing.'

'What happened? Why are you being so cagey about all this with me? It's not like you.'

'It's difficult for me to talk easily about it. The usual happened, we didn't make it. No one's fault. The pressure of work, the relationship folded.'

'Then she went on to marry Eddie Butcher?'

'Exactly.' He glanced across at Willis and rolled his eyes. 'You couldn't write it, could you?'

'No, because it doesn't ring true.'

'It did to me, at the time. I was heartbroken.'

'How did they meet?'

'I don't know. I'm not sure. It's tricky, Eb.'

'So, what did Della have to say last night?'

'Nothing that helps. I gave her a lift back to her hotel near Gatwick. She was quiet. She didn't understand why Eddie had been targeted and she didn't think he had been into anything other than legitimately building villas. She's as much in the dark as we are.'

'And you believed her?'

'Yes, I think so.'

'So what now?' asked Willis as she looked across at Carter.

'We treat it like we would any other inquiry.'

Willis kept her eyes on Carter's profile. A lot of things

were running through her mind. It was the first time in five years she didn't feel she had Carter's trust. Something new had just happened between them. Carter hadn't wanted her involved in a vital part of an inquiry. He had personal reasons. Willis could understand that but they were part-ners – and, if Carter didn't trust her enough to confide in her, then they were *not* partners.

'Were you going to tell me?' she asked.

'Not if I didn't have to.'

She shook her head, confused.

'Eb, this is tricky ground. I feel the need to tread care-fully. I don't want you dragged into quicksand with me.'

'Is that what you see this as, potential quicksand?'

'A part of me does. I can't lie. We all have things in our past, but they don't all end up in a murder inquiry.'

'Quicksand or not, I am in this with you.'

He nodded but she could see she hadn't convinced him.

'If nothing else, you're a heavy bastard and you'll sink faster than me and I can stand on you to get out.'

They took the road off the roundabout towards the small industrial estate named The Paddocks and pulled up at the gates. It was a smart estate, surrounded by a barbed-wire-topped steel fence. There were big notices telling people to beware of the patrol dogs. They pulled up and Carter peered past the guard on the gate, who was sheltering from the elements in a small hut.

'Pretty high security for a builders' yard. The place looks deserted. Morning, what you guarding here?' Carter said to the security guard. 'The Crown Jewels?' He grinned.

'Yeah, it looks like it, don't it? You wouldn't believe how much stuff gets nicked from sites.'

'Where is everyone?'

'Winding down for Christmas, I think. Most people knocked off this week except Mr Manson in Paradise Villas.'

'That's who we've come to see.' Carter showed his warrant card.

'Are you here about Eddie?'

'Yes, that's right.'

'I was sick to my stomach when I heard of what they did to him, poor bloke.'

'When was the last time you saw Eddie Butcher?'

'It was the day before Bonfire Night, the 4th. He was here for a few hours in the afternoon.'

'Did he say anything to you? What was he here for, do you know?'

'He was in his office most of the time. He seemed fine. We were talking about the celebrations, the firework displays and he said he was thinking of heading home to Spain by that evening, he wasn't going to stay around for them. We had a joke and a laugh.'

'How did he seem?'

'He was his usual chatty self. He was the kind of bloke who always gives you the time of day. He was a friendly sort. There's Mr Manson.'

A man was walking to a white Range Rover. Carter called out to him and he stopped in his tracks and waited for them to reach him. He was still jiggling the keys in his hand, still looking hopeful that he could leave any second.

Manson had a once-boyish face, but now it gained a little puffiness in his jawline. His blond hair was receding. He had large sapphire-blue eyes. He was wearing jeans and a blue Aran cardigan. He looked as if he could have been in a boy band once.

'Mr Manson?' Carter showed his warrant card. 'You've met my colleague before, Detective Sergeant Willis?'

Willis waved a hand in the air with a warrant card attached. She was standing a few feet away as she got a feel for the place and began taking photos.

'What's this about?' Manson was looking past Carter towards Willis with a frown on his face.

'Can we have a chat, please?' Carter glanced back to Willis. 'Don't mind her, she doesn't get out of the office very often. I'll be honest with you,' said Carter, slipping into his cheeky-chappy routine in the hope that Manson might loosen up. It was always Carter's defence against people who spoke with a posh accent. He never felt at ease. 'Eddie Butcher's murder is really proving difficult to solve, even finding out what he was doing over here seems an impossibility. He's not the easiest man to research, if you know what I mean. People are reluctant to speak to the police.'

'Really?' Manson tried to look genuinely puzzled.

'It's probably because a lot of his friends were ex-cons. Some of them not even retired villains, pretty active. You must have seen some sights, met some real types.'

Manson shrugged. 'I didn't socialise with Eddie outside work. I met the clients, obviously, but I never saw them like that, maybe they were ex-cons. Maybe, some of them are not the most ... I don't know. Sorry, I don't know what to say.'

'I'm not trying to put you on the spot. They were clients, I suppose, and you built villas for them? They were Eddie's contacts.'

Manson was still distracted as he talked and kept one eye on Willis who was walking around the exterior of the warehouse and disappeared out of sight.

'Do you mind if my colleague takes a look around while we chat?' Carter smiled. 'Can you open up the warehouse, please? We'll be as quick as we can.'

Manson shrugged, 'Okay, but it's been done already.' He walked back over to open up the side door to the warehouse.

'We're struggling to come up with a reason Eddie was killed, especially in that manner. It's the kind of death we'd associate with someone having trodden on the wrong toes, crossed someone they shouldn't. Is that at all possible in this case, do you think?'

Manson shook his head. 'I can't think of anyone that Eddie had fallen out with.'

'And you and Eddie got on well? You must have after working together for how many years?'

'Fifteen.'

'Exactly. That's longer than most marriages last. You must have known each other inside out. You still got on like a house on fire?'

'We had no problems. We usually agreed on most things.'

'No dodgy clients pissed off with the service? Anyone come to mind?'

'No.' He shook his head. 'I can't think of anyone, but then I wasn't always with Eddie. He lived in Spain and I lived here.'

'But, whoever it was, they chose to kill him here.'

Manson seemed to be thinking things through. He rubbed his face with his hands. His eyes were rimmed. He was having difficulty standing still.

Carter looked past him into the warehouse.

'Would you feel better if we stepped inside?'

Manson was watching Willis as she examined the contents of some boxes.

'What are you working on right now? Do you make anything here?'

'No, we hold some things for shipping out to the building sites. We're working on the same projects as we've been working on this last eight months. We're building one villa on the Costa del Sol and updating an existing one for a client out there.'

'Both of them are going smoothly enough?'

'Yes, on target.'

'Paid for?'

'No, not yet, it doesn't work like that in this business. At this stage, we have a lot of money outlaid on them. Were waiting for interim payments on both.'

'Who are the clients?'

'I'm not being funny, Inspector, but this is my livelihood. I'm the one who's going to lose everything if they decide to pull out, or just not pay because Eddie's not here any more. Without Eddie, my livelihood could all disappear and I have my own money in this business.'

'Why would it just disappear? It's obviously a good business and you must have built a good reputation. Now surely you're the brains behind all this. How much do you own?'

'I have a five per cent share in the business. I wasn't the brains in the outfit. Eddie had all the charisma and the contacts. All I did was work out the logistics.'

'You're being modest, I'm sure. Has something happened to make you think Eddie's death is going to make a big difference to this business?'

He shook his head. 'I don't know. I was not the figure-head. It's always tricky, precarious. I don't know what will happen to the business now.'

'And you liked Eddie Butcher? I mean you thought he was a good boss?'

'Yeah, he was okay. You know, he didn't mess you about. He expected a good job done but he left you to get on with it.'

'That's good. I really hate that, someone looking over your shoulder, pointing out the bleeding obvious. Micromanagement, eh? But sometimes it was short of money. We've been looking at the accounts for the last few years. What's been going on? Is it the world recession? I didn't think that actually affected the super-wealthy.'

'It's touched people all the way to the top, I think, but Eddie and I liked to keep a modest cash flow going. We didn't work more than we felt like and we made what we needed. Sometimes there are millions in the account and other times we are a million overdrawn. That's the nature of a luxury business. It never bothered Eddie. I learned to be the same.'

'It's a whole new world to me.' Carter laughed. 'I worry about going a few hundred quid overdrawn, let alone a million.' Manson smiled. 'I'm going to need to know a bit more about what Eddie was working on. I just have to eliminate possible causes. I can see you run a tight ship here. I'm not looking to cause you problems, just want to solve the murder of a man who seems to have been a good friend of yours.'

'Yeah, of course, I understand. But, like I said, I don't want the customers to panic.'

Carter smiled. 'Got ya . . . this is sensitive, I understand, don't worry.'

Manson went into the office, came back after a few minutes, and handed Carter an envelope.

'This is the information on the two villas we're working on, clients' names, et cetera.'

'Appreciate it. I'm going to make sure any contact with them is kept to a minimum.

'Has anyone from the family been out here, since Eddie was killed?'

He shook his head. 'I haven't really had much contact with them. I've met them, but that's about it.'

'His family have a bit of a reputation,' said Carter.

'Yes, so I heard. Like I said, I only met Tony a couple of times.'

'The thing is, I can see it would be tricky for you. I bet a lot of people you've built villas for are actually Tony's friends. You must have a few Mafia bosses taking a swim in a pool you built.'

'Could be. Look, sorry, that wasn't my side of the operation. I'm the chippy, the site manager; I'm the man who works out how stuff is going to get done; I'm not the one who has dinners with the clients.'

'And Eddie did?'

'He lived in Spain. He saw the clients regularly. We had local contractors we trusted. I went back and forth when I needed to check on projects out there and Eddie and I met at the sites, if we needed to, but I know he saw a lot of past clients socially. I expect Marbella is one big club. Everyone knows everyone else?'

'So, Eddie looked after the clients and he was good at that. He was a charmer, you say? He did well from all this, didn't he?'

'Yes, I suppose so.'

'What about you? Do you get to own one of these villas that you build?'

Manson shook his head. 'The wife and I own a small place in France.'

'Really, that's it?' Carter asked.

Manson nodded.

'That's great, though, isn't it? I'd be happy just having a caravan in Margate.'

Manson laughed. 'It's not as great as it sounds. Every time I go over there I see stuff that needs doing to the place. It ends up being a working holiday.'

'Have you always been a developer?'

'I've been in the building trade since leaving school. One of those jobs I fell into. I started off making bespoke kitchens.'

'Well, good on ya! How did you and Eddie come to go into business together, in the first place? How did he even find you?'

'I built a kitchen for him and he liked my work, we got on well. He thought I'd be up to the job and the rest is history.'

'He was right. You and he have done well together. Are you from this area?'

'I'm from Hertfordshire.'

'Do you still have family there?'

'In Rickmansworth, yes. Sorry? What is this relevant to?'

'Just trying to get a bigger picture of Eddie, beyond the ex-criminal headlines. I just wanted to understand the nature of your relationship.'

'Nature?'

'I mean, you were happy working together? Did you feel five per cent in a business when you did the donkey's share of the work was good enough?'

'Yes. Of course. I mean I always earned a good wage. I was grateful to Eddie.'

'But did you ever see yourself taking a bigger share? Was it ever discussed?'

Willis came back out of the warehouse.

'No, it wasn't.' Manson looked at his watch. 'It wasn't what I would have wanted. I didn't have the risk that Eddie did. I didn't need to worry about the financial side of things.'

'Okay, I'll let you get on. Thanks for these,' Carter said, holding up the envelope.

Back in the car, Carter waved at Manson, who wasn't watching them. He'd already got into his car and started the engine.

'Find anything?' asked Carter as they were back on the road.

'There has been some activity going on, boxes moved, that kind of thing. I took another set of samples. It seems to be looking very bare in there. I wonder why they'd need such a big warehouse.'

'Manson said they often have building materials collected there ready to ship to sites,' Carter said. 'But there's something I don't trust about him. He's too polite about everything. I got the feeling he thought I was an idiot.'

'I thought you always counted that as a success when people thought that.'

'You're right, but he's scared.' Carter smiled. 'Natural, I suppose. He must wonder if he's next on someone's list. Even, if he's not scared about dying like Eddie, he has a whole livelihood to lose. Still, something about him is not ringing true to me. I want him checked out thoroughly.

Where did Manson come from? He said Eddie found him when Manson made a kitchen for him. Sounds like Eddie was really taken with him. Turned out he was right, they must have made a lot of money, but Manson always got five per cent of the profit and the profit has dwindled to nothing. How come Manson isn't mentioning that? How is he managing with a gold Rolex on his wrist and driving a new car? Was Eddie doing a lot more than building villas?'

'I'll get Pam on to it right now,' said Willis as she took out her phone and made a call to Pam. When she finished she looked up from her notebook. 'Where are we headed now?' She didn't recognise the route.

'You want the full history, the complete picture? Then we'll head down to Ramsgate and visit Della Vincetti's family. It's about time I went back.'

Chapter 10

They parked up on the seafront at Ramsgate and walked back into town; the wind and rain had eased slightly as they walked up a steep hill above the marina and along to the row of restaurants in the Victoria Westcliff Arcade. Fredo's Ristorante was at the end, tucked into the cliff side. They opened the door to a wonderful warm mix of the welcoming smell of pizza dough and slow-cooked tomato sauces, Marsala wine and herbs.

The restaurant was split-level, with arches separating the two sections. The old brick walls were painted off-white, and were dotted with paintings of Italy.

A blonde, middle-aged woman looked up from serving customers and gave them a smile that said, I'll be with you in a second; and then she took a double take.

'I don't believe it! Dan, how are you?' She walked across and paused. Shocked but happy, she hugged him.

Carter hugged her and kissed her on both cheeks.

'I'm well, Connie; you're looking just the same. How do you do it? You don't look a day older. Let me introduce my colleague. Ebony, this is Connie.'

Connie took Ebony's outstretched hand and covered it with both of hers. 'Oh, your hands are cold. For goodness' sake! I can't believe it.' She looked at Dan, still shaking her head. 'What are you doing here? I mean, come in, come in.'

'Well, I thought we'd get some lunch, for a start,' said Carter.

'Of course. I'll call Fredo. Wait a minute. Let me take this order through. Come and sit down.' They walked beneath the arches and down the step into the main section of the restaurant then down further into a small private area.

Fredo was led out from the kitchen, wiping his hands. He stopped in his tracks when he saw Carter.

'Bloody hell,' he said in his Italian accent. 'I can't believe my eyes. Look at you, you're grown up. You're a man now.' He stood beside Carter and put his arm around his shoulders. Willis thought Fredo looked about to cry.

'Fredo, this is my colleague Ebony.' She stood to shake Fredo's hand.

'Please sit down. Can you believe we knew this man when he was like a boy.' He slapped Carter on his chest.

'Is that mentally or physically?' Willis said. 'Because in one way he probably hasn't changed.'

Fredo laughed loudly. He couldn't take his eyes from Carter.

'Come on, please, sit down and we'll eat together. The restaurant is not busy and we have our nephew, Paulo, working in the kitchen now. He can cope on his own. You sit. I'll be back.'

Fredo went into the kitchen and then returned minus his apron and with two bottles of wine in his hands. Connie came to join them, in between seeing to the other customers in the restaurant.

'Your parents, Dan? How are they?' Fredo looked across the table at Willis. 'Excuse us, won't you? It's been a long time.'

'Of course, go ahead. I'm so looking forward to eating here.' Willis was starving now. The smell of the restaurant was enough to elevate her hunger to stratospheric heights. She had what Carter called 'hollow legs': it didn't matter what she ate, there was always room for more.

'Mama is in great shape, she's busy with all her grand-children,' answered Carter. 'I have a son, Archie, now. But he's one of eight grandchildren that she helps look after. But Dad's not been so good. He's in remission right now, but he's had throat cancer.'

'I'm sorry to hear that. Send them our love,' said Fredo. 'Bring them with you next time you come. It must be at least twelve years. I don't know where those years have gone. I'm sure Della would love to see them too. We talked about you just the other day, with Della, didn't we, Connie?' She nodded.

'When she came for the funeral?' asked Carter.

'Yes. We didn't go to it, of course,' said Fredo. 'We said our goodbyes to Eddie in our own way. We didn't like all that with the black horses and the carriage, and then, look how it all went wrong.'

Connie brought out plates of antipasti and a bottle of wine; a man was with her, helping her carry the food.

'Here is Fredo's nephew, Paulo.' She did the introductions.

'I remember you,' Carter said as he stood for them to shake hands. 'You were still in short trousers then.' Carter scrutinised Paulo's face and scanned his memory banks. 'You were the snotty-nosed kid who always wanted me to play football with him in the park.'

'Yes, I am glad I made such an impression on you,' he laughed. 'I am never allowed to forget you, even if I wanted to: my aunt and uncle speak of you often.' Paulo mimicked, 'Dan used to make it like this, Dan's way was the best, et cetera, et cetera. You are a lot to live up to.' He smiled.

Dan shook his head, touched but embarrassed. 'It was a long time ago. I learned how to cook here.'

Paulo left for the kitchen and they ate. Willis was glad not to be the one having to talk. She loved Italian food. Over their partnership, Carter had taken her into some of the best Italian cafés in London. He was a great cook, as well, they were right. The food on the table was her idea of heaven. As they finished one plate of antipasti, Paulo came out with lobster ravioli and fresh, stone-baked pizzas.

'Did she come here?' Carter asked as he started eating.

'Yes, she came here for an afternoon,' said Fredo, and Connie stopped eating to hear what he was going to say. 'Her heart is broken,' continued Fredo. 'She has so much to cope with, my poor little Della.'

Connie nodded. 'You saw her, Dan?'

'Very briefly. I gave her a lift after the wake. She didn't want to stay at the country park with the others; I can understand why.'

'She was grateful for that.'

Fredo proposed a toast.

'To happier times,' Fredo said, then shook his head sadly as he looked across at Willis. 'That's the problem, Ebony. You fall in love with your daughter's boyfriend. You want her to stay with him for ever, to have beautiful babies and to take over your business some day, but then they go and spoil your dream by making a mistake.'

'We can't say it was a mistake, Fredo. It was her choice,'

Connie said, looking slightly anxious now as she listened to Fredo spill his heart across the table.

'I know, I understand. But for me? It was a big mistake. It's one hell of a family she married into. I think she sees trouble ahead. This is a tough time for Della.'

Carter looked at Connie, who nodded. 'She doesn't tell us much. But ...'

'It's like marrying into the Mafia,' added Fredo in a whisper. 'She cannot go where she want, or see who she want. The family do not accept her; they never have. We are very worried for her.'

'Can you help her, Dan?' asked Connie.

Willis watched Carter's reaction closely as he stared into his wine glass. She could see that it was a big thing for a proud, private woman like Connie to beg for help for her daughter.

'I can try but I'm not sure how, or whether she'd want my help. At the moment we are working on trying to find Eddie's killer.'

'Huh ...' Fredo shook his head. 'Good luck with that. We heard what they did to him. This was one Mafia to another; I don't think you're ever going to find who is responsible.'

'Then you think Eddie was involved with organised crime? With something he shouldn't have been?' asked Carter.

'No, not him, but surely the family is,' answered Fredo. 'I know that Eddie wanted to break away from them; Della told us that they were going to move. Eddie was getting ready to turn his back on the family.'

A silence ensued, while Carter drank his wine.

'Is that what brings you here?' asked Connie. 'For

information about Eddie?' Willis glanced Carter's way as an uncomfortable feeling had landed at the table.

'No. I was just reminded of times gone by, that's all.'

'Della said it was nice seeing you again,' said Connie with a smile.

Carter nodded. 'Yeah, it was nice to see her too, after all these years. She's as beautiful as ever.' Connie and Fredo looked at one another and Connie smiled and nodded.

'I can't tell you how much she could do with a friend right now, Dan,' she said.

'I understand, I will do my best,' said Carter. He looked across at Willis.

Willis asked, 'Have you had anyone come in here looking for Della or talking to you about Eddie?'

'I can't think of anyone,' answered Connie, looking across at Fredo, who shook his head to confirm. 'No one strange.'

'Dan, if this was a Mafia execution of Eddie,' Connie asked, 'does that mean all of us could be in danger?'

Carter paused before answering. He looked at Willis, who hesitated to answer for him.

'We don't know the answer to that yet, Connie,' replied Carter. 'We think it could have something to do with Eddie's brother, Tony.'

'That no-good piece of shit,' said Fredo, throwing his napkin on the table in front of him and sitting back in his chair in disgust. 'We always knew he would be trouble for Eddie and Della.'

'Did Della ever talk about Tony and Eddie being involved in something illegal together?' asked Carter.

'No, of course not. Eddie was straight.' Connie bristled. 'He built top-of-the-range luxury villas for people all around the world.'

'He was no Boy Scout,' said Carter. 'He set up the business with stolen money.'

'It's a long time ago,' Fredo said defensively.

'People were beaten up, doused in petrol, they thought they were going to die. The robberies they were involved in were brutal,' Carter answered.

Carter stopped eating and wiped his mouth with the napkin. The table had become tense.

Fredo stared at his wine and shook his head slowly. 'This is all in the past, Dan. He served his time in prison.'

'Yeah, but he kept the spoils. The money from the diamonds was there waiting for him when he got out. His Paradise Villas was set up with it.'

'What can we say, Dan?' Fredo looked up. 'Is this important now?' he asked. 'Is this still a reason to kill him?'

Carter shook his head. 'No.'

'Dan, we understand exactly the way you feel. But, we have learned to live with these facts over the years,' Connie said. 'We know about his past but the man we knew was gentle and kind. He was a good husband to Della. He didn't deserve to die like that. No one deserves that.'

'No, of course. That's for certain,' Carter answered. 'We will do our best to find out who did it, and why. We are looking into his company, just in case there was trouble with a client of his. We talked to the manager at Paradise Villas before we came here today; do you know him?'

'Billy Manson? Yes, we know him well,' answered Connie. 'When Eddie was over here working he'd come and see us and bring Billy with him. They often ate in here and Billy's even been here with his family a few times. He has two great kids and a lovely wife, Jo.'

'Eddie and Billy seemed like good friends,' agreed Fredo,

'not just colleagues. I know Eddie relied on Billy to run the business for him. He trusted him, so can you. Billy will tell you the truth.'

'But we haven't seen Billy for about a year now.'

'What about Eddie? When was the last time you saw him?'

'About six months ago,' answered Connie.

'Was that usual?' Carter looked from Connie to Fredo.

'No, we were thinking it was a long time since we saw him,' answered Fredo. 'Della said he had been working hard, that was all.'

'She said Eddie was ready to start afresh, leave the family,' Connie added.

'Now it's too late,' said Fredo. 'Poor Della.'

Chapter 11

Della got back to the villa after her talk with Tony; she had a rest and then got up and ran herself a bath. Her head and heart felt in freefall. She was trying hard to take one emotion at a time and not feel so overwhelmed that she fell apart. The one thing she was sure about was that Eddie's family wouldn't be waiting to catch her if she fell, they'd have already placed the daggers out.

Slipping into the warm water, she submerged her head and listened to the hum of silence in her waterlogged ears.

She listened to her own breathing, felt the tickle of the warm water creep across her scalp. She opened her eyes and saw Tony's grinning face.

As she raised herself up out of the water, Tony's hand grasped her throat and she felt the water rush into her nose as she fought for breath. She instinctively pulled at his hands around her neck but changed her defence to attack and punched hard into his face and throat. The last blow sucked all air from his windpipe and his face was out of her view as she rose in one leap forward and out of the bath. She stood naked, coldly angry, coughing. She watched him choking, retching on the floor. She was shaking with anger and with adrenalin.

'Get out of my fucking house, Tony. You ever come in here again uninvited, I will kill you.'

Tony rolled onto his side and lay staring up at her, his eyes red from the effort. He clutched at his throat. Now he was so wiry and thin, all his ribs stuck out like a fossil.

Tony considered her for a moment and then he smiled and raised himself to his feet, breathing hard. His face was dripping wet. His eyes were black and mad. He was nodding with some deep understanding that had just dawned on him.

'Okay, princess. You have it your way. I can come in any time with the bulldozers. I can start knocking the walls down around you, and I will.'

'You don't own my house.'

'I will soon. I spoke to the lawyer; now we have a new will. It signs everything, and I mean everything, over to Yours Truly. You, my little caged bird, are free. Free to fly away. And' – Tony turned to leave after wiping his face with a towel nearby – 'I suggest you fuck off before I bury you in this place. Pack your bags and leave. You better be nice to me – I'm the only thing stopping you getting sliced up like Eddie right now. Of course, they would take their time with you.'

Della felt the vomit rise acidic in her throat as she locked the door after Tony had gone and made a dash for the toilet. She tasted bitter bile as she retched. The porcelain toilet was cold beneath her hands as she gripped the sides.

Afterwards, she stood, washed her face and looked at the blotchy reflection staring back at her and averted her eyes. This was no time to feel sorry for herself; she was too scared to be a baby now. She was going to have to fight for everything she had left. Tony had some mad, vicious plan; she could see it in his whole demeanour. He looked delirious about it. Tony clearly knew a lot more than he was saying about Eddie's death.

She went back to lie on her bed to try to calm herself. Could Eddie have left her so unprotected? He must have known this would happen. After an hour of staring at the ceiling and thinking things through she got up and went into the dressing room and opened the shoe closet. Then she knelt and uncovered Eddie's personal safe. Her hands were shaking as she turned the combination. Surely, there must be deeds to the villa somewhere? She tried to open it. Twice she went wrong. Eddie had put in an anti-theft device. She knew she had one more attempt before it would be blocked. She went to Eddie's side of the bed and pulled out the drawer. There was the book he always kept there. Della knew what page he'd told her the code was on. It was the sum of their birthdays. Hers was the 12th of February; his was the 9th of July. She added up the combination of numbers and turned to page 30. She took the first sentence on the page and the first letters of each word and wrote down the corresponding number to the position of the letter in the alphabet. Then she went across to the safe and carefully fed in the numbers. Her hands were still shaking as she reached inside and pulled out the files.

Chapter 12

'So, you were one of the family, basically?' Willis said to Carter as they drove back towards London. The rolling grey mass of low cloud was inching over them ahead. The day had already turned dark at four o'clock. The cold air was settling in. The atmosphere in the car was even colder.

'Yes, I suppose I was.' He looked across at Willis. She was staring at him intently. He'd seen the look before. It meant she didn't understand, didn't accept some piece of the puzzle. If he had thought that giving her a bit more of the picture would help her, ease her mind, it hadn't worked. He felt a slash of anger rise in him. It wasn't often he'd had to justify himself to his colleagues.

'And you haven't been back since you and Della split up?'

'No, I just didn't think it was appropriate.' He tapped the steering wheel, irritated.

'No, maybe not. What do think will happen to Della now?'

'I don't know.' He shrugged, pretending indifference. 'She lives too close to Tony to be safe. If she asked me I'd tell her sell up and leave, find a new life.'

'Is her life in danger?'

'Got to be. If Eddie's was, then so is hers.'

'The family were prickly when you talked about Eddie's past. Can they really think of him as an honest businessman?'

'I suppose it's because Eddie kept a low profile after he came out of the nick. He was pretty young when he went inside. The Butcher brothers were two of many done for a spate of high-profile diamond and gold heists across Europe. They were part of a slick operation. They were paid well for their silence. One thing they didn't do is grass anyone up. Eddie went into property building with his share, while Tony went into building himself a drugs empire.'

'How did it feel today?' Willis had pushed back in her seat. She was watching Carter's reaction to her questions.

Carter glanced across and gave a shrug.

'Let's keep this to what's relevant. I'm getting tired of being cross-examined on personal issues. What it seemed like to me was a family who didn't want to attend the funeral of their son-in-law, someone they were fond of, because they're scared. They think he was killed because of something Tony's involved in.'

'They like Manson, the manager of Paradise Villas,' said Willis.

'Yes, they know him and his family. That flies in the face of what he told me. They have no reason to lie so he must be.'

Chapter 13

Marco rapped on the door.

'You ready, princess?'

Della watched the door, as if she expected Marco to burst through it, and mow her down in a hail of bullets.

'Are you talking to me?' she answered and waited, listening. She heard a shuffle as Marco's weight shifted and he leaned against the door. She knew he would be grinning. 'Call me "señora" or Mrs Butcher.'

'*Si, señora.*'

'Wait for me in the car. I'll be down in ten minutes.'

'*Si, señora.*'

They drove in silence to Tony's villa. Marco left the car with the valet and escorted her inside. How things were changing, thought Della. Now she was watched every minute, every second. A few days ago Marco would not have escorted her anywhere. Now, he had the right to walk in with her. Soon, he would be above her in the pecking order; she must reclaim some ground and fast before it disappeared beneath her feet.

Laurence stepped forward to greet her as she walked into the trophy room in Villa Cassandra.

'Hello, Della.'

Frank Sinatra was playing on the music system. The lighting was subdued. 'Eddie for ever' was lit in candles on the veranda facing the mountains. The rest of the family were already there.

Della looked across at Tony; he had dressed up for the occasion. He was wearing his whole ensemble: black floppy hat, pink ruffle-fronted silk shirt and black dinner trousers with a satin strip down the sides. But he had shrunk so much since he first bought them that all of the clothes needed taking in and the trousers were obviously held up with a belt that had to be pulled in so much it gathered the material around his waist. She felt a flip inside her stomach, which was a mix of anger and fear, but the anger had the edge.

Harold and Tony were talking on the veranda facing the sea. The evening outside was dark. The fountains were lit. The guest houses were all aired and open. The place was alive.

As Laurence went to kiss Della, she moved her head so the kiss landed on her cheek. Suddenly the question hit her: a few weeks after her husband's death was she fair game?

Laurence drew back instinctively, wounded, embarrassed. She instantly regretted being oversensitive: she needed all the friends she could get. She'd always trusted Laurence. Eddie spoke well of him. He seemed to understand and smiled warmly as he touched her arm. She felt the touch, realised it had been over a month since anyone touched her with affection. She was grateful to Laurence.

'How are you holding up?' Laurence's voice was lowered.

His eyes were questioning as he caught her looking around the room nervously.

'It's hard to say,' she answered with an attempt at a smile.

He nodded. She touched his hand as she walked away from him, further into the room. Della walked towards Sandra and got an acidic smile from her mother-in-law. Della also noticed a hint of triumph in Sandra's demeanour as she sat on the far white sofa, facing the room, holding audience. Debbie was sitting beside her.

Sandra stopped talking and watched Della approach.

'Hello, Sandra.'

She looked Della up and down. Della had ignored Tony's request to dress sexy and had come in her usual 'Jackie Kennedy-style' simple navy shift dress, cardigan, kitten heels, pearls, her hair pinned up. Eddie always said there was no need to gild the lily. He loved to see her with minimal make-up, with simple clothes that were stylish but classic. Tonight she'd made sure she had put enough make-up on that she wouldn't melt under scrutiny. She intended to hold her ground even if it was trying to swallow her whole. She was still shaking from Tony's attack on her, but now a new feeling was growing inside her: self-preservation was sharpening her senses and making her brave.

Sandra looked hung-over and edging into drunk again. She looked as if she'd gone to bed in her make-up and just applied more on top in the morning. Her eyes were black with kohl and her face was over-tanned, caked. Her hair was silver blond and scraped up to a bun on top of her head with a hairpiece attached, like a blond Catherine wheel. She looked like a Barbie gone to seed. She was from the school of 'more is more' when it came to overtly sexual. She hadn't changed her make-up routine since the sixties. The eyeliner was too heavy and the lashes too long and the skirts too short.

Debbie had joined in the theme tonight: she'd donned a black playsuit and silver stilettos, a thick silver chain looped around her hips. She had enormous diamonds hanging from her ears. No matter how much money she spent on things to make her look pretty, they never did. The more beautiful the jewel around Debbie's neck, the more wizened she looked in comparison.

Sandra steadied her glass and her gaze as she focused on Della. 'Where did you go last night? We agreed we'd all stay in Giddewell,' she said.

'I didn't agree to stay anywhere. I needed some peace.'

Debbie whispered in Sandra's ear. Sandra laughed and nodded.

'Yeah, don't feel like you have to stay around on our account, if you need peace. We realise you must want to move on now. The quicker the better, as far as we're concerned.'

Harold's voice interrupted. 'A toast to Eddie.' His voice came out deep and cockney. 'He'll be sadly missed.'

Harold was the shortest of all the brothers and the most violent-looking. He had the dark-red complexion of someone who had lived a rough life without com-promise. No amount of expensive clothes or good food could alter it. He drank too much and he spent all the money he ever earned on partying with the rougher edge of society. Eddie always said he was a man ruled by his vices and someone you could never trust. He meant to do the right thing but it was always open to interpretation. His liking for the rougher side of life included his women, whom he now picked up from escort agencies and pimps who'd come to know him over the years.

Della accepted a glass of wine from Sheena.

Tony seconded Harold's toast: 'To my little brother, may you cause havoc in hell.' Tony started laughing in the silence of the room and Sandra glared at him.

Debbie looked embarrassed and stood. 'Let's eat,' she announced and led the way through the double archway and into the dining area.

Tony began almost dancing his way across with them, herding people forward, as skittish as a spider.

As Harold passed her, Della held him back by the arm.

'You were with Eddie when he was in London. What was Eddie doing there?'

Tony turned and double-backed, double-quick. He leaned in to her face.

'Not now, you hear me?'

'Harold?' she persisted, ignoring Tony.

'Nothing that I could have prevented,' Harold answered, looking cornered.

Tony put his hand on Harold's back to propel him forward.

'Business,' he said, 'and business doesn't always go as planned.'

'What business? Eddie was a property developer, not a drug dealer.' Della raised her voice. 'I have the right to know.'

Tony turned back, incensed. 'I said be quiet! I never said it was anything to do with drugs, now did I? You're being disrespectful, you know that? You're in my house and you show some fucking respect or get out.'

Della averted her face as she felt Tony's spittle land on it. Laurence came over and intervened. He placed a hand on Tony's arm. 'She's just upset. We've all been through a lot the last month. Della wants to know as much as you can tell her about how her husband died. That's perfectly reasonable. We all want to know.'

'All right. Okay. Hey!' Tony held up his palms in the air but his face was still fuming. 'I'm like the rest of you. I'm the first one who wants answers. But one thing you got to know, princess: Eddie was a lot of things that he didn't share with you. He had his secrets. That's all I'm saying. You were on a need-to-know basis. We all were.' Tony turned and went to walk away.

'I don't believe that,' she called after him. The room went quiet.

'Oi! Someone get Della a drink, for fuck's sake.' Tony didn't look at Della. The room waited nervously as he shouted out again, 'Sheena, where the fuck are you?'

'I don't want one,' Della said, 'and I'm not hungry.'

Tony shrugged. 'Suit yourself, your ladyship,' he said, and went to take his place at the dinner table.

Laurence led Della away to the veranda as the rest of the family sat down to eat.

'I don't belong here, Laurence.'

'I'm sorry for all this, Della. It isn't fair, not after you've been through so much.'

'It's almost as if they blame me for his death.'

'They always have to find someone to blame. They lead one another on. Do you want me to run you home?'

'No, that's kind, thanks, Laurence. I could do with the fresh air.'

She looked at Laurence and caught him glancing at Sandra. She was staring at them.

'I won't keep you; but just tell me, Laurence: what Tony says about Eddie being involved in something criminal, is it true, do you think?'

'I don't know, I never get involved with Tony's business. But, Eddie was a bad boy when you met him.' Laurence smiled sympathetically.

'Led on by his older brother. He did everything Tony told him to back then.'

'How do you know he still didn't?'

Behind her Della saw the family lift their glasses a second time.

Fuck him, fuck them all, Della said to herself, but deep inside she knew that her world was for ever changed. She was Eddie's wife; now he was dead.

'Laurence, get in here,' Sandra called. 'I want you to leave,' she shouted at Della.

'What do you mean?' Della resisted Laurence's hand on her arm as he tried to stop her reacting. She shrugged him off and he walked away towards the dining table.

'You know what I mean.' Sandra sat back in her chair. 'You're not welcome here any more. We tolerated you because of Eddie but, now he's gone, you can go.'

'I don't take orders from you. I can stay or go, as I please.'

'No, that's where you're wrong,' Sandra said and Tony was grinning. 'You'll be on your way, soon enough.' Sandra looked away and began a conversation with Debbie.

Della walked across to the table.

'Excuse me?'

'You heard.' Sandra smiled. 'We've always known what

you are. You don't belong here now. I'll make you an offer from my own purse. I'll give you two million quid. You sign over Eddie's villa to me and you disappear and don't come back.

'Fuck you, Sandra.'

Chapter 14

Carter took a call in the car just as they hit the outskirts of London.

'That was my informant; he's got some information for me. I'll get out in Whitechapel on the way back,' Carter said, finishing the call.

'What about the meeting? Do you want us to wait?'

'Yes, wait. I'll be back for that later. Eb, I'd rather you didn't mention any more about Della and her family, please. I don't want people to ask unnecessary questions that might confuse the issue. I need to talk to the chief inspector first. Plus, I don't want to put them in danger. If the rest of the Butcher family don't know about the Vincettis, so much the better.'

'Of course.'

Willis took over the driving seat as she dropped Carter outside Whitechapel Tube Station.

He watched Willis drive away and then he took a left past the sari shops and the market stalls on the wide road. It was five p.m. and the streets were getting busy with people on the way home. He stepped into one of the sari shop doorways to answer his phone.

'All right, babe?' Cabrina's voice came over the phone.

'Hello, sexy, how's my son?'

'Missing his dad.'

'Well you know I would be there if I could.'

'Yeah, the weather's fantastic. The resort is incredible. They even have a babysitting service so me and Dawn have been out a couple of times.'

'Sounds great.'

'Yeah, well, it's actually not that great. Dawn hooked up with a bloke on the first day. I haven't seen her since. It's me and my little man, Archie, enjoying the happy hour and the two-for-one deals on cocktails.' Cabrina laughed drily. 'I seriously wish we hadn't booked for two weeks. Is there any chance of you coming out?'

'I don't see how, babe.'

'Thought not.'

'I won't do it to you again, I promise. You stay and relax, spend some money, I'll cover it.'

'Don't make promises you can't keep.'

'What? I'll put money on your credit card for you.'

'Not that.'

'No, you're right, I can't promise it will never happen again but I'll do my damnedest to make sure. I'm going to make it up to you.'

'Yeah, I know. I'll hold you to it. I can't wait to come home. I miss you.'

'Me too, got to go, babe. Be good.'

'Why do you say that?'

'What?'

'Be good. You haven't said that to me for years.'

'It's just a figure of speech. I suppose it's because I worry about you on your own. You could fall for some local stud.'

'Yeah, right. He'd have to get past the stroppy five-year-old first. Do you still love me, Dan?'

'Of course, Cabrina. What is this? Don't be daft.'

'This wasn't just an excuse because you didn't want to spend time with us?'

'You know that's ridiculous. Why wouldn't I want to spend time with the two people I love most in all the world?'

He heard Cabrina sigh. There was a pause, in which he knew she would be biting her lip. She was tearful, he knew the silence.

'Try and enjoy yourself, babe. I'm just here working hard. Bring me a present back, some fake Ray-Bans or something. I'll ring you tomorrow, promise. Kiss Archie for me.'

Carter put his phone back in his pocket and pushed open one of the double doors of the Blind Beggar pub, which was once a brewery, built on the site of an old coaching house. It was reminiscent of walking into a Western saloon with its long bar to the right and an open sitting area with tables and chairs straight ahead. It was rough and ready. The tables and chairs were mismatched, straight-backed and wooden. The ceiling was painted deep red. The floor was wooden. There was a screen to show sports hanging down from the corner of the ceiling.

There were just a few customers sitting in a lounge area to the back left of the pub where a fire was lit. It added a welcome warmth to what was otherwise quite an austere, working man's pub. A woman was using the Wi-Fi facilities near the fire and the entrance to the pool room. She was tapping away on her laptop. The pub was her office.

But its main claim to fame was its history with two local lads, the Kray brothers.

Carter ordered a glass of Chilean Merlot. The pub wasn't busy. He was a few minutes early.

'Been busy?' Carter asked the barman, who looked as if he'd come straight off the set of *Deliverance*: big beard, missing teeth, chequered shirt and braces.

'So-so.' He hadn't learned the necessary skills to be a good barman. He didn't like talking. Someone had told him not to smile.

As Carter took his drink and sat down on one of the long wooden pews against the far left wall, a group of people came through the doors bringing with them a blast of cold air. They were led by a female tour guide.

'We're not buying a drink,' she announced. 'Just showing people what a great pub this is.' The barman took no notice; he was used to it. He continued with his task of polishing the beer taps.

The woman led the five people on the tour to stand directly in front of Carter.

'Here is where George Cornell was sitting when he was murdered by Ronnie Kray.'

'Yeah, I've just finished cleaning up the mess,' Carter said, winking at one of the women. She giggled.

The tour guide was not impressed: she was expecting Carter to relocate, which he didn't feel inclined to do. She moved them quickly along to the next poster on the wall detailing the Krays' lives in the area. Carter was joined at the table by a man with an orange juice in his hand and a small dog beside him.

'You trying to scare me?' Carter nodded towards the orange juice. 'All right, Melvin? Scamp?'

'Just trying to prepare myself for the festive season, that's all. It's a busy time for me. I'm expected to have a drink with my punters and there are a lot of tourists heading this way.'

'Of course, all these eager tourists wanting to know the murderous side of the good old East End.'

'When you retire you can give me a hand if you like.'

'Yeah, maybe, thanks, mate. But I'm a way off that and, when I do retire, I'll try to avoid any job which has murder in its job description.'

'Offer stays open. You might change your mind. It's a growing trade. What we need is more funerals like Eddie Butcher's. Pity he wasn't as notorious as the Krays but lucky they're all on this patch. It's a hotspot.'

'I can see that. You have competition.' Carter turned to watch and listen to the tour guide: she was running through the Krays' life history.

'Don't worry about her. That's Janice. She doesn't know how to sell it. She's only got three stars on TripAdvisor. Twenty quid a head she charges and it's not worth it.'

'She charges the same as you, then.'

'Exactly, but mine's top-drawer.' He laughed. 'Genuine article, links to the actual family and all that.'

'An affair and a bastard child is stretching family connections.'

'It don't matter. It still counts. Anyway, I've put it up now, it's twenty-five.'

Carter laughed. 'Bargain.'

'Let's move.' Melvin picked up his drink. 'Want to go in the garden?'

'Not really. It's frigging cold. Even Scamp's not keen.'

The dog had gone to sit by the woman on the laptop near the fire.

'They have a patio heater. Come on. Scamp!'

Carter stood, picking up his wine. 'It just makes me want a cigarette whenever I go into the garden in a pub,' he said, following Melvin. 'If I'm truthful, I want a cigarette wherever I go,' moaned Carter, as they stepped into the nicely laid-out garden area with covered seats and water features.

They walked past the Christmas tree with hanging icicle lights, and sat down near the patio heater. Melvin began rolling a cigarette. Scamp jumped on his lap. Melvin Pratt was a man in his early forties who had grown up in the area, in the shadow of the Krays. His dad had been a friend to the Krays and a petty criminal who boxed with the brothers in the gym down the road. His mother's cousin was rumoured to have had an affair and a child with Reggie. Melvin had always been at the edge of success. He'd been doing well on a market stall selling bric-a-brac until the Trading Standards Department closed him down. He'd been a delivery man for the brewery until his back went. He'd raised a kid who, it turned out, wasn't his, and then his wife left him for another woman. Now he had carved out a niche for himself in the community that owed him.

He took out his phone and handed it to Carter to see the photos on it. Carter began swiping the photos.

'I didn't even know half of these people were still alive,' Carter said as Melvin grinned proudly.

'Yeah, I got some proper old-school villains. I haven't put these on my website yet but they're going to look great. I'm going to wipe out the competition with this. Everyone will see that I'm the genuine article, someone who knew the Krays, who knows the gangsters. Still does.'

'Yeah, can't argue with that.' Carter swiped through, looking for faces he had missed on the day. Most of the ones he saw were known to him. He stopped at a scene from the Blind Beggar in the evening.

'Who's that?'

'No idea; I was three sheets by that time. Let me see again.' He took the phone from Carter and began stretching the photo as he squinted at it. 'Oh yeah. He knew Eddie.'

Carter began sending the photos he wanted across to his phone.

'Oi! Give me that, there could be personal stuff on that. Tell me first which ones you're having.'

'Finished now.' Carter handed back the phone. He slid a hundred pounds across in a tight roll. Melvin took it and smoked his cigarette while they waited for the barman to leave. He'd come outside to switch on the fairy lights.

'Tell me, did you see anything interesting that evening?'

'I saw a few of your mates working. Some of them very good but you have to be from the East End to really talk to the old boys. Luckily for you, I am. The talk was all about Harold and Tony having failed their brother.'

'What were they saying?'

'Everyone was talking about how this was down to them. If not directly ordered, then it was a deal gone wrong. People liked Eddie. They were badmouthing Tony. Seems like he's bringing a lot of foreign muscle into these streets. Harold has been stirring up the young gangs; no one likes it. It means nothing but trouble for us. We have gang fights daily now. Sooner or later riot police going to be living on these streets. Then the gentrification process will be on hold, disaster!'

'Let's hope it won't come to that. What else are people saying? Did they think that one of the young gangs could have done it?'

He shook his head.

'I know a couple of the lads in the gangs. I asked them what it was all about, all the fighting, and the turf wars. They said it's all about the drug cartels. But Harold is losing his grip and there's a new man in town.'

'Is there anyone I should be talking to?'

'One of the photos on my phone I was saving for you.'

Melvin brought up an image from a locked folder. It was a man walking along the road outside St Matthew's Church.

'This guy is your new man. His name is Marco. We've seen a bit of him recently. He works for Tony and the Mendez cartel.'

'Was he here for the funeral?'

'I didn't see him.'

'Where did you get this?'

'I took this photo when I was sitting with Lev in the bakery. He pointed out this guy as he walked down the road. Then he came in.'

'What was he like?' Carter asked.

'Funny mix. Spoke English with a South American accent but he was mixed with white. Tall guy, heavy-set-looking, tough, ugly.'

'What did he want in Lev's?'

'Usual: a bagel, smoked salmon, cream cheese.' Melvin grinned. Carter reached for his wallet.

'What else?'

'Not much. I got the feeling he came in to check me out. He sat there staring at me, so I tried to make conversation, offered him a tour. I was friendly. He wanted to know what I knew about the old buildings around the church. I told him there wasn't much I didn't know. I was born and brought up in the area, I told him.'

'Was he interested in a building in particular?'

'Didn't seem so,' Melvin said. 'I told him that I could tell him a lot more if he paid me for a tour. He got a call and he got up to leave. On his way out he threatened me.'

Carter frowned. 'How?'

'He told me if he saw me taking any photos of him on my phone, he'd shove the phone somewhere the sun don't shine.'

'What about Lev? What did he do?'

'He didn't do or say anything while the man was in the bakery,' Melvin said. 'Lev just pretended to be really busy. I caught him watching us. After the man had left Lev told me I should think of staying away from the area for a bit.'

'Why?' Carter asked.

'He wouldn't say. He just shook his head with a "Don't say I didn't warn you" type of look.'

'Did it worry you?'

'Me?' Melvin laughed. 'No, of course not. I've lived with worse than him. He ought to have been here with the Kray generation.'

'These new ones are a lot worse, believe me,' Carter said. 'Keep yourself safe, Melvin. You've done enough for me now. If you see this guy Marco coming your way, then turn round.'

Melvin snorted. 'I can't do that, no way. This is my business we're talking about. I'm not going to alter my route just to suit him. If he keeps hanging around here, that's his problem.'

Chapter 15

'Something you want to get off your chest, Harold?'

Harold had asked if he could speak to Tony in his office. He left the others arguing around the dinner table. After a few drinks, past grievances were exhumed for a re-examine, but proved just as rotten as when they were buried first time round. Sandra was hell-bent on getting as drunk as possible; she was quietly fuming that Della had talked to her like that. Laurence was brooding and Debbie was doing her best to be a good hostess.

Tony opened his desk drawer and took out a bag of cocaine. It expanded onto the desk like a collapsing snowball.

He tore open the top and shovelled out a large mound with his fingers. He set about the process of chopping and cutting, scraping it and smoothing any lumps with a diligence that consumed him for ten minutes while Harold watched and waited. Finished, Tony rolled a note and offered it across to Harold who half-heartedly snorted up a part of a line and wiped it back out of his nose into his hand.

'We shouldn't be treating Eddie's widow like that.'

Tony's head swivelled back and forth, as if he were trying

to free his neck from a tight collar, and then his eyes settled on Harold.

'Like what?'

'You intend taking everything she has away from her? Can you do that? Take everything from Della?'

'Everything.' Tony smiled sickly sweet. He stood.

'Why take the business from her? At least leave her that.'

'I've been waiting a long time to get my hands on that business and all the other little projects that Eddie thought I didn't know about.'

'The police will never stop watching it, if you have anything to do with Paradise Villas,' said Harold. 'You won't be able to launder money through it. You won't even be allowed to build a garden shed. It's no use to you now.'

'Laurence will run it. It's time he earned his place in this family.' Tony was getting irritable with Harold's continued questioning of his methods. 'Laurence is even more respectable than Eddie was.'

'Maybe, but I can't see Della going quietly. We both know she's clever, stubborn.'

'Leave it to me,' Tony said with a sigh, as if it always came down to the same solution. Tony had to do everything himself.

'What do you want me to do when I get back to the UK? We have to do something about Eddie, people are expecting it. I don't know if they're going to believe that Francisco got the payment.'

'Yes, they will, at least for a few days. This is a good opportunity for these young gangs. We're going to need some men we trust around us when it gets bigger than we can handle. We act fast and furious and we kill the fuckers before they kill us. Promise them a part of the drugs distribution after it leaves here. Promise them anything but make them kill every last one of the Mendez cartel in the UK.'

Harold shook his head, worried. 'How do we know they killed Eddie?'

'Who else could it have been? You have any suspects you want to name?'

Harold shook his head. He stayed where he was. Tony leaned back in his Italian leather chair and rocked as he continued drinking whisky from a cut-glass tumbler, stolen from the *Godfather* set.

Tony eyeballed Harold before exploding in a shower of spit and facial expressions that would have scared someone doing the haka.

'Are you fucking kidding me, Harold? Let me ask you something. Did you see what they did to Eddie? Did you? Did you?'

'Of course I did. I identified his body.'

'Who else would have done that but the cartel? They want their money, Harold. We need to get hold of a hundred million and we need it now. When they realise Francisco's dead and the money still isn't in their hands then they will come for each of us. You must strike first. Get some balls, Harold. What the fuck has happened to you? You've gone soft.'

Harold spoke: 'The cartel don't care about the money: it's the principle.'

Tony opened his eyes slowly and focused on Harold. He was in his customary-post snorting position of leaning back, head tilted backwards, eyes closed to stop them from watering. His Adam's apple moved up and down his throat.

'A Colombian drugs cartel with principles, huh? You're more stupid than I thought.'

'They want proof the shipment went missing,' continued Harold cautiously, hurt but nervous. 'If it was confiscated by the police in Amsterdam, they want to see the papers. They said they can see there is no shortage of top-grade cocaine in the UK right now.'

'Look and listen, Harold. Eric the smackhead, or some other nobody, stole their shipment. It's being snorted in every corner of Amsterdam, right now. What does it matter any more? We have a war on now and we're going to win it or die.'

Harold wasn't ready to drop the subject. There was a lot sloshing around in his mind. He knew his days as Tony's sidekick were numbered. He knew Marco was the young buck in the rut but he didn't know if that meant he had to die, or if he could just accept retirement. Another thing he didn't feel right about: he seriously hadn't seen Eddie's death coming. Eddie was the best one of the bunch. That made Harold more nervous than ever. If they could kill Eddie, they could kill any of them.

Tony gave a bored roll of the eyes and made a tick-tock motion with his head.

'Are you fucking in or out?' he screamed in Harold's sweating face.

Harold chewed on the inside of his lip. His rubbery features had begun to blur into dark purple.

'They're not going to forgive us, Tony. You made me part of this. You went behind my back and organised Marco to step in and get the shipment, and then he killed our man in Amsterdam. Why the need to cheat them?'

Tony slammed his palms on the desk and the cocaine

dust showered it. 'In or out, out, yes? I don't want their forgiveness. They can stick it up their Colombian arses. I want to cause them maximum damage all along their chain. I want them to sweat while we get together enough money to go over their heads to the real men in the game.'

Harold paused as realisation kicked in. 'You don't want to fuck with these guys, Tony.'

'Don't I? Really, Harold? It's too late for that. We're taking over, Harold, and you better be ready. You want to be my right-hand man still? This is your time to shine, Harold. I need someone who is a hundred and ten per cent. That you, Harold, hey?'

Chapter 16

'Any more on Billy Manson, the manager from Paradise Villas?' Carter asked, as he came in and sat down to attend the meeting with Chief Inspector Bowie. It was seven p.m. Willis and Robbo were already there in Bowie's office.

'How did his alibi fit in with events, Robbo?'

'His wife confirmed that they were at the council fireworks display,' answered Robbo. 'There's CCTV footage; we can see his wife Jo pushing the buggy with their youngest child in it. The other child is walking beside. We can't see Manson himself. His wife said that they separated while Manson went off to get them something to eat. It's too crowded to pick them up again.'

'So, we can't categorically rule him out,' said Bowie, 'but what would be his motive?'

'He has a five per cent share in Paradise Villas,' answered Carter with a half-shrug. 'It's not likely, but this could all have been about him wanting a bigger slice or a disagreement about the way the business was going. He seemed to be really sacred of the knock-on effect with clients if they are put off by the nature of Eddie's death.'

'I can understand that, even allowing for the type of clients Eddie had, they're going to wonder what kind of person gets killed like this. They're going to wonder whose toes he trod on. If Manson is in the frame then we need to ask ourselves what his plan would be,' Bowie said from behind his desk. 'What would he gain from killing his business partner?'

'It could be he gains nothing, but he is covering up some wrongdoing that could hurt his business. What if Eddie had started to go in a direction Manson didn't approve of?'

'What did you think of him when you met him?' asked Bowie.

Carter answered, 'Not my type. Public school gone wrong. Probably carried the hopes and aspirations of pushy middle-class parents who sent him to a low-quality, fee-paying school and he didn't make the grade, even then. He came out only good at working with his hands and they couldn't afford or didn't have the contacts to find him a job on the old boys' network. So Manson ends up making bespoke kitchens for a living, not a bad job by anybody's standards, but he still hankers after this rich lifestyle. He still feels like he just isn't good enough. That's what Eddie saw in him when he met him. He saw a well-spoken, well-dressed carpenter, who might be perfect in his business. But, fifteen years down the line, did it all go wrong?'

Willis was staring at Carter with an astounded expression on her face.

'What?' asked Carter. 'Do you think you're the only one with an insight into people's characters?' He grinned at her. 'So, I'd like to delve deeper into the life of Billy Manson.'

'Up to you, but we don't have time to waste resources,' said Bowie. 'What did you find there at the Paradise Villas warehouse?'

'There had definitely been some activity there in the last two weeks,' Willis said. 'I took some more samples.'

'What is going on there?' asked Bowie. 'What do they do there?'

'The Paddocks is not that big a business park. There are about twelve units,' answered Willis. 'Paradise Villas occupies one of the biggest. It has a warehouse facility, an office and a workshop. What you'd expect in an industrial unit.'

'The other units on the site are a mix: printers, teak furniture importer, nothing of particular interest,' said Carter. 'It has twenty-four-hour security round the site.'

'What's being made in the workshop?' asked Bowie.

Carter looked at Willis to answer.

'Not a lot, so far as we can see,' she replied, 'and, according to Manson, they buy everything in and it gets collected together to ship in the same container out to a job. When we went there, there were just boxes containing marble fireplaces, pretty average-looking.'

'They farm the work out,' added Carter. 'I suppose they have a tried and tested formula and just tweak it for individual requests. Robbo, did you check out any more information on the villas they're working on right now?'

'One he's building, the other doing alterations – that's something he seems to offer – an after-service. The alteration is for a timeshare magnate who's been inside once for cheating customers. His name is Peter Tully and he has links to the criminal fraternity here and in Europe. He's one I think we should go and talk to. The new villa is still in its foundations stage – the owner is a football manager. We're talking to him at the moment. He seems to be above board.'

'And you saw Della Butcher?' asked Bowie, looking at Carter. 'You gave her a lift to a hotel, I hear.'

All eyes were on Carter as Bowie asked the question. Willis hadn't told anyone, but thought Carter would have to watch himself. She tried not to look at him, but, when she did, she saw that he was trying his best not to look fazed; he was expecting this question. Willis moved her gaze towards Chief Inspector Bowie. Something was obvious to her – he already knew about Carter and Della but he was disowning that knowledge.

'I talked to her briefly on the night of the wake.' Carter was doing his best to stay relaxed. 'I provided the transport when she decided to leave the wake and stay in a hotel near the airport. She said Eddie had been the same as always in the month before he died although he did intend to break away from the family and he and Della were talking about moving.'

'That must have been quite a big thing on the horizon. Would Tony have been all right about that? Did he have something to say about it, do we know?'

'Della wasn't sure whether Tony knew or not.'

Bowie nodded. 'Do we need to talk to Della officially?'

'We may do. I'm keeping an open mind but for now I think she's as much in the dark as we are,' Carter answered. 'I got some useful information this afternoon from my informant. I got these photos from his phone, of people of interest who were around and in the pubs the evening of Eddie's funeral.'

Carter nodded to Robbo, who had already loaded them onto his laptop and turned it round to show the others.

'The identity of most of these has already been confirmed by Intel,' said Robbo.

'But there is one man that my informant wanted me to see. He wasn't at the funeral, but he was here around

November the 6th when Eddie was murdered. He's been seen with Harold and is now known to be Tony Butcher's new right-hand man.'

Robbo obliged with a photo of Marco.

'What do we know about him?' asked Bowie.

'Very little right now. I've just shown this to Robbo, so we'll start on this straight away. We know his name, Marco Zapata, and we know he has a connection to a new and rising Colombian drugs cartel. No doubt, if we have informants with pictures of him on their phones, then the NCA, Organised Crime Command, will have a whole file on him. I believe we need to open up this investigation to them. They have all the contacts that can save us a lot of time. We need to work together.'

'Plus, the Spanish police always inform the NCA when one of the family is on the move,' said Robbo. 'They carry out twenty-four-hour surveillance on Tony Butcher. Marco Zapata will feature in that.'

'And do the NCA always follow Eddie when he comes to the UK?' asked Bowie.

'Apparently so,' answered Robbo. 'But only when it relates to Tony or Harold.'

'Then we need to see the history of that,' said Bowie. 'Every visit he made in the last three years and all the sur-veillance on the family that they've carried out. We need to request cooperation from the Spanish police.'

'Again we need to liaise with the NCA to save us time.'

'Harold will have a lot of the answers we need,' said Bowie.

'I'll interview him again,' said Willis. 'I'll put some pressure on this time. He was not expecting Eddie's death; I could see that when I spoke to him before. Whatever happened, something went wrong. If it wasn't his fault he might feel like covering himself.'

'Bring Harold in for questioning under caution?' asked Bowie. 'After all we are investigating the murder of a British citizen on British soil and, if necessary, we should take a trip out to talk to Tony.'

'Softly-softly,' said Carter. 'If we rush things Harold will refuse to talk at all. If we keep things just about his brother's death, no mention of the cartels, no mention of Tony, then we might get something out of him he didn't mean to give.'

'They're due to fly back here tomorrow,' Robbo said, looking at his notes.

'Okay, we'll meet and greet at the airport,' Carter said. 'Let's put some gentle pressure on them.'

Carter caught up with Willis as they left the meeting.

'Spare a few minutes?'

'Can it be over something in the canteen?' she asked. 'I'm starving.'

'Naturally.'

'All right, Teen?' Willis asked as she walked in and saw her working on the hot-drinks counter.

'Ebbers! Haven't seen you for ages. Do you still live in my house? I was wondering if you'd moved out.'

'Yeah, sorry, Teen, it's a bit like that at the moment.'

'I know, busy time. You text me if you're going to get an evening off and we'll hit the town.'

'Or maybe just stay in and get a takeaway and a couple of beers?' suggested Willis.

'That'll be the one; same as always. Do you want a curry now? We've got it on the menu tonight.'

'Sure.'

'Is it edible?' asked Carter.

'Depends how hungry you are,' answered Tina. 'Ebbers always likes it.'

'Then I'll say no thanks.' Carter put a chicken-salad sandwich on his tray and ordered a tea. Willis ordered a Coca-Cola with her curry and Tina loaded up their trays at the till. They walked across to sit at a table in the far corner. The canteen was at the end of the dinner service.

Willis began demolishing her congealing curry and Carter picked at his dry sandwich before dissecting it and picking out the chicken. He pushed it to one side and waited for Willis to look up.

'Eb, I haven't been completely straight with you about something to do with the investigation,' he said.

Willis stopped eating and waited.

'Is it more about Della? I could see the chief inspector knew about your relationship with her. He didn't seem best pleased that you'd given her a lift to the hotel. I wonder what he'd have thought if he knew we went to see her parents.'

'Yeah, I don't know. But, he's worrying unnecessarily.'

'Does he know her? You were all on Operation Argos together, weren't you? I knew she was an officer after tracing her real name. I've been waiting to hear it from you.'

'Yeah, we were, and he did know her. But, not in the same way as I did. We started a relationship. I was already in the force and Della wanted to join. She came through quickly and then was recruited for Operation Argos. No one knew that we were in a relationship, they would never have let us work together if they had known. It seemed so exciting for us. To be undercover together was just incredible.' He paused, Willis didn't interrupt. She nodded. Some of the story she had guessed.

'We both spoke Italian. We made a convincing duo. We were brought together to work undercover in an Italian restaurant, where the Butchers discussed nearly all the business. It was a small, family-run Italian restaurant in Walthamstow – Trattoria Verde, it was called. I know what you're going to say.' He held up his hand. 'And you'd be right. We should never have gone into work undercover when we were in a relationship, but we did. We thought it was made for us. In our naivety, we didn't see anything wrong.'

Willis watched Carter as he went through the details of his past. She could tell it was painful. It was something he hadn't had to think about for a long time and now it was bringing him so much stress.

'It was a great time for me. I thought I'd landed on my feet: beautiful girl, Italian father. I thought my future lay with her family. You saw how much we all meant to each other. If Della hadn't wanted to join the police force, we would probably be together now.

'But, by the end of two years, the relationship was under too much strain and it was virtually over. She started to drift away from me; the talk became about materialistic things: where were we going with our lives; what could we hope to achieve? The police force wasn't going to be something she'd stay in, she said. The restaurant was too much like hard work for little reward. But, basically, I would have been happy on a desert island with her. I didn't want to think about what she was telling me. She'd changed. Or maybe she was always like that and I chose not to see it. Either way, we were under enormous strain and still trying to do the job we were paid to do. Bearing in mind that Della had come straight out of cadet school and into undercover work. She fitted their needs so exactly. It was all too much for her. It was just too hard.'

'When did you find out she was involved with Eddie Butcher?'

'I knew there was some flirting going on. I knew I was losing her and I thought there must be someone else, but I didn't find out who, or how much they were involved, until the operation crashed.'

'Was she responsible for the crash?'

'I honestly don't know.'

'But it would seem reasonable to assume she was.'

'No, not really. It could have been anyone or it could have been a simple mistake made by loose talk.'

'What do you want to do about her now? What do you think about this investigation?'

'What do you mean?'

'You said you used to wait tables for the Butchers. That means they must all know you. They're going to recognise you if you go near them. Did they know Della was a police officer?'

'I don't know.'

'If they recognise you they'll suspect her. If they don't already know it all, then they will find out. We've seen the way they deal with people. They are merciless. They might think she's still working as an undercover cop. You could be putting her whole family in danger.'

'No. I don't see it like that. I'll let you do the inter- viewing. I'll keep a low profile. I don't have to be seen by anyone. It's a long time ago. They're not going to remember a waiter.'

'Unless they know that's not what you were.'

'I owe it to Della to find out who murdered her husband.'

'I don't think you owe her anything. She chose her own path in life.'

'Okay, then there's the added bonus that Della could lead us right into the centre of Tony's organisation. It could lead to us shutting down a major drugs route into the UK.'

Chapter 17

'You know, in some cultures, Della would have been put in that ground with Eddie,' Sandra said to the three men. Laurence had gone to bed. Harold was sitting slightly apart from the others; his mood hadn't been helped by too much excess. He was so tired that he felt like a walking zombie with an overactive brain. Tony was still as manic as a meerkat.

'Or,' contributed Marco, 'in some countries, if Eddie had been cremated, she would have had to jump into the burning fire with her husband's corpse.' Marco laughed and danced.

'Christ, you're a sick fuck,' said Harold.

'There is a big fire pit over at Della's,' Marco said, grinning at Sandra; she had come alive again and was sitting at the edge of her seat snorting more cocaine.

'The fire pit is just about big enough to put her into,' she said, wiping her nose furiously as it burned. 'It'll take a while of course.'

'At least ten hours, slow roasting.' Marco laughed. Sandra squealed with delight. Harold sat in the corner of the sofa. He was regretting staying up. He should have just retreated like Laurence, but then he wasn't anything like

Laurence and he had a lot to answer for. He had allowed his younger brother to be tortured and executed. He, the enforcer, was looking as if he couldn't even protect his own family. Harold had already decided that he must take matters into his own hands. That this madness that Marco brought to the Butchers was a step too far.

'Because, we'd make sure it was slow,' said Sandra. 'It can take a long time to roast to death. Slowly the skin blisters and burns through and it would start to peel like wallpaper down a wall and then it would fly into the air like lace, burning in the night sky.' Tony was beside himself with excitement. Harold was staring at his mother, horror-struck. Marco was laughing hard.

Sandra hadn't finished. 'She's a skinny little runt. Not a lot of fat to work with. But, still, it takes a long time for the toxins to build up in organs from the shock and the pain and the fact that she won't have no skin left to protect that skinny little body.'

'We need to do it,' Tony said, spitting more than talking. 'Come on, let's go. We need to head down to Della and roast her.'

Harold was shaking his head. Marco was still laughing.

'Hey, Harold,' said Tony, 'you better get out there, you and Marco, and get digging before our friend downstairs starts to smell.'

'What friend?' asked Sandra.

'You don't need to know, Mum.'

'Have you got a body in this house?'

Tony didn't answer her.

'Harold?'

He nodded.

Chapter 18

Carter walked into Chief Inspector Bowie's office. 'You wanted to see me?' he said.

'Pull the blind, let's have some privacy so we're not interrupted,' said Bowie.

Carter came to sit opposite Bowie.

'We need to be frank with one another,' said Bowie. 'We've known each other for a long time, Dan. I know this case is personal to you because of Della. I know we wasted two years of our lives undercover last time for Operation Argos. But, what I'm really concerned about now is that we have a conflict of interests going on here. What about Della?'

'What about her?'

'I checked with the hotel where she was staying near Gatwick. She took a long time to check in that night.'

'We went for a drive. We talked. She is a key witness for us.'

'She is also your ex.'

'That was a long time ago.'

'Promise me you'll be careful with this, Carter. Don't let your heart catch you unawares and let your guard down. We don't know that she's Snow White in all this.'

'Finished?' Carter got up to leave.

'Please hear me out. We messed up in 2003. We messed up big time. I don't want to have to explain myself to my superiors and tell them how we got too cosy with the woman who may have been responsible for the failure of Operation Argos and who is enjoying a new, intimate relationship with the SIO investigating her husband's murder.'

'You won't. Just leave me to do my job. The way I look at it, it's a helping hand to bringing Tony down. Della has the kind of insider knowledge we can only dream about.'

'As long as you keep a clear head when dealing with her.'

Carter went outside for some fresh air. He walked down the street and popped out one of his nicotine chewing gums from its packet. He'd been an on/off smoker all his adult life. He'd switched his actual cigarette addiction across to the gum, for the moment.

He walked down the waterlogged street. The cold fresh air whipped around corners and hit him in the face. The residue of a storm from across the Atlantic. The sky was a moving bank of grey cloud. No stars were visible tonight. Carter stopped and took out his phone. He'd had a missed call from Cabrina, damn! He'd said he would call her. He looked at his watch. It was too late now: ten thirty. He told himself he ran the risk of waking Archie up. He'd text her a 'goodnight' instead. But, really, Carter's mind was too preoccupied. He looked at his other missed calls. Della had tried ringing him an hour ago, just before he went in to talk to the chief inspector. Carter stared at the screen. It was funny to see Della's name written on the list of callers again. Carter knew Bowie was right. He had to make sure he didn't let his feelings carry him to a place that never really existed.

He pressed the call button and she answered after a few rings.

'Oh, Dan, am I grateful you phoned me back. I'm sorry I keep ringing you. I don't know who else to talk to.'

'That's okay. How are things?'

'Not good. Worse than ever, if I'm honest. The family have turned on me.'

'Where are you now?'

'I'm sitting on my patio, looking at the stars.'

'No stars here tonight.'

'Still, I'd rather be where you are.'

'You have the option, Della. You must leave there if you're so worried. Check into a hotel somewhere.'

'This is my home. I feel like everything's falling apart, Dan.'

'What's happened?'

'Oh, the usual hate-filled rhetoric from Sandra. Harold saying nothing about who killed Eddie, or why, but he has guilt written all over his face. Tony is getting madder by the day. He says Eddie had some sort of secret life that got him killed. Laurence is just being himself. I'm not sure about what he feels. He's laid-back about the whole thing. Considering what happened to Eddie, I don't know how that can be possible. Maybe he thinks none of it affects him.

'Tony tried to rape me earlier on today. He obviously has keys and passcodes to here.'

'Can you make your house more secure?'

'I get the feeling they'll find me if I leave. Marco, this moron, is staying here in my villa. Tony's sent him down to watch me. He's my jailer, as far as I can tell.' She sighed. 'Sorry, Dan. Christ knows, you're probably the last person who wants me ringing him up and asking for support.'

'I think you need to get out till all this calms down, Della. I won't lie, I've already had a ticking-off from Bowie.'

'What does he say?'

'Getting too close, once bitten, that kind of thing.'

'But, we were kids then.'

'Does it feel like that long ago to you?' Carter asked.

'No, you're right. It feels like yesterday. I heard you went to see Mum and Dad?'

'I did. It was lovely to see them looking so well. But, I shan't go again. We need to keep them out of this.'

'I know,' Della said. 'None of the Butchers know about them. Or I seriously hope they don't. Mum said you came with your partner. She's a lovely woman, good appetite, apparently.'

'Ha, yeah, that's my colleague, Ebony.'

'They said you have a kid now. Are you married?' Della asked.

'No, but we will bite the bullet someday, I expect.'

'What's she called?'

'My girlfriend's name is Cabrina.'

'And your son?'

'Archie.'

'Archie? What a great name. We were never blessed with children.'

'Not too late.'

'I better hurry up,' Della replied. 'I'm not far behind you, remember.'

'Two years.'

'Yes.'

'I better go, Della.' Carter sighed.

'Yes, I understand. Night, Dan.'

'Night. Lock all your doors.'

Carter stood for a few minutes in thought and then he rang Cabrina.

'Hello, babe, sorry if it's late.'

'No, don't be silly, I was just dreaming about you.'

'Something sexy, I hope.'

'Of course. I can't believe how much I'm missing you.'

'Me too. Where's the little man?'

'He's in here with me, taking up all the bed. He had a lovely day on the beach. He made a friend, a little girl called Sky.'

'Sweet.'

'Yes, so cute, they played for hours. I've gone really brown already.'

'I'm looking forward to checking you for tan lines.'

She giggled. Carter grinned to himself. 'Love you, babe,' he said on a sigh.

'And you. Night.'

'Night.'

Carter put his phone back in his pocket and headed back to Fletcher House.

Chapter 19

Della poured herself another glass of wine and put some more logs on the fire pit and then she sat back down and tilted her chair back and looked at the stars. By eleven she had finished a bottle of wine. She looked up to see Sandra on her patio.

'You going to invite me in for a drink?'

'Christ! Don't I get any privacy in my own home? Does everyone have keys to my place?'

'Sorry, didn't mean to disturb you, came to say sorry about this evening. Came to make peace. I don't have keys. I walked up the lane and through the almond grove.'

'Really?' Della looked out towards the dark and squinted at a light that flickered in the darkness. 'Who else is out there?'

'No one. I came on my own.'

'What were you doing out there?'

'I was taking a stroll, saw your fire and thought I needed to really explain things and apologise, of course. Things are so difficult for all of us, but I don't want to fall out.' She looked around. 'You been burning stuff?'

'Not really, just relaxing.'

'I brought some wine with me. Will you drink with me?

Let's drink to our Eddie. No matter what you think, Della, I know how much Eddie adored you and you did him.'

'Okay. Yes. I suppose so.'

Della held up her empty glass and Sandra filled it.

'This is French. You like that, don't you?'

'I prefer it, yes.'

'Can I sit here?' She pulled up another lounger. 'Cheers!' She raised her glass. 'I don't want to fall out now. We need one another. We're family, after all. You're still a Butcher. Cheers! To Eddie, the best son a mother could have.'

'Cheers!'

'Let's get steaming drunk together and talk bullshit through the night. Then we'll have breakfast by the fire, watch the sun come up and it will be a new start for us. How about that? Cheers!'

'Cheers, Sandra! I'd like that. Eddie and I often watched the sun come up sat here. It's magnificent, isn't it?'

'Best time of the day. Come on, drink up. I want to hear all about the good times you and Eddie shared.'

Della leaned across to have her glass refilled by Sandra and nearly fell out of the chair.

'Sorry.'

'No problem, I've got it.' Sandra filled Della's glass and stood to hand it to her.

'I must be more drunk than I thought. I better ease off or I'm not going to make it till dawn. I'll be asleep in this chair.'

'You must be so tired, aren't you?'

'Tonight it seems to be catching up with me.'

Della looked at Sandra and she couldn't see her straight any more. It wasn't like drink. It wasn't double vision. It was split into so many parts, frames, like looking into a distorted mirror at the fairground. She heard Tony's laughter, his voice, he was singing: 'Burn, baby, burn . . .'

Della looked towards the fire and it multiplied, and Tony sprang at her.

'Leave me alone. Get out of my house.'

'Whose house?'

'I want you to go, all of you. Leave!' Della clutched at the side of her chair to help steady herself and stand but her hand missed and she fell sideways. Her hand contacted the cold patio floor. She heard Sandra laugh. Della flipped onto her knees and began to crawl away as Sandra's laughter kept ringing and she heard the crackling of the logs, felt the heat of the fire pit as she rolled too close and tried to push herself away. She crawled into the cool darkness. Tony's legs blocked her way. She tried to move past them but she felt her back painfully squashed. She felt her face pushed into the concrete. Pain as her ribcage was squashed. Tony's weight bounced on her back.

'Get off her.' Della heard Debbie's voice. 'That's enough. Let her go.' Debbie's voice came into Della's consciousness. 'Leave her, I said. What the fuck is happening here? Sandra, what's going on? Is she stoned?' Debbie asked.

'Yeah. We found her like that. Tony and I were just calling on her. We found her drunk. She's a slut, a slag. With all her fine graces, she tried it on with Tony. I saw it myself.'

Della shook her head, she vomited on the patio. She was swaying like a sick animal. On her knees. She puked several times.

Debbie looked at Sandra.

'You go and I'll tend to her.'

Tony started laughing. He picked Della up from under her armpits and he shook her in the air like a trophy.

'Reckon she weighs eight stone, at two hundred degrees – what's that? About ten hours?' He laughed. Sandra started laughing hysterically.

'Tony, tell your wife to go back to her own house. Tell her to mind her own business. I fancy a barbecue.'

'Tony, don't do this. This isn't right. This is madness.'

'Debbie, get the fuck out of here. Do as you're told.' Tony let Della drop and she tried to crawl forwards again.

'Della is part of this family, you ought to leave her alone. Sandra? Come on, it's not right, this. Tony, what are you doing?'

'Just a little fun, Debbie.' He nudged Della with his foot and she groaned. She was like a stick insect moving painfully slowly from one leaf to another. She wobbled on her stick-thin limbs, hands and knees. She wobbled and shook as she inched her way forward.

Tony kicked her in her stomach and she exhaled in a groan and fought for breath as she rolled onto her side and curled up.

'Tony!'

'What, Debbie? You think this is bad? You see how my brother died?'

'That had nothing to do with Della.'

'Didn't it?' screamed Sandra. 'She's been a snake in the grass for so long, turning him against his own family, encouraging him to move away, turn his back on us all. She's the reason why Eddie did what he did and now we are facing a fucking Colombian death squad because of her.'

'I don't understand.'

'No, you don't, and you should be grateful for that. Go back to the villa, Debbie, and thank your lucky fucking stars you don't understand the problems this woman has caused.'

As Della heard the row starting between them she tried to get to her feet. She stumbled among the stunted old trees and the scrubby bushes out towards the wasteland and the almond grove. She tried so hard to stay on her feet and move but it was as if her legs were spaghetti dropped into boiling water. They buckled beneath her. She crawled forwards, dragging herself away from the villa and towards the stone hut she could see in the distance. Beneath her hands the ground softened. She heard voices again and heard her own voice, desperate, crying, pleading with her body to move. But above her own voice she heard the sound of a child crying. She dug with her fingers into the soft earth that seemed to be collapsing beneath her. The voice called to her, a child in pain, a child asking for help. It seemed to be coming from beneath her hands.

She dug as the pain shot deep into the bones in her fingers. She pulled away at the earth where she could get a hold and it seemed to give at her touch. She was getting close to the child now. She felt the line of a body beneath her hands. She dug deeper as the child called louder and Della speeded up her efforts until her fingers traced the outline of a face in the earth. She worked harder, to scrape away the earth, and the moonlight cast a shadow behind her as someone stood watching. Her fingers found the open eyes of Francisco.

Marco stood laughing behind her.

Chapter 20

10 December

Carter had written three headings on the whiteboard beside the video screen.

Eddie was killed by a client of his from
Paradise Villas

Eddie stepped into new territory and was
killed because of it

Eddie was killed because of brother
Tony's activities

An officer from the National Crime Agency, the Organised Crime Command division, had agreed to work with them and share their intelligence. At the officer's request, they were gathered in the video room. Fifteen chairs were laid out in front of a desk with a video screen behind. Five of the chairs were occupied. As well as Robbo, Willis, Carter and DCI Bowie, there was also Pam. Carter had decided that the first words of the OCC officer should be heard by a limited few. Bowie had invited himself. Carter had wanted it to be an informal meeting in Robbo's office but that wasn't what Ross, the OCC detective inspector, had wanted.

Carter introduced the tall, dark-haired man, who was wearing a smart, well-fitting, dark-blue suit and a patterned shirt, with pink tones. He looked like someone who loved buying clothes, who would have a colour-coded wardrobe and who never put on more than an extra pound before taking action. His face had the smoothness of a younger man than his forty-two years. There was a feminine quality to his long thin hands.

'This is David Ross – he's an inspector in the National Crime Agency, Organised Crime Command. Welcome, thanks for coming.'

'Thank you and good morning.' He spoke from his position behind the desk with an open laptop connected to the video screen behind him. His voice had a hint of Northern in it.

'Thank you for inviting me in to work alongside you in your investigation into Eddie Butcher's death. I have been given authority to share some relevant information with you. I'd like to begin by pointing out that' – he turned to face the whiteboard and Carter's headings – 'at this present time, I can probably only help with just one of these scenarios. Tony Butcher has been in our sights for a long time. We have him under constant surveillance.'

A photo of Eddie Butcher with his brother Tony came on the screen behind him.

He turned to look at the screen.

'By "we", I mean that it is an international effort with the Spanish police.'

Ross flicked through some photos of the Butchers and Eddie with Harold.

'Because we monitor their comings and goings, their activities, to a certain extent we also monitor Eddie Butcher. Eddie has not been of any real interest to the British police force for ten years now. He has been building villas for ex-cons and has been paying his taxes so he's left alone. But, when Eddie was with either one of his brothers, we took notice and we were also alerted by the Spanish police when Eddie, or any of the family, were on the move.'

More close-up photos and aerial shots of the two villas came onto the screen. There were photos of Eddie and Harold outside Lineker's Bar in Puerto Banús. There were photos of Eddie at a black-tie charity golfers' event.

'Here we were taking photos of all those members attending what was, on the surface, a charity dinner, but in reality was a get-together of most of the drug barons and ex-cons living in Marbella. There is no doubt Eddie mixed with these sort. He knew and liked them, but was he one? We have no intelligence linking him with any organised crime.

'The surveillance on Eddie was low-key. So the information I'm about to share with you was collated as part of our ongoing investigation into Tony Butcher's worryingly expanding drugs empire and Harold "the Enforcer" Butcher. There's a lot of footage, which I've tried to edit for you. Here is what we know of the last visit Eddie made to the UK.'

Ross started a slideshow of images, which began with photos of Eddie at the wheel of his G wagon.

'Here, Monday, October the 26th, Eddie is on his way to the airport with his wife Della in the passenger seat.

They are on their way to the Málaga International Airport, where Eddie boards a plane to the UK. Later we see Della arrive back home on her own.

'But a day later, we have the real cause for our interest. This man, Marco Zapata, also leaves for the UK. He's the illegitimate son of one of the cartel families. The Zapata are rising stars in the distribution network. They're taking over the distribution of much of the cocaine into America and now Europe. They don't grow, they don't manufacture: they *move* the cocaine.

'We have hit a time when the Colombian cartels are fractured and, instead of the massive cartels we've seen in the past, smaller ones have taken on specific roles: distribution, manufacture, America or Europe, et cetera. No one large cartel now rules them. They try to coexist. There are many more openings for entrepreneurs like Tony, but he will need the help of someone like Marco. But Marco didn't rise very far in the Zapata cartel. He started his career as a hitman, and he was not welcomed into the fold. There was sibling rivalry. So, he took off for Europe on his own to try and muscle in on some bigger action, and there he found Tony. When Marco first arrived in Spain, he was linked to a shipment of arms that was traced to a Colombian death squad unit. The arms included automatic rifles, grenades and an anti-tank missile. But Marco escaped prosecution and he's been working for Tony for the last nine months. He's been doing essentially the same job as Harold does, but he's been doing it in Spain.

'We've been tracking Marco. He's been to the UK and to Amsterdam several times. He was there, the Amsterdam police tell us, when a man was murdered, his throat cut, and he was found floating in the canal. That man was believed to be the Mendez cartel's, responsible for switching the cocaine from one container ship to another when it comes over from South America. When it arrives in Spain, it's up to another team of Tony's to come up with ways of getting it to the UK. The Amsterdam police believe that this man's death was down to Marco. He was seen with him on the day he disappeared. But they don't have enough to charge him with so they've agreed to shelve their investigation so that we can watch Marco and hopefully get him some other way. We are not sure who Marco holds allegiance to.'

Ross paused to check his notes.

'We believe Tony must have ordered the death of the man in Amsterdam. The Mendez cartel came looking for what had happened to the drugs shipment that Tony says never arrived, and what happened to the money that Tony said he already paid to the dead man in Amsterdam. We are convinced that Eddie's death has to do with this shift in power. We are thinking this was either a case of mistaken identity or, more possible, revenge. The Mendez cartel may want to continue doing business with Tony, so they kill Eddie as a warning, as a punishment for transgressing. But we know it can't end there. This is a major problem that's about to hit our streets, with two warring cartels playing out their feud in the East End and all the gangs flexing their muscles ready for the fight. I know that we will work better as a team if we can come together on this. Any questions?'

'What progress has been made with catching Tony Butcher?' asked Robbo. 'What is the position right now?'

'We believe that Tony and Marco are setting up an operation together and looking to get rid of any opposition to the Zapata family taking over the Mendez routes. But who do they count as opposition? Definitely any Mendez cartel members. That's a lot of people involved to get rid of; it filters down to the young gangs in the capital's streets. That's been Harold's job in recent months. He's recruiting from the young gangs. He's promising them big rewards. We have undercover officers working here and in Spain. We are as close as we can get to Tony.'

'There was talk before of Tony getting off because of police corruption,' said Willis.

'Do you mean in Spain or here?'

'Both.'

'Well, there's no doubt it's a problem. It's frustrating for the Spanish police. They come close to getting one of these barons like Tony and all their work comes to nothing when the evidence is "accidentally" handed back to the suspect, or is lost. All we can do is keep trying to tighten the strings. As for corruption here, it's still a problem. We all know the police pay is not enough and we know any officer that goes undercover in an operation runs the risk of switching sides, of accepting pay-offs. We know all about blurred lines but we are hopeful this time will be different. We have plenty to put Tony behind bars with, we have cocaine shipments that have come over which can be directly linked to Tony, but we can't get him until he decides to step back on British soil. For now, he causes havoc from the confines of his villa.'

'Tony will be safely tucked away in his villa while he'll have caused a war on the streets of the East End,' said Robbo.

Willis raised her hand to ask another question.

'I know that you are concerned with Tony but, if Eddie was trying to set himself up in cocaine distribution, could he have set up a deal all by himself with a cartel? Maybe he was approached. Perhaps he double-crossed Tony.'

'Possible,' answered Ross, 'then we need to consider a few things: was it with the Mendez family, who supply Tony, or someone else, i.e. the Zapata? Did Tony know about it and authorise it and it went wrong, or did Tony know nothing about it? Why would he do it at this time? I would like to bring Harold and Laurence back in for an interview here at the station.'

'We will pick them up as soon as they get back on UK soil,' said Carter.

'The missing lawyer Francisco must have been kept alive long enough to witness changes to Eddie's will. We should ask Laurence and Harold about him. Laurence might give something away.'

Ross looked at his watch. 'Okay, I need to get back. I would like to propose I go to Spain and interview Tony, under the guise of investigating a lead about his brother's death. DS Willis and I could interview the other members of his family out there and any of Eddie's other close associates and friends. We can certainly decide if this villa theory is worth pursuing. I think they will all want to be seen to cooperate if it's the murder squad rather than NCA.

'Okay, the sooner the better,' Carter said, looking at Willis, who nodded her agreement.

Chapter 21

Ross caught up with Willis as she stayed behind after the meeting.

'Do you want to grab a drink? I'd like to go through things with you if we're going to be working together.'

'Okay ...' She hesitated. 'Canteen all right for you?'

He screwed up his face. 'I was hoping for something a bit more edible. I know a restaurant just a short drive from here on Upper Street. Would you be keen? Just to grab a quick lunch?'

'Can we make it back within the hour?'

'Within two hours, anyway,' answered Ross. 'After all, it is a meeting, it's work. It will take what it takes.'

'Okay, sir.'

It was a short ride to the restaurant, but a long time between courses. Meanwhile Willis had all her notes on the table. Ross gave them his full attention and they achieved a lot. Willis happily tucked into a pudding while Ross was sipping coffee.

'You married, Willis?' he asked. She shook her head while sucking the sticky-toffee residue from her spoon. 'I was,' he said, nodding knowingly.

Willis shovelled in the rest of her pudding and held her hand up for the waitress.

'Coffee, please.'

'No cheese board?' Ross smirked good-humouredly. Willis considered it and then shook her head. Ross continued talking: 'I was married for fifteen years. The job pretty much destroys any chance of a happy marriage.'

Willis shrugged. 'Lots of people manage it. Dan Carter's not married but he has a long-term partner, it works for them. I guess it depends on choosing the right partner. Lots of professions would be the same: doctors, nurses, explorers, Navy, Army, people who work on oil rigs ...' She looked up at him. 'Do you want me to go on with the list?'

'I got it, thanks.' He lifted his hand for her to stop. 'Absolutely, you're right. Carter seems like a good bloke; you're obviously close. Do you know his family?'

'Yes. I know them well.'

'That's a great thing. You know, I tried really hard to juggle it: family life, marriage, but working the hours we do – it was always going to fail.'

'The affair didn't do it, then?'

He looked up from his coffee a little surprised. 'Ah ... you've been doing a bit of research on me?'

Willis shrugged. 'Basic stuff. I wanted to know about your career and I found out about your marriage problems along the way.' She pushed her empty bowl to one side, and checked her phone for messages. She turned her phone over and put it on the table in front of her. 'We should get back, sir.'

'You're right. Sorry to take you away from your desk, or your colleagues.'

She held eye contact with him and shook her head. 'I'm happy to work with you, sir. I'm looking forward to it. But I don't need to know about your private life. I don't expect us to become best friends. I'm just hoping we work well together. That matters most to me.'

'Do you think we can?'

'I hope so. This job means an awful lot to a lot of people.'

'We can agree on that. This is a big job. In the end, it could be massive, could affect all of our lives. I've spent my entire time in the NCA trying to bring Tony Butcher to justice. I've been planning it for so long. He does so much harm in the UK. He's responsible for so much of the drugs abuse on the streets. I want this to be the most significant arrest of my whole career so far. I want my daughters to grow up knowing that their dad helped bring down one of the biggest villains the UK has ever produced.'

Willis was studying him. She'd learned about his career. He came in as an inspector; he was one of the graduate class: psychology degree. But he had earned respect.

'I read that you were in the MIT before NCA was set up,' she said.

'That's right. I loved it, but I'm not done changing departments. I believe everyone has a limited life in each specialist department, otherwise you become overfamiliar and you stop seeing the opportunities. You need to keep a fresh outlook. You don't want to go stale.'

'I guess that's true of some things. But I believe in continually striving for perfection and then hanging on to it. I don't believe in spreading myself too thin. I'm committing my career to being the best murder detective I can possibly be,' replied Willis. 'I don't ever want to change departments.'

'And what about your career prospects if you stay where you are? They are very limited.'

She shrugged. 'If I make it to inspector, I wouldn't want

any more. I'm not a "people person". I like the investigation more than I like talking to the press.' She smiled at Ross's frown. 'Don't worry: I'm not the least bothered. I am gradually growing into my own skin and realising what I'm good at.'

'Which is?'

'Well, maybe you answer that for me at the end of this investigation. But I can tell you what Dan Carter says I'm not good at and need to work on.'

He smiled. 'Go on.'

'Making friends, or pretending to make friends in order to get information out of people. I'm always told I need to lighten up, too. Carter would like to see me dance on a few more tables, let my hair down a bit.' She rolled her eyes, embarrassed.

'What does he say you're good at?'

'Observing people's weaknesses. Seeing beneath the bullshit. Carter usually does the talking while I do the watching. He also says I'm a magnet for anyone with mental-health issues, which I don't consider to be an asset, to be honest.'

He smiled, studied her. 'You're an interesting person. Probably a graduate, and yet you are still a sergeant, so you must have chosen to come in at the bottom of the ladder, unlike me.'

'You didn't research me then?'

'No, I didn't. But I can take a guess. You took a degree in politics? Psychology?'

'Criminal law and forensics.'

'Very impressive. Middle-class, maybe single white mum, black dad? Your pronunciation of certain words, your use of the cutlery, your knowledge, or lack of, of the menu, you're a strange mix.' She smiled at him. He continued: 'There are gaps, things you didn't learn in your childhood, despite your underlying middle-class accent. I can almost hear a Welsh note in the way you pronounce certain words.'

Willis was fully focused on Ross now. She was intrigued by his appraisal of her: he was much more accurate than she thought he would be. She'd spent a lot of her childhood in children's homes. The three longest stints had been in Wales.

'There's a challenging childhood. There's a bright child who struggled with her home life.'

'Very good.' She smiled across the table. 'So, you've gone down the clichéd route of mixed race but well spoken and come up with: single white middle-class mother deserted by her black boyfriend and all the stigma of being the only girl of colour in a posh school.'

'Well, if the cap fits …'

'It doesn't. Hello?' Willis turned and signalled for the waitress. 'Bill, please.'

'I'll get this,' said Ross. 'Look, I'm sorry. I didn't mean to offend you.'

'You didn't. That's one thing I'm good at – not getting offended.'

'I didn't find out about you, I'm at a disadvantage and you are obviously a much more thorough police officer than me; but I think we get on well enough. I mean, I think we are both determined to get this right. I'm a hard worker. I don't mind the hours. All I have is my work. I have heard you're also driven by work. That's great. I'm completely focused.'

'What about your daughters?'

'Millie and Beatrice? Five and seven years old. I see them

every other weekend. My ex, Belinda, is very accommodating. She and her new partner never mind changing things around if I need to. Like when we go to Spain, to Marbella, it won't be a problem.'

'Excuse me.' Willis looked at her phone. 'DI Carter just sent me a message. It seems Harold and Laurence are booked on the flight back here this afternoon. They will be landing at Gatwick. Shall we have them picked up?'

'I think that's a good idea. You have facilities in the station next to Fletcher House, to interview and hold them?'

'Yes.'

Willis took the bill from the waitress and passed it across to Ross. 'I'll take you to somewhere better next time,' she said. 'Carter has introduced me to some great Italian restaurants.'

'He's going to be a hard act to follow.'

'I'm not looking to replace him, sir.'

Chapter 22

Tony stood and shuffled off into his office, sliding his bare feet along the marble floor. Harold was sitting in the Don's office, in an armchair, asleep. He looked ashen.

Tony came to stand in front of him and nudged him, so that it brought Harold awake with a jolt. He handed him the orange juice Debbie had brought him.

Harold took the juice and drank it straight back. He shook his head awake and rubbed his face. His five-o'clock shadow sounded like sandpaper beneath his hand. His nails were dirty. His hands were sore. He stared at Tony accusingly.

'Don't look so worried, Harold. I know what I'm doing,' Tony said, watching him curiously.

Harold sat looking at the floor for a few minutes, then began shaking his head slowly.

'Last night wasn't right, Tony. If I hadn't pulled Della out of that hole, Marco would have buried her along with Francisco or Mum would have burned her alive.'

'Rubbish! Just a bit of fun, that's all. She needs taking down a peg or two. Eddie should have done it long ago.' Tony went to sit behind his desk.

'I didn't do right by Eddie. I should have stopped him going that day,' Harold said, staring out into space.

'But you didn't, and neither did I, and we have to live with that,' answered Tony. 'All we can do is make them pay for it now. And we will, right?'

'Right.'

'Excuse me, Harold, I can't hear you.'

'Right, Tony, okay? Right, bloody right.'

'That's it, Harold, get that anger stoked. We're going to need plenty of it. Heads are going to roll when you get home.'

Tony walked past Laurence on his way out onto the veranda muttering to himself while smoking a cigarette.

Laurence drank his coffee and watched him. He was wondering just how mad Tony could get before a meltdown. Tony turned and stopped at that moment and he looked straight through the glass at Laurence, as if he knew his thoughts. Then he came scurrying back into the room and came to stand in front of Laurence at the table.

'Talk?'

'Sure.' Laurence picked up his coffee and followed Tony into his office.

'Where's Harold?' Laurence asked. He hadn't seen Harold pass.

'Harold's gone to pack.'

'Okay.' Laurence sat in one of the armchairs and waited for Tony to get settled behind his desk. He studied his brother. Tony's eyes looked sore. His face had a strange fierce blush. He smelled of stale sweat, bonfire and dirt.

'What happened last night?' Laurence asked as Tony seemed to be fiddling with something in his drawer. 'Mum looks really ill today.'

'Uh . . .' Tony rolled his eyes to the ceiling as he pretended to struggle to recall. 'Nothing, few drinks too many, that's all, but we needed to let off steam. No, Mum is fine, Mum is grand.'

'You going to be okay here when we've gone?' Laurence asked.

Tony's eyes opened wide as he thought about the answer to the question.

'Have to be now Eddie's gone. There are going to have to be big adjustments. We're going to miss him. The world has to carry on.'

'Of course, but we need to know why he was murdered. We are all at risk until then. Harold and I are heading back to the UK knowing *full well* that we face the same death as Eddie, unless we find out who did it.'

'Is that all you care about?'

'I care about what happened to Eddie the way he would care about it if it happened to me.'

'Hey, lighten up – you won't be a target. Eddie meddled in something he shouldn't have and it all went badly wrong.'

'You know what went wrong?'

'He pissed off the wrong people. In this world, you can't afford to do that. We all know that. You know that, don't you, Laurence? Even in your world, you know there are people to be avoided, villains who you really don't want to do business with?'

'I have to choose my clients carefully, it's true.'

'We are proud of you. Proud of the start we gave you in life. I never minded giving you my share of what the old man left us. Lucky the old man bought up the properties he did. He was a shrewd old bastard and you've done well with the property-management company. You've become quite a businessman now with it all. Is it all going well?'

'Yes. It could always be better. What do you mean I won't be a target? Eddie was a legitimate businessman, wasn't he? His only mistake was belonging to this family and perhaps living half a mile from you.'

'Well, I'm not saying anything. But, Eddie was a lot of things to a lot of people. Maybe he spread himself too thin, made promises he couldn't keep. It has nothing to do with you; you will be safe.' Laurence was churning things over in his brain. Tony continued: 'I saw you bought up a place in Bethnal Green. What are you going to do with it? Why is it still empty?' Tony had worked his face into a picture of concentrated interest but one of his eyes had developed a tic in the last twenty-four hours and he kept trying to stop it by pulling at his eye. It was swollen and sore now.

'I thought it was a good investment. The area is getting gentrified. I'll go for change of use if no one wants to make it into a gastro pub. I can turn it into flats.' Laurence was distracted, annoyed. He was exasperated, talking about his business as if it were a normal day at the office. He didn't like any of the others interfering in his world of legitimate business. He saw them as naive to the real world of people earning proper livings.

Tony's face was starting to turn into a mask of boredom and the tic was intensifying.

'Don't worry about my business, Tony. When you're in the legit world you take some knocks. I don't mind being patient. Okay, I'm going,' said Laurence. 'I can see you have a lot on your mind,' he added sarcastically, replacing his coffee cup in its saucer as he watched Tony snort a large line of coke.

Tony smiled at Laurence's intended slight.

'I'm not worried, far from it. I want you to take over Paradise Villas.'

Laurence was taken aback. He sat down again.

'Really? Why? I presumed that it would stay as it is. That Della would at some time step in to keep it profitable, or that it would be left to Billy Manson to manage it for her.'

'It's "legit", right? Right up your street, then?' Tony grinned. 'You're the clever one in the family. You can expand, in time, branch out, try new things. I give it to you as a present.'

'I hadn't thought about it.'

'We will have the paperwork drawn up and fax it to you. Leave it to the manager Billy Manson to guide you through it, get the hang of it.'

'Why do that? I can just come in, with a fresh start, after all it's Eddie's name that people bought into. Manson is just the builder. I can get plenty of those. I am a Butcher brother, after all.'

'You are indeed. But I trust Manson to continue doing a good job until people get used to things. Be careful not to rush in there. We need Manson to stay for now. In the future? Well, who knows?'

'What about Della? She must have a large share of Paradise Villas. You can't take that away from her altogether.'

'Eddie didn't leave it to her but we can still be generous, if we choose. If *you* choose. Give her a slice of the profit, if things work out well, if she behaves herself. After all, she's never actually done anything to deserve it.'

'She was Eddie's wife. What more did you expect her to do?'

'Okay. Never let it be said we did her wrong. You make a profit and she will benefit, won't she? You've always fancied her – maybe take her as well as the business?'

Tony laughed.

After Laurence had left, Tony went to speak to Sandra in her room. She was lying in bed, propped up with pillows, a cooling eye mask on.

She lifted one side of the mask to look at Tony as he came into the room.

'Mum? Laurence is going to take over Paradise Villas and Harold is going back to the UK today to track down the people who killed Eddie. They're going to be dead meat.'

Sandra didn't comment.

'She's not going to go quietly,' she said, referring to Della.

'I'll deal with it.'

'No, I want to know how you intend to do that. I don't want any fuck-ups.'

'I've said I can do it.'

'What you say and what you deliver are two different things. You will have to scare her big time. You make sure every bone in her body feels crushed, every drop of self-esteem is squashed and you make sure she's scared shitless. I don't want her ever coming back. You sure about fixing Eddie's villa? I want that place.'

'I know. It's fixed. It's as good as yours.'

'All legal?'

'I got Eddie's probate solicitor to change the will.'

'How?'

'Made him an offer.'

'Would you stop with the *Godfather* stuff. It's so fucking

irritating. Was that the corpse that Della found? That was funny.' Sandra chuckled. Tony spent a few minutes laughing too loudly. Sandra had begun to clutch her head in pain.

'I want to be in there before the spring. Make me fucking happy. Because right now I'm having a hard job swallowing what happened to Eddie.'

'Harold is going to have the plot of land at the back. We're all going to be living within half a mile of one another. It will be great.'

'If Harold's going to have builders working on the plot of land, you better make sure they don't dig up something that shouldn't be out there. The earth is much too hard to dig deep. You're a moron sometimes, Tony.'

'It's okay, we've thought about that, Marco and me. We're tidying up the place.'

'Why is that weirdo Marco still here? Get rid of him, we don't need him.'

'We do, Mum. He's got all the right connections. He's going to take over from Harold so he can retire. It'll be okay, Mum. You don't need to worry about any of it. I'll take care of it all. Laurence looks interested in taking up his place in the family,' said Tony.

'Don't you dare, Tony.' Sandra sat up in bed, wincing. She slumped back a little and picked up a bottle of Lucozade. 'He's still wet behind the ears. I don't want him ending up like Eddie. I can't lose another son.'

Chapter 23

While Willis was at lunch with Ross, Bowie and Carter were in Robbo's office, going through what they'd learned at the meeting.

'What did you think about what he had to say?' asked Bowie.

'It was good to get clarification of some aspects to do with Tony and the new deal,' said Carter, 'but, if we were just after an answer to why Eddie was killed we're further away than ever. But ... nobody's kidding anyone else about that aspect. This is all about getting Tony.'

'And the NCA need us to do it,' said Robbo. 'You heard him: they need the cover of investigating Eddie's murder to be able to interview people close to Tony.'

'Don't be so sure, Robbo,' said Bowie. 'They'll hitch a ride along with us just as far as we're useful, then they'll flag down another car.'

'We make the most it then. We use them just as much as they use us. We can't odds it anyway. This is their department, their domain,' said Carter.

'He wasn't interested in discussing the other ideas,' added Bowie. 'He doesn't see Eddie's death being anything to do with buying and selling villas, nor does he consider Eddie to be drug baron material.'

'We still have to be thorough. We know Eddie had money problems,' said Carter. 'His manager at Paradise Villas, Billy Manson, says they were insignificant and the norm, but we know that ten years ago he was in a much stronger position that he is now. Maybe he was getting lazy. Maybe it was proving too hard to make the kind of living he wanted from it and he decided, you know what? I'll do what Tony does.'

'Pam, did you find any evidence of Eddie having offshore bank accounts?' asked Robbo. 'Was he the director of more than Paradise Villas? Does he have hidden money that we can't see yet?'

Pam answered, 'A few bank accounts. I've not found secret billions anywhere so far. I think Eddie was pretty straightforward with his money dealings. He could have chosen to become a tax exile, taken Gibraltar citizenship and then just lived in Marbella. He had options he didn't take. He paid his taxes here. But, we know a lot of his work was done for cash. Most of it, I would expect, so he probably didn't declare a lot of his earnings.'

'He seemed to have a good work–life balance,' said Carter. 'I still can't see him bothering to become a drugs baron. He must have seen how Tony lives and thought it can't be worth it. But someone, something, could have put pressure on him to do it.'

'So, hypothetically, Eddie would have needed the money for what?' asked Bowie.

'Not for anything to do with his business,' answered Pam. 'It seems to struggle on paper only. Both Eddie and the manager, Billy Manson, enjoy a great lifestyle from it.'

'And, Eddie could have found money easily if he needed it, I'm sure. Tony would have been able to bail him out a few million if he'd had to pay off a client when a villa went wrong,' said Robbo. 'And again, what Ross said, did that mean he went in with his brother Tony or did he cross him? Which cartel would he have been doing business with?'

'We will hope Willis has a decisive result from Spain. We know that Tony is mad as a box of frogs, so Willis is a good one to send. She will keep a calm head.'

Bowie was deep in thought.

'Okay, I'm happy with working alongside the NCA, even though I think they are glory hunters. This was never just about finding out who killed Eddie.' He looked at both Carter and Robbo. 'This was always going to be about trying to rectify the wrongs of 2003. This is our chance.'

Chapter 24

Della came awake in a flash of pain to see Debbie standing over her. 'What are you doing here, Debbie?'

Della rolled to one side and half sat up as she reached for some water. Debbie walked across to the window and drew back the curtains. Della squinted.

'What time is it?' She sat up in bed, wincing as she did so.

'It's two in the afternoon.'

'Why are you here? Why am I in so much pain? It hurts when I breathe. Everything feels bruised. What the hell happened to me?'

'Things got a little out of hand last night.'

'Got out of hand? What do you mean?'

'I'm glad you're okay now. I left Sheena to look after you overnight.'

'Jesus Christ, Debbie, what the hell is going on?'

'Shush, keep calm.'

'Keep calm? I'm beginning to think something awful happened last night.'

'You live to tell the tale, that's the main thing.'

Debbie straightened the curtains. She stared out at the day. She had been in and out every couple of hours since Sheena called her at three in the morning to say Della looked like she was having a reaction to the drugs. Sandra had put a mixture of uppers and downers in Della's drink. It was some prescribed and some more that Sandra kept for parties.

'I remember Sandra turning up. What did she do, spike my drink?' Debbie didn't answer. 'Christ, I thought as much. I always knew things would be difficult for me if Eddie was killed but I never thought that the family would turn on me like this. They tried to kill me.' She looked at her hands. 'And I remember digging in the soil. Christ Almighty, what's out there?' Della sat bolt upright. 'Debbie, for Christ's sake, I remember hearing a child calling for help in Spanish. She was out by the stone hut. We have to go and look, Debbie. I'm telling you, there's a child out there.'

'Stay where you are and rest. Sheena said that's what you told her. I went up there to look – there is no one there. There's nothing there to see. There's no sign of any child. You must have been hallucinating.'

'I'm telling you, I heard—'

'You were off your face.'

'Yeah, why was that? Sandra's trying to kill me.'

'No, she just wants to scare you.'

'Why can't they leave me alone, Debbie? Isn't it enough that I lose my husband? What do they want from me?' Debbie sighed. She ran her fingers down the side of the curtain. Della continued: 'Tony is out of control, Debbie. I've seen the bruises on you. I know you cover for him but he tried to rape me. Is that the kind of monster you want to be married to?'

'Marco tried to rape you, not Tony.'

'What are you talking about?'

'In the almond grove. Harold found you; he carried you back here. He helped me put you to bed.'

Della shook her head to try to clear it

'I'm not talking about then. Tony broke in here while I was in the bath, earlier on, in the evening. He would have raped me if I hadn't fought him off.' Della struggled to talk, she took a drink of water.

Debbie was staring at her. If Della had expected her to explode and call her a liar, it wasn't happening.

'I need your help, Debbie. This is what they'd do to you as well; you know that, don't you? Sandra is a poisonous old bitch and she doesn't care about anyone but herself. She uses everyone, even Tony.'

'I know.'

Debbie walked out and left Della on her own. She lay there thinking and then she went into the bathroom and switched on the lights around the mirror. The marble was cold under her feet. The walls were cold to her touch. Her mind was jumping from one event to another, confused. Which part of Eddie's story was real? Had he been having problems with money? Yes, he could have. Would he have shared that with her? Probably not. But did he know he was going into a situation that could kill him? She didn't think so.

She remembered Eddie's expression as she dropped him off at the airport. He'd turned back towards her as he carried his case, she remembered thinking he was getting soppy in his old age. He was finally showing her some real affection, some trust.

'Eddie?' She looked into the mirror and smiled as tears distorted her vision and she saw him standing behind her.

'What do I do now, Eddie? Tony has me a prisoner in my

own home. My life here is over. I don't want to start again without you, Eddie.'

'Sorry, babe.'

'What am I supposed to do without you? I gave up everything for you and now I find out that you betrayed me? It's too hard to take in.'

'Don't believe it. You know in your heart that I wouldn't go back to the old ways. You know I loved you.'

'Yes, but the last few months were so hard between us, so strained. I even thought you were having an affair.'

'I never would, Della.'

'Maybe. But, maybe, I never really knew you.'

'You knew me warts and all. You fell in love with a bad boy and you tamed him.'

She laughed. 'Yes, I did.'

'You know what you have to do, Della.'

She nodded. 'Come out fighting.'

She got dressed and checked that she was on her own as she walked through the villa. She realised she still felt really rough. She felt as if she were still drunk and really hung-over at the same time. But, something needed looking at. If Debbie was right, plans were already being made to cover their tracks and clear the area. She had to look today.

The day was bright and sunny and warm again, the air had cleared from the rain. Della got a bottle of water from the fridge and walked out onto her patio, past the remnants of the fire from the night before. She slipped trainers on and headed off into the wasteland at the back of the villa. She followed the path that led to the old stone hut at the far end of the almond grove. As she walked she tried hard to remember what had happened the night before. She'd only snatches of memory and she didn't know what sequence they came in. She remembered the fire and Sandra and she remembered that there were so many other people. As she walked forward she kept glancing around. She was so anxious, as if she were about to experience a panic attack. She felt the rush of fear that she had felt last night. She knew she'd run, crawled, for her life along this path.

Now as she approached the small stone hut, its wooden door hanging off its hinges, she felt the fear heighten. She felt it squash her lungs as if she were about to be attacked, but she could see there was no one around. The silence was only broken by the sound of the crunching beneath her feet. Della walked, head down, staring at the broken twigs, the swept undergrowth. It was flattened.

Della kept her eyes on the hut and racked her memory. She saw herself in the darkness. She remembered seeing the looming hut as she crawled forwards. She had been trying to reach the hut, but she hadn't made it and her hands had sunk into soft earth. She remembered feeling her knees sink into the earth and then she had heard the child.

She crouched down and examined the earth. There were marks where hands had patted and smoothed it over. Della stood and went to the hut and pulled open the wooden door. Inside was so dark that Della got out her phone to get a better look. She bent double, went inside and took some photos. She smelled the air. There was some lingering scent that she couldn't quite recognise and there was the smell of wet earth where the rain had seeped in and settled. Della tried to work out if a child could have been inside. There was nothing left inside. The earth floor looked clean, thought Della, too clean. Where was the natural debris? It was too staged.

As she turned to come out she froze. The scene from the previous evening came back to her. Tony and Sandra and Marco? They were there with her when ... She remembered the face in the earth; now she knew what she had remembered was real – someone had been buried in the ground in front of her.

Della stood for a while trying hard to put the whole picture together. She stared at the flattened earth. She walked a few paces forwards and pressed her foot into the ground. It gave slightly on the freshly dug earth. She recoiled and she remembered being pressed into the earth and not being able to breathe.

She ran back to the villa. She spent the afternoon in her bedroom. She heard Marco coming and going. She had expected to hear from Laurence before he left for the airport with Harold. He always used to come down to spend the last hour with her and Eddie whenever he came to stay at Villa Cassandra, then Eddie would give him a lift to the airport. But not this time. She heard Marco throw his keys onto the kitchen counter. She guessed he must have taken them all to Málaga Airport.

Della went into the bathroom and bent over as she held the cold shower over her throbbing head. The pain was blinding; she was bruised on her legs, on her arms, her stomach. Her ribcage was turning black with bruising. Her neck was strained as if she had whiplash. She was still struggling to grasp what had occurred the night before. How out of control they had all become! She was feeling a type of blind panic she wasn't sure she could deal with.

When she came back into the bedroom she saw that she'd had a missed call from Laurence. She rang him back. He was ringing from a UK airport. She could hear the sounds of planes being announced in the background.

'They attacked me last night, Laurence.'

'What do you mean? Who?'

'Sandra, Tony, Marco. All of them. Did you know?'

'Of course not. Della, there's no way I would have let them hurt you. What happened?'

'They were going to kill me. I'm bruised and battered, Laurie. You have to help me.'

'I will come back to Spain as soon as I can, Della. I intend to help you in every way I can. Keep calm. Just tell me what happened last night.'

'Sandra slipped something in my drink.'

'You're sure?'

'Yes. Debbie confirmed it.'

'She wouldn't have done that.'

'If I just stay here I'll end up in a shallow grave like the lawyer who Tony got to alter Eddie's will. I phoned his practice to speak to him, he's not been seen for two days and I have some pretty horrible memories from last night, one of which was seeing him! Oh my God, Laurence, I'm just sitting here, waiting to be murdered.'

'Della, you need to keep calm.'

'I'm going to have to do something. You weren't there. Sandra will do anything to get rid of me. I'm telling you, Laurence: they're after my blood.'

'I said I'll help you, Della. Tony has asked me to take over Paradise Villas and I have agreed, but only to stop it going under.'

'You see! That's my business, by right. What the hell is going on?'

'Tony has got it signed over to himself. He's managed to

have Eddie's will altered. I don't know how. I hope it's not what you think; but, if there's any truth in that, if you think you're right about a body out there, then don't go near it. Tony is worse than I've ever seen him.'

'How can he do this to me?'

'I don't know. But rest assured: I'm looking after your interests, Della. And, maybe it's best this way for now, give things a chance to settle down. As soon as things calm down, I'll get it signed back to you, I promise, and I'll make sure I look after it for you in the meantime.'

'Why does he even want Eddie's business? What does he need it for?'

'He says he wants to see it expand.'

'Expand? Bollocks! He wants to launder money through it, I expect. You be careful, Laurence, he'll have you breaking the law before you know it.'

'I'll be careful.'

'He's a bastard taking that away from me.'

'I know. I understand, Della, but it's not gone. I'm caretaking it for you. I'm going to give it back to you when I can, promise. You know, I've always been fond of you, Della.'

'Eddie would be grateful to you, Laurie.'

'I'm doing this for both of you, but especially for you, Della. You deserve it: you were a loyal wife to Eddie. He didn't deserve you.'

Laurence caught Harold up as they came through passport control and out into the Arrivals lounge. They didn't get far before they were escorted by police officers and driven to Archway Police Station.

*

Della put the phone back on the bedside table and sat staring at it. What were these drop-in comments people kept making about Eddie? What did Laurence mean, Eddie didn't deserve her? Eddie was a good man. They had a wonderful life. They laughed, they loved. They had everything when they were together. That last thought struck her: when they were together. Who was he the rest of the time? She went back to the safe in the dressing room. She had just a few documents left in there now. They included the detailed drawings of the villa. Della had written everything else she needed to know from Eddie's correspondence in her phone, in her notebook, in emails, in code. Della had been busy. She picked up the phone and rang Carter. It went straight to voicemail.

Chapter 25

Willis finished reading the post-mortem results on her way into the interview room.

'How were things in Marbella?' she asked.

Harold stared coldly back at her from across the table. His face was blotched from alcohol, tiredness. He shook his head.

'None of your business. What was it about – picking me up from the airport? We've had a difficult few days – I need a rest. I don't need to be hounded by you lot. You have no fucking respect.'

'No swearing, please. We're not hounding you, Harold. We're keeping family members up to date with the way the investigation into your brother's murder is going.'

Harold switched his attention to Ross. He stared back. He picked up a pen and began writing notes while still maintaining some eye contact with Harold.

'How about Tony?' asked Willis. 'Did he have any ideas who could have done it? You must have discussed it.'

'Why should he? He's the same as the rest of us – we don't know who did it.'

'We've been running through some theories, there's one that we're working on – that maybe Eddie was killed in a case of mistaken identity. After all, Tony is not just hiding from the police in that villa. He's hiding from the cartel he ripped off, isn't he?'

Harold was listening hard while pretending to stare out at space. He swallowed. He wiped an irritating trickle of sweat that had begun at his temple and was now beginning its descent, doglegging its way down.

'No comment.'

'The cartels are not people to mess with. I'm surprised you decided to come back here. I thought you'd also be hiding away in Tony's villa. After all, if they killed Eddie, they won't hesitate to kill you.'

'Eddie's death had nothing to do with Tony or me.'

'So why did they torture him?' She passed over more photos. 'What did they want to learn from him?'

'I have no idea.' Harold's face was beginning to solidify, turn white.

'We have just received some test results back on Eddie. He didn't die when they fired a bullet into his brain.' Harold looked up expectantly, waiting. 'He died from stress on his heart. He suffered a heart attack while he was being tortured, minutes before the gun was fired into his skull. But, we've been wondering why someone wanted it to look like he'd been executed.' Harold shook his head. He was thinking things through. 'Any idea? What does that sound like to you, Harold? A botch job? Who would want information that badly from Eddie? Who, Harold? Who are they?'

'I will tell you the same as I told you before. I left him at ten-thirty in the morning outside the café. I don't know where he went and I don't know what he'd got himself into.'

'We don't believe you. We're wondering if Tony had something to do with it. And by Tony I mean you and Tony, after all, you're his deputy, aren't you? Surely you know his every move. Or maybe not. We know about the missing Mendez cartel money. You must have known the cartel would come looking for it. What was Eddie's job? To try and feed the cartel with a lie? Did Eddie even know about the missing cocaine that wasn't really missing, was already being cut and sold on the streets? And, what about the money? Did he walk straight into the trap? Did you let him walk into it, Harold?'

'No comment. I don't know what you're talking about.'

Ross showed him a photo of Marco. 'Let's talk about this man.' He showed him another photo of Harold and Marco together.

'No comment.'

'This was taken a week before Eddie was killed. This man is called Marco Zapata. He is the son of one of the cartel families in Colombia, not just any cartel family. You don't seem surprised at anything I say. It wasn't a surprise that the Mendez family probably tortured and executed your brother because you sold him down the river. They were never going to believe your bullshit about the cocaine never having reached the UK, were they? They were never going to swallow the one about the Amsterdam connection having shafted you. They could see for themselves that there's enough pure cocaine on the streets that has their own brand stamped all over it. So then you try telling them that the money went missing. You really think they're stupid, Harold?'

'No comment.'

'Actually, let me rephrase that: does *Tony* really think

you're that stupid, Harold? Obviously he does, because he's allowed you to sacrifice your brother for the missing money. Greed over flesh and blood. Isn't that right, Harold?'

'No comment.'

'Well, you can rest assured, Harold, when you meet the same fate as Eddie, or when Sandra or Laurence does, because surely it must be a matter of time. Then Detective Sergeant Willis here and I will have the self-satisfaction of knowing we tried to prevent it happening but you didn't cooperate. You better inform Sandra she's going to need twenty-four-hour protection when she steps outside the villa, maybe even inside it, and that will probably still not be enough. If you were prepared to cooperate with us fully, then we would give her that protection. But, so long as you continue to insist this has nothing to do with the cartels, your brother Tony and a drugs war, then there's nothing we can do. You're a sitting target. But this could be your lucky day, Harold – I'm in a position to offer you a deal.' Willis looked Ross's way, Carter was talking in her ear: 'What the hell? He's here to make a deal. He's supposed to be just an observer in there. What's going on, Willis?'

'Okay, thanks for coming, Harold,' Willis said as she pushed back her chair.

'Wait a minute, wait a fucking minute,' Harold said as he stayed where he was. 'I want to hear what this monkey has to say.'

'I am in a position to offer you a deal. I work for the National Crime Agency.'

'I know who you are. I've seen you before.'

'We know that Tony is a ticking time bomb. Now, he's going to make a move to go way up the ladder in the cocaine dynasty but he's not going to make it. Tony has overstretched himself and getting Eddie killed proves it. He's so keen to aim for the stars he's forgetting to protect the earth his feet are standing on. Tony will not succeed in this. Marco is not what he seems, and it will all come tumbling down around the Butcher family's ears. You help us to set up a trap for Marco and the cartels and we'll guarantee you a prison sentence of less than fifteen years. That's the best we can do – you can be out in seven on good behaviour. Tony will never know it was you. We'll make sure you're caught at the same time.'

Chapter 26

Carter was waiting for them in the observation room. Harold had already left.

He stopped Ross in the doorway. 'What the hell did you just do in there?'

'I did what I was instructed to do. I had the power to offer Harold a deal.'

'What happened to working together? What happened to good old-fashioned rules of conduct here?'

'Nothing. If I had talked to you about it first, you would have had to take it to Chief Inspector Bowie and it would have slowed it down again. Eddie Butcher is dead and you are no nearer to catching his killer. Plus, we are not getting to Tony fast enough; we'll lose this opportunity. We believe that this is all about Tony's new connection with the Zapata family. We know for a fact that Marco is the black sheep of the family. We think he's trying to ingratiate himself with his family and he's doing it on the back of Tony's megalomania. If we don't hurry, Tony is going to get killed by the Mendez family, or by the Zapata or even by Marco. We don't know how far his ambitions stretch.

'They must have put their own time limit on the missing money and it's already passed because they've executed

Eddie just to show Tony they are coming. Harold knows this is true. He's an old man now; he wants his pipe and slippers. He's not going to see it into next week unless he gets help.'

'He's never going to tell us any more than he has already,' said Carter.

'Maybe, but Harold knows he'll be safer inside jail than out of it,' Ross said. 'He can buy a lot of protection inside and he can contain it. Out here? He's a sitting target. Tony will have ordered Harold to organise the wiping-out of any of the Mendez cartel here. Harold will use the young gangs to do that. It will be a bigger bloodbath on the streets than we've seen. Plus, there will be no going back afterwards. Once vendettas start between these gangs, they escalate. They'll want a big bit of the new Zapata pie. They have the chance to be on it right from the start. That's a hell of an opportunity for these young gangs. But Harold will be thinking that it's a lot of work for an old man. He doesn't need any more than he's got already. He's probably thinking, he could downsize easily to a smaller mansion and live the rest of his life playing golf. If I was the Mendez cartel I would have strengthened numbers over here in the last two months since the money went missing and I would assume that's why the death squad is setting up its stall here. They're anticipating a lot of work.'

Carter was thinking it through. Willis knew him well enough to know that he approved of Ross's actions. He would have done it himself if he'd had the authority.

'So, what else have NCA authorised you to do that you're waiting to surprise us with? What else have you got in the bag?'

'It's an ongoing situation,' replied Ross. 'We would be

willing to make a few deals, compromise a few notches on the ethical scale to get Tony and to stop the carnage he inflicts on the UK. We have to throw everything at it now before it's too late and we end up with a bigger drug problem, gang problem, organised crime problem than ever before. This is the chance now to stop Tony and the cartels.'

'I wonder if Harold will go for it,' said Carter. 'He seems to have already written off any chance of justice for Eddie. He's not even looking for it. He must know that it doesn't exist. Tony's obviously managed to work his way out of responsibility just enough to leave Harold thinking that the investigation into Eddie's death is now closed.'

'What about Laurence?' asked Willis.

'I think it's time to give him a reality check,' said Ross.

Chapter 27

Billy Manson parked his white Range Rover on the harbour at Ramsgate. He picked a box from the back seat and headed up the hill to Fredo's Ristorante.

'Billy!' Connie was preparing the tables for the lunch service. She greeted Manson warmly. He walked in carrying the box and put it on the bar while he went in for a hug.

Connie held on to him. 'How's it all going?' she asked, pulling back to observe him. 'You look tired, Billy. You been looking after yourself?'

'I'm okay, Connie, don't worry about me. How is Della coping? I haven't wanted to bother her. But send her my best wishes. She knows where I am if she needs me.'

'Thank you, Billy. She's struggling but she's a tough cookie, as you know. How are Jo and the kids? Looking forward to Christmas, I expect. Can you get time off? You must be very busy now, doing Eddie's work as well as your own?'

'The kids are very excited. Look, we are thinking of going away for a month; we could do with a break. Plus, I don't know what will be happening with the business.'

'What do you mean? Surely it will continue? It's such a fantastic thing you have going there.'

'Maybe. I was hoping Della would take it over but it

seems there's a chance Eddie either didn't sort things out properly, in the event of his death, or there's been some manoeuvring going on by the Butcher family. Either way, it's not Della's business now: it's Tony Butcher's.'

'That can't be.' Connie was shocked.

'I got a call from Tony himself last night, really late. I mean three in the morning, telling me that Laurence will be coming to work with me and that they really wanted me to stay on, et cetera. But it sounded like bullshit.'

'I don't understand.'

'No, well, I wish I didn't, but it sounds like they're taking over.'

Connie was speechless.

'Look, I wondered if you'd mind looking after this box of things for me,' said Manson. 'It's nothing important, just stuff of Eddie's: personal papers and stuff. I'm not sure he'd have wanted Tony getting hold of them.'

'Of course. Shall we give it to Della when she comes over next?'

'I'd like to go through it with her, so if you could wait till we're all together. There are a few things in there that I know Eddie would want me to give her myself. Some things need explaining. Eddie and I didn't always do things the easiest way or the clearest.'

'Of course not. You and Eddie were a great team.'

Manson walked back down towards his car and he made a call on the way.

'Hello?'

'Jo, it's me.'

'I didn't recognise the number.'

'I know, it's a new phone. Use this number for me, for now.'

'Why? What's going on? Are you okay? You sound out of breath.'

'I'm fine.'

'Where did you go last night? I've been worried sick.'

'Sorry. I got a call about business. I ended up shifting some materials all night.'

'Poor Eddie. I didn't realise they did all that to him. I read about it this morning. Why would someone do that? I feel so sorry for Della. Do the police know who did it yet?'

'No.'

'Billy, are we safe? I worry for the kids.'

'We'll be okay, Jo, but I think we should get out and have a holiday for a month until it all blows over. Get the kids packed and get us on flights to Thailand. We'll have Christmas there. You book it. It doesn't matter what it costs. Get us on a flight as soon as you can.'

Chapter 28

'He hasn't got anything worth hearing,' Carter said in Willis's earpiece after twenty minutes of interviewing Laurence. 'Let's call it a day.'

'When was the last time you saw Eddie alive?' Willis asked, ignoring Carter. He'd been irritable even before she'd started the interview. Ross wasn't present: he'd gone back to the day job. There was another officer standing by the door.

Laurence sighed. 'I saw him three times when he was over here in the two weeks before his death. The last time was three days before he went missing. You know all this. I've told you it I don't know how many times.'

'What was that meeting like?'

'It was a quick coffee to talk through some recent acquisitions I'd made. They hadn't gone as well as I'd hoped and I needed Eddie's advice. I needed him to look them over and see how much they'd cost to renovate.'

'Where were these properties?'

'It's an old warehouse in Shoreditch and a closed-down pub – the Albert, in Bethnal Green.'

Willis slid a pad and paper across the table. 'Addresses, please.'

Laurence shrugged irritably.

'I don't have the exact postcodes to hand.'

'Street number and name and area will do. We'll call you if we need to gain access.'

'Okay.' He wiped his face, the strain and tiredness showing.

'What about the business that Eddie has? Paradise Villas. Was it going as well as he'd hoped? Did you talk about that also?'

'No, we didn't. I never thought Eddie had problems with Paradise Villas. He had it all in hand.'

'It wasn't making as much money as it had done, was it?'

'There was a lot of competition from other developers. Eddie had downscaled quite a bit. He didn't want to work that hard any more. He'd made enough.'

'Do you know the manager there, Billy Manson?

'I've met him once or twice.'

'How recently?'

'Before Eddie died, when Eddie first came over in the middle of October, we'd been to see my acquisitions. We went for a drink in Shoreditch. Manson was with him when I got there.'

'Did everything seem okay between them?'

'Things seemed a bit tense; they'd worked together for so many years, there were bound to be times when they got on one another's nerves. What's this about? Is Manson under suspicion?'

'No, we're just trying to get a fuller picture of Eddie's last couple of weeks, that's all. He didn't seem worried to you?'

'He seemed a bit stressed. I suppose he was a bit more so than usual. He's usually laid-back. He looked a bit tired, distracted.'

'Would he have confided in you if something was wrong?'

'Maybe. But I am always considered the baby of the family. I hope he would have confided in me, yes, but I can't be sure. We discussed projects that I was working on. He told me about the villas he was building.'

'And now, is it right that you will be taking over Paradise Villas?'

'News travels.'

'Was that something you and Eddie had ever discussed? Was it always on the cards?'

Laurence thought about his answer but then shrugged non-committally.

'Did you meet the lawyer, Mr Francisco, who wrote up Eddie's will and witnessed the changes made to it? Did you meet him when you were in Marbella?'

'I have met him before, but, no, I didn't see him this time.'

'He's gone missing, along with his seven-year-old daughter. He was last seen when he visited Tony on the day of Eddie's funeral.'

'Well, I was here in London then, so, I don't see your point.'

'You didn't see him in these last two days?'

'No, sorry.' Laurence was beginning to prickle.

'He seems to have had time to draw up a new will. The original document left everything to his widow, Della. Now this new one, which appears to have arrived from nowhere, leaves everything to Tony. Do you think that's strange?'

'I don't know about that.'

'His widow being left nothing?'

'I'll make sure Della's well provided for. I'll take care of these things for her. I don't know what's happened about Eddie's will. Tony has his ways of doing things.'

Willis was studying Laurence.

'I think you loved your brother, Laurence. I hear Eddie was a good bloke, and I don't think he deserved to die like this.' Willis opened her file and started to pass over the crime-scene photos from the car park. 'What if I told you that your family could have been directly responsible? That one of Tony's deals went wrong and Eddie paid the price?'

He looked at her angrily. 'You have no idea,' he said. 'I know that you lot don't give a shit about our family or about who really killed Eddie. We Butchers don't expect justice to be delivered by you. Eddie's death had nothing to do with Tony or Harold or anyone with Butcher as a surname.'

'Why? Because, after all, Tony is an upstanding figure in society who just happens to have a sideline of importing a ton of cocaine a month into the UK.'

'I know nothing about that.'

'Okay. You can go, Laurence, but I want you to know we consider you to be in great personal danger. If Eddie can be tortured to death, then so can you.'

'Thanks for your advice. I'll take care of myself.'

Willis walked down the corridor so far with him, then headed back to talk to Carter. She found him still in the observation room but in a private conversation on the phone. She hung back as he took a few minutes to end it. He came off the phone looking worried.

'Is Cabrina okay?' Willis asked.

He nodded, distracted. 'Fine.'

'Your dad okay?'

He nodded.

'Can we talk?' he asked.

Willis stepped back inside the observation room and closed the door. She perched on the desk there.

'What did you think about Laurence?' asked Carter. 'If I was him I'd be seriously worried about my health. What have the cartels got to lose by killing him too?'

Willis replied, 'He doesn't seem to have any idea what's going on all around him, unless he's just really clever at seeming naive. The Butcher family have protected him, haven't they? Now, Tony's given him Paradise Villas to keep him happy, to bring him into the fold.'

'Or to make sure Paradise Villas is steered in the right direction.'

'Either way, he seems to have drawn a line under his brother's death.'

'Are you all right about going to Spain, Eb?'

'Fine. I'm quite looking forward to it.'

'What are your thoughts about Ross? What kind of man is he?' asked Carter. 'He ran us a bit of a dance in there, didn't he? I want to be sure about him before we go any further into this deal with the NCA.'

'Broken marriage, two girls, he's a Saturday dad. He likes to think of himself as a victim; everything is out of his control. Nothing was his fault. He hasn't learned any-thing from his broken marriage. He is always searching for the next high. Work is an adrenalin sport to him. He gets bored, he moves to another department.'

'But?'

'But he's very clever, eccentric, impulsive. He has a low boredom threshold and he is obsessed with bringing Tony to justice, plus, and it's a *big* plus, for me, he's drip-feeding us information relevant to Eddie at the moment, but, if we get him on our side, I think the floodgates will open. It's a win–win situation, if we're lucky. If not, we may still get Tony and Harold shut down.'

Carter picked at his fingers, deep in thought. He looked tired, thought Willis. He was full of cold.

He switched off the lights in the observation room as he opened the door to the corridor.

'You coming?'

'Dan?'

Carter half stepped back inside.

'What is it, Eb?'

'Are you okay?'

'I am fine, Eb. I've got man flu, that's all.'

'That's the third time I've seen you take a private call and get funny with me when I've come within earshot. Even when it's Cabrina on the phone you don't usually need privacy and you don't usually say more than a couple of sentences. Whoever it is on the other end of the phone means a lot to you.'

'You know who it is. It's Della. She's going through a great deal out there.'

'Why are you talking to her?'

'She's not a suspect in any of this. She needs my help. They are trying to kill her over there in Spain. The Butcher family are literally trying to kill her.'

'What does she expect you to do about it?'

He shook his head. 'I'm not sure. What can I do?'

'Find her husband's killer and hope that she gets herself out of there fast.'

'And go where? Where is she going to be safe?'

'Can we do a deal with witness protection for her?'

He shook his head. 'I don't know. I don't even think

that's what she'd want; after all, what she wants is justice for her husband and to be left with the estate he intended to leave her. Tony is threatening to bulldoze her house down around her ears. Laurence has been given the business. She knows there's nothing I can do for her; all I can provide is a friendly voice on the other end of the phone, which is what I am doing. When you and Ross go to Spain, you can try to talk to her, see if you can help her circumstances in any way, okay, Eb?'

She nodded. 'I don't mind doing that. What I don't want to be is a go-between for two old lovebirds who are thinking of rebuilding their nest.'

'Don't be ridiculous. It will never be like that.'

'That's what you say, what you think now; but I know you still feel raw about the relationship break-up. You still feel maybe she was the one that got away. But I just want to point out that we're all getting tired, we're all beginning to feel overstressed with this investigation. The last thing you need is to feel emotionally involved in it too. Do you want to step back from it? Do you think you should?'

'No, Eb, I don't. Can we leave this now? She's a friend, nothing more, and I'm being a friend back to her. Enough said. I've had a call from my informant – I'm going to be gone a few hours. See if you can get any more information about Manson. I'll catch up with you as soon as I get back. And, Eb?'

'Yes?'

'I know you mean well. But back off.'

Chapter 29

Della heard the sound of Marco as he came flat-footed through the French windows to the back of the house and the barbecue area.

'What are you doing?' She'd lit the fire pit. She was sitting on the patio overlooking the base of the mountains and the almond grove that descended for an acre before the perimeter wall and the start of the ascent.

'None of your business.' She didn't turn to answer him and, after a few minutes, she heard him thudding heavy, barefooted across the marble as he went back inside the villa.

'I'm going to sleep,' he called.

Della felt revulsion at his presence in her home, the way he came and went as he pleased. She knew she had to get him out somehow. But she had to come up with something good. The last three days she'd spent going meticulously through her life. She was living on adrenalin. The incident in the almond grove had set something in her mind that Della could not shift. It was her or them. It was live or die. She was shocked that Tony thought he had the right to destroy her, to physically and mentally beat her into a pulp and to leave her buried like

Francisco, in a shallow grave. The one thing she knew was that he was so wrong. Eddie hadn't chosen her at random. He'd seen the strength in her that she knew she once had. She'd gone a little soft around the edges but, even when she'd fought Tony off in the bathroom, she'd been surprised how training had kicked in. She was a policewoman and she was Della Vincetti long before she was ever a Butcher.

She lifted the last of the papers she'd hidden from his view beneath her chair, and began feeding them into the fire. The breeze caught them and sent burning embers up into the deep sapphire-blue sky. Eddie's secrets went up in smoke. After she'd finished, she switched on the patio lights and told the maid to light the wood burner in the house and to prepare dinner. She told her not to awaken Marco.

Della went inside to shower. She poured herself more chilled white into a crystal glass, heavy in her manicured hands, and she took it with her into her room, locking the door after she closed it. She sat on her bed and thought hard. Things had to happen now. She looked at her phone. She wanted to call Carter again. She wanted to hear his reassuring voice. She knew he couldn't help while she stayed in Spain. She'd already decided to get out for now. She'd have to make it on her own. She'd have to play the shrewdest card she'd every played.

She waited till she could hear Marco moving around the kitchen: the clash of the fridge door as he slammed it shut, the rattle of bottles.

She put on her bathrobe and went out into the kitchen. Marco was watching the television mounted on the wall. He was sitting on a bar stool and swivelling it around as he listened to the commentator talking in Spanish on the music station. A rapper was being interviewed.

He stopped swivelling to watch Della as she passed and went to the fridge. She moved around in a sensuous cloud of perfume. Her gold jewellery glistened on her brown skin. Her blond hair curled down her back.

Marco followed her with his eyes. He picked up a hand towel and was wiping the sweat from his body as he watched her. She turned with a bottle of wine in her hand.

'Drink?' she asked.

'Sure.' He looked surprised. He was used to her ignoring him.

He grinned as he pushed the bottle of beer to one side and turned off the TV sound.

She smiled. 'Cheers!' She sat on the stool next to him.

'You getting ready to go somewhere?' he asked.

'I was thinking of inviting myself to dinner at Villa Cassandra. But there's plenty of time. Tony will be needing some down time. I've seen him get this wound-up before. It usually ends in him taking a bucketload of tranquillisers and sleeping for a week.'

'Ha-ha. You hate Tony, right?'

'I do now. He had my husband killed.'

Marco shrugged. 'Maybe, or maybe it was not his fault.'

'And maybe it was yours.'

'Mine? No. Why?'

'Because you and Tony are hatching some plan. Eddie must have found himself in the middle of something he knew nothing about.'

'How come you think you know so much about it?'

'Why shouldn't I? You think I don't keep my eyes and ears open? You think I'm as stupid as Tony likes to think I am? Tony doesn't know everything; he doesn't have all the answers.' She smiled sweetly at Marco as she allowed her robe to open up and show her bare tanned legs.

Marco looked at her curiously. He reached over to top up her glass as she continued: 'I've spent the last few days going through Eddie's affairs. I've seen papers here in this villa that no one but Eddie and his lawyer has ever seen. I know what his plans were and they did not include dying for Tony or taking part in any cheap drugs deal.'

'Cheap? None of it comes cheap, princess.'

'Except my husband's life, it seems. It's taken a little while to sink in but now I understand a few things very clearly. Tony thinks I am going to go without a fight. He is wrong. If you think I don't have friends in high places, you are wrong. I can get my hands on a lot of money. I have a lot of options in life.'

'How much is a lot?'

'Upwards from a hundred million. That's what this is all about, isn't it? It's always about money with Tony.'

'Jesus!' He grinned.

She laughed. 'Never underestimate me. I could be a good friend to you.'

He grinned stupidly. 'I am sure you could. But I don't know why you would want to be.'

'I have a deal I want to put to Tony.'

'So what is this, real or no?'

'Oh, it's definitely real. Phone Tony and tell him I have a proposition to put to him. Tell him to expect me for dinner.'

He laughed. '*Si, señora.*'

Back in her room, Della tried Carter's number again. She left a message.

'I need to see you, Dan. I've decided what I'm going to do and I'm coming to the UK. I'll ring you when I get there. I'm so grateful to you, Dan. I'm sorry to put all this on you. I know it's a difficult situation for you but I feel like I have the answer to it. Can't wait to see you.'

Chapter 30

Carter looked around him as he walked into St Matthew's Church in Bethnal Green.

'What have you got for me, Melvin? Why are we meeting here?'

They were alone but Melvin kept looking around as if he expected to be jumped.

'You okay, Melvin?' Carter asked. Melvin didn't look good. He sometimes had bouts of depression.

He shook his head. He was walking backwards up towards the front of the church, between the chairs that had replaced pews when the church became more of a community centre. Now it provided a meeting place and playgroup facility in the week as well as multifaith religious services.

'Did you find out any more for me?' asked Carter.

Melvin nodded. 'But I need more money. I can't work.' He looked up at Carter, panic in his eyes. 'Scamp is gone.' He started crying.

'Whoa, slow down. What's the problem, Melvin? I thought business was good? What do you mean Scamp has gone? Where?'

'I let him out the front for a pee and he vanished.'

'Did you ring up Battersea Dogs Home?'

'Yes. It's not good. He's gone. They've killed him. Scamp never hurt anyone. Did he?'

'He'll come back. I'll make enquiries for you; I'll put up a reward for his return. Two hundred quid, how's that? Come on, Melvin, come here.' Carter held open his arms and Melvin sobbed into Carter's coat. 'Come on, let's sit down here for a while and talk.'

'I can't work. I'm too worried.' He blew his nose in the hanky Carter handed him.

'What about the staff in the Blind Beggar? Do they know anything?'

'I haven't asked them. I've been too scared, in case he comes back and finds me gone. I don't dare leave my house; this is the first time I've come out. I've left the door open just in case he comes when I'm not there.'

'You shouldn't do that. You better get off home. Have you been to the doc's, Melvin? You're getting ill again.' He kept shaking his head. 'Look, here we are.' Carter took out his wallet and pulled out all the notes he had.

'There's a couple of hundred quid there. You go home and get a photo of Scamp and text it to me and I'll alert the patrol cars to look out for him, okay? I'll get in touch with the dog wardens.'

'Thank you, Inspector. I did have something to tell you. It may not be much but I've seen that man again. You asked me about a man in one of the photos. I saw him in a café. He was with someone. I took this picture for you. I pretended to be looking at the menu. I hope that's clear. I'll send it to you now.'

Carter looked at the photo.

'When was this taken, Melvin?'

'This was taken two days ago. It's that bloke I showed you before.'

'Who, this guy?' Carter tapped on the photo and enlarged it. 'You never showed me him before.'

'Didn't I? I've seen him around here a few times, talking to the big ugly bloke. Do you know him?'

'Yes, his name is Manson. Does that mean anything to you?'

Melvin shook his head. 'I've just been keeping a lookout for the big ugly one with the bun.'

'Marco.'

'That's him. Haven't seen him for a week or two.'

'Who is Manson with?'

'I couldn't risk getting a better shot of him. I thought you might know him. He's a really dodgy bloke. He's been in the area about a month. I've seen him around but he isn't friendly. He speaks to Lev now and again, but no one seems to want to talk long with him. I tried a conversation with him once, in the pub. He speaks good English, with a South American accent. You can ask Lev about him. I don't know what's going on around here but everyone's scared. Even Lev.'

'You need to rest up, Melvin. You're getting ill. You go and see the doc, okay? I'll start asking about Scamp for you.'

He nodded, but his eyes were still on the door as if he expected an ambush.

Carter watched Melvin leave and then he sent the photo of Manson across to Robbo with the message, 'Any ideas?'

Carter walked down to the Old Jewish Bakery. Lev was serving customers. The windows were steaming up. Carter ordered a coffee and he sat at the window seat. Lev was talking to his customers, who seemed like regulars picking up their usual preordered bagels. Lev was washing out the containers, getting ready to close for the day. Carter waited until the last customer had gone. Carter had been reading the information on the walls about Lev's grandfather, who started the bakery. It was a tale of endurance and resilience, a heartwarming tale.

'That's a great history you have there, Lev.'

'It is.' He was cleaning down the surfaces.

'You've seen some changes around here, but fundamentally things stay the same. I suppose you're looking forward to the gentrification happening?'

He smiled, nodded.

Carter showed Lev the photo on his phone of Manson and the mystery man.

'Do you know who this is, Lev?'

'I don't recognise them, sorry.'

'Sure?'

'Positive, Inspector.'

'Melvin seems to think he saw you with one of these guys, South American, been around about a month.'

Lev stopped what he was doing to look at the photo again and then shook his head.

'Well, it's a bad photo. But have you heard of the name Manson?'

'No, sorry.'

'Well, it's no problem. Just not sure what Melvin is talking about. He seems like he's getting ill again.'

'Yes, I thought that when he came in here earlier. He's lost his dog.'

'What about that? He thinks someone took it.'

Lev shook his head in disbelief. 'He just lets it out to shit in the front garden, it gets out the gate, I see it sometimes going through the bins here.'

'Well, you keep an eye out for me.' He handed Lev a card. 'And you ring me if you think of a name for that man.'

'Of course.'

Chapter 31

'We're looking through the footage from the funeral again to see if we can see your man in there,' said Robbo. 'Meanwhile, Pam has dug up more on Manson.'

Pam handed Carter and Willis a file each, before the start of the sub meeting in Robbo's office.

'I've been looking into his lifestyle for you,' she said as Robbo, Carter and Willis opened up their files and began reading.

'I'm waiting for confirmation on a couple of things, but this is what I have on him so far,' she said as she went back behind her desk. 'Plus, I've just had it confirmed from the dealership that Manson paid cash for his brand-new Range Rover. That was three months ago in October.'

Robbo handed out coffee as Willis and Carter read through the file. He'd already read it as Pam compiled it.

Afterwards Carter closed his and put it on the desk.

'Good work, Pam. We need to put some surveillance on Manson. We'll request his phone records and have his phone bugged.'

'I don't think he's using his contract phone exclusively. He was photographed on another device outside Paradise Villas,' said Pam, 'when we studied the CCTV after Eddie died.'

'Let's re-examine that footage and make sure we didn't miss anything,' said Carter.

'I'll take another look,' answered Robbo.

'One thing has just come in,' said Pam. 'We've been monitoring the use on the company credit card and Jo Manson has just purchased tickets for the family to fly off to Thailand for a month for Christmas.'

'That's an afterthought then. Snap decision. He must be getting nervous,' said Robbo. 'Who books so late for a family holiday at Christmas? They would have to pay dear for tickets now.'

'First class,' said Pam. 'It cost them almost thirteen thousand.'

'When are they due to fly?' asked Carter.

'They're due to go tomorrow evening,' answered Pam.

'Do we let him go, guv?' asked Willis.

He shook his head decisively. 'After reading this report? We don't let him go anywhere. Manson has come back in the frame here.'

'I agree,' said Willis. 'He could do a runner.'

'The property in Thailand is owned by him, Pam, is that right?'

'Yes, and there are four other properties registered to his name abroad in: Florida, Thailand Costa Rica and Mexico. They were paid for outright.'

'When were they bought?' asked Willis.

'All in the last eighteen months.'

'So, seems he's been working extra hard at Paradise Villas. Is there any record of that kind of bonus coming his way?' asked Robbo.

'None I can find,' answered Pam, 'but it looks like he's got his fingers in a few pies. He has links to companies registered in Miami, the Caymans, Madeira. I'm beginning to find his name on the directorship of several companies.'

'Companies that do what?'

'Mostly manufacture: teak furnishings, marble fireplaces, ceramics, artisan furniture.'

'We saw fireplaces when we went out there,' said Willis.

'Here's a list of the other products his companies supply.' Pam passed it round.

'So, all of these manufactured goods can be legitimately traced to things that could be used in building and fitting out the villas?' said Carter as he read it.

'Yes, I think they definitely can,' answered Pam.

'Was Eddie part of these companies?' asked Robbo. 'Was he also a director?'

'No, just Manson's name is on the company details. They were set up between eighteen and twelve months ago.'

'So maybe that was the way he made extra money,' suggested Carter. 'He supplied the building materials? He supplied some things that went into these luxury villas? Is there anything sinister in that? Eddie was downsizing, Eddie had made it clear he was just coasting along. Manson got paid a good salary but it wasn't going to go up, while Eddie wouldn't give Manson any more than a five per cent share of the business, and the business wasn't growing; so Manson made his own luck. Maybe it was a win–win situation.'

'It depends whether Eddie knew that – and why did it all happen in the last year?'

Carter congratulated Pam. 'Good work, we definitely have enough here to warrant another chat with Manson. He's been very selective with the truth.'

Ross passed outside in the corridor and knocked on Robbo's door.

'Is this a private meeting or can I join in?' he asked with a smile, looking ever more as if he'd stepped off the set of a film.

'Yeah, grab a chair; you can help us on this one,' Carter said. Willis made room for him next to her. But she did it without a smile. She wasn't sure whether she liked him. He had purposely made her look small in the interview with Harold. She wasn't sure that was a good sign for a potential work colleague.

Ross glanced at the file on the desktop.

'Manson? Paradise Villas manager? Is that who we're discussing here?'

'Yeah, but he's much more than a manager,' replied Carter. 'He told us he just owned five per cent of the shares in Eddie's company but Pam's discovered that he has a share in several of the foreign companies who supply the fixtures, fittings, building materials to build those villas. You name it, he's got a stake in it, he's a very entrepreneurial guy.'

'Did he own those with Eddie?'

'Not that I can see,' answered Pam.

'We saw some boxes with "Dream Stone Fireplace Company" printed on when we went out there,' Carter said as he handed Ross the list of companies.

'Let's have a look at some of these,' said Ross, opening up his laptop and typing in the name.

'This company is based not far from their place in Swanley, is that right?'

'That's the one,' answered Pam.

He came up with the some images of fireplaces.

'These them?' He showed Willis.

'Yes. They're all pretty much the same type of thing. The ones I saw weren't so elaborate. They were plain blocks of marble.'

Ross started typing on his keyboard.

'What are you doing?' Willis asked him as she looked over his shoulder.

'Sending them a request for a quote. There are no testimonials on this site, which is odd. I want to see what they can offer me.' He sent the email request, then looked up at Carter. 'So what else is there on Manson?'

'He drives a brand-new expensive car that he paid for with cash. He has second homes in other countries. We have photos of him meeting with . . .' He handed the picture over to Ross. 'Recognise him?'

Ross scrutinised it. 'Not off the top of my head, but look at his body language: he looks like he's the one taking the verbal bashing here. Where did you get this?'

'My informant, who's a local man. It was taken in a café on Whitechapel High Street.'

'Did he hear what they were saying?'

'No.'

'He'd no idea who Manson was; he'd seen him with Marco before now, so he took this for me, thought it would be of interest.'

'Perhaps this man was acting as a messenger for Tony. But why meet in the East End? Something of interest there for them? Or is there a point in the choice of meeting place? Are they trying to intimidate Manson?'

'Manson is suddenly going to fly out to his house in Thailand for Christmas. We're debating whether to let him go,' said Carter.

'If it was my investigation, I would,' answered Ross.

'I wouldn't,' said Willis. 'He can do a runner.'

'He has kids, family to consider, before he'd do that,' said Ross.

'Yes, but they're young and he can rehome everyone,' said Robbo. 'Plus, if he's in any way involved in Eddie's death, or if he knows something significant about it, if he's in danger, he'll run.'

'I agree with Robbo and Willis,' said Carter. 'Make the call, Eb. Tell him he's not going anywhere until this investigation is finished, and put an alert out at the airports.'

Willis went across to sign in at Robbo's desk and get hold of Manson.

'Do you have more information to share with us?' Carter turned to ask Ross.

'I have a file to share, yes. This ...' He took out a file from his backpack. 'This is a year's worth of surveillance records on Eddie Butcher. Now that Marco's made an appearance in connection with Manson, I'll see what else I can find for you to help with a link there. I'll get the team on the mystery man as well.

'We followed Harold, not Eddie. You have your own CCTV footage of where Eddie went next, don't you?'

Robbo nodded. 'We lose him when he's walking back along Whitechapel Road.'

'What's happening now to Tony, at the villa, according to Spanish police?' Carter asked Ross.

'They say that the missing lawyer Francisco, who was dealing with Eddie Butcher's will, was also the bookkeeper for the Mendez cartel. The Spanish police say that they registered Francisco as visiting Villa Cassandra, being driven by Marco Zapata. Here are some stills from the day; this was the day of Eddie's funeral, the 8th.'

He took out an envelope from his briefcase and slid photos from inside.

'This is him arriving with Marco. This is him leaving and shots of him being dropped off in the centre of town. It's too busy to get a clear shot of him then. They're more interested in Marco. Have a look . . .'

Willis studied the photos.

'You can spot the difference, if you look hard enough,' she said.

'Yes, at first glance it was a clever double for him but we've identified the person we think it is: it's the gardener, a retired expat; he's the maintenance man, pool man and head gardener. He also oversees Eddie's grounds, down the road. His name is Danny Miller.' Ross handed around a picture of Miller. He was wearing Francisco's suit.

'Do we know Danny Miller?'

'He was in jail at the same time as Tony; we presume he met him in there. Miller was in for burglary and GBH. He's worked for Tony for the last ten years. Before that, he'd done a string of jobs in Spain, mainly centred around working in bars.'

'So, will the Spanish police order a search of Tony's villa?'

He nodded. 'They're asking us if we wish to be present.'

Carter smiled. 'Any reason not to?'

'None I can think of,' answered Ross. 'It will be quite an insight into him.'

'Have you ever met him before, Ross?' asked Robbo.

'Once or twice. I've interviewed him before at a Spanish police station, but never been to his home.'

Willis came off the phone. 'I got hold of Manson; he wasn't best pleased,' she said.

'Let's hope he's got insurance,' said Ross.

'Can you go back to your informant and get him to find out more about Manson and Marco and what they were doing together?' asked Ross.

'My informant has got mental-health problems. I can't use him again,' answered Carter.

After the meeting, Ross asked to talk to Willis at her desk.

'I think we should plan the itinerary for our Spanish trip now. We need to work out who we see first. We'll need to hire a car. I reckon we'll be away for a few days. You okay with that?'

'Yes, fine, canteen okay? I have a lot to sort out at my desk before we go.'

'Canteen's fine.' Willis led Ross through to Archway Police Station and down to the canteen in the basement. Tina raised an eyebrow as she saw Willis walking in with Ross.

'Teen, this is Ross.' Tina went to wipe her hand on her overall to go in for a handshake but Ross had already passed by with a wave and was choosing a salad from the fridge cabinet.

Willis smiled but shook her head at Tina. 'See you later Teen. Actually, I probably won't be around tonight. I'll text you,' Willis said as Ross came back and smiled at Tina.

Willis led them to a table.

'When are the Spanish authorities wanting to visit Tony?' she asked.

'As soon as we get there. They'll wait for us.'

'Really? Shall we fly out first thing?' asked Willis.

'Yes, Can you email me over your passport number, date of birth, that kind of thing, and I'll ask my secretary to get the tickets,' Ross said. 'And then, shall I see you at the airport?'

'Yes,' answered Willis, distracted.

'What's bugging you? Is it the deal I offered Harold without telling you I was going to do it?'

'Partly. It did make me look stupid. I don't know whether we'll achieve much by going out there.'

'Carter was also caught off guard. It's not as if I singled you out.'

'Doesn't make it any better.'

'Listen, there will be secrets you keep from me. Things that we don't cross over on, and that's fair enough. I know, for instance, that DI Dan Carter was once involved with Della Butcher. You didn't tell me that, did you?'

'She's not a suspect.'

'No, I get it, which is why I've not passed the information on.'

'How did you find out?'

'Operation Argos? I got access to files from the time. I presume you would have done the same. I also had a meeting with Chief Inspector Bowie to clarify my role in all this and I put the past to him. Are you worried that Carter's involvement jeopardises the investigation? After all, it looks like this was the real deal for Carter at least? This was lurve . . .' Ross drawled.

Willis shook her head as she stared into her coffee cup.

'Then we'll just have to hope it brings something valuable to the table and doesn't cause Carter too many problems. We'll talk to Tony. That'll be an interesting experience; I'm looking forward to it. He can't refuse to answer questions about his brother's murder.'

Chapter 32

'What did Ross want?' Carter asked.

'To talk through our Spanish trip,' Willis answered.

'You okay with that?'

'Of course.'

'Sorry I snapped at you, earlier.'

'That's okay, don't mention it. There's a lot at stake. You have a lot to think about.'

'But it shouldn't ever interfere with the job,' Carter replied.

'I don't think it's doing that. You're aware of it. You'll weather it. I can take a bit of abuse now and again.' She smiled.

'Slight exaggeration.' He smiled back at her. 'Shall we drive down and talk with Manson and ask him about the Thailand trip? Did you get the results back from the samples you took the other day?'

'Yeah, nothing. The same composition as last time.'

'Did Robbo relook at the CCTV?'

'He's doing it now.'

'Okay, let's go and talk to him before we head off. I won't keep you working all night. I expect you need to pack for tomorrow. That should take you five minutes at least.' He grinned.

Jo Manson was preparing the dinner when the knock on the door made her jump.

'Billy?' she whispered hoarsely.

'Okay, stay calm. I'll go. Keep the kids in the kitchen and close the door.' Manson hopped up onto the worktop and took something from the roof of the cupboard. He tucked it into the back of his trousers.

'Where did you get that?' Jo stared, shocked.

'Never mind, Jo, just lock yourselves in here. Keep the kids away from the windows. Take them into the utility room and out through the garage if you hear something is wrong.'

'What?'

'Just do it, Jo, for fuck's sake!'

She nodded, shell-shocked.

The children, Lana and Bertie, were sitting in the family room off the kitchen, around them an expanse of glass, and Jo went across to flick the switch and activate the blinds to hide the blackness beyond the glass. They lived in adjoining fields in the Kent countryside.

Jo stopped her work, held her breath, as she listened to Billy going to answer the second knock at the front door.

'Hello again, Mr Manson.' Jo was about to grab the children and run when she heard Billy reply, 'Inspector?'

'You remember my colleague, DS Willis?'

'Of course.'

'Can we come in, please? We thought we'd better come down here in person and explain why we can't allow you to go to Thailand,' Carter said as he took a step inside the front door.

'Come in, follow me.' Manson led them inside the chic modern home with an abundance of white walls and wooden floors, large feature windows and exposed steel beams. Carter took off his shoes; Willis reluctantly did the same. Manson was barefooted. The floor was heated beneath the hardwood.

Manson led them into a long room with a gable end. It had a white pod-shaped wood burner that was built into the centre of the room. They sat near it on Scandinavian-looking furniture that was more comfortable than it looked. Expensive art that Carter couldn't understand, and would never have bought, hung in huge canvases on the feature walls.

'What was the problem with us spending Christmas abroad?' asked Manson, sitting on the edge of the sofa. He was visibly nervous. He hadn't washed his hair in a few days. He looked exhausted. He was wearing scruffy tracksuit bottoms and a dirty T-shirt.

'I'm sorry, but it was necessary.' Carter smiled.

'Am I a suspect?'

'You have a lovely home. Did you build it?' Carter asked, looking around.

'I had a hand in it, yes, thank you. You didn't answer my question.'

'No, because that's tricky. I'd like to give you the chance of telling us the truth first. You weren't a suspect yesterday until we did a bit of digging and now we are reconsidering our position.'

'Truth? About what?'

'Let's start with the Thailand trip. Where were you and your family going to stay?'

Manson blushed crimson at the same time as he half

laughed and shook his head. 'What relevance does this have? What does it matter where we were going to stay?'

'Because you haven't been completely honest about your assets.'

'I didn't tell you that I owned a house out there? What does that matter? You never asked me.'

'No, that's true, but then we discovered this was one of many properties that you'd bought outright in the last eighteen months and we were wondering whether they were funded by the many companies you'd set up to supply materials to Paradise Villas.'

'The short answer to that is yes. I have some interests in other companies. These provide me with extra income. As I told you, I only have a five per cent share in Paradise Villas. It doesn't bring in the profit that it used to.'

'So you branched out?'

'Yes.'

'Seems like the sensible thing to have done.'

'Yes, and I have a good accountant who gives me good advice and I have offshore bank accounts. Nothing I do is illegal.'

'Did Eddie know about these connections?'

'Of course. He thought it was great that we knew where the goods were coming from. We could control the quality.'

'Must have been time-consuming, setting all that up.'

'It was. Which is why I ended up buying places out in Asia, South America.'

'You have a place in Mexico, is that right? That's not a place I associate with furniture.'

'It's on the coast. It's a base for me to source things from.'

'What things?' Carter smiled.

'Bespoke art pieces. I have someone who makes bronzes

of polo ponies in Argentina. I have a modern Aztec design company in Peru.'

'Anything from Colombia? You have friends from there, I think.'

As Manson shook his head slowly he was trying to hide the understanding from his expression.

'Marco Zapata?'

'Who? I don't know that name, sorry.'

'You've never met with a man called that?'

Manson was shaking his head but his face had paled as he was pretending to search his memory. He tapped his fingers together nervously.

'I don't think I should say any more at this point. I don't know where this is leading but it doesn't feel comfortable.'

'This is just a friendly chat to clear the air, Mr Manson. It can all be sorted here and now if you cooperate. If you insist on denying what we already know to be true, then we're going to have to continue this discussion down at the police station. It's up to you. If you have nothing to hide, then what are you so nervous about?'

'I am nervous because I am suddenly in a world I know nothing about. Eddie Butcher died a horrible death and I am scared for me and my family. That's why I wanted to go to Thailand, just in the hope you might have caught whoever did it by the time we came back. My wife is close to a breakdown because she's so scared.'

'What have you decided to do, now that the family are taking over?'

Manson shook his head, he seemed calmer. 'I haven't decided yet. I'll wait and see.'

'What about all the fixtures and fittings you make, the

teak furnishings and the rest of it? Won't they need to be sold?'

'I only manufacture to order.'

Carter showed Manson the photo of him with the mystery man from the cafe. 'Who is this?'

Manson contemplated shaking his head but spluttered out the name Justino.

'Justino who?'

Manson shrugged. 'I honestly don't know anything more about him; he was a contact from a Peruvian artefacts company. They wanted me to buy some of their works, but I didn't bother in the end.'

'Do you have a number for him?' asked Willis.

'Sorry, I didn't bother keeping it. Who is he? Why was my photo taken with him?'

'We're just looking into any strangers in the area, that's all.' Willis answered.

'Okay, well thanks for your time,' said Carter. 'Sorry we couldn't help with the Thailand thing. If we had got a bit further in the investigation and if people were a bit more forthcoming, then it might have been different. Getting information from anyone who knew Eddie Butcher is like pulling teeth. Still I expect you know that already. We'll keep you informed. If you think of anything you reckon can help this investigation, then contact us.' Carter handed Manson a card. 'The sooner we solve this the sooner you can get on with your life and, if you are contacted by Marco Zapata again, please ring me straight away.'

Manson stood, nodding, looking relieved and very eager to be left alone.

*

Once they had driven out of sight Willis turned to Carter: 'I'd like to take another look in the warehouse. I want to check on any activity there. I've sent Robbo the name Justino to see what he can find out.'

'The Peruvian artefacts company sounded like crap – but the name Justino may just be the truth. We'll go to the warehouse now, no problem,' answered Carter. 'It's only twenty minutes' drive.'

'But, we don't have a search warrant,' Willis said. 'I'll be in Spain tomorrow.'

'Then we'll try being nice to the security guard and see where it gets us. Leave it to me to do the talking. We know where your charms get us.' He looked over and winked. She shook her head smiling. 'One of these days I'll surprise you and I'll charm the pants off someone.'

'Live in hope, Willis. Live in hope.'

*

'We won't be long in there, it's just something we need to check. We'll bring the keys straight back. Thanks, mate,' Carter said as the security guard opened the gate for them.

'It's okay. It's empty, anyway. They've moved all the stock.'

'When did that happen?'

'Billy Manson did it last night. By the time my shift ended at eight in the morning, it was all gone.'

'Where did it go? Do you know?' asked Willis.

'No idea, sorry. Must have been fairly local because he made two trips.'

'Okay, thanks, mate.' Carter handed the keys across to Willis as they drove in and parked. Willis went round to the boot and took out her scenes of crime kit. She picked up some booties to cover their shoes.

'Empty,' said Carter. As they stood in the cold warehouse, their breath came out white as Willis shone her torch around the inside.

Willis handed Carter a pair of the booties.

'What are we doing here again?' He sighed at the prospect of getting down and searching the dirt floor.

'I'm just curious, now that the boxes have gone.'

'Okay, fair enough. Do you need me? Can I go and be curious elsewhere?'

'I can manage.'

'Okay, well I'll go back and chat to the security guard and see if he can remember anything else. Call me if you need me.'

Carter walked back out of the building, putting the booties into the car as he passed. 'So, mate, it's lucky you've got a heater in there. Talk about freezing. You always do night shifts, do you?'

'Yeah, you get used to it. Although it's a bit boring.' The security guard was in his late forties; he looked like he had been in the forces at some point. He had a tattoo on his neck that was a badly drawn Betty Boop. His face had more lines than it should have, but he had an uprightness about him that said: military, meltdown, second chance.

'What do you do all night?' asked Carter, genuinely curious. He had hated working on surveillance in his time. Some people were good at just observing, Carter was not. He loved to talk. He was easily distracted.

'I talk to the dog mostly.'

'Where's the dog?' Carter looked around, a shot of adrenalin crossed his heart. He hated guard dogs. He'd been bitten by an Alsatian once and the more he moved the more it tore at the flesh of his leg.

'He's off sick. I've left him at home. Apart from that, I read a lot.'

'So, last night, when Manson was here, must have made a welcome change. Gave you something to look at, at least.'

'Yeah, it was a bit random, moving stuff in the middle of the night. He turned up here at half three. But, it's not the first time he's done that.'

'On his own?'

'Yes.'

'Must have been something to move all those boxes on his own?'

'He has a mini-forklift. He's used to it. We get a load arriving every month.'

'Have you seen where the things come from?'

'From a lot of places. But a lot of the time they come from Spain, Amsterdam. They're part of a container load.'

'Which all ends up here before it's sent off to build villas?'

'I don't know about that. From here the stuff in the warehouse gets taken by Manson somewhere, must be the same place, I reckon. It takes him about the same time to do the offloading and delivery every time.'

'Does Eddie ever do it?'

'I've never seen Eddie even be here when the warehouse is emptied. Usually when Eddie's here there's just an empty space in there.'

'Could you hazard a guess where he took them last night?'

'Well, it takes him a good hour to load it, must take him the same to unload it the other end. He's gone for about two to three hours. There are lots of industrial estates he could shift it to, I suppose, or maybe it's a lockup some-where. I've got no real idea, sorry.'

'What about the van? Is it his?'

'Oh yes, I'm sure about that. I can give you the number plate for that because we have to register all that kind of thing.' He checked in his book and wrote it down on a piece of paper. 'Here we are, make, model, number. Hope that helps.'

'You've been great, thanks, mate.' Carter looked over to where Willis was locking up the warehouse. 'Hope the dog feels better soon.'

'Yeah, thanks.'

Carter walked back across to the car. Willis was putting her bag back in the boot.

'Interesting,' Carter said as he flashed his headlights and waved at the security guard.

'I found nothing that looked promising,' answered Willis as she checked her phone to see the time.

'You want dropping straight home, or do you have time for a drink?'

'Need to go home, sorry. You must be feeling better.'

'What way?'

'Your man flu?'

'Yes, cracked it now. Just not keen on the empty-flat syndrome.'

'Now, there's an admission. I might just make Cabrina's day and tell her what you just said.'

'You wouldn't?'

'Of course not.'

'It's just that you'd think I'd be able to sleep being alone in the flat. But no. I'm lying there staring at the ceiling.'

'Do you really want to go for a drink? I can spare the time.'

'No, get out of here! I'm okay. You're right, you probably have to be gone early in the morning.'

'I have to leave the house at five thirty to be precise.'

'Shit, that's not funny. I'm okay, Eb, honestly. I'll take you home now, then I'll get on with some work.'

Carter dropped Willis off and drove just a few streets before he pulled over and checked his phone. He sent off a couple of texts and then he rang Chief Inspector Bowie.

'What's up?' Bowie asked.

'Nothing, just thought you might fancy a pint.'

'Sorry, headed home. What time's the meeting tomorrow?'

'I'm waiting for an update from Robbo on a few things, but I'll be in early.'

Carter finished the call to Bowie, then he called Robbo.

'We had an interesting visit to Billy Manson's house in the Kent countryside, and we also went to his warehouse tonight. Manson's doing something he didn't want Eddie to know about. Whether it's just making money on the side, supplementing his income, or something more, I don't know. I'm going to text you over the details on a white van that Manson uses to move goods from The Paddocks industrial estate. I need you to check where this van was in a radius of about fifty miles from Paradise Villas. We're looking for a second warehouse or storage facility. For some reason Manson finds it necessary to shift these boxes in the middle of the night. You know what?'

'I'll start on it now.'

'Do you fancy going for a pint this evening?'

'Sorry, I'm abstaining at the moment but I have plenty of strong coffee and two spare bags of Haribo that I've managed to squirrel away from Willis's greedy eyes, if you feel like company while we work.'

'I'm suddenly very tired.'

Robbo laughed. 'You headed straight home, then?'

'*Yes*, what is it with you, Robbo? You turned into my nanny suddenly?'

'Sorry, just picking up on something Willis said, that's all, about this investigation being personal for you. You want my opinion about it all?'

'No, not really, but I don't expect that's going to stop you.'

'I know how personal this is to you. I remember you two as a couple. You and Della were like two peas in a pod. I remember thinking you were almost like the perfect pair. You were too similar, perhaps, to make it. Della is a female version of you, Dan. You be careful, because she knows how to pull your strings. She always did.'

'I don't need your advice, thanks.'

'Yes, you do. You remember that she was mercenary, in the end? She chose money over love. She wanted all the things a policeman's salary could never bring her. Not unless that officer was on the take.'

'She says it was love.'

'Bullshit. She was blinded by cash, not love. I saw it happening. I know how much you loved each other, but she nearly broke you, Dan. Don't for Christ's sake let her try and do it again.'

Chapter 33

Della walked into Tony's with Marco beside her. She was wearing a short dress and heels.

'Debbie and Sandra joining us for dinner?' she asked, looking around at the empty room. The fake candles had been switched on in the windows. The doors to the verandas were closed against the building gusts of wind that heralded a storm coming.

'Drink!' he called out at the top of his voice and Sheena appeared, carrying a tray. For Della there was an unopened bottle of Chablis, which Sheena opened and poured into crystal glasses for her and Marco. A bottle of whisky was already on the table for Tony with an ice bucket.

'It's just us this evening. You look gorgeous, my dear, radiant,' said Tony, clearly savouring the scene. 'Please excuse me while I go and change for dinner.' He hurried away.

Della went to the music station and chose a playlist.

'Let's put some music on, shall we? Can you dance, Marco?'

'Me? Sure. I'm from Colombia, remember? All we Latinos can dance.'

'Come on, then, Mr Latino, give me a masterclass.'

She began moving to the music. He stood, put his glass down and walked over.

He took hold of her and they began dancing. Della had been to ballroom-dancing classes when she was young. She'd stopped it when she was fourteen but she'd been good and she still was.

They started to tango and Marco led her around the trophy room. He didn't notice Tony, who was standing by the entrance, watching mesmerised. He began a slow clap. He still had his shorts on, but he'd put on a white silk shirt, open at the neck, and he had a black Spanish dancer's hat on his head.

Della started laughing. Tony came forward to take over from Marco. He made up his own dance – twirling Della around and catching her in his arms. Every time he caught her he tried to kiss her.

Sandra walked in. 'Tony!'

Della allowed herself the chance to catch her breath and stood laughing as she doubled over and fanned her face with her hand.

'What's going on here?'

Della just ignored Sandra and allowed Tony to answer.

'Nothing, Mum.'

'What is it, Sandra?' Della asked with a sweet smile.

Sandra took her time in answering; her eyes bore into Della. Marco was taking it all in, a big grin on his face.

'What's on the menu for dinner tonight, Sandra?' asked Della. 'Not some cocktail you've prepared for me, I hope. It's a favour I'd like to return one day.'

'Huh. You'll have to get up early to catch me out.'

'Mum, you joining us for dinner?' Tony asked.

'Got better things to do.' Sandra turned and walked out.

Sheena announced that dinner was served. It was Tony's favourite: steak and chips. Tony pulled out Della's chair for her to sit and he backed away, bowing, and went to sit at his place at the head of the long table.

On his right side was Della and on his left was Marco. Marco attacked his steak with all the finesse of a starving hyena. Della cut slithers of meat and moved the food around her plate. Tony poured her some champagne, which he was careful to open in front of her.

'Well, I think, in retrospect, I should have been just as happy to enjoy just your company, my dear,' Tony said as he watched Marco eat and turned away disgusted. Marco looked up and saw them staring and shrugged, continued eating.

Tony turned back to Della and raised his glass. 'So lovely to see you, princess. I hear from Marco that you have a proposition to put to me. I am all ears, darling. Please, do go on.'

'I know where to find a large stash of uncut diamonds and cash. Eddie hid them. They are the missing diamonds from the Great Diamond Heist.'

There was a rare silence from Tony as his face betrayed the workings of his brain and he chewed over the information. He was visibly shaken.

'You know quite a bit about it, then? You know Eddie lied to me?'

'I was Eddie's wife. We didn't have too many secrets. I don't have the exact location, but I have a few ideas on how to find it.'

'Did Eddie tell you?'

'He left me clues. And, I knew Eddie better than anyone. I understood the way his mind worked. He left me papers in the villa. I've burned them now. I've spread the information out so that only I can access it: private email accounts, codes. Kill me, you kill any chance of ever finding it.'

'How much is there?'

'More than three hundred million's worth, some of the rarest gems of all time. Eddie was waiting to bring them onto the market one by one.'

Marco stopped eating and watched as Debbie came into the room. Della could guess what had happened: Sandra had told her to get some make-up on and get in there. She was greeted by Tony.

'Debbie, baby, come on in and sit down. I didn't think you were getting up again today. Call Sheena and tell her to bring you dinner.'

Tony looked slightly tense now that Debbie had entered the room. Debbie wasn't going anywhere. She knew her place was to make sure she heard everything.

'What's Della doing here?' Debbie addressed Tony.

'Della has come with a proposition for us, baby. She has some fascinating news. Come and sit down and you can hear all about it.'

'Oh, yes? What is it?'

'It's about the diamonds. The precious gemstones that Eddie always said he knew nothing about. The jewels that he was hiding all these years. Our jewels.'

'You always said he was lying.'

'I did, didn't I, my dear? And I was fucking well right. But, this wasn't Della's fault and now, clever little thing that she is' – he gave her a sickly smile – 'she knows where it is. Such a lot of it, too.'

'How much?' asked Debbie as Sheena brought her a cup of coffee and cleared their plates. Tony grabbed her wrist as she took his.

'A lot. Sheena, bring us a bottle of good champagne, the best.'

'How do you know where they are?' asked Debbie, addressing Della directly.

'Eddie has left me instructions, but they are only for me to follow. One step leads to another, and has to be done by me. The jewels are not all in one place.'

'Ha! Bullshit!' said Debbie. 'She's bluffing, Tony.'

Marco was watching everyone with interest.

'We could only ever bring them out and sell them a few at a time,' said Della. 'You know that's true. Every diamond has to be traceable, that is until it goes through a few hands, and then no one seems to remember where it came from. Uncut diamonds are easier. There are a lot of those.'

'We need proof,' said Debbie.

'Debbie is right, Della. If you can show me a couple of these gems, then I will believe you. You take them to Harold to verify; he handled enough of the original jewels to know their worth.'

'How are we going to sell them?' asked Debbie. 'It'll take for fucking ever.'

'Maybe we won't have to,' said Tony. 'We can swap them for a shipment, eh, Marco?'

He nodded, sucking on a wooden toothpick.

'Diamonds are always welcome.'

Tony addressed Della: 'The cartels will be watching you.'

'I'll have to be clever, then.'

He laughed. 'You know what, Della? I think you will be.'

'I can't do it all on my own and I know you will send Marco to watch me anyway, so he may as well come with me from the start.' She turned to look at Marco. 'So long as you don't get in the way. If I ask for help then I expect it, but if I don't ask I don't want to be followed or questioned. You're there to keep me alive. Is that clear?'

'Absolutely. I would do that,' Marco replied.

'What is the deal?' asked Tony. 'What do you want from it?'

'You had Eddie's will altered. I want the original reinstated.'

'That might be tricky.'

'I want my house signed back to me. I don't care about Paradise Villas – Laurence can run it – but I want a share of the profits and I want my house back straight away, or there's no deal.'

Tony held up his hand. 'I did it with your best interests at heart.'

Della shook her head. 'If I am to trust you in this new venture I need to know what happened to my husband. I need the truth. No truth, no diamonds.'

Tony sighed. Marco was watching him intently, as was Debbie.

'Nothing I could do to save him; nothing I could have prevented. You must believe me in that. Yes, I will admit that Eddie met his death because of a deal with the cartels that went wrong. They were owed money when a shipment went missing. They should never have picked on Eddie, but they did. He was in the wrong place at the wrong time. I am truly sorry, princess.'

Tony bowed his head for several minutes.

Della nodded, satisfied that at last she had something like the truth.

Tony lifted his head again.

'I agree to your terms, Della. You show me the diamonds and I'll give you back everything that was Eddie's.'

'No, you'll have the house signed back over to me, my villa, my land, straight away; you'll have the papers drawn up immediately.'

'What about Sandra?' said Debbie.

'What about her?' answered Tony.

'Well, she's going to be madder than a cornered cat when she finds out she's not going to be living in Della's villa by the spring.'

'Debbie, please, don't spoil this wonderful moment that we're having here. Della and I have finally come to an understanding. Champagne, ah, very good. Open it, Marco. Let's make a toast.' Marco popped the cork and Debbie accepted a glass of champagne. She even managed a smile.

'To the biggest diamond haul in history,' said Tony.

'To the diamonds and to Eddie,' said Debbie.

'To Eddie.' Della raised her glass.

Half an hour later, Tony and Debbie stood on the mosaic sundial in the hallway watching the tail lights of the G wagon disappear down their driveway.

'Did that sound too good to be true to you?' Debbie asked. She shivered. It wasn't a cold night but she was tired.

'Perhaps, but it sounds a lot of fun,' Tony sniggered. 'It's a small risk, worth taking, baby.'

'Why don't you just give her back what's hers, Tony, and let her live her life. I feel sorry for her. She doesn't want any of this. She wants to be left alone. She's doing this because she thinks you will kill her otherwise.'

Tony didn't answer for a few more seconds as the security guard's gun flashed in the light of the closing gates. The fountains were on their night sequence. The stray dogs were barking somewhere on the road.

'How do you know any of this is real? I know she's scared. She could be just trying to save her skin.'

'You know what this is, Debbie? This an opportunity made in heaven. Eddie messed up. I gave him every opportunity to hand it over, but would he? Would he shit! Now his little wife is going to hand it over to me on a plate. Then we'll have everything. And, you know, you're right. I would have killed her, and I probably still will.'

Della went home to pack. She wasn't packing for a holiday: she was packing for a fight. A massive task ahead. She put in a mix of outfits and she went to get down a box of things she'd had hidden away for years. They weren't hidden from Eddie and they were only memories but she was looking for one specific thing. She found it. It was a knife given to her by a Hong Kong detective. She'd been at the beginning of her training when he'd come over for a case concerning people trafficking. She'd been assigned to drive him around. His name was Johnny Mann. He was half Chinese and half British. He had taken her into Chinatown and pointed out the triads and opened her eyes to their secret signs. He had shown her what to look for: the gang whistles, the mysterious hand signals, the meanings of their names and ranks. He had taught her a little of his speciality: shuriken throwing, the ancient art of street weaponry. He'd also taught her how to use chopsticks and how to demand mind-blowing sex. They hadn't stayed in touch but she thought of him often.

Della took the box out of its cloth bag and opened it. It was a throwing knife, he said. He had one he called Delilah. He called hers Lola. His was custom-made for him. It had the right weight for him to be able to throw it straight, direct it. It was tied to the wrist and concealed in the cuff of a jacket. Della had practised with her knife when she first was given it and then it had been hidden in the memory box for the last fifteen years. She took it out of the box, and Sellotaped it to the inside of her hair straighteners so that it would not show up on the scanner.

Chapter 34

11 December

In the morning Willis caught a bus and changed trains twice on the Tube to arrive at Archway Underground Station in plenty of time. She got a lift to the airport from Roger, a dog-handler colleague from Archway Police Station who was going back towards his Stansted home after a night shift. The cost of housing was pushing people to live far out.

Ross got a taxi to the airport from his home in Hampstead. It was a studio flat he'd bought after the divorce. It was near to the girls, who were still young enough for them all to camp in the one room when they came to stay. On his days off he went to the art galleries and to the interiors shops to browse. If he was off on a Sunday he went to sit in one of the many cafés and order breakfast and read the newspapers before buying himself an expensive bottle of wine and a takeaway of some beautifully packaged cake treats for later. He took them home to his empty flat. In his bin were the remnants of many fancy boxes of uneaten cake and many empty bottles.

Willis got there in plenty of time. She got herself a coffee and wandered around looking at the destinations on the check-ins. She'd already found out where their flight was going from.

She clutched her passport in her hand as she waited for Ross.

'Where's your bag?' Ross surprised her by coming up behind her.

Willis was standing at the check-in gate for the flight to Málaga.

'Is that all you're taking?' he asked. She was offered the chance of bringing a suitcase. Ross was paying for one to go in the hold, but she had declined. She had brought her backpack to fit in the overhead lockers instead.

'Yes, thought I'd buy whatever else I need when we get there.'

'This isn't a shopping trip, you know,' he teased.

'I was just meaning shampoo, that kind of thing.'

'I know. I'm only messing.'

Willis had packed almost her entire work wardrobe, which consisted of two pairs of black trousers and three blue shirts. She had her black, plain, leather work shoes on her feet and she was wearing her usual black puffa jacket. She had packed the hat she'd worn on surveillance at the funeral. To travel she had on jeans and a T-shirt.

They checked in and went through to the departure lounge. Ross walked around the duty free and tried out the gadgets. Willis got out her iPad and began checking the itinerary. They were due to arrive at eleven twenty that morning; it was just short of a three-hour flight from Stansted. Then it was straight to the hire car and head for Marbella and the men they wanted to talk to.

The plane took off on time and Willis got the window seat. She went very quiet as she stared at the dawn, just beginning to lighten the sky. It was only the second time Willis had been abroad.

'You okay?' Ross asked. She nodded and fiddled with her seat belt.

Ross smiled to himself. It had been many years since getting on an early flight excited him. It was the last time he and his wife and kids had gone skiing. They were always very early flights. They were lovely holidays. At least, he consoled himself, the holidays were good, even if the rest of the marriage wasn't the best. Even if the day-to-day was a struggle, the holidays were full of laughter. That was one thing he missed: the sound of his wife being happy. He had a lot to regret. Now, all he could do was try to be the best dad and wish his ex-wife well in her new life. That thought still carved a chunk out of his heart. The way Lisa had played him also made him wince. She'd never meant to have more than a fling with him. He'd thrown his marriage away for a fling.

'What is it?' asked Willis, watching Ross shake his head.

'Nothing.'

At ten that morning, Carter was looking at CCTV footage with Robbo. Manson's white van was difficult to find. He'd driven down lanes. He'd avoided getting back on the M25.

'We dropped in some samples late last night. Have they gone off?' asked Carter.

'Yes, they'll get the results back to us asap,' answered Robbo. 'What were they from?'

'Willis took them from the floor of the warehouse at Paradise Villas.'

'She'll be on the plane with Ross now,' Robbo said, pausing the screen as he looked for a reaction from Carter.

'She'll be loving it.' Carter smiled.

'What, she doesn't get away much?'

'Yeah, only time was with Tina from the canteen. Doubt she'll remember anything about that.'

'Was Ross the right man to go with her, do you think?'

'I don't think we had a choice. We were almost invited because we had Ross. He has such tight links with the national police out there. He probably knows them better than he knows us. You know he offered Harold a deal?'

'Yes, Willis told me. What was interesting was that, the way she explained it, it might still be on the cards. He didn't say no.'

'Harold's tired. He's scared, maybe for the first time in his life. And he's not comfortable with what's being asked of him. At heart he's an old-style robber, not a drug baron.'

'But Harold will never set anyone up. He'll never be a snitch, not in a million years,' said Robbo.

'No, but he may just step out of the way at a strategic time. He may not quite follow Tony's orders to the letter, who knows? I think we should approach him again.'

'Who's keeping in touch with him? How was it left?'

'He has Ross's number. I kept my face out of view.'

'Just in case? I thought you told Willis they'd never remember you.'

'Yeah. But then I thought about it. I used to serve Harold his morning coffee most days. I think if he's good with faces, he might just remember.'

On his way back to his office, Carter got a call.

'It's me. Can we meet?'

'Della? Sorry I didn't get back to you last night. It's a busy time for me.'

'I understand, Dan. I've just arrived in London. I have some information for you. I have something I think you should hear. What do you think? Can you meet me?'

'Where?'

'London Bridge? The pub we used to go to? What was it called, the one on the river?'

'Old Thames Inn?'

'That's it.'

'When?'

'Can you meet me in an hour?'

'No problem.'

Carter didn't wait around. He picked up his coat from his office and left Fletcher House before he had to answer anyone's questions. A taxi was waiting for him at the end of the road, at the back of Archway Police Station.

Della was waiting for him at a table just inside the door.

The wind and rain were gusting around the tables and chairs outside. The Thames was a washout in grey. Carter was blown inside.

She was drinking coffee. He took off his coat and hung it on the coat rack just inside the door.

'You could have brought a bit of that Marbella sunshine with you,' he joked. She smiled but looked anxious. She fiddled with her cup. 'Can I get you another?'

'Please.'

'Coffee? Latte?' She nodded.

When he got back he sat down beside her.

'How are you bearing up?'

She took a few seconds to begin speaking.

'I'm doing my best.'

'Of course you are. It can't be easy. Must be like being inside a nightmare.' He wanted to hug her but he wasn't going to.

'It's too hard out there. Tony is completely off his rocker. He's had Eddie's will altered. I think Tony has murdered Eddie's lawyer, who drew up the will with him. I think he got him to alter the will before he killed him.'

'Have you evidence?'

'I'm pretty sure I know where he buried the body. I'm also sure that there was a child involved. Francisco's daughter went missing at the same time.'

'Can you steer the police towards the burial site? They already suspect that Tony abducted him. No one mentioned the daughter to me.'

'They need to look at the wasteland behind my villa. There's an almond grove there and a small stone hut, it's near there. But I can't be sure it's still there, or even what it was I saw. I had one hell of a night, that night. When your mother-in-law drugs you and your brother-in-law tries to rape you before your husband's been in the ground a week. This has brought out a side of Eddie's family that not even I could have imagined.'

'Tony?'

'Yeah, Harold I can handle, he's straightforward. Laurence has always stayed away from the madness. He's weak and he's a spoiled brat, but he's harmless. Tony is out of control with his best friend Marco the maniac.'

'I'm sorry, Della.' Carter reached out to cover her hand with his. 'It's so tough on you, I know.'

'Yeah.' She bit back the tears. 'I loved him, Dan. I know that's hard for you to believe. Everyone saw me as a gold digger. Even Eddie did, for a while. It wasn't till the last time I saw him when I dropped him off at the airport that I really believed he did love me, trust me and he really did want to break away from the rest of the Butchers.'

'What happened to stop it? If that was his plan, why didn't he go ahead with it? Could he have been up to something you didn't know about?'

'I'd love to say no, but I can't be sure. I've been through his private papers. There's stuff in there I wasn't expecting, but I can't see any massive drug deals on the horizon.'

'Manson has companies that supplied goods to Paradise Villas. Did you know that?'

'Eddie never mentioned it, but is there a problem with that?'

'Manson wasn't owning up to offshore bank accounts as quickly as I'd have liked.'

'Can you blame him?'

'Maybe not, but this is a murder investigation of his friend and boss. Eddie had downscaled his work while Manson had turned his up. Money is his driving force.'

'Everyone wants to make it big at some time in their life. Eddie had done that. We had all we needed. Now he wanted to stay alive to enjoy it.'

'Not everyone.'

She looked at him in amusement and then shook her head. 'Most people want to make it big just to see what it feels like. I can see you still like your designer clothes, Dan. You're still wearing the gold bracelet I bought you on our first anniversary.'

Carter shook his head. He didn't want to get drawn into a slanging match about integrity and what was truly important to him. 'Do you know Manson well?' he asked instead.

'Of course. I've met him many times. He and Eddie were close. He's even been out to stay at the villa a few times. Eddie trusted him implicitly. There's no way Manson could have anything to do with Eddie's death.'

'Maybe not directly, but he's scared. He's trying to run.'

'I don't blame him. We're all scared.'

'Did Eddie ever discuss problems with clients?'

'Eddie didn't really discuss work with me. It just ticked along. He and Manson got on with it. The only time I ever saw any of the villas he built was when they were finished and he'd show me some photos. If it was someone we knew, then I might be invited to the house-warming, some big bash there, but that's it really. Dan, don't waste your time chasing leads like that. Believe me, Tony had my husband killed. Tony set him up. They ripped off the cartels. Harold was told to tell me some lies. Between the both of them I think I know a few things for certain. It was Tony who tried to rip off the cartels by claiming that a shipment had gone missing. He sent Eddie into a situation that he was never going to come out of. Why Eddie went, I don't know. I'm seriously beginning to wonder if I knew my husband. But then I come back to the same thought: Eddie, a drug baron? No way. I know that Tony set Eddie up. Whether he expected him to get killed I don't know, but, whatever plan he had, it hasn't worked. He's still looking for a lot of money. Tony told me so much, the rest I got from Marco, who seems to see me as a better bet than Tony at the moment.' Carter looked at her curiously. 'It's not like that. Marco is worried: his neck's on the line, too. He told me that there's a massive shipment of cocaine on a container ship on its way over here right now from Mexico. It has to be paid for when it arrives. The Zapata want payment on arrival because they don't trust Tony, and Marco has a lot to prove to them. Tony already has the money from ripping off the Mendez cartel on the last shipment to go towards it, but now he has to come up with a huge hundred million pounds. Even for Tony, that's a lot. Now, Dan ...' Della took a breath. She had a worried smile on her face. 'I have an idea. Please hear me out. I know this is going to sound mad. I want to get Tony, Dan, like we always planned in Operation Argos. I can help you. We can help each other.' Carter nodded. Della continued, 'I've told Tony I know where the biggest stash of diamonds from the Great Diamond Heist is.'

'What? Why? What were you thinking? Did he believe it?'

She nodded. 'Tony's always believed there's a big stash of jewels somewhere. Eddie and I used to laugh about it. But Tony seriously suspected that, when Eddie got out from their stint in prison, he moved the diamonds. Tony believes that, if Eddie had wanted to, he could have put his hand on them and Eddie always led him on.'

'Della, I'm going to have to ask: is there any truth in it?'

'None. Of course not. Eddie's task was to launder the diamonds he was given and to keep quiet about the role of the others. He did time so others didn't have to. They all knew their part. No one had the complete knowledge or trust; otherwise the others would have got to it by now. They were all a bunch of thieves, after all. I told him I'd found papers, codes, safety-deposit boxes, information that only I could access, all that bullshit, and he believes it. He's sent me over here with Marco to find it. He thinks the diamonds will buy him the new cocaine deal with a new cartel. In theory, he's right. Diamonds would do nicely for the cartel.' Carter was nodding his head, staring out into the grey on the Thames. 'I want you to put this proposal forward, Dan. I want you to propose that I work with you undercover and we draw Tony out of Spain and we set him up.'

Carter looked at her incredulously. His mind was working through the negatives. He shook his head, but he was still working through the list.

'The Spanish police would have to be part of the operation. They would have to back off in order for him to leave the villa. There's a million things that can go wrong with this. If we had a year to plan it, it would be different.'

'Yeah, I know. All that will have to be done. But there will already be undercover operatives working in Spain. There'll be a structure in place that we can build on.'

Carter smiled. 'Still the police officer at heart.'

'Heart? Not so much. Mind? Definitely.'

'You're right. There may be people ready to go into action. There are a few police officers in his pay.'

'I can probably get names for you. They're the same ones who always turn up and pretend to question him. I know they're on his payroll. What I would do is lead him right to the diamonds and make sure it hits a snag at the last minute. He'll think I'm double-crossing him and he'll have to come over here. If he thinks the deal rests on him coming, he'll come. Whatever he's involved himself in, it's bigger than anything before and he knows he has to get it right.'

'It's too risky for you to be involved in any scheme to catch Tony, Della, you must know that.'

'I don't have many choices left to me, Dan. I get Tony or Tony gets me. He will kill me, I'm certain of it. But

I'm still in the heart of the Butcher clan. I can bring Tony down, Dan.'

Dan searched her face and saw sincerity and the negatives in his mind began to flip to positives. Could he believe her this time? A part of him wanted to and another part told him he shouldn't really care what happened to the woman who broke his heart and possibly screwed up years of work on Operation Argos. A woman who chose cash over love. If she betrayed him once, could she do it again? Easily. But something else told him this was an ideal way to get Tony and to finally put things in his past to bed. Why was it when he ended that thought he ended it in bed?

Carter stared into his coffee cup. 'It can't be entrapment,' he said.

'Then we'll need to make sure it all goes smoothly. But, the idea obviously interests you?'

Carter tapped his fingers on the desk as his brain ran through the things they would need to achieve to get Tony. 'What's in it for you, Della? Is it just to avenge Eddie? It's a hell of a risk.'

'Tony will have me killed anyway. Maybe Harold or Marco will do it or maybe they'll hire a mercenary; but he will do it. He's taken everything from me, Dan. I have to get it back. I can't bring Eddie back, but I can bring him his own style of justice. Tony will tolerate me while he thinks I can find the diamonds. The minute he thinks I've found them, he'll have me killed. But there'll have to be some face-to-face deal that only he can do. He'll come if he has to. What are you thinking, Dan?'

'I'm thinking that this is more for the National Crime Agency teams than us. They will have all the contacts.'

'My plan won't work if I get handed over to an NCA

team. I work with you or I don't go ahead with it. You're the only one I trust, Dan. I can't afford for anyone else to be involved and it get back to Tony. I don't want to end up like Eddie. There are people in Tony's pay in the Met, we know that for certain.'

'Give me a minute.' Carter put on his coat and stepped outside and made a quick call to Bowie. He kept his coat on when he came back in.

He nodded. 'Let's go.'

Chapter 35

After waiting to pick up Ross's bag from the luggage carousel Willis and Ross went to the car-hire desk and filled out the forms for their hire car. An hour of hanging around in the underground car park, and they were on their way in a black Audi convertible, which filled Ross with glee, as he couldn't wait to get the top down as soon as they were leaving the airport.

They drove along the coastal road to Marbella. Willis got a text from an unknown number: 'This is Detective Garcia from the Spanish police. We are starting our meeting in the Marbella police headquarters at one. Please attend.'

'We're supposed to be at a meeting at the police station in Marbella in forty minutes,' said Willis. She was already looking up the map reference on her phone. She leaned over and put the instructions into the satnav.

'They could have given us a bit more notice,' complained Ross.

'I suppose they know we came on the morning flight.'

'The hotel we're staying at has a pool. We should try and wrap this up in the next couple of hours and then we can book in and have a dip. Did you bring a cozzie?'

'No. I didn't think about it.'

'You're kidding! Jesus, Willis. So, when you knew we were coming to Spain for work, did you think that meant constant work?'

'Yes, I suppose I did.'

'This is Spain. They work differently here. I've been here many times. There's more socialising and working, more sunbathing and swimming and working, more eating, drinking . . .'

'Any actual working?'

'Not if I can help it. The hotel will sell swimming costumes. You can buy one there.'

Willis realised she probably should have brought more than fifty euros spending money with her. She didn't own a credit card. She had a mortal fear of getting into debt. She saved her money: she was hoping to buy a flat for her and Tina to share but, every time she thought she might be getting near to it, the prices went up again. She never seemed to have enough.

'Any news about tomorrow, or an update from the Spanish detectives we're meeting? Do we know their names?'

Willis read the email. 'Garcia just sent the text; Ramirez is the more senior.'

'Great names. You know they call them the Marbella Vice? Their life is spent searching luxury yachts and on speedboat chases.'

She looked at him with a roll of the eyes.

'You wait, you'll see. You'll never see more money than in Marbella. It's the playground of the rich and more rich.'

They arrived and parked on the street nearby, then they walked up the steps into the police station and were met by a good-looking policeman who introduced himself as Detective Garcia. He had on a blue-striped shirt, dark blue trousers. He had a gold strap to his Rolex. He smiled with perfect white teeth and a hint of George Clooney in the brown eyes. His accent was thick Spanish but his choice of vocabulary was more American than UK English.

'Do you speak Spanish?' He looked at both of them. They shook their heads.

'No problem. I hope my English is good enough. Welcome. Good you made it,' he said. 'Let me take you to meet my colleague and we'll run through what's going down tomorrow,' Garcia said as he escorted them through a door and past security. They stopped briefly at an office along the way and were joined by Ramirez. He was a less smooth-looking detective with a moody look about him and a hint of stubble. He had thick eyebrows and dark green eyes. He had the look of a man who had been stunning in his youth but had got old too quickly and now didn't care what he looked like.

Ramirez spoke to Garcia, and then they picked up their laptops and file boxes and led the way further into the building.

'Come with us, please. We're going somewhere private.'

'Is it just going to be us?' asked Ross as they walked along the stifling hot corridor. The sun was blazing in. Ross kept his aviator sunglasses on. Willis had lost her sunglasses on a day out with Tina in Hyde Park, and she hadn't replaced them.

'Just us, yes. We try and keep knowledge about raids on suspected high-profile criminals to a need-to-know basis,' said Ramirez, who spoke near-perfect English.

'We have a problem here in Marbella, with corruption, with bribery.'

'Unfortunately, it's the same the world over,' answered Ross.

'Is this your first time in Marbella?'

Ross shook his head. 'It's an interesting place – a bit like the Essex dream.' Neither policeman understood Ross but they nodded and grinned. He qualified: 'I mean, it's full of people showing how much money they have. Super cars, Saudi princes, billion-pound yachts. Marbella is famous for the Saudi royals, the wealthiest people in the world, isn't it?'

'Yes, and the wealth keeps growing. The recession hits the medium wealthy and the poor but it doesn't hit the super-rich.'

'Many people live here in Marbella but have Gibraltar citizenship for tax reasons, don't they?' Willis said.

'Yes, definitely,' Garcia answered. '"Showing off" is a national pastime here, making sure everyone sees that you are somebody.' He smiled at Willis as he led them through two more security doors and into an air-conditioned meeting room.

'Is it your first time in Spain?' he asked her.

'Yes,' said Willis. 'It's very dramatic scenery. The coast looked beautiful, all the white buildings with terracotta roofs. The sea was so blue. It's idyllic.'

'Yes, lots of Brits agree. We have over three hundred thousand in Marbella alone. They love it.'

'Oh dear, sounds like a huge amount. Is it a problem for you?'

'Sometimes. But it isn't only the Brits who have brought problems with them: all over Europe people come to

Marbella because it is full of the super-rich who like to party. With money comes criminals: drugs, guns, feuds.'

'It's got quite a reputation,' said Willis. 'Must be quite a challenge to be a police officer here.'

'Yes, the streets hide so many warring drugs gangs now. We are not sure where it will all end. It's got so bad. We get murders all the time, shoot-outs.'

Willis sat down at one of the desks and took out her laptop and notepad. Ross was hovering. He went to perch on a desk a few feet away from her. He had his arms crossed. He still hadn't taken off his sunglasses. He was checking out the Spanish detectives as they talked in Spanish and prepared a laptop. Willis raised an eyebrow. He smiled, took off his glasses, folded them neatly and put them back into their case in his bag.

Ramirez opened the files he'd brought with him and handed them out a section each.

'We're going to run a few photos on the laptop for you to show you what the operation will involve tomorrow and what we're looking for. We have a plan here of Tony Butcher's property. There are four buildings in all. We will concentrate on the main house.' He brought up a blueprint of the estate.

'We know that at present there are three family members,' said Garcia. 'Tony, his wife Debbie and Tony's mother Sandra. Besides them are six servants. They have their own house on the grounds. We will come in via the gate here; there is a twenty-four-hour guard on duty. As soon as this happens we will move quickly to stop any evidence being destroyed.'

'What about Della Butcher?'

'Her villa is here on the plan. The two villas share

adjoining almond groves at the back. Della and Marco Zapata left for the UK this morning.'

'Can you tell us about the missing man, Francisco?' asked Willis.

'He owns one of Marbella's leading legal and accountancy firms. He's responsible for moving billions of dollars of virtual money around the world for the super-rich here in Marbella. He is a shy man, quite unassuming. He doesn't enjoy the same lifestyle as his clients. He is a family man with one daughter. What he does is mostly legal. His offices handle most kinds of financial work. But, naturally, because he deals with the super-rich, he also looks after the cartel's money. He will pretend he doesn't know it, but he must have an idea,' said Garcia.

Ramirez agreed: 'Francisco is a genius in his field of hiding his clients' assets. But, because of the type of people who live here, he has also taken on some clients that have direct links to organised crime. These are mainly the British and the South American connections. The Russian mafia look after their own finances.'

'Thanks for inviting us to come tomorrow,' said Ross. 'Willis and I will be fascinated to take a look at the big man himself. He can't refuse to answer questions about the murder of his brother.'

They looked at one another and Ramirez shrugged.

'Sometimes Tony Butcher is screaming at us like a toddler having a tantrum; sometimes he wants us to stay for dinner. We never know which Tony we will find.'

'So, what do you hope to achieve in the raid tomorrow?' asked Willis.

Ramirez answered, 'Best scenario? We hope to find some evidence that Francisco is still alive.'

'This is a respected local man, with a small daughter, who is also missing,' said Garcia. 'It will bring huge problems down on us if he has been murdered. Tony will not be safe, anywhere. The death squad will find him, and God knows how many others will die with him.'

'You have the photos of him arriving and a double leaving with Marco Zapata?' Ross said. 'Chances are Francisco is dead.'

'Yes, correct, but we don't have a body.'

'What reason do you think Tony would have for killing Francisco?' asked Ross.

'We both know why, otherwise a member of the Organised Crime Command wouldn't be here, would he?' Ramirez smiled at Ross. 'Tony has cheated on his supplier, the Mendez cartel. We know it. You know it. He has kept the money he's supposed to pay for the cocaine. Francisco is the man whose firm launders the money back to the cartel. There will be gangs fighting on the streets here to settle the score and, at the same time, to use this opportunity to force their way to the front.'

'We will be looking for evidence of the murder tomorrow, but hoping to find none,' said Ramirez.

'Have you raided Tony Butcher's place before?' asked Willis.

'Many times over the years.'

'What about his brother Eddie?' asked Ross. 'Did you ever raid his premises?'

'Eddie Butcher? No,' answered Garcia, 'we had no need to go in there. He was a respected man here in Marbella. He donated a lot of money to local charities. He was a man with a bad past but a good future.'

'Who ended up tortured to death,' added Willis.

'The Mendez cartel did not want to kill Tony, not at this moment, so they kill his brother instead. They wanted to warn him,' said Ramirez.

'Someone kills someone from the family of a rival dealer, and then we have the start of a war that can end up being continued for years,' answered Garcia. 'We have had enough.'

Ramirez nodded his agreement. 'Now that the violence is spilling onto the streets we have to be more active and stop it at the source.'

'What's Tony's main way of getting the drugs to the UK?' Willis asked. She knew that Ross had answered the question, but she also realised he was choosing to take a bit of a back seat.

'Tony has many ways,' answered Garcia. 'The way of getting the biggest amount across is by getting it shipped straight across the Atlantic in container ships to the UK from South America, sometimes changing ship in Antwerp or Amsterdam. We see it smuggled inside bananas, yams, baskets, crockery, flowers, breast implants.'

'Once,' said Ramirez, 'we had a shipment of bananas sent here to Valencia and the smuggler failed to collect his cocaine from the banana shipment at the dock, and the bananas ended up being delivered for sale in Lidl with kilos of cocaine in the boxes.' He laughed.

'We see it made to look like wooden pallets, bags of charcoal, woven into baskets; they even use carrier pigeons and jet skis,' said Ramirez. 'If only the cocaine cooks who come up with all these ideas would turn their hand to something legal! They are geniuses.'

'So, it seems like they're always coming up with new ways,' said Willis.

'That's correct,' answered Ramirez, who had begun to stare at Ross, a little uneasy with his silence. 'It's a case of getting it distributed in as many ways as possible. But you are very well aware of the problems, Detective Ross? I see by the information we received you have close links with us.'

Ross nodded. He smiled and shrugged. 'I've been involved in a few arrests but Tony's always been the one.'

'We have had him under surveillance for the whole of my career in this town,' answered Ramirez.

'Is it right that Tony never leaves his villa?' asked Willis. 'He must be able to get out if he wanted.'

'Tony could leave,' said Garcia. 'He could probably even get on a plane easily enough with a false passport. People find it easy to move around here, to hide in the mountains, and keep away from the police. Spain is a big country. They have a network of criminals who help one another here. They could not stay here otherwise. Many of them have contacts within the police force who tip them off when we are planning a raid.'

'But Tony has become too scared to go far now,' added Ramirez. 'I think he is suffering from paranoia. All this time locked away has made him fear the outside too much and he knows his actions are causing wars outside his villa.'

'How does he manage all the movement of tons of cocaine from his villa if he never leaves it?' asked Willis.

'He can carry on his empire from inside his walls,' said Garcia. 'He orders it and he leaves others around him to work out how something will be done. He just sits in his villa and demands it. He relies on his family and a few others here on the Costa del Sol. There are a few of his old buddies here and some new and very dangerous ones.

Tony is not as good as others with modern technology. He pays others to have banks of computers and complicated passcodes, move money around the world, to make deals for him.'

'What about the rest of the family? How much are they all involved?' asked Willis. 'We know Harold's the Enforcer, he's not a genius.'

Ramirez nodded. 'Harold is getting too old for the job. Now he has Marco Zapata to help him. But Marco is away right now, which is helpful to us. We can deal with Tony more easily without him.'

'What about the others?' asked Willis. 'What's his wife like? She's from the UK originally?'

'They have been married for twenty years or more,' answered Garcia. 'We never see her in town any more. She used to come out with girlfriends and you would see her in the bars, but no more. She is a prisoner there now, we think. Della Butcher, Eddie's wife, keeps very separate from the others. She and Eddie were usually seen together if they were in town. Eddie liked to show off on his yacht, in his cars.'

'What level of surveillance do you carry out on a day-to-day level on Tony?' asked Ross.

'We have communications surveillance when he is in certain places in his house, anywhere on the verandas area. We track and follow any of the cars coming and going. We will try to plant surveillance devices now in this raid but Tony is clever at finding them. Tony has every latest gadget regarding surveillance.'

'What about Sandra?' Ross asked.

Ramirez laughed and shook his head. 'Best not to make eye contact with her.'

Garcia grinned and nodded. 'Yes, she bit me once. She is an old cougar.'

'He had to get a shot in the arm,' laughed Ramirez, 'for rabies.'

'Exactly, she is a rabid dog.' Garcia rolled up his sleeve to show a small scar on his tanned arm. 'If she is in a bad mood she is worse than an angry cat.'

'Is she actively involved in Tony's drug smuggling?' asked Willis.

'No, we don't think so, but she is Tony's support. She has a special bond with him. She has been accused of assault, even murder, in the last twenty years, but every time she gets off. She's a lot like Tony.'

'Be sure, if Sandra wanted you dead, she would do it herself,' said Garcia. 'She never minds getting her hands dirty.'

Chapter 36

Carter got Della a bottle of water as they waited in the pub for Bowie to join them. They had caught a taxi to Archway. The pub there was used to their holding impromptu meetings. It had plenty of private booth areas for them to talk. It was two thirty in the afternoon and very quiet. Perfect for what they needed.

'I can't stay away much longer, Dan,' said Della. 'Marco will be back soon.'

'Where did you say you were going?' asked Carter.

'I didn't. He went to see Harold. I don't know what for. He knows I have some things to do on my own but I don't want to push my luck. I said I'd see him later.'

'Has he called you?' Carter asked.

'No. We all have two phones. I'm happy for you to monitor mine but only if it can be done without the slightest chance of Marco realising.'

'All these things will have to be set up for you,' Carter said. The enormity of the task was weighing heavily on him.

Carter looked up as the door to the pub opened. Bowie headed towards them, ordering a coffee on the way.

Della stood as he got to the table and greeted him.

'Hello, Simon. I'll have to call you sir now. You've come a long way since we were cadets.'

'Hello, Della. Yes, it's been a long time. I'm sorry these aren't better circumstances to meet under. You have my sympathies. We are doing all we can to find out who did this to Eddie.' Bowie sat down. Carter could see how guarded he was. Bowie had been in Operation Argos. None of them had forgotten Della's betrayal. But Carter knew he had to go straight to the top and get Bowie's approval if Della's plan was on the cards at all. There would be opposition down the ranks.

'Carter briefly outlined your proposal on the phone to me.'

Carter was nodding quietly. The one thing he really knew was that Operation Argos was a personal failing for the whole team. Any chance of rewriting history and Carter knew Bowie would want to hear about it.

Della kept her voice low as the waitress came over with Bowie's coffee.

'I think we can help each other,' she said.

'If it goes wrong, Della, it could get you killed,' Bowie said.

'I know that, but I still prefer those odds to staying in my villa and waiting for either the death squad or Tony to kill me. I presume you also think that Eddie's death had everything to do with Tony?'

Bowie was cautious. 'We agree with you that Tony might have set Eddie up,' said Bowie. 'If he was killed by a death squad we will have a hard job nailing the person responsible.'

'I know that. I understand. But I'd be happy with getting the man who ordered it. I hold him responsible for Eddie's murder. Him and Marco Zapata did it between them.'

Bowie opened three packets of sugars and stirred them into his coffee.

'Go ahead, Della, tell me what you have,' said Bowie.

'What I'm offering you is a chance to lure Tony out of the villa. He's desperate to get his hands on a lot of money and I've told him I know where the missing haul from the Great Diamond Heist is.'

'Did Eddie ever talk about the missing diamonds?'

'Yes. He said it was a dead end. He said that the haul was long since split up and converted into cash. That's what Eddie believed. Of course, he kept a few.' She smiled.

'And Tony?' Bowie sipped his coffee.

'He's always thought Eddie was hiding something. The robberies took place in London, Antwerp and Dubai over a period of two days and then the diamonds were filtered into the system but it couldn't be rushed. They had to have time to avoid suspicion. Both Tony and Eddie came out of prison to big cash payments, as I am sure you know, but the link to the main haul was lost when a few of the others involved in the London end of things were murdered. The chain to the stash was broken. Eddie came out of prison before Tony. Tony always thought Eddie shafted him.'

'You say that Eddie kept a few?'

'I need immunity on this if I'm going to help you. I only found out after Eddie was killed that I'm wearing a set made from the blue diamonds that were stolen. I will get hold of the few Eddie left in safety-deposit boxes and I'll use them as bait to show the cartel. Marco is brokering the deal.'

'He travelled over with you, didn't he?' said Bowie.

Carter watched Bowie. He wasn't sure whether Bowie was buying into any of it.

'Yes. I have sold Tony the idea that I need Marco to keep me alive and see me through to the diamonds. The truth is, I know he is the key to Tony now. Marco is ruthlessly ambitious and nothing matters to him but his own advancement. He's got a big interest in helping me. He wants what Tony has, I know it. Marco would happily slit everyone's throat to get to the top and he sees Tony as an easy route. He's waiting for me to hand him the goods, then he'll kill me, Tony and the rest of the family, no problem. It was his idea to switch over to his family's cartel. He has so much to prove to them and he's assured them he can deliver.

'The diamonds would be a perfect currency for him. I could see, when I told him about it, that he thought all his Christmases had come at once.'

'Exactly. He wouldn't have to pretend to launder it,' said Bowie. 'But, now you're over here, Tony's going to make sure Harold and Marco keep tails on you. How are you going to manage?'

'I've told them the deal is off if they tail me. I know they'll try but I'm going to leave that to you, to a certain extent. I might need a double. I might just be able to give them the slip. After all, they don't have the luxury of CCTV to monitor where I'm going. But there'll be three of them to keep tabs on. I don't trust Laurence, either. He's happily stolen my husband's business from me. I want that back. Eddie expected me to keep that under our roof. I've told Tony he has to give me back what's mine by rights. He's signed my house back to me, that's a start.'

'We can set you up in an apartment and have the whole place rigged,' suggested Bowie.

'We are in one of the family's apartments at the moment.

The one Eddie was staying in. I think it will be too tricky to move, but you can get one ready for me to run to. I can ask to move to other premises for practical reasons. The Butchers must know they are watched.'

'Yes, that could work. We have several options around town. We'll get one ready,' said Carter. 'We'll have to swing into action fast if we want to find you a double.'

'What's your plan for all this, Della?'

'Tony wants some proof from me that I can find the diamonds. I can come up with something to show Harold. Something genuine. I need the rest in place – uncut diamonds, a lot of them. They need to look convincing, maybe coated in diamond dust, I don't know.'

'We can look into, and arrange that,' said Bowie. 'So, you pretend to have found the stash of missing diamonds, and Harold sees the proof you have and gets back to Tony with a "Yes, this is genuine." Then what?'

Della sighed. 'Here's what I've been thinking, what I have to work with: Eddie had several safety-deposit boxes that are still current. I will go inside and pretend to empty those, perhaps find something relevant I can show Marco and Harold. I have told Tony that I burned papers relating to codes for boxes, people's names to contact, all clues that only I can follow. What do I mean by that? I don't even know!'

Carter was nodding. Bowie was watching and waiting.

'Two things we cannot control,' said Carter, 'the cartels, and the deal.'

'Tony will have to do that. All we have to do is find him the diamonds and then he will have the funds to do the deal. I'm sure of this. I can work on Marco so that he keeps feeding Tony, fanning the flames. Then, just as it looks like it's all going through, I can double-cross him. If we take Marco out of the equation as well, then Tony will have to come himself. Nothing would keep him away.'

Bowie glanced at Carter. The excitement of what could be was winning Bowie over.

'It's tricky, but it may be possible,' said Bowie. 'We're going to have to rely heavily on undercover intelligence if we are to find out where and when the deal will happen. I'm worried that a lot will be on your shoulders, Della. The more we talk it through, the more dangerous it becomes for you. We're going to have to involve others.'

'Maybe not till the end,' said Carter. 'We can start this off and see where it leads.'

'The public can never know about you, Della. How is that going to suit you?' asked Bowie.

She nodded. 'I know I'll be a snitch and a grass and I'll be for ever hunted if the truth comes out, but you forget: I've always been that. I was an undercover cop. Only Eddie knew about that. I've lived with that secret, I can live with another.' She looked at Carter, who was frowning. She smiled. 'I really don't have a choice with this, Dan. I come out fighting or I die.'

'Not if you get witness protection. New identity.'

'And give up my home, my lifestyle? Have to be anonymous for the rest of my life – live my life in fear, always looking over my shoulder? I can't do it, Dan. I want what is mine. I want it returned to me. Eddie didn't mean to leave me with this mess. He obviously underestimated his family, but I won't. I know exactly what they are capable of now.'

'The first step is to get some diamonds, a mix of uncut and cut, and fix up a couple of places for you to look for missing clues from Eddie,' said Bowie. 'They will follow you, so we better make sure you lead them a dance. It wouldn't hurt to take Marco along on one of the parts of the trail. They have to be totally committed to it.'

'Yes, I agree. Tomorrow I'm going to Hatton Garden. I can take him with me then.'

'What's in the safety-deposit box there?' asked Carter. Della smiled at him.

'Shall we just leave it on a need-to-know basis? I've told you I can provide the high-quality diamonds to secure the deal. Let's just pretend that I'm an ordinary person going into an ordinary safety-deposit box to find who knows what. What I come out with has nothing to do with the investigation.'

Bowie looked at Carter, who nodded.

'You're right: need-to-know basis,' said Bowie.

'Tomorrow you need to hire a car and make sure you lose the boys while we meet up and we exchange a phone, a wire, we go through the finer points,' said Carter. 'We should have a fair bit of it worked out by that time.'

Della got ready to leave. Carter stood.

'You okay, Della?'

She smiled at him reassuringly. 'Don't worry, Dan. I'll see you tomorrow.'

'Here.' Bowie passed her over a phone. 'It's traceable. We've made it look like you've been using it for ages. It's got false contacts, messages, et cetera. Carter here is under a contact called Danielle Sprint. I'm under Mum Sprint.

If you can't get hold of either there's the crime analyst Robbo.'

'Robbo? I remember him.'

'Robbo is under a pizza company called Roberto's.'

'Okay, got it, thanks.'

'Text me when you're ready to meet tomorrow,' said Carter. He watched Della leave and sat back down.

'Drink?' asked Bowie. He shook his head.

'She has no idea what she's letting herself in for.'

'Best that way, I think, don't you?' said Bowie.

Carter nodded. He was distracted, worried. He looked up at Bowie. 'We better make this work, then. Can we access enough good-quality raw diamonds?'

'It's possible. They need to come from a believable source: the right mines from the time. We better get hold of a jeweller to help with this. What about Maxi Seymour? He's an ex-copper.'

'Good idea. We can remind him of the fact he owes us for getting his stolen diamonds back to him last time he was robbed.'

Carter nodded. 'I'll get on it today. I better get Maxi to help us get hold of enough of the good stuff mixed with glass, to make it believable. We need to be ready for the deal. Obviously, we're still talking about a large risk if the diamonds disappear.' Carter waited for Bowie as he took a few seconds to stare into his coffee cup.

'There's no doubt this is a hell of a gamble, Dan. Having to explain that we trusted an ex-policewoman turned ex-con's wife with several hundred thousand quid's worth of diamonds that she could just fuck off with?'

'The what-ifs are massive,' said Carter. 'Losing a few

hundred thousands' worth of diamonds would definitely be a big one but allowing a few hundred millions' worth of cocaine into the UK is worse. Della wouldn't be so stupid as to run off with the diamonds. We might not catch her but the Butchers as sure as hell would.'

Bowie nodded. 'At some point we will have to involve the NCA,' he said. 'Ross needs to know that we have a plan; we're going to need the NCA's help in tracking the shipment of cocaine into the UK. If he's going to be working closely with us, he probably should know the whole truth.'

'This will mean putting Della at even more risk,' said Carter. 'What if it goes wrong?'

'Then we give Della her witness protection and that's it. She disappears and we carry on as normal. She knows the risks.'

'But what if she gets killed? Are you saying she's disposable?'

'I'm saying, things happen when criminals shaft one another. No one will think that it's an unlikely scenario. The news will be Della was after the diamonds, of course. Why wouldn't she be? Her husband died the same way, once a criminal always a criminal, all that shit,' Bowie said, exasperated.

'Christ, that's harsh. That doesn't sit right with me.'

'Then, you think about it good and hard, Dan, and you let me know what does sit right with you. This could be the chance to right some wrongs for 2003. A lot of what was wrong was Della. How do we know we can trust her any more now than we could then? I'm willing to let her take the risks. She owes us.' Carter was about object but Bowie put up his hand by way of an apology. 'Look ... look, I'm sorry, Dan. I understand your concerns. But I think Della can look after herself. I think she's a lot more capable than you give her credit for.'

'This better not be about revenge for the failure of that mission,' Carter said, 'because I seriously don't believe that had anything to do with Della. It could have been anyone.'

'I know. I'm sorry. I'm feeling the pressure too. I am prepared to back this plan, I assure you. I have every faith in your judgement. How do you see it working?'

'Okay, well we start by making absolutely sure that Della has everything she needs to do what she says she will,' said Carter. 'We are going to have to take most of the direction from her. She is also going to be our main source of information about the shipment and its arrival.'

'The man Marco will be a major problem. He's like her shadow.'

'Then she'll have to find a way of using him,' said Carter. 'We said it can't be a set-up, but we're going to have to know every move Tony makes with the new deal. It has to be all manoeuvred by us. Place, time.'

'What if they demand the transaction happens in Spain?' asked Bowie.

'No, that can't be,' Carter answered. 'Then all this will have been for nothing. We need this arrest to be on UK soil. So long as Tony remains wanted for crimes in Spain we will never get him in court here. It has to be here. We have to make it impossible for it to take place anywhere else. The diamonds must remain elusive till the last moment. Della will have a big task on her hands. She's going to need all the help we can give her. She's going to need our support.' Carter looked at Bowie for his assurance.

'I understand,' Bowie said, 'but what about the rest of

the team? How much are they going to know about Della? There'll be a lot of hostility and I doubt if you'll find one officer who would trust her.'

'Only those closest will know her identity. Everyone else will know her as Contact X in all meetings. All most of the team need to know is that she is an insider who knows when and where the deal will take place.'

'Robbo?'

'Yes. He is going to have to help us coordinate.'

'We've already agreed Ross will have to find out sooner or later. Ross and Willis will both be right in the middle of this.'

'That's it, then. That's enough. Contact X must be protected by the five of us.'

Chapter 37

Willis and Ross left the meeting and checked into their hotel. They went to their serviced apartment within the holiday hotel complex.

'I thought we'd be better off in an apartment so that we can discuss things with more privacy,' said Ross as he pushed the door open and held his foot against it for Willis.

The balcony window was open in the lounge area. The breeze smelled of the sea. It was dusk.

'It's great.' Willis walked through and put her bag down in the middle of the tiled floor and stepped out onto the balcony. The lights of Marbella stretched brightly beneath them.

Ross was looking over the apartment.

'You can take the room with the double bed. That's fine by me,' he called out.

'What's the alternative?' answered Willis.

'Another room, with twin beds.'

'Either's good for me.'

'Okay, then, thanks. I'll take the big bed. I tend to fall out of single ones.'

Willis experienced a wave of excitement as, standing in the evening air, she felt the warmth on her skin and breathed in the smell of tropical vegetation.

'Fancy a dip?' asked Ross.

'I need to buy a costume.'

'Okay, well I'm afraid I'm not waiting.' He appeared behind her changed into his long swimming shorts. 'I suppose you could just wear your bra and pants and wrap a towel round you. Does it look busy down there?' Ross came to look down from the balcony. The pool was empty.

'I suppose this is the off-season. But they said it was heated.'

'Do you think that will be okay?'

'What, the bra-and-pants thing?' She nodded.

'Fine. They expect it of us Brits, anyway. No, I'm only joking. Put a robe on – there's one in the bathroom – and we'll go for a dip. We deserve it after the day we've had. Then we can have dinner, beer on the terrace here and an early night.'

Willis went into the bathroom to get changed and put on the robe. She followed Ross out and down the stairs and left her robe on a sunlounger and dived into the water. She swam beneath the surface. It was wonderful to feel her hot skin soothed by the cold waters. She swam length after length of crawl before she came up for air at the end of the pool.

'You're a fantastic swimmer.'

'Thanks.' She propped herself up by her elbows and looked at the lights around the pool.

'Feels great, doesn't it?' Ross rested his head on the side of the pool and stared up at the dark sky. 'We used to come to Spain most years. Even before we had kids. Then we'd live for one holiday to the next. We saw a lot of the world, Belinda and me. We had a lot of fun.'

Willis wiped the water as it dripped into her eyes.

'Did you ever go to Jamaica?' she asked.

'We went to Antigua,' answered Ross. 'And Barbados. We loved it. The Caribbean has the most perfect temperature – it's thirty degrees all year round and the breeze never stops. I think it's heaven. Is that where your family originated?'

'My dad did. My mum, as you so rightly guessed, was British.'

'Was? Is she dead?'

'Not exactly. She's not well. She's in a psychiatric hospital.'

'I'm sorry. What about your dad?'

'I have never met him. He didn't know about me till recently. We've been in touch but we haven't met yet.'

'You should go out there.'

'Yes, I know. I will one day. What was going on with you today? You went quiet in the meeting. I could tell that Ramirez was wondering what was the matter too.'

'Did I?'

'What were you thinking?'

'I was probably just tired.'

'It wasn't that. You were really watching them. You didn't want to answer Ramirez when he said about having information on you. What was your thinking?'

'Okay, I was just trying to avoid asking too many questions. I don't want to give them anything they don't already have.'

'But, how can we work together if we're not sharing information?'

'I have no idea who they are. They could both be in Tony's pay for all I know.'

'Is that likely?'

Ross shrugged. 'I'm going in now,' he said, waiting for her to rise from the water. 'I'm getting hungry.'

They wrapped their towels around themselves and trotted back up to their apartment.

Willis changed into her new tunic top and jeans. She had washed her hair and left it to balloon out over her shoulders.

'You look lovely,' Ross said to her as she came out of the bathroom. She'd brought an eyeliner pencil with her as emergency make-up and she'd put it to use. On the way to the restaurant Willis got a call from Carter.

'I need to take this.' She pointed to the phone; Ross nodded. He walked on.

'Okay,' she said to Carter, 'what is it?'

'Della Butcher has come here with a deal. She has told Tony she can find hundreds of millions of pounds' worth of missing diamonds from the Great Diamond Heist. It's bullshit, but she thinks she can convince him. He's desperate to believe it. He needs the money: he's got himself in trouble with the cartels and he's trying to switch suppliers, as we know. She's offered to try and set him up for us.'

So, what's your call on this, Dan?'

'Bowie and I have talked it through with Robbo. We think it's worth the risk. But we will keep it to just the few that need to know. The more people that we tell, the less likely it is to succeed. Tony still has people in his pay in the Met.'

'Plus, Della stands a big chance of being killed.'

'Yes. She knows that very well.'

'What did Robbo say?'

'He took some convincing. We all did. But we've decided to go with it. It could work – straight trade-off, diamonds for cocaine. It will be a helluva coup if it comes off.'

Willis mulled things over before she replied.

'Does this alter what Ross and I are about to do?'

'We can let Ross in on this when you feel the time is right. The thing is, Eb, the minute we tell them, we run the risk of losing it. The NCA will want to take it off our hands and Della won't cooperate with them. She will cut her losses and run, I'm sure.'

'She just wants you?'

'Crudely put, yes. She wants the team she knows and trusts.'

'Even though they don't trust her?'

'There was never proof that she brought down Operation Argos.'

'Maybe we should lose it. This is really a job for the NCA instead of a major investigation.'

'And, in normal circumstances, I would agree, but this is so personal. This is all about a family that me, Bowie, Robbo, all those involved in Operation Argos, know so well. We are the ones who have a chance of finally getting a result, not Ross and the NCA.'

'I think this is too risky for Della. I mean, if this goes wrong, she will be dead at the end of it.'

'She wants to take the risk.'

'You okay with all this, Dan?'

'Yeah, thanks for asking. I'm good with this. This is work. This is about a woman who I trust as a fellow officer and it's about a massively important operation which could change the face of the UK drugs market, stamp out a whole distribution network.'

'Okay, I get it. You tell me what you want me to look out for when I get to Tony's, tell me how you want me to play it, and I will.'

'You make sure that when you think about telling Ross, you can be sure he understands he can be part of it but he can't take this over. Don't tell him who Della is straight-away – we are referring to her as Contact X. If he agrees to our terms, then fine. You judge it, but make sure you get it right, Eb – loose tongues cost lives.'

Willis caught up with Ross. The hotel restaurant had just a few people in that evening. They were shown to a window seat with a candle.

'Can we sit further to the back?' asked Willis.

Once they were settled they ordered a beer each and Willis drank from the bottle. Ross laughed.

'I don't know, bra and pants and bottled beer – you're a classy date!'

For a few seconds she stared at him, and then she smiled.

'Can we talk about today?'

'Again?'

'Yes, it's bothering me. I'm supposed to be your partner on this job and I don't know sometimes if we're working for different teams or we're even in the same game.'

'You know I'm authorised to share certain things with you,' said Ross. 'If I tell you everything I know about this case, it will just confuse things. We both have our secrets and I'm all right with that. We both have our hands tied, to a certain extent. Let's just tell one another what we know the other needs to hear, no more, no less.'

'What kind of thing is too much detail?'

He smiled. 'Like, all the people who are on the edge of Tony's life. All the bent policemen he has collected over his time. Not just Tony, all the freemasons within the force. Harold has a fair few of the Met in his pay. I have learned the hard way to trust no one when it comes to huge sums of money. We all know we're paid a pittance. The temptation is too much for lots of people.'

'Did Harold get in touch with you? What is the likelihood of him wanting to deal?'

Ross smiled and shrugged.

'I need him to come to me personally. Like I said, he has a few Met officers who would broker a deal for us, but I'm not talking to anyone but the man himself.'

'How can you do your job as a police officer if you don't trust your colleagues?'

'I am a one-man band. I told you that. I spend a few years in a department then I move on. I'm a troubleshooter. I identify a problem, I eradicate it, I move on.'

'But you're stuck on this, aren't you?'

'Yes, I've hit a big Butcher-shaped wall. I want to get Tony Butcher more than I've ever wanted anything. He has become the case I cannot crack, but I don't even get a chance to try because he will not step outside his villa. I've been here before, Ebony, and I have a horrible feeling I'll be here again.'

'Okay, thanks for explaining it to me.' Willis picked up her beer again.

'That's it?' Ross asked, amused.

She nodded. 'I respect what you're saying. It makes sense to me. But . . .'

'Thank you.' He raised his bottle against hers. 'But what?'

'I know what it's like to mistrust everyone. I know how it is to watch your back to such an extent that you never turn and face anyone. I know you think it's called "not letting your guard down", but without that trust you can't grow as a human being. It's cowardice and naivety and ignorance, in its own way. No matter how many times life lets you down you need to go in wide-eyed and hopeful to every day.'

'You are Miss Wide-Eyed and Hopeful, are you?'

'Compared to what I was? Yes I am.'

'And what were you?'

'I'm not telling you that. I'm on a need-to-know basis, remember? Until the day you tell me you care about me as a person, you care about me as a colleague, then we don't need to know any more about one another.'

Chapter 38

Carter walked into the bar on Upper Street and ordered a glass of chilled Sauvignon Blanc. It was one of those formulaic-type bars where the trends mattered most. He and Cabrina usually called in on one of their rare nights out. It would be for pre-dinner drinks. Carter was trying to remember the last time he had been in there. He realised they hadn't been out for an evening for months. They'd both been away with their mates for stag and hen dos but they hadn't been out together for ages. That thought made him feel guilty. It would have been his fault. His long hours completely wrecked any plans Cabrina ever made. There were very few weeks when Carter made it home when he said he would.

When she got back from Tenerife he'd take her away for a weekend, get his mum to look after Archie. Of course it would have to wait for the Butcher investigation to be over.

He took his drink over to a leather cube to sit where he could see the door but he was out of the draught. He snacked on dried edamame beans and checked his texts while he waited for Maxi Seymour to arrive. He thought about the conversation with Bowie and he wondered if Bowie had another agenda. Bowie was very good at climbing the career ladder on the backs of others. He was even better at blaming others when things went wrong. Not just Della's head would roll if this went wrong. Carter would be in for the chop and Bowie would blame everything on him. Not just that, would he try to implicate Carter? Would he cite his past relationship with Della as the reason for the failure of this mission and Argos? Carter couldn't help but muse over it. After Argos he had to deal with the massive fallout. He'd had to deal with his failures professionally and personally. Della had run off with Eddie and Carter had been posted to the back of beyond to try to rebuild his career. He'd met Cabrina when he'd been on a night out with one of the officers from the station. He'd thought she was a bit gobby and a bit brash but also quick-witted and bright, chic in killer heels and a tight dress. She had the kind of confidence he loved in a sexy, feminine woman. She could give him a run for his money. She told him he would have to step up his game if he wanted her. She'd given him back his sparkle and his fight. She'd been just what the doctor ordered. Was he on the rebound when he met her? Of course.

'Oi! You daydreaming? What's she called? I might know her. Is she leggy with double Ds?'

A well-dressed man in a camel-coloured Crombie three-quarter coat with a brown velvet collar and a narrow-brimmed black hat appeared by Carter's side without his noticing. Maxi Seymour was always immaculate but also slightly off centre in his style.

Carter stood and shook his hand.

'Long time, Maxi.'

'Too long. I thought you would have been in to buy the better half a wedding ring by now.'

'Can't afford it. You're too pricey. Got anything knocked off?'

'As it happens ...' Maxi grinned and then slapped Carter on the back. 'You ready for another?' He pointed to Carter's half-glass of wine.

'Yeah, why not?'

The waiter came to take their order and then Maxi drank half of his pint of real ale down in one go.

'Nothing like a hard day's work to whet the appetite for a night out.'

'You haven't done a hard day's graft in years, not since you left the force.'

'Ha! Very true.'

Carter smiled.

'Good to see you, Maxi. How's business?'

'It's good. How's things in the force? I hope you haven't found my name on any hit list. My shop's been done five times already in the last ten years.'

'I know. I'm sorry we can't do more to prevent it. Intelligence on that kind of robbery is nearly impossible to come by. But at least we managed to get quite a lot of it back last time. I expect the insurance covers it, does it?'

'In my case it does. In my shop everything has a trace. In deposit boxes it's a different story, as you know. We worked on that case together, remember? Those slick bastards who coordinated ... what was it? Five robberies in two days? A museum exhibition in Dubai, safety-deposit boxes in London, a depot for diamond dealers in Antwerp? Did I miss one or two?'

'A jeweller's in Switzerland and a hotel holding a diamond fair in Paris. Operation Argos?'

'That's the one. Tony Butcher used his ill-gotten gains

from the robberies to set up his drug empire, didn't he? Christ we were so near to cracking the biggest job of our lives. If it hadn't gone wrong this end, you'd be head of the Met now. If it wasn't for that bitch – what was she called?'

'Yeah, well, who knows what went wrong? But it's not that easy to make commissioner, I'm afraid. But you're right, it would have been massive.'

'That's why I left the force. I thought, Two years down the drain and I've got that on my record – failed spectacularly. No, thanks. I also realised how much money I could make from selling diamond rings. Beats dealing with the criminal fraternity. But you did okay in the end. More than okay: you're an inspector in the murder squad now. What did you need from me?'

'I need some help, on the quiet,' answered Carter as he sipped his wine. Music came over the speakers and Carter leaned forwards so as not to have to shout.

'What is it? If I can, I will,' answered Maxi. 'Never too old for a bit of excitement.'

'If I wanted to con someone into thinking I had found the missing diamonds from the Great Diamond Heist, how would I go about that? What would three hundred million's worth of diamonds from that heist look like?'

For a minute Maxi stared unblinking at Carter while his mind went to diamond paradise and he checked off the best wish list he'd ever been allowed to imagine.

'The Great Diamond Heist?'

'Yes.'

'Christ!'

Carter could see Maxi didn't want to come down from the dream, but Carter didn't have all day.

'Maxi? Only a few have to be real. Tell me where the

best fakes are and tell me how I can put together the uncut stones. Where do you get them? Tell me what that would look like.'

'It could look like as many stones as you could hold in your hand or a truckload, depends on the carat.'

'Go with somewhere in between.'

'Uncuts are the best currency if you want to sell on the black market. No one knows where they came from. Theoretically, mostly you go by the colour and by the purity and the stone they're found in but, for argument's sake, they can't be traced and you can make up their history. Three hundred million in diamonds would look like a big box of uncut glassy-looking chunks of rock – half as big as your hand, some of them – some of which would be incredible to look at: even in a raw state, you'd see the facets and the fluorescence, the clarity. They would be huge and cut just enough to show their potential brilliance. They could be worth as much as twenty, thirty million in one stone.'

'Did you ever see a diamond like that?'

'I saw one but I never held one.'

'Can you help us get hold of enough convincing fakes to fool someone? We can get hold of a few good real ones to start the ball rolling.'

'Where from?'

'I can't tell you but I know they will be from the same time as the Great Diamond Heist and from the correct sources.'

Maxi smiled. 'You'd have to let me work on it. I'd also need to know the budget.'

'We need it done straight away. The finished thing has to be in our hands in the next week. Because this is so sensitive you'd have to be very discreet, but that's why I came to you – you know what we need from you.'

Maxi nodded. His eyes stayed on Carter as he thought it over for a minute.

'I'm going to have to say ... I can do it.' He grinned.

Carter phoned Robbo. He was sitting at his desk, working a little later than he should. Carter knew he would be. He had yet to discuss the prickly subject of Della's involvement with him. He felt he owed him an explanation as one of the few to know that she was involved.

'Maxi Seymour has agreed to help us. He's taking over the sourcing of as many diamonds as he can find.'

'How's he doing that?' asked Robbo.

'Calling in favours, telling people he needs to borrow diamonds to put on a big display. Have you heard from Eb?' asked Carter.

'No, but I dare say she'll be in touch if she's got anything useful.'

'Thought she would have rung to say goodnight at least.'

'Yeah, kids today? What are they like!' Robbo joked.

'I haven't had time to talk to you about Della,' Carter blurted.

'No.'

Carter could hear in the tone that Robbo wasn't going to make it easy for him.

'It was an offer I couldn't refuse.' He smiled into the phone.

'Could turn out to be a Trojan Horse.'

'It could, but without her, it's looking more like a donkey.'

'I'm glad you can see the funny side,' Robbo said, 'because, as I recall, she screwed us over last time.'

'As much as I appreciate you sharing my burden, she screwed *me* over, no one else. Operation Argos failed for other reasons than Della – she maintains that she managed to keep her identity secret throughout and only Eddie knew she was an undercover and that wasn't until after the operation had failed. It's easy to make a scapegoat out of her, but it's not right.'

'Okay, well it's your call; you're the SIO on this. I'm just following orders. A lot of lives are reliant on her telling you the truth this time. Where is she now?' asked Robbo.

'She's at the Butchers' flat in Shoreditch. She's waiting for Harold and Marco to come back.'

'The one thing I have to say in her favour was that she had balls and she's going to need them now.'

Chapter 39

'Melvin! For goodness' sake rein it in!'

Chrissie, the barmaid in the Blind Beggar, shouted across to Melvin as he stumbled and spilled his pint over another unhappy customer.

Chrissie came from behind the bar with a bunch of napkins to soak up the beer from the man's coat. 'I'm so sorry, sir. He's lost his dog and he's beside himself with worry.'

Melvin raised his hand as an apology and backed off towards the fireplace. But then the muttering started again.

'I know a lot of things about some people in here. I could tell you things.'

Lev from the Old Jewish Bakery drank his pint down and stepped across to talk to Melvin.

'Come on, Melvin, we're calling it a night for you – time for you to get home. I will see you home.'

'Get off me. You fucking hypocrite. Who you working for, eh?'

Chrissie finished placating the wet customer and came across to escort Melvin to the door.

'It's all right, Lev. I'll handle it. Come on, Melvin, you've had enough, time to go home and sleep it off.'

'Get off me. I don't need to be told anything by *you.*'

Melvin shrugged her off, defiant. 'Or you, Lev. You should be ashamed of yourself, mixing with that sort. You're supposed to be all about the old East End, the Bethnal Green of the past, and yet you just roll over and take it, don't you?'

'That's enough, Melvin,' Lev said, stepping closer. In the background the sound of someone laughing was the only other sound in the bar.

'Oi, I've been nice so far,' said Chrissie, getting a firmer grip on his arm. 'I don't need to be. I'm telling you to bugger off home now and I expect you to listen to me, all right? Unless you want to be barred?'

Melvin raised his hand with the beer in it and slopped another wave onto the floor. Chrissie took the glass from him and steered him towards the door as he started to sob.

'Stop, just a minute, please, Chrissie, please. Has anyone seen my dog?' Melvin stopped to turn and address the people in the bar. 'He's called Scamp. He's a little brown dog with a collar with a bone on it. There's a reward. I've a hundred nicker for anyone who returns him to me.'

'Who gave you that? You snitch.'

Harold Butcher was watching the proceedings – he was having his first pint back on home turf. From the back of the bar the laughing grew louder. Marco walked in; he'd come in from the garden, where he'd been having a cigarette. He was wearing a leather jacket and had a thick scarf wrapped around his neck. He wasn't used to the cold. He started slow clapping and laughing as Melvin tried to stand up straight.

Harold walked up to Melvin and put his arm around his shoulder.

'I'll keep a lookout for your dog, no problem. Now, fuck off home and sleep it off, before you get yourself in trouble.'

'Thank you, Harold, you're a good man.' He slapped him on the shoulder. 'Not like some of you other arseholes in here.' Melvin took a step towards the door and then changed his mind. 'I know you,' he shouted at Marco. 'You bastard. You piece of shit. I'm not scared off, you know. I know a lot of things about a lot of people. Fuck you! I mean it, you scumbag. Don't you try and scare me from my home, my job. I'm part of this community and I won't be kicked out. I belong here.'

'No one's trying to kick you out of your home.' Harold tried again to steer him back towards the door. The pub had fallen silent, all chatter dulled, as they had no choice but listen to Melvin rant.

'They are, Harold. He doesn't want me to do my tours any more. He wants me to go away. But I'm not going to. You bring my dog back now, right this minute. Do you hear me?' he shouted back over Harold's shoulder.

Melvin lost his balance and crashed into the doors. Harold picked him up by his coat collar and half walked, half lifted him to the street outside.

'You're upsetting folks; now fuck off, mate.'

Harold dipped into his pocket and pressed a roll of notes into Melvin's hand.

'For old time's sake. Now go home, stay there for the next couple of weeks. Take a holiday. Don't come in here again shouting your mouth off, do you hear me? Do you?'

Melvin nodded, his head hung down onto his chest. He swayed on his feet.

'You want me to call you a cab?' Harold asked after him.

'No, you're very kind to me, Harold, but I can walk. You're a good man, Harold.'

'We go back a long way, Melvin, that's why I want you to promise me you'll stay out of here, stay away from this area for a while. Promise?'

Melvin kept nodding as he walked away with a backward wave Harold's way. Harold watched him stagger up the street and turn the corner before he returned to the pub. Marco had ordered another drink. The pub had already forgotten all about Melvin.

'This one's on the house.' Chrissie the landlady passed over a double Scotch Harold's way. 'Poor old Melvin. He's as harmless as a fly, but he'll get himself in trouble one of these days.'

'What's happened to his dog?' asked Harold. Marco was smiling to himself. Harold looked at him and the anger flashed into Harold's face.

Marco held up his hands. 'Apologies, you just seem so caring, that's all. It's not a side of you I know.'

Chrissie smiled and nodded as she rested her hand on Harold's arm.

'I appreciate it, Harold. You're a gent. When he gets in one of these states you can't believe anything he says. He'll start hallucinating next.' She glowered at Marco before returning behind the bar.

Harold looked at his phone and lowered his voice as he leaned in. 'We just got word – Tony's going to be getting a visit from the Spanish police tomorrow morning.'

Marco looked unsurprised. 'Looking for?'

'Francisco, I guess. The double act you tried to pull didn't fool them for long.'

'They will find nothing. We cleaned it good.'

'I'm pretty sure they know that. But they're just going through the motions.'

'Will they search Eddie's property?' asked Marco, a little concerned.

'I doubt it. Even if they do, it won't matter: we have it covered. Have you heard from Della?' asked Harold.

'Yes. She'll meet us back at the apartment.'

'What's the deal with you, Marco? You tell me what's really going on.'

'Surely you know everything, Mr Right-Hand Man, Mr Enforcer.'

'You'd be wise not to take the piss out of me, Marco.'

'Apologies.' Marco looked around for a drink. Harold took his arm and held it. He smiled. 'I don't object to bowing out of the limelight. You want to take over from me, you're welcome, as long as I'm retired and still alive. But you'll need my help if you want to fill my shoes. Tony has these grand schemes but they're all in his head, and that's not a nice place to be sometimes.'

Marco went to turn away from Harold and Harold grabbed him by the neck and pulled him down to within an inch of his face.

'You got my brother killed. I don't trust you, Marco. Over here, I command the troops. I could dig you in between the ribs with a nice thin blade, no fuss, clean, and walk out of here, and I'll be scot-free before you hit the ground dead. Even if you asked for help, you wouldn't get it. They don't like you round here. You're pissing them off. You get me?'

'Yes.'

'My back is being watched here twenty-four/seven. Who's watching yours, Marco?'

'Once again I apologise. We're friends here, Harold, on the same side.'

'I think you're on your own team of one,' answered Harold. 'You setting up this deal with your family?' Marco nodded. 'You've kept the money from the Mendez family and you're looking to add to it to move on to bigger deals?'

'That's the gist of it, yes. This is the time now, to act, to push forwards.'

'I heard your family chucked you out. They didn't like a bastard in the family.'

'There will always be problems between siblings. My family will have a new respect for me. They will see what I have to offer. Tony has built his network of distributors. He is an octopus with his tentacles stretching across Europe. We have a lot to offer the right cartel.' Harold was watching Marco intently. He nodded.

'Let's go and talk to Della. I want to hear what the princess has to say.'

Marco stopped him when they reached their car.

'You know, Della needs watching very closely. We should put a tail on her. She has little time to prove herself. The Mendez cartel are thinking about the signed statement from Francisco, about the funds. They will be looking for confirmation of that and they will not get it. I say, in one week's time this city's streets will begin to run with blood unless we make the new deal and fast. Uncertainty will lead to more bloodshed. Are your troops ready?'

Harold opened the driver's door and paused as he looked across to Marco.

'Born ready.'

Marco laughed. 'You know what, Harold? I'm going to attend to some business here. I'll catch you later.'

'Where are you going?'

'Old friends have been in touch. I need to see how they are. I will be back later.'

Chapter 40

Della was waiting for Harold when he returned that evening.

The apartment was a penthouse in Shoreditch: 1 Shoreditch Mews, Flat 18. It occupied the whole top two floors of an old warehouse. It was white and open-plan. It had a roof garden with Perspex sides. The bedrooms were on the lower floor.

Della felt nervous as she waited in the open-plan sitting area. The automatic blinds had been closed. The automatic candles had sprung into life. She heard one pair of feet coming up the stairs to the top level.

Harold appeared above the Perspex parapet.

'Where's Marco?' Della asked as she reached forwards to pick up her glass of wine.

'He said he had business.'

She considered that answer with a look of disdain on her face.

'Are you having him followed?'

'Should I?'

'Of course.'

Harold shrugged. 'My guess, he's meeting with Colombian friends.'

He poured himself a whisky from the decanter. He topped it up with ginger ale.

'I heard all about your deal. Is it for real? I have a feeling it's just bullshit, made to bide you some time, but I can't figure out why you'd bother. Why not just leave Marbella? I'll get you some funds. I'll take care of you. You're Eddie's widow, after all. I don't hold with the disrespect that's being shown. Own up to me, and I'll get you on a flight to South America. How does that sound?' He came to sit near her and put his feet up on the table.

'Thank you, Harold, but I'm not bullshitting. I can get the diamonds. You know I appreciate it and I know you mean it, but I don't feel like running. I want what's mine and I will fight for it. Eddie left me all that information for a reason. Eddie must have known all this would happen. This is all the protection he could give me in the end. He left me something that Tony wants more than anything.'

'Oh, yeah, he has wet dreams about that stash of diamonds.' Harold grinned as he brought his drink over to sit on the sofa with Della. 'He's talked about it and nothing else for as long as I can remember. But you will be the first to be killed if it goes wrong. If Tony makes a deal.'

'I heard that the deal is already done. The shipment is on its way. Tony can't back out now. Neither can any of us.'

'Then you better find them diamonds quick and let's get it done.'

'You sound like you've had enough of it all, Harold.'

'I have. This will be my last job for Tony, then I go into retirement. I sit around and get fat in the sun, drinking beer.'

'So you have a vested interest in this happening?'

He nodded. 'But what worries me is, is revenge top of

your list here, Della? Because, if it is, then you won't succeed. Tony doesn't feel remorse. Tony doesn't have that in his make-up.'

'Do you?'

'Well, it's debatable, after all these years. But I'd never have ordered or stood by and allowed Eddie to be killed.'

'Do you know that's what Tony did?'

'Tony didn't pull the trigger. Now, let's get back to business, Della. I'm going to be your best friend here. I'm going to look after you the best way I can, but you're going to have to trust me.'

'And not Marco?'

Harold shrugged. 'Marco is working for himself in all this. Don't turn your back on Marco for one second. He already wants you followed everywhere. If you don't want that, you have to trust me. You better tell me more so that I can help you find the diamonds. I need to be sure the stash exists. I don't want to lose my head.'

'You want proof, Harold? I understand that. But, this is going to be done the way I want it, Harold, or not at all.'

'Okay, I get it. What do you want from me?' Harold asked.

'Protection. For a start, we should move from here. Eddie was staying here before he was killed. This apartment smells of a trap to me. The police must be watching us twenty-four/seven.'

'The place isn't rigged. I had it checked out.'

'Still, everyone knows we're here. It's not safe. I want a new apartment that's not associated with the Butcher clan. If things kick off with the Mendez cartel I don't want to be in here like a sitting duck.'

'It makes sense. I'll see what I can organise.'

'No offence, but all your friends are involved in this. I can still pose as a normal human being and no one will suspect a thing. I'll rent my own apartment. You two can do your own thing.'

'Maybe, we'll see about it.'

'Hello? I thought we were in a hurry. You want to take a month to work this out, then go ahead, but I think we'll be pretty much in the shit by that time. Can I just point out the obvious, Harold? And that is that Tony's sitting pretty in Villa Cassandra while we are out here and about to die just like Eddie. I suggest that we three stick together and we make a sensible plan that's going to see us through all this. Now, I have said that I can find the diamonds. I believe I can. I just need to stay alive long enough to do it. Do you understand?'

'Yes.'

The bell went for the intercom.

'You expecting someone?' asked Harold. Della shook her head.

'Who is it?' Della asked as she watched Harold walk over and look at the webcam image from the front door.

'Laurence.'

'Well, are you going to let him in?'

'Sure, just be careful what you say.'

'Come up.' Harold pressed the buzzer.

'Have you eaten? I bring food. The best Indian in town,' Laurence announced.

'Thanks, Laurence, you're very kind.' Della got up to go and greet him. 'Just the smell of chicken tikka masala is enough to make me ravenous.'

'You okay, Della?' Laurence hugged her. 'It's nice to have you here.'

'Thanks, Laurence; I think it's nice to be here, except it's gone so cold. The Christmas lights are pretty here. I forget what a magical time of year it is to come to London.'

'It's the only time I wish I had kids,' laughed Laurie, excited. 'Don't put any bets on a white Christmas just yet, though. They say there's a few storms headed our way. How long are you planning on staying?'

'I'm not sure.' She took the takeaway bag from him.

Harold had been distracted, looking at his phone. Messages were coming in. He took a call and went into his bedroom to talk.

'I have to go out for a while,' he said when he emerged a few minutes later. 'I'll see you soon, Laurie.' He picked up his keys and left.

Laurence looked at her. 'Something I said? I've only been here a few minutes!'

Della smiled. 'It's great. For whatever reason, we have a bit of peace.'

Laurence laughed. 'It's going to be pretty hardcore sharing with those two monkeys, isn't it? You can come and stay at mine. I have plenty of room.'

'Thanks, but I need to spend time with family and friends. I haven't seen some of them for ages. You know how it is.' She smiled at him. She realised he'd made an effort to come and see her. He was stinking of expensive aftershave. He had the just-shaved look to his baby face. 'It's kind of you. Are you going somewhere else after this?' she asked in hope.

He shook his head. 'Not unless you're keen.'

'Me? No I'm going to bed early, I'm afraid.'

He nodded as he walked across to put some music on and pour himself a glass of wine as he topped up Della's glass.

Della went into the kitchen. Laurie was watching her as she got plates out and opened up the containers.

'I didn't know you had family in London,' he said. 'How come we never saw them?'

'Ah, well, it's a well-kept secret.' Della returned, smiling, with a tray and the food. 'Let's eat.' She put the plates out on the table.

They sat opposite one another and struggled for something to talk about, maybe because so much of what she might say she couldn't. Laurence was awkwardness personified. They exchanged meaningless comments about the quality of the food and smiled at one another over their wine. Della put it down to tiredness. It was beginning to feel too intimate. She was almost hoping Marco would come back to herald the end of the evening. Everyone hated Marco.

'Would you be interested in meeting Billy Manson with me? I want to crack on with the projects that Eddie had going.'

'Yes, of course,' she said, relieved. 'I've got a pretty full schedule, but let me know when you're thinking of it.'

'Tomorrow?'

'That's probably fine. I'll send you a text with my new number to use here.'

She picked up the new smartphone that Bowie had given her.

'How many phones do you have? You picking up bad habits already, Della?'

'My Samsung is playing up. I'll get it sorted when I get back to Spain. I've had this one for a while. Just good to have a backup. There, I've sent you a text. Let me know what time and I'll try and make it.'

'Give your broken phone to me. I'll get it fixed or replaced for you. It's no bother.'

'I left it at home, but thanks, anyway. You're very kind, Laurence.'

'Do you need a car while you're here? I've got one you can borrow.'

'It's okay. I've gone with the usual car hire firm that Eddie always used. I pick it up tomorrow morning, it's all arranged.'

'Cancel it; you don't need it. I told you, I'll sort one out for you.'

Della looked up from her plate.

'It's kind, Laurence, but I can do things for myself.'

'Why? Eddie always took care of you; now I will.' He smiled. 'It's a pleasure.'

'It's kind of you, Laurence, but I'll be okay on my own. I'm going back to who I once was.'

'And who was that?'

'Della Cipriani.'

'The waitress? The one who used to bring me a strawberry milkshake?'

'Funny you remember that.' Though Della wasn't finding it funny.

'Of course, I was in love with you back then. I was a teenager in love. I had no idea you had eyes for Eddie. I remember thinking you and that waiter were an item. I thought he was my competition. Not good old Eddie.'

Della pushed her plate away and picked up her wine.

'You have a remarkable memory; if a little askew. You were very young, after all. You know what, Laurence? I'm sorry, but I am so tired. It's just come on in a wave and I can feel a migraine starting. Would you mind if we call it a night? I need to get to sleep soon, to try and stop it getting a hold. I need to take some pills.'

'Oh, what a shame. The evening was just getting started. Are you sure you wouldn't like me to stay and give you a neck massage – that's the latest thing for migraines?'

'That's kind of you, but I don't think that would be appropriate, do you?'

He shrugged. 'We are not your average couple. Appropriate doesn't come into it, does it, Della? We come from an "every man for himself" background. Rules don't apply to us Butchers.'

'We are not a couple, Laurence. I've just buried my husband, your brother. I'm beginning to feel uncomfortable here.'

'Not my intention, of course. I just wanted you to know that I feel deep affection for you and I will be here when you need me. I'll call by in the morning when you've rested.'

'I might not be here. I've got lots of things I want to achieve while I'm here in the UK.'

'What things?'

'Just things he left for me to do. That's all.'

'The car? You'll need the car.'

'I told you, I've booked one now, it's paid for. I'm going to pick it up first thing. You don't need to bother. Thank you, though.'

'I'll give you a lift to the hire company. Which one is it?'

'I forget. I'll check later.'

'Check it now. I need to know.'

'No, Laurence. I don't need a lift. Thanks for coming. I need you to go now. My head is pounding.'

Laurence picked up his coat from where he'd thrown it

over the back of a chair and he started down the stairs, and then stopped.

'I'll text you about the meeting with Manson. That's if you're still interested in knowing about your ex-husband's business. That's if you care what happens to it.'

'*Late* husband, not ex. Night, Laurence.'

Chapter 41

12 December

At just gone four in the morning, Ross and Willis walked out of their apartment into darkness. They walked quietly along their landing and down the outside stairs and across by the pool to the reception area.

They stood in the quiet foyer of the hotel as they waited. The air conditioning was fierce and Ross shivered. He couldn't stop yawning. Willis had slept just enough. She never needed a lot. She had the ability to sleep deeply and quickly. She felt refreshed and raring to go. She was beyond excited about the day. She was a morning person, even on a normal day she was used to getting up early and into work. But today she'd woken to the sound of night time in Marbella: the drone of bars and cars. She'd slept with her window open. The light flooded into the room from the electric light on the landing. It buzzed as moths hit it.

They had made coffee in their apartment and Willis had found plastic cups to bring it downstairs, so Ross stood sipping it as they stared out at the darkness.

'Okay, here we go,' Willis said, as she caught a glimmer of car headlights turning to come to the hotel.

'It's just one car. I don't think it can be them,' said Ross.

They watched as the headlights went out and the two detectives pushed open the doors to the foyer and walked across to them.

'Ay up, it's the Marbella Vice again.' Ross gave a side smile to Willis, whose eyes were fixed on the Spaniards walking their way over and giving a nonchalant wave towards the women on the reception desk.

'You ready for this?' Garcia rubbed his hands in anticipation as he got near.

'Absolutely.' Ross grinned back at Garcia as he went across to the bin by the reception desk to throw in his empty coffee cup. He and Willis followed them out to their car.

Garcia took the wheel. Willis glanced at Ross. He didn't look her way; he was staring out of the window.

Ramirez turned back from the passenger seat.

'How's the hotel? Okay?'

'It's good, thanks. Tell me, how many officers will be coming in with us for the raid?' asked Ross.

'We're having the Special Ops officers to come and help us with this,' answered Garcia. 'There will be fifteen of us altogether. We have made slight changes to the way we will enter the premises but our position is the same as we showed you at the meeting: we attack from the front gate.'

Ramirez shut off the headlights as they came within sight of Villa Cassandra. The police van was parked away from the road. Black figures began emerging from the back of the van. They were fully equipped with semiautomatic rifles and helmets with visas. They stopped briefly to liaise with Garcia and Ramirez and then they took their positions along the perimeter of the premises.

Ross and Willis donned flak jackets and waited out of sight of the main gate until the signal was given, and they saw the black figures of the Special Operations forces scaling the walls and running along the top of the wall before they dropped down into the garden. The next sound was the frantic deep barking of angry dogs. The sound of a whelp as they were tranquilized. Lights went on in the house. An alarm sounded and the guard on duty on the gate stood back, his hands raised, before opening the front gate. Willis and Ross followed Garcia and Ramirez as they burst into Tony's premises and sprinted up the driveway and round to the back way through the kitchens and servants' quarters. They went through the kitchens and into a massive, well-equipped gym. An indoor pool and numerous steam and sauna rooms followed as Ross and Willis made their way out of the lower floor.

'In here.' Ramirez had gone on ahead and he called them into a room that was within the centre of the building. It was a space where it looked like there had been a bank of computer stacks. The abandoned connections were hanging down, ripped out.

Garcia pulled open a box of phones and packs of SIM cards.

'Must be three hundred at least.' Garcia held up handfuls of the cards. 'Unfortunately, it's not illegal to have SIM cards.'

'What the fuck is going on? You wake us up at five in the bleeding morning, for no good reason.'

They caught up with Tony in the trophy room.

'What is this about?' The early-morning wake-up had found Tony fully awake and dressed in his usual vest and shorts.

Ramirez answered, 'We have reason to believe Señor Francisco is being held somewhere on this property.'

'Who?'

'Señor Francisco, the lawyer who visited you, brought here by Marco Zapata on the day of your brother Eddie's funeral. Is that clear enough for you?'

'How the hell do I know what happened to Francisco? We dropped him back in the middle of Marbella after we concluded our business. Is that what all this is about?'

'His daughter is also missing. Do you know anything about her?'

'Nothing. I didn't know he had a daughter.'

'We will need to take a look around.'

'Go ahead. Try not to nick anything this time. Who are these two?' Tony addressed Garcia, who answered him in Spanish. Tony was watching Willis and Ross closely.

'Tony Butcher?' Willis went straight for the introduction.

'Who are you?'

'DS Willis from Major Investigation Team 17. We are handling the investigation into your brother's death, sir, and this is Detective Inspector Ross.'

'You've got a nerve.' Sandra came to stand in the trophy room in her sweeping kimono-style white silk dressing gown, which was far too thin and silky to stay closed. She glared at the detectives as she lit a cigarette. All of Tony's cocaine had been tidied away. It was now hidden in the cavity beneath the swimming pool. It was a feature Eddie had built in to the villa.

'Is there anyone else in the property?' Ramirez asked.

'The staff,' answered Debbie, who had said little since she walked into the trophy room seconds after Sandra, and seemed to accept the raid as part and parcel of life.

Willis called Ross aside and they went to a corner of the room to talk.

'Something's very wrong with all this,' said Willis. Ross nodded.

'The officers searching are just going through the motions. No one expects to find anything. They've quite obviously been tipped off.' Garcia came across to talk to the English detectives.

'I don't think we are going to be lucky today.'

'If we think Francisco is buried somewhere in this property, we need to bring the specialist forensic team in here,' said Ross. 'This isn't going to get us anywhere.'

Garcia blinked a couple of times at Ross while he made sure he understood what Ross was saying.

He shook his head melodramatically from side to side. 'Not without proof.'

'What were you hoping to see here? Francisco nailed up next to the lion head or hanging over the giraffe's neck?'

Garcia's eyes took a narrow amusement. 'Hah-ha! That would be just fine, wouldn't it? We will always be in a delicate situation here, Ross.'

'Okay, well that's your business. We would like to interview the family about Eddie's death, that's why we're here.'

'Go ahead,' said Garcia, a flash of anger in his manner as he walked off.

'Mr Butcher, can we talk to you about Eddie's murder?' He nodded. 'Can we talk in private?'

'Office.' He stood and came from behind the dining table

as he strode back through the trophy room and Ross and Willis followed.

'We would like to speak to you both afterwards, please,' said Willis as they passed Sandra and Debbie. Debbie nodded, Sandra turned her back.

Inside the Don's office Ross took stock as he walked in and stood looking at it all as if he were in a flashback situation.

'This office?' he started to say, looking around him. 'This office looks very familiar, it's like—'

'Not *like*,' said Tony, amused but irritated. 'It *is* a replica of the Don's office in the *Godfather* trilogy.'

'Of course it is. Impressive,' said Ross. 'Can we sit down?'

'Sit.' Tony waved his arm in the direction of the leather sofa. 'You come to make me an offer I can't refuse?'

Ross smiled, Willis frowned; she'd never seen the *Godfather* movies.

'Mr Butcher,' she said, as she decided to sit on the chair rather than next to Ross, 'I know that you were here at the time of your brother's murder but, because of the nature of his death, I need to ask some questions.'

'What do you mean?'

'I mean, I'll ask some questions and hopefully you'll be able to answer them.'

'Don't be a smart-fucking-arse with me, girl, you're a long way from home.' Tony swivelled on his chair as he glared at Willis.

'Are you threatening me, Mr Butcher?' Willis felt the anger solidify into a calm she had learned from Carter. She was grateful for it. The room had Tony's testosterone bouncing off its walls.

'Just stating the fucking obvious. In case you hadn't noticed.'

'Can we turn up the lighting in here, please?' Ross asked.

Tony thought about it but then reached down and touched a switch and the lights behind the pretend windows and their louvre blinds turned to full daylight.

'There are questions about the way your brother died,' continued Willis. 'Given the nature of his line of work, does it seem strange to you that he was tortured and killed in the way he was?'

Tony shrugged. 'Everything is strange to me about my brother's death. Why kill a man who builds houses for a living?'

'Except when he builds them for dangerous people,' said Ross.

Tony nodded. 'If I had been there, I might have prevented it.'

'How?'

Tony breathed in through his nose and held the breath a few seconds then exploded with, 'By killing them before they killed him.'

'So, you admit his death had something to do with the people you know?'

'I admit nothing. He was executed for some reason that had nothing to do with me.'

'His death was made to look like an execution,' Willis said.

Tony went into a blinking spasm as he thought about what she had said.

'Made to?'

'Yes, he was shot in the head minutes after he was

actually already dead. His heart gave way, the toxins built up from torture. It would have been obvious he was dead. Someone wanted some information from him very badly. They wanted it to look like an execution.'

Tony's eyes settled on Ross.

'That's right. We now know Eddie died from a heart attack brought on by the stress of the torture.'

'Okay, that's all we need, thanks,' said Ross. 'We'll be here for a few days if you need to get in touch via the police station.'

Tony was still staring out into space when they got up to leave the Don's office.

Willis held on to Ross as he walked forwards to where Sandra and Debbie were sitting on the white sofa, waiting their turn to be interviewed.

'I want to go outside and have a look at the land around Eddie's villa.'

Ross nodded. 'I understand what you're saying.' He called Garcia over and told him what Willis wanted to do.

'Why?' asked Garcia. 'We don't have permission; we don't have a search warrant for that villa.'

'I don't need one to look at the outside of it.'

'No, of course not, but we don't want this raid compromised. We have been planning this for a long time. You go where you are not supposed to and that's it. Everything is wasted.'

'Excuse me for a moment,' said Ross. 'Let me understand what you're saying here. My colleague is asking to walk out on a piece of no-man's-land and look for the missing man and child and you're saying that Tony didn't give us permission?'

'No, I'm not saying that.'

'Good, because, I have a lot of questions about this raid.' Garcia went across to Debbie.

'This British policewoman wants to look at the grounds between here and Eddie Butcher's villa.'

Debbie looked from one officer to another. Sandra stared on, cigarette in hand. She'd been given a coffee. 'There is no one occupying my brother Eddie's villa at the moment,' Debbie replied. 'His widow has gone away for a short break. I don't have a key.'

'But I can walk from here to there, right?' Willis asked.

'Sure, if you want to you can, but you need to be careful: there are dogs roaming sometimes in the early mornings. You need to take a stick.'

'I'll be okay.'

'I'll send Sheena, our housekeeper, with you,' said Debbie.

Willis took Ross aside.

'Is that okay, sir? We're only being shown what we were supposed to see. I need to look further. We've had some intelligence from home and I need to go and check it out.'

He nodded his agreement. 'This is a sham. All the computers were gone. They've left just enough evidence to make it look like they were caught unawares, but they weren't. Be careful; stay on your phone. I'll talk to Debbie and Sandra while you're gone.'

'Ma'am?' Sheena was waiting for Willis when she walked out to the front of the villa. Willis left Ross and followed Sheena.

'Are we going via the almond grove, the land at the back of the house?'

'No, ma'am, it's better by the road.'

'Can we get to it by going this way?' Willis pointed away from the road; she had already seen the route, between the two villas, on Google Earth. She knew the route was straightforward.'

'Very poor ground underfoot, ma'am. You cannot see what is there.'

'That's okay. I'd like you to take me via the back of the villa, please.'

Sheena stopped and turned and looked behind Willis, as if looking to see if they were being followed.

'Follow me, please, ma'am.' Willis followed Sheena along to the side of the lane and the path that led off, across the wasteland.

'Is that Eddie's place?'

'Yes, ma'am.'

'Sheena, it's just us here. Nothing you say will go further, can you tell me what has been happening here?'

'Sorry, ma'am? What do you mean? I don't understand.'

'Okay, I'm looking for something here.' The light had reached the day now and the sky was full of soft, blushing peach, and slithers of gold and purple. The ground, the olive and almond trees were like an impressionist oil painting in the softest of lights.

Willis looked at the stone hut that came into view on her left.

'Can you just wait back here, Sheena? I just need to get my bearings.'

'Ma'am.'

Willis walked forward with the crunch of dried undergrowth and chippings beneath her feet. As the light came rapidly to the day there was a perfect stillness. Somewhere a rooster crowed. A fire glowed from beside the stone hut. A man was standing by it. He stared at Willis as she approached. He didn't look like a farmer to her. He looked like the photo of one of Tony's staff, Danny Miller.

Willis approached. The early-morning breeze was gusting the sparks.

'Is that dangerous?' she asked. 'I mean there are sparks flying.'

'I've got it under control.'

Willis held up her warrant card.

'UK Metropolitan Police, investigating the murder of Eddie Butcher. What's your name, please, sir?'

'Danny Miller, I'm the gardener here.'

'For this villa?'

'Mainly for Tony Butcher's, but I help out anywhere I'm needed.'

'What's your job helping out here?'

'Just burning rubbish.'

'Whose is this piece of land?'

'It's nobody's.'

'But you're allowed to come and bring your rubbish to burn on it? Is that legal?'

'It's legal enough.'

Willis walked nearer.

'What exactly are you burning? The smoke smells pretty nasty.'

'Just some old unwanted bits of furniture and things that have been dumped on the land here.'

'Like what?'

'There was a dead dog. It was attracting all the scavengers. I thought it best to burn it. I didn't realise how long it would take or how much heat I had to get in the fire to

do it.' In the red glow of the ashes bursting, Willis's eyes
smarted as the smoke drifted her way. She walked around
to the hut and peered inside. Just then Miller poured on
more petrol and the fire exploded into a balloon of flames.

Chapter 42

Ross stood in the Don's office and stared at the fake windows, the three choices of lighting settings to appear behind them: bright, afternoon, and evening sunset. The only thing wrong with the authenticity of the office, in relation to the *Godfather* films, was the smell, or lack of it. What smell there was was of new leather and cleaning polish. It smelled like a set. It didn't feel real.

'This is great.' Ross grinned at Tony. 'It's a nice touch. Is that what they call you around here? Don Corleone? Or just the Don?'

Tony sat down behind his desk as he waited for the officers to finish their cursory look around the rest of the place.

'Ha-ha. What they call me is Mr Butcher. You like this room; you're going to love what I got downstairs. You want to see the original car from the film, a 1953 Buick Special?'

'That's impressive.'

'You want to see?'

'Love to.'

Tony opened up the door at the back of the office and led the way down the corridor, towards the garage. He opened the door into the forecourt.

'How many cars have you got here?' Ross asked as the halogen strip lights illuminated the corners of the large garage and rows of vehicles under covers.

'Fifty-three last time I counted,' Tony said as he flicked on more lights.

'Where can you drive them round here?'

'I take them around my grounds. I have a driver who keeps them ticking over. I can't actually take them that far myself, at the moment.'

'But you could leave this villa if you wanted, couldn't you? We both know security is pretty lax here. I mean how often do you go for drinks with these guys, Ramirez and Garcia?'

'I told you, never. They visit me from time to time, of course, in an official capacity, like today.'

'But you knew they were coming.'

'I don't know what you're implying.' Tony grinned.

He stripped off the cover from one of the cars to show Ross a shiny red Mustang beneath.

'No that's not the one,' he said. 'I'm going to have to go and look at the floor plan. I can't remember where the *Godfather* film cars are.'

'That's okay, I can wait.' Ross watched as Tony walked across between the cars and opened a door. He switched on a light inside. Ross stepped back a couple of discreet paces so that he could get a look inside. It was a simple control room, but the smell coming from it was unmistakable. Someone had spilled a lot of bleach on the floor.

Ross started walking towards the entrance; the smell was eye-watering.

'Did you find it?'

'Still looking. The floor plan's a bit confusing. Come and see for yourself.'

Beneath the smell of bleach there was a thick musty smell of turned meat.

Ross inched forwards and felt that prickle in his skin that was his fight-or-flight mechanism waking his nerve endings. It pricked at him like needles as it said, Don't go near that door. He could no longer see Tony and there was just the faint orange and red glow coming from lights on a switchboard inside the room. Ross heard the click of a revolver.

Chapter 43

Della awoke early and lay in her bed listening to the noise from the road outside. She'd seen Marco and Harold in the early hours of the morning. Some ground rules were established. Both men seemed to be in sombre mode. The reality seemed to be hitting them all. The enormity of what was happening. More could go wrong than right.

She checked her phone as she lay there: she had a message from Laurence. It made her skin prickle – made her anxious, seeing Laurence in this new light. Eddie had always joked about his kid brother being in love with Della, but she hadn't taken it seriously. Complications of that sort were the last thing she needed, but, on the other hand, she thought to herself, it could be useful for staying alive. He might be a help to her, in the end.

Della thought about seeing her mum and dad. She ached to see them. She hadn't properly given in to tears about Eddie, and she longed to be hugged by her warm loving family. But, she must get on with the job first. She'd be going down that way, towards Ramsgate, soon enough. She was going to pick up the hire car and meet Carter, but there was someone else she wanted to see first. She sent a text to Carter to tell him she'd be in touch mid-afternoon.

Della decided to get up and get out before the other two stirred and she might have to answer questions. She'd catch breakfast on the move. She showered in her *en suite* and pulled on jeans and a sweatshirt as well as a parka to keep out the bitter cold. When she got outside, she hailed a black cab to take her to Tower Bridge and the car-hire company.

She took the lease on a white VW Up, a small town car, and then drove to Islington Upper Street and pulled up on a side road, paid at the parking metre and walked back along Upper Street. She found what she was looking for: a smart-looking, black-fronted beauty salon: Visage.

A blonde woman in her forties walked towards her as Della waited by the reception desk. The woman was smiling, holding out her arms.

'Hello, Della, it's so good to see you.' She gave her a hug.

'It's good to see you, too, Tracy. How is my favourite cousin?'

'I'm good, thanks. Come on, let's go and grab a coffee and you can tell me what I can do for you. It was lovely to get your message.'

They walked up the road to the small café and ordered coffee.

'When did you get back from the cruise ships?' Della asked. 'And how's your grandson, Jackson?'

'Jackson is wonderful, thanks, and I've been back a year now. I'm sorry I couldn't make it to Eddie's funeral. I know we weren't supposed to go, but I was going to just stand in the crowd. In the end, Jackson was ill and I couldn't make it. I ended up having to take a week off work to look after him. He's living with me now. I'm looking after him full-time. My daughter hasn't been doing so well recently.'

'I'm sorry to hear that, Tracy. It looks like you're working in a nice salon?'

'Yes, feels like I'm getting somewhere again. The owner of Visage has been really good to me. I pay to use the place. It feels more like I'm my own boss.'

'Is that what you want to do, own your own beauty salon?'

'God, yes. I've got so many ideas, Della. There's so much I want to achieve.'

'You still love it?' Tracy nodded. She had toned down her look in the last couple of years. She had gone from ageing porn star to a soft, older beauty that saw her lose the heavy eyebrows and the long lashes in favour of the natural look. 'Do you still help out in theatre make-up?' asked Della.

'I do, now and again, to keep my hand in. I've always loved it. But Jackson takes a lot of my time. He's a gorgeous little boy but a handful.'

Della smiled, nodded. She sipped her coffee.

Tracy looked at her enquiringly. 'What brings you over here now, Della?'

'I want you to do me a favour, Tracy. Well, it's more than a favour: I need help. The police still don't know why Eddie was killed or who did it, which is why I didn't want any of you coming to the funeral. I have come here to help them find out who killed Eddie, but it's dangerous and I need all the help I can get.'

'Anything I can do I'll be happy to, Della. You've been so kind to me.'

'Thanks, Tracy. I know we joked about it once before but I need you to try and change my appearance. I need you to make me a latex mask. I want to create a new me: wig, dress, make-up – everything new. I'll pay you, Tracy.'

Tracy held up her hand. 'You're family, and you've been good to Jackson and me. Just pay my costs and we'll get on it straight away.'

'Tracy, you don't know how grateful I am.'

'No problem. The mask will take about three hours to get it right. The rest we can go shopping for afterwards. I have wigs you can try on, see what you like, or I can get one for you cost price. When do you want to get it done?'

'As fast as we can – now, if possible,' Tracy said with a hopeful look.

Tracy got out her diary. 'Let me just go and check my books. If it looks free this morning, we'll do it.' She smiled up at Della and nodded. 'Yes, you ready? I can do it in the salon. I have everything we need there.'

Chapter 44

Carter was on his way to work when he got a call from Chrissie, the barmaid at the Blind Beggar. He drove straight there.

'Where did you find him?' asked Carter as Scamp looked ecstatic to see him and started jumping up at him.

'Someone brought him in this morning when I opened up. They said they found him. I don't know where, or whether they even did. It was just a scuddy-looking kid in a hoody and trackies twenty times too big for him. But he looks like he's been cared for okay. Melvin will be over the moon.'

'Why did you ring me? Don't you know where Melvin lives?'

'Oh, I know, but I was told I had to tell you first.'

'Was it because of the reward? Did you get the kid's number?'

She shook her head. 'Look, I was just given this piece of paper with your name and number on it by the lad. He just told me to ring it. He didn't ask for the money. I'm pretty sure he didn't know there was a reward, otherwise he would have wanted it, definitely; he looked like he slept on the streets. He gave me your card and he said I was to ring you and you should take the dog round to Melvin's.'

'Did that make any sense to you?'

She was not making eye contact with Carter, as she rearranged the furniture, ready for opening. She stopped, paused, her hands on the back of a chair she was about to push under.

'Yes, it kind of does. People know you know one another, if you understand what I'm getting at. Melvin's been shouting his mouth off. Maybe that's why they asked for you. People know about him being a snitch, *your* snitch. Last night he was threatening to tell all about other people's business. I tried to make him be quiet, we all did. We know he's harmless. He has nothing of real value to tell you, anyway, I'm sure. He just does it for effect. It's a bit sad. He's a sweet man really. When you take Scamp back, I want you to warn him to be discreet. That's what this is all about. These are dangerous times. He'll be happy he's got Scamp back, but it was a warning to him. Tell him to take a break. Tell him it might be better he kept away from here for a while.'

'All right, Chrissie; I hear what you're saying. It was probably the drink talking – I gave him some money to drown his sorrows, probably not the wisest of things to do.'

'Yeah, it wasn't. I had to throw him out in the end, spilling his drink over customers, shouting out threats. Even threatened Lev from the bakery. Luckily, Harold Butcher showed him the way out for me. He took him outside. I think he sent him home.'

'What time was that?'

'Late, about eleven. Look' – she went behind the bar – 'you say hello from me. I bet he's got one hell of a hangover. And, look, take this bag of scraps from the kitchen for

Scamp just in case Melvin hasn't the inclination to go to the shops.'

'Will do, thanks, Chrissie.' Carter noticed she didn't make eye contact as she handed him the bag.

Carter took hold of Scamp's lead and walked out of the pub in the direction of Melvin's house. It was the ground-floor flat in a three-storey terraced house that bordered the gardens around the church.

Carter knocked and knocked again. The bell was broken. He looked around for a possible hiding place for a key. There had been some attempts by Melvin at keeping the small front garden tidy. But people threw in litter as they passed and the shrubs had grown too large for the small space. The litter caught in the bushes. There was also the problem with dog shit.

'He's in there, I know he is,' a man shouted down from the window above. 'He came back drunk as a skunk last night. I had a mind to call the Old Bill. He was banging and crashing so loud, probably fallen asleep in the hallway, wouldn't be the first time. He started cooking stuff at about midnight. I could smell it all the way up here.'

'Was he on his own?' asked Carter.

'He came home on his own, but I heard someone else's voice later on.'

'Thank you.' Carter raised his hand and was about to knock again when the door gave to his touch and he pushed it open.

Scamp was panting with excitement as he strained on his leash and sprang inside into the dark hallway, but the dog turned, tail between his legs, and came rushing back out past Carter. He stood whimpering. Carter called out, 'Melvin?'

Chapter 45

'Come out, Señor Butcher.' Garcia stopped at the control-room door and kept his revolver in line with the door's edge. Ross looked at him as if to say there was no need to be so heavy-handed, that Ross was handling it.

Garcia looked at him incredulously as if he couldn't believe that Ross had ended up alone with Tony and on his terms.

Ross blanked him: he wasn't about to explain himself to the Spanish detective.

The sound of Tony's laughter grew from just inside the darkness. It bounced off the concrete walls of the control room. Garcia shook his head at Ross as if to say, Don't take risks like that, but, if you do, don't count on me to rescue you again.

'Come out, Tony,' repeated Garcia.

'Of course.' Tony Butcher appeared from behind the door, stepping out of the darkness. 'Hey, just trying to show off to your friend here, wasn't I, Ross? He wanted to see the Godfather's car. I just can't remember which one it is.'

Ross stepped inside the control room and shone his torch across the floor.

'Mr Butcher, what is this room used for?'

'Storing gas containers, as you see. It has the climate control for the cars, that's all.'

Garcia stepped in behind Ross and he flicked on the lights.

'The floor looks like it's had something organic spilled on it,' said Ross as he squatted down and shone his light across the floor. 'Besides the smell of rotting meat, there's bleach,' said Ross.

Tony started walking back through the cars, into the garage.

'Ask the maids, they're the only ones who clean in here,' he said with a wave back over his shoulder.

Garcia spoke into his radio and the voice of Ramirez came back in reply. 'We are leaving, Inspector Ross,' said Garcia. 'It seems we have found nothing of interest here.'

Ross shook his head, nonplussed.

'How? How is that possible?'

Ross watched Tony disappear in a flap of cheesecloth and a slapping of leather sandals, and then he turned to Garcia.

'What was your brief here? Was this a social visit? I mean, I notice you're all on first-name terms here.'

'Mr Butcher is cooperating. We're done here. There's nothing more for us to do. We gave you a chance to question him over his brother's death and we looked for signs that Francisco and his daughter were here, and we found no sign.'

'We definitely need to bring the forensics team in here, and we haven't interviewed the other family members yet.'

'Ramirez has ordered the team in, it's time to leave.'

'Do you want to stay until they arrive, so that we don't risk further contamination of the site?'

'It is all in hand. No need to stay.'

Garcia walked smartly towards the garage exit. Ross caught up with him as they walked out to the side of the house.

'Where is Sergeant Willis?' Garcia asked Ramirez as they approached him standing with his officers by the gate to the property.

'She is not back yet,' he replied.

'Can you call her, please? We need to go right now.'

Ross dialled her number. It went straight to voicemail. He left a message.

'No luck – she'll come back to me as soon as she can.'

Garcia walked away. They came round to stand at the front of the villa. The squad were beginning to exit the villa, carrying bags.

Ross started to walk on the road behind the villa.

'Where are you going?'

'To look for my partner.'

'I'm here.'

Willis walked up, looking worse for wear.

'You okay?' She nodded. 'Willis?' She nodded again.

'What happened out there? Any luck?'

She shook her head. Sheena was walking past her, back to the house.

'Will there be a debriefing now?' Ross asked as they took off their jackets and watched the few boxes of evidence being carried out of Tony's house. Tony was standing watching them from the entrance. He was chatting to Ramirez as if they were old friends. Garcia looked at Ross's expression.

'This is a small town.'

'So was this always going to be a pointless exercise? Is he always tipped off?'

'Not always.'

'But he was this time?'

'It seems so. Detective Willis, what did you find over at the other villa?' Garcia asked.

'I found a gardener, Danny Miller, burning a very intense bonfire that smelled like a barbecue.'

'How did he explain it?' asked Ross.

'That a dog had died and he was burning the carcass.' Willis didn't look Ross's way as she turned to look back at the house. Sandra had come to stand with Tony and watch them leave.

Ross leaned across to Willis in the car.

'What happened out there?'

She shook her head. She couldn't talk, and her eyes flicked to the back of Garcia and Ramirez.

Inside the briefing room, the evidence boxes were piled onto the empty desks as the officers who had taken part in the raid came to sit and listen to what Ramirez had to say. He spoke in Spanish and Garcia translated for Willis and Ross.

'It's disappointing, basically. There was no indication that Francisco was there. There was nothing to implicate Tony Butcher in anything that might have happened to Señor Francisco or his daughter. We have registered them as missing persons and we will treat the case as such.'

Ross and Willis sat listening until they were asked if they had any thoughts, any questions after the raid.

Ross went to say something but changed his mind and shook his head.

'It was interesting' was all he ended up saying and he and Willis excused themselves at the end of the meeting and were about to leave.

'You need a lift back to your hotel?' Garcia asked as he caught up with them.

'No, it's okay, we can make our own way back.'

'You want to run through with us what you want to do for the rest of your stay?'

'We have a couple of people to see on the list of people Eddie was building villas for.'

'Do you want to catch up later? I feel there's a lot we need to talk about. Today didn't go so well and I want to discuss the implications of that.'

'Implications?'

'Maybe that's not the right word. What about the ramifications?'

'That's a good word.' Ross smiled but he didn't look friendly.

Garcia shrugged. His face had dropped its friendly smile and now looked irritated.

'We'll call you; maybe we can have dinner later? We'll show you what makes Marbella such an interesting place.'

'That sounds like a good idea.' Ross smiled, nodded, and shook his hand. Willis was already walking away. She gave a wave but her eyes were looking somewhere on the horizon.

'What the bloody hell is going on here?' Ross said as they walked away from the police station and headed down towards the beach.

Willis shook her head. 'There was evidence of several people having been in the area of the hut. I saw what I would say was a child's hair clip. It was just inside the hut, in the dust. I managed to pick it up without the gardener seeing.' She showed Ross.

'It's a new clip, definitely. My girls wear ones like this. Are you saying that the maid saw you pick it up?'

'Yes, she did, and what was strange was I don't think it came as a shock to her.'

'It's very weird here. We'll hit the road, we have plenty to do for the rest of the day. It will be nice to get the roof down. I'll buy you lunch first. We need to be away from here to talk it through.'

As they passed through the town of Fuengirola, Ross pulled up and parked on a narrow side road.

'Fancy a wander? There's a big market here, I read about it. We could get some lunch before we go and see the first one on our list.'

'Okay, I don't mind, if you think we have time.' She watched Ross roll up his shirtsleeves and she did the same.

'I'm going to grab some shorts from my bag,' Ross said, hand on the door ready to open it and get his bag from the boot. 'Do you want your bag?'

'I didn't bring anything else with me, just my jeans and a T-shirt.'

'Well, that's a bit cooler than black, anyway.'

He went to get their bags and they changed in the car.

The market was a brightly coloured mix of food and other goods. It took up the length of a wide tree-lined road.

Willis was looking at some sunglasses when Ross appeared by her side with a white, traditional, cotton tunic in his hand.

'What about this, Willis? With a pair of shorts?'

'You'll look great,' she said as she picked up another pair of glasses to try on.

'Not for me, for you.'

She took it off him and held it up to have a good look at it.

'Okay. That could work for me. Thanks. Where did you get it from?' He turned and pointed to a woman on a stall who was waving. 'I'll be over in a minute.'

Ross left her looking at the glasses. She was choosing a pair for Carter and one for Tina. By the time she wandered across, he'd paid for the blouse. He handed it to her.

'Thanks,' she muttered, embarrassed. 'You shouldn't do that.'

'What? It's a present between friends.'

'We don't really know each other as friends.'

'No, well, I hope we will, by the end of the week. The more we know one another, the better we'll work as a team.'

Willis couldn't argue with that, even though she felt awkward accepting the gift. She stared at the bag in her hands as she wandered away from the stall in search of a casual pair of trousers to wear with it. She glanced across at Ross and laughed, he was trying on a bullfighter's hat. He picked up a cape and swirled it in the air.

'Oh, God,' laughed Willis. 'I'm not with you.'

'I'm going to buy flamenco outfits for my girls. Eb, can you give me a hand?'

She walked across and greeted the toothless stallholder, who seemed to love smiling.

'What colour do you think?'

'I have no idea.'

'What would you have liked when you were a girl?'

'I would have hated all of them. I probably would have liked the matador's outfit best.'

'Well, they're very "girly" girls so I'll get one yellow and one pink.' He picked up the outfits and handed them over to the stallholder. Ross reached in his pocket.

'How much?'

'Aren't you going to haggle?'

'No.'

'Why?'

'Because it's not a lot of money.'

'That's beside the point. You have to haggle, otherwise he's not doing his job properly. And the next tourist that comes along will have to pay even more and so on, it will just keep creeping up,' Willis said.

'Life's too short to haggle,' he said, handing over the money and then turning to her. 'Anyway, did you haggle for the sunglasses you bought?'

'No, because he had a deal going on when you bought more than one pair: they were three for ten euros.'

'You could have gone for four for ten or three for nine or four for eight. You just didn't try.'

'Shut up.' She smiled.

'Come on, let's have a beer and lunch.' Ross picked up his flamenco dresses and steered her towards a café.

Chapter 46

'What is it, Scamp, eh?' Carter tied Scamp's lead to the handle of the bin cupboard and made sure he couldn't get away before he took a step back into the house.

'Melvin?' Carter walked a couple of paces into the hallway. Straight ahead of him, down at the end of the hall, he could see an upright fridge and the edge of a worktop and what he presumed was the glass-fronted door to the kitchen. There were other doors – one on the left and two on the right. The first of the doors to his right was closed. He knocked, heard nothing, then turned the handle and stepped into a dark bedroom that smelled of unwashed clothes and damp. The carpet was sticky beneath his feet. Carter stayed in the doorway and waited for his eyes to adjust to the dark. The bed was empty. The duvet was half on, half off.

Carter stepped back into the hallway. There was light from a room on the left filtering in through the slightly open door. Carter stopped, called again. No reply. He could smell the kitchen; someone had been cooking. The smell of roasting meat still hung in the air, not fresh, but stale, fat-congealed, charred, tinges of crackling, a hint of pulled pork. He lifted his chin to smell it again, deeper. He turned towards the partially open door on the left. Carter took a step nearer; he tried gently pushing the door open but it was jammed. He applied more pressure. He felt his weight pushing against something that was slowly giving; he heard the roll of castors.

His burned legs were spread. His cock was cut at the base of the shaft. The blood had dried down his leg. His testicles were scorched like black coals. Skin hung as curled paper off his legs, crotch, arms, torso. It hung, curled and blackened in neat pulled strips. Someone had taken time over the torture. It was an expert's touch of extracting maximum pain. Each strip of skin began with a slice and ended with a curl of crackling. Carter took a step inside the room and then recoiled. Every part of Carter's instinct told him to look away, to run, to throw up. Every part, except the police officer part. He walked towards Melvin, who was sitting in the armchair behind the door.

Melvin's arms were limp by his side but his hands were twisted palms up. His head was tilted back and from his gaping neck wound, slit beneath the chin, his tongue stuck out and was pulled down towards his sternum.

Four hours later, Della was done. She looked at herself in the mirror. Tracy fiddled with the long fringe on the shoulder-length brunette wig, swept the fringe to one side.

'There, pretty sure no one would think you're wearing a mask. You'll be okay with fixing this on yourself with more liquid latex?'

'Definitely.' Della smiled at her reflection. She could see the face of a woman whom no one would look twice at. It was a hard face. It was a face that would be difficult to remember.

'It suits you to go dark. The eyebrows look dramatic; they change your look completely. You'll need to dye them if you want them to stay that dark. Use this brown dye and then add black with pencil, otherwise they'll be too obvious without the mask. I think they're important to finish the look. You just need to go and buy a new wardrobe now. I would stick to dark colours. What about going for trouser suits instead of your usual dresses or jeans? A smart Armani suit maybe. That would look fab with a straight wig like this.' Tracy took Della's brunette wig off and placed a long black one on. She made sure the shorter fringe was sitting properly. 'That's pretty chic. I prefer this one. It goes with your Roman nose, the cheekbones.'

'So do I but, unfortunately, I don't want to look great: I want to look like someone who doesn't want to be recognised. The other wig is the one.'

Tracy swapped it back.

'Great, thanks, Tracy. I love my new face.' She laughed. 'You're a genius. I need to buy some cheap leggings, a big hoody, I need to scour a few charity shops, I think, and I need to take a passport photo now.'

'Can you get a passport?' Tracy asked, and then immediately shook her head. 'No, don't answer that.'

'Yes. I can, if I pay enough. Eddie's left me some names of people who can help.'

'I'll take the photo for you here, I use a good camera for taking photos of the models downstairs.' Tracy picked up a camera case from the shelf at the side of the room and she cleared some space.

'Come and stand here against this sheet. This will be fine. Tracy took several photos. 'Where do you want me to send the photos?'

'Better email me them to this phone, please, Tracy.' She gave her the number.

'Here, take it all off now and we'll put it in a plastic box for you, I'll bag up everything you need.'

'What do I owe you, Trace?'

'Nothing, you've often been kind to me in the past. If you could have Jackson and me out to stay, when you're home and things have settled down? He would love it.'

'It's a deal.' She hugged her.

'Anything else you need, just ring me,' said Tracy.

Della used the reception phone on her way out of the salon. 'Where do you want to meet?'

'Holloway Road, drive along it towards Archway from Highbury and Islington, left turn just before you pass Holloway Tube Station on your left, Hornsey Street. I'll be waiting along there. If you are going to put it into your satnav, you'll have to make sure it can be erased.'

'That's okay. I think I'll be able to find this.'

'I'll wait for you outside and we'll get the car off the road into the underground car park.'

Carter was standing just where he said he would be when Della pulled up beside him and he got into the passenger seat and gave her instructions for parking in the underground car park. He used his security code to gain entrance. There were mostly empty spaces.

'This is a new development. I don't remember any of this being here.'

'Yes, new stuff being built all the time. But this place still has a few empty flats.

'This is a fairly new acquisition by the police. My office is just up the road, maybe it's a bit near, but I would feel better if I could get to you quickly.'

They took the lift up to the third floor and Carter opened the door to an apartment that was smelling unlived in.

'The furnishings are a bit Spartan, I know.'

'It's fine.' She smiled reassuringly at Carter. 'Thanks for choosing this one for me. I know how grotty they can be. Are you okay, Dan? You look done in. Is there anything I should know?'

'I'm fine.' Carter was thinking to himself that there were a million things Della shouldn't know. There wasn't one positive thing he could tell her. He had decided it was best to withhold the information about Melvin and his necktie. 'Let's concentrate on you.' He smiled. 'What happened when you got to Shoreditch Mews, after leaving us yesterday?'

'Nothing happened – not much, anyway. Laurence turned up acting weird, like he owned me. Marco was nowhere to be seen until about one in the morning, when he turned up looking like he'd been cage fighting. And Harold was his usual monosyllabic self. He disappeared again for most of the evening. He didn't want to talk when he came in just before Marco, in the early hours. Marco was still up but they don't really speak to one another. They're not the best of mates, neither one trusts the other, but both of them are pretty focused on what Tony wants.

'I had to make sure, if they want to get the diamonds, they both understand these are my rules. I think Marco will be meeting with the Zapata cartel this evening. He said so.'

'We can put a tail on him. Do you think you can get a bug on him somewhere?'

'I think if I try, and I fail, I'll probably end up like Eddie.

But, he's going to expect to be followed, watched. He's going to be suspicious if you don't try.'

'I feel so much stress about all this, Della. I wish you'd just run. I wish you'd hide away and we'll figure out some other way of letting you live your life in peace. I feel responsible. It's almost unbearable.'

'Dan' – she smiled – 'you know it's not possible for me to run, but I thank you from the bottom of my heart for your concern. Whatever happens, I know you'll do your best, and that's usually good enough. Just think like a detective, Dan, not like a friend.'

Carter nodded. 'You said you had to follow leads, check security boxes, pretend to meet old cons. Have you worked out how it will look best?'

'Yes, I'm starting with the security box this afternoon. I think I will go out to the countryside in Kent after that. That's where Tony always thought the stash was hidden, in a lockup somewhere.'

'What's going to be in the security box to help your story?' Carter gave her a sideways smile.

She held up her hands. 'I really don't know, believe me. It was Eddie's style to sit on stuff, save it for a rainy day. Probably there will be cash. Maybe there will be jewellery. He used to give me a lot of jewellery. I know there will be something useful in there for us because he left me instructions about it.'

'When does the shipment arrive from Mexico?'

'I'm not sure even Marco knows that yet. I'll find out from him as soon as he does but we're talking days not weeks.' She smiled, nodded. 'It will be all right, Dan. I told you, just keep your detective's head on and we'll be fine.'

'And you keep your wits about you.'

Della opened the curtains a little and looked down at the courtyard below.

'I will, I promise. This is the most important week of my life, Dan. I have to do or die. I know you can only help me so far. I know you'll do your best for me, like you always did.' She turned back from the window and smiled at him. He bowed his head.

'Am I allowed a hug?' she asked, cocking her head to one side and smiling.

He opened his arms.

In the courtyard below Laurence stepped out of vision of the apartment. He'd followed Della with the tracker he'd put in her handbag. During the day he'd lost her for a few hours when she went into a beauty salon on Upper Street but then he'd picked up her trail again and it had led him here, right into the arms of her old lover. He looked at his phone: he had a good photo of them both.

Chapter 47

Ross was laughing and joking with the café owner as he ordered tapas from the menu in perfect Spanish.

Willis was staring at him.

'What?' He smiled when he had finished talking to the owner.

'You can speak Spanish? You told Ramirez and Garcia that you couldn't.'

He shrugged, nodded. 'I've been out here on many occasions. They must have seen that. Pretty sure they knew I could understand what they were saying because they were careful. They were cautious.'

'Did you hear anything that would lead you to be sure about them? That they were corrupt?'

'I've heard that they work in interesting ways from others. Garcia comes from a family of criminals and Ramirez has accepted hospitality from Butcher, stayed in his ski chalet in the Sierra Nevada, that kind of thing. But I have also heard they have been responsible for the arrest of two big drug barons. One was over here from South America. Another was Spanish.'

'Are they selective, then, in who they go after?'

'That's the point, isn't it?' Ross poured out his beer into

the glass provided. Willis was drinking Pepsi. 'Are they choosy about when to be good policemen and when to be bad? And does the good outweigh the bad or is it always tipped in Tony Butcher's favour? Or is it the way they work?'

Ross's phone signalled he had a VIP email.

'Excuse me.' He picked it up to check it. 'Interesting,' he said as he turned it round and showed it to Willis. 'This is a message back from the Dream Stone Fireplace Company. Or, to be precise, the message has boomeranged back to me undelivered. They can't be trading at all with the public. It all stays in-house. What about Manson?'

'It'll be interesting to talk to people today who had villas built by Eddie Butcher and Billy Manson,' replied Willis. 'I want to hear what the people who did business with him thought of him.'

'The main thing is to talk to the people he's building for right now,' said Ross. 'If there is a dispute, we need to find out. I would love to look around a place properly. You okay? You're quiet. What news is there from home?'

'There's been a development with Della Butcher.'

'Yeah, I know about the deal with the diamonds. Thanks for deciding to tell me about it, though, I appreciate that you're not one for holding secrets between partners.'

'Who told you?'

'Chief Inspector Bowie was obliged to, in the end. If we are to catch Tony we had to know something as big as this. What are your thoughts on it?'

'It seems like an enormous risk for Della. It's the riskiest plan altogether. To pretend to have the diamonds to give to a cartel in exchange for their cocaine. Is that going to work? And Della hasn't even really got them?

She's lying to a cartel at the same time as she's taking their cocaine.'

'It won't be her. All she has to do is convince Marco and Harold and therefore Tony that she has the diamonds. They have to know where they are and then the deal can be done. Counterfeit money has been used before to lure and trap drug dealers. We think it will work.'

'We?'

'The department.'

'I suppose so.' Willis wasn't convinced. 'But this is one cartel taking over another. If it goes wrong, a lot of people will be at risk.'

'Yes. If it goes wrong Della will be dead. This is a risky business. We are in prevention now, not dealing with the aftermath. This is drug dealing, not murder. Everything about this is risky. If it goes wrong, if Della ends up dead, she probably won't be the only one, and the news will read that she was killed by the same drug dealers that killed her husband. Tony, Harold, probably the whole family will be executed by one cartel or the other – or both.'

'If it goes wrong, we may not catch the cocaine dealers but we may still seize the shipment, which is reputed to be the biggest ever to cross the Atlantic. For me it's a win–win situation. Would I risk it if I were Della? Having seen Tony today, realising what he's capable of, yes I probably would. Who would want Tony in their life?'

'What are we going to do about Ramirez and Garcia?' asked Willis.

'I think we should meet them tonight, let them show us a good time, watch how they are in this place. I'd like to see the extent of their corruption, how people talk to them, treat them. We should learn a lot by watching them with their friends. Then we'll head home tomorrow. Agreed?'

'Agreed. I want to get back now. I want to be on hand with this plan of Della's.'

'You also want to watch over your partner, and see he doesn't stray.'

'You know that's not going to happen. Carter is unorthodox but he's smart and he's a step ahead of most detectives. You wouldn't think so, but it's instinctive to him. I don't have any worries about him.'

Chapter 48

After finishing with their visits to look at a few of the villas Eddie had built and to talk to the expat owners, they got in the car to drive back to the hotel.

Ross looked across at Willis as he fastened his seat belt and prepared to drive off.

'Nobody who actually knows anything of value is going to talk to us. I've had enough. I'd rather spend my time having a nice cool swim than talk to lowlife, high-living scum.'

'I thought you were enjoying it.'

'What, talking to Mr Silver Fox, barrow boy turned billionaire by ripping off ordinary folks? No thanks.'

'Should we talk to one of the others on our list?' Willis scanned through the names on her iPad.

'No. We could waste a week getting around half of these luxury villas and by then I will rethink my universe and I will turn to you and say, "You know what, my dear? Crime really does pay." And we'll drive off into the sunset like an alternative Thelma and Louise and live the rest of our lives on oysters and champagne.'

Willis frowned. 'You're quite bonkers.'

'I know. Being a bit mad keeps me sane.'

They spent the next fifty minutes of the drive in silence as
Willis rested her head back on the seat and closed her eyes.
The warm air made her feel happy as they drove by the sea
again on the coastal road. It filled her senses with a special
memory of the rare occasions in her life that she had ever
gone to the beach. The long coach ride, full of its own special intrigue, followed by the pile-out onto the beach of all
the children from the home, and then the hours of laughter.
Those were happy times in her childhood. There weren't
many and they never included her mother. Willis thought
about what Ross said. Being a bit mad hadn't kept her mother
at all sane. But, then, her mother wasn't just a bit mad.

'You okay?' Ross asked. 'You've gone quiet.'

'Fine, just enjoying the scenery.'

'What do you want to do about this evening?' asked
Ross. 'I sense you're not that keen on seeing the bright
lights of Puerto Banús?'

'It's just I haven't come prepared. I don't have anything
to wear. I don't have any money. I think it's not my kind
of thing. I have so much work to catch up on.'

Ross raised his hand for her to stop. 'Okay, I get it, but
do me a favour and just come out for a few hours. We can
really check these guys out in their natural habitat. This
is all on me. I will claim it back on expenses. Wear your
jeans and the white top again. It's perfect for this place.'

'Okay.' Willis's phone went off. 'Robbo?'

'The second set of samples you took from the Paradise
Villas warehouse are back.'

'Good, anything?'

'Where the boxes were resting?'

'Yes?'

'Corresponds to distinct indentations, gatherings of

dust and raised deposits of soil around the box edges, corners . . . Remember, you took photographs?'

'*Yes*,' Willis emphasised. She was getting irritated with
Robbo.

'They found substantial traces of Grade A Colombian
cocaine mixed with a small amount of stone composite.
Looks likely someone's been making fireplaces out of com-
pressed cocaine.'

Willis sat up in the passenger seat and turned wide-eyed
to Ross.

'When are you coming back here?' Robbo asked.

'Tomorrow. Have you told Carter?'

'I can't get hold of him at the moment but I will tell him
asap.'

'Manson has to be at the heart of this,' said Willis. 'With
or without Eddie.'

'Get Ross to help us on this. He had photos of Manson
and Marco. We need him to check for more of the same. Any
photo which includes Manson at all and sightings of the white
van. We need that second location – the place he transports
the boxes to. I'm thinking it must a laboratory of a fairly big
size. The process of extracting the cocaine from these large
features must involve quite a bit of space. It shouldn't be too
hard to find business parks with that capability.'

'Okay, will talk to him now. See you tomorrow, Robbo.'
Willis came off the phone.

Ross's head swivelled back and forth, from road to
Willis, waiting.

'Cocaine comes in many forms,' teased Willis.

'Don't do this,' Ross groaned. 'Just get on with it, for
goodness' sake.'

'It's disguised in things like gel bras, woven Inca baskets, fresh yams with the centres hollowed out and, wait for it, bespoke, composite, marble fireplace surrounds.'

'God, you're kidding me. It was staring us in the bloody face all the time,' Ross said as he swerved to avoid a chicken who had decided to cross the road at that moment.

'Not quite,' Willis frowned.

'Almost,' replied Ross.

Ross drove along the mountain road back towards the coast. He switched the mute button on the satnav so he could concentrate.

'Where does that put Manson?' he asked. 'Does he work for Tony?'

'We need to have more on Manson if you can help with that.'

'Sure, I'll get on it. He's definitely made some bad life choices, if he thinks he can start working for the cartels and have some control over it. Unless he is the innocent party here? What if it was Eddie that was doing a sideline in making things out of cocaine and Manson's just realised what he's landed in?' said Ross. 'What's Carter going to do? What's his take on this?'

'I don't know yet. Robbo hasn't spoken to him yet.' Ross glanced across at Willis; she ignored it. She had her eyes glued to the road ahead. The narrow lanes didn't allow for the speeds Ross liked to drive.

'We definitely have a few more questions to ask Manson,' she said.

'Surely, now, this should be handed completely over to the NCA. This is our territory. It's quite clear we are never going to solve this murder. This is way more complicated than just a murder and we both know the murder was just the cherry on the cake.'

'It was always our case. We're hanging on to it,' answered Willis.

He laughed drily. 'We've been specialising in bringing Tony Butcher down for so many years I've gone grey, or I would have if I'd let it happen. We have all the contacts in place now. We are very near. This is bigger than Eddie Butcher's murder.'

'Did you know about Manson?'

'No, not directly.'

'That's a no, then.'

'I accept we have been useful to one another but now the murder squad should step aside. The National Crime Agency has the powers that you don't. We can cross boundaries; impound goods in customs; we have immigration powers. We are set up to deal with this situation.'

'So, you never thought it might be made into things like fireplaces and put into expensive villas?'

'No.'

Chapter 49

Carter left and went back to Melvin's flat in Bethnal Green. He sat outside in his car. The body had been removed but the place was quiet with the work of the white-suited forensics officers, bringing a type of serenity in the methodical search of Melvin's last minutes. Carter got out and came to stand at the door to the flat.

Sandford, the chief forensics officer, passed across the corridor in front of the door, and came back to talk to Carter.

'Have you got anything for me?' asked Carter. 'It looked similar to Eddie Butcher's injuries to me.'

Sandford nodded. 'We might be in luck this time. He was killed where you found him; we might find something of the killer here. How far did you walk into the flat?'

'Not far. You saw where the body was, just inside the lounge? I smelled it first, the smell of roasting flesh.'

'I'm amazed he didn't just set the house on fire. He'd used the blowtorch on just about every inch of the man's skin.'

'It was never his intention to hide the evidence with a fire. This man loves torturing his victims for no good reason, it seems. The killer wanted me to find Melvin like that. He sent me a message with Melvin's missing dog. This man is a frigging monster.'

'Did you know the deceased?'

'Yeah, we used to talk.'

'As in?'

'He was an informant, of sorts, but just a casual arrangement; he never told me anything worth knowing in all the years I knew him. Certainly, nothing worth killing him over. The most he did was take photos of people on the evening of Eddie Butcher's funeral. One of those used to be in a Colombian death squad.'

'That would explain things.'

'He was a nice bloke, been through the mill. Not the luckiest chap. He gave tours of this area, showing people where the Krays lived, that kind of thing. But he hadn't worked for a couple of weeks. He was scared. Someone took his dog. He told me they were trying to frighten him off from giving his tours.'

'I guess he didn't listen.' Sandford was standing still and listening to Carter for once. Normally he walked away when Carter started talking. The two irritated one another. Sandford was a rugby man and Carter was football. Carter spent money on designer clothes, he loved shopping. Sandford let his wife buy his clothes for him from Marks & Spencer.

Sandford smiled at Carter kindly. He had registered that this was different from the many murder sites they'd worked together. This was personal. And then Sandford remembered he needed to be somewhere else.

'I'll leave you to it. You don't need me bothering you,' said Carter. Sandford had already gone back in to continue his work. As Carter looked past him he could see the pieces of charred, curled skin stuck on the armchair.

'By the way, what did you do with the dog?' Sandford turned to ask.

'Pam, who works with Robbo, has taken it.'

Carter walked back along the road to the Blind Beggar, looking at Melvin's photos on his phone. He had a look at Melvin's social media to see who had written on it. There were a few messages from locals. There were lots of reviews from happy clients who had experienced one of his East End Gangster tours. Carter decided he'd walk the tour himself. First he went to see Chrissie at the Blind Beggar and ordered a coffee. The barman went off to make it, annoyed: it always pissed him off when people ordered coffee in a pub. Chrissie came through from the back and stopped in her tracks when she saw Carter.

'Can I have a word?' he asked.

She nodded. They went through to the garden at the back, where they would have privacy.

'Did you hear about Melvin?'

'Yes. I feel sick to my stomach. Is it true he took hours to die?'

'He was tortured for a long time. He died by having his throat slit, at the end.'

'Sick bastard.'

'Got anyone in mind when you say that?'

She turned away. 'I can only repeat what I already told you about what happened last night. Like I said, Harold and Lev were in, and the tall strange-looking blond man with the bun; he left with Harold. There were a handful of others. They all saw Melvin drunk. They were all quite kind to him, really, except when he started getting aggressive. He started accusing them of trying to stop him working, stealing his dog, he got nasty. Even Harold tried to make him calm down but he couldn't.'

'Harold left at the same time as Melvin, you said?'

'No, Harold and the blond man left half an hour after.' She shook her head. 'This isn't Harold's style. I know Harold Butcher's style. I've seen it many times over the years. Harold is a mean, quick-tempered man, but he wouldn't torture someone just for fun. I've said all I know.'

'Okay, thanks.' Carter looked at Melvin's route for his tour, although he already knew it would take a circular route past the gym where the Krays boxed, past their old house, their school.

Carter walked down to St Matthew's and along past the railway bridge and the ballerina graffiti. He crossed over and headed towards Lev's bakery. He could see Lev watching him.

'Hello, Lev, how's it going?'

The café was empty. Lev was keeping himself very busy behind the counter, chopping iceberg lettuce.

'It's going okay, thank you, Inspector.'

'You heard what happened to Melvin?'

Lev nodded. His eyes made fleeting eye contact with Carter's before he tipped the lettuce into a serving container and wiped his hands on his apron.

'I hear you were in the pub last night when Melvin was there.'

Lev nodded.

'What kind of state was he in?'

Lev shrugged, as if there was nothing really unusual in the evening.

'He was drunk. He'd lost his dog. It's understandable.'

Lev moved on to carving thin slices of cucumber with a mandolin cutter.

'He was sure someone had taken the dog,' Lev said as he concentrated on making the wafer-thin cucumber slices and trying to stop his fingers getting near the blade.

'I think he was right. Someone did have his dog. I don't know who or why.' Carter got out a photo of Marco to show Lev. 'How do you know him?'

'I don't know him, Inspector. I know *of* him.' Lev stopped slicing and squinted at the photo. Carter knew what he was doing: he was trying to put a location to it.

'That was taken from this bakery, taken from your shop by Melvin.'

'He came in here most days.'

'He said he was here when this man, Marco Zapata, came in. What did Zapata want?'

Lev raised his shoulders in an exaggerated 'Am I supposed to remember details like that?' He resumed slicing the cucumber.

'Did you go in the Blind Beggar to meet with Marco Zapata last night?'

'Damn and blast!' Lev quickly grabbed some kitchen towel and wrapped it around a bleeding finger. He threw the cucumber in the bin as blood began dripping over it. 'I've shaved the top of my finger off.' He looked at Carter half-accusingly. Lev reached beneath the counter and pulled out a few plasters, then went to the corner of the bakery and put his bleeding finger under the cold tap.

'Yeah, that looks nasty,' said Carter in a tone and with an expression that said the opposite.

'Look, Inspector, I know of Marco Zapata.'

'What do you know?'

'That he's friends with the Butcher family.'

'Does that surprise you?'

'No, not really. They are all Mafia, aren't they? They will all join up when they want something that benefits them all.'

'What is it they want, do you think?'

Lev shrugged, he pulled his finger from under the cold water and wrapped it tightly to stop the bleeding.

'You're asking the wrong person. I serve them coffee and bagels, make polite conversation, laugh at their jokes and I give them a donation now and again. For that, I get left alone. I don't have any reason to gossip or to speculate. I don't want to lose my life.'

'But you choose to drink in a pub where they go?'

'I haven't seen Marco Zapata in there before. I don't go there often, maybe once a month. It's my local. Do you need any more reasons?'

'So last night was a once-a-month outing for you?'

He nodded.

'What did people say about Melvin's behaviour?'

'Nothing really. He was just loud and drunk.'

'Did you hear what Melvin said to Marco, or Harold?'

'He said the same to all of us, that he knew things, that one of us had stolen his dog.' Lev put plasters over his fingertip and then two latex gloves on top of that as the blood still seeped through and began filling the finger in the glove.

'My God,' he said irritably. 'Inspector, do you mind? I have to call my cousin to help. I can't cut the ingredients with this hand like this.'

'That's okay. Where is he, local?'

'Yes.'

'You want to call him?'

'I'll do it in a minute. When you're done with questions.'

'Okay, I just want to ask you something else, Lev, and I know you're not going to want to answer it but I need you to. Did you hear who killed Eddie Butcher?'

'No, I didn't.'

'I can tell you something for nothing, Lev, Eddie and Melvin were both killed by someone specialising in the Colombian cartel's form of torture.

'Melvin was killed because he was making a stand against the likes of Marco. If you locals don't stand up to it, Lev, this place will sink deeper into drugs and gangs; is that what you want? I've walked Melvin's route for his tour. It always went past here, always past the church, the old pub. Did something about the tour piss Marco off?'

Lev shook his head but at the same time he stood tall and faced Carter.

'I can't help you. Sorry, Inspector. I wish I could but I don't know why Melvin was killed.'

Carter looked at the poster on the wall, the news clippings of Lev's history, how his grandfather had come to the UK and had worked his way up to own the bakery and his famous bagels.

'Your grandfather would be turning in his grave. If Melvin got killed for doing a tour of this area and pissing off some thug, what's going to happen to you and your family along the line? Where's the line in the sand, Lev?'

Chapter 50

After Carter had gone, Della had a good look around the apartment for hidden cameras. She didn't find any. She put the television on while she went into the bathroom and got out all the things she had from Tracy. She looked at the latex mask and the dark wig. She had a big holdall-type bag, a short duffle coat with a hood, old trainers of Tracy's, a dark blue baggy tracksuit and a T-shirt. She had an outfit she would never have worn in real life. She locked the things away in the cupboard and took the key with her. Then she drove back to the apartment.

She drove to 1 Shoreditch Mews and parked her hire car. She let herself into the apartment and walked up the stairs. There was the sound of a blaring television and football on.

Marco glanced her way. He was sitting on the sofa with his feet on the coffee table, watching the sports.

'Where have you been?'

'I told you, I have business to attend to. You look like shit. Go and have a shower and a shave. I need you to do some work for me this afternoon.'

He turned back to look at the television and Della went into the kitchen to make herself a coffee. She stood by the machine, listening to Marco swearing at the television and then the sound of him getting up and switching it off. He stood behind her.

'What work, princess?'

'Don't call me that; I already told you not to.' Della felt Marco breathing on her neck. She shivered. 'And go and wash, you absolutely stink.'

Marco laughed as he swaggered out and Della heard the *en suite* bathroom door slam in his bedroom.

She went into her room and put the diamond into the safe in the wardrobe. The safe was only a small one. These flats had been designed and built for travelling businessmen to use instead of hotels.

She came back out and got her coffee as Marco came out of his bedroom with a bathrobe on.

'So, what's the plan, my lady?'

Della scowled at him; she picked up her coffee and went to sit at the Perspex dining table. He came to sit opposite her. He sat with his knees splayed; he slouched over the table. He grinned.

Della stared at him. 'I'm going to Hatton Garden to get what I need from the safety-deposit box. I'm going to need you close by.'

'I should come inside with you,' Marco said.

'No thanks. Stand outside and look like you are taking the job seriously and not casing the joint. Put a suit on.'

Marco's mood was souring. Whatever amusement he had hoped to gain from winding Della up, it wasn't happening. Now his face dropped visibly. He stood and allowed his dressing gown to fall fully apart. He had shaved his pubic hair. He had a semi. He looked at her and grinned.

Della didn't blink. 'Get dressed.'

The front door opened and closed and she heard the sound of footsteps. Harold's unmistakable light feet. He had never lost the boxer's physique, like an old feather-weight you wouldn't mess with. He was almost silent on his feet.

He came up level with Marco and ignored him and walked past into the kitchen. He poured himself a coffee and brought it across to sit opposite Della. Marco left the room.

'What are you up to, Della?'

'Up to? You know what I'm up to. I'm finding the diamonds.'

'You know what I mean.'

'No, I'm sorry, Harold, I don't.'

'Where did you go this morning? What were you doing?'

'Did you have me followed? Because, if you did, Harold, the deal is off, and try telling that to Tony?'

'Laurence came here at eight this morning. He seemed to think you had made arrangements with him. You start getting cosy with Laurence before your husband's cold in his grave and you're not the person I thought you were, Della. Not at all.'

'Why did he think that?' Della felt a wave of relief come over her. But then she could never be sure about Harold. He would definitely have her followed, but she was sure they didn't see her beyond Tracy's this morn-ing. Even then, she had walked around several routes before ending up at the beauty salon. She thought she was safe.

'Then we have Marco with his tongue and his dick hanging out. This is turning into a *Carry On* film. You better stop playing whatever game you think you're playing and get on with trying to stay alive.'

'I'm focused, Harold, just try and keep the animals in their cages.'

'Laurence wouldn't just hit on you without encouragement.'

'Wouldn't he?'

Harold looked away as he thought about it, and then he raised his palms above the table and sighed.

'Okay, I accept, he's probably always had a thing for you and that animal in there is not fussy.'

'Thanks.'

'You know what I mean. You are a beautiful woman, Della, in your prime. You will get through this. We both of us stand to gain our freedom from this deal. Tony has promised me I can retire when this is all in place. I will build on the plot behind you. I hope I can be a friend to you, Della. My feuding days are over.'

'The people I am going to meet with will know what a set-up looks and feels like. They will run a mile from me if they get a whiff of betrayal. I need to be left alone to meet and talk with these people. They don't even know they have the information I'm looking for. Don't, I repeat, don't fuck it up, Harold. We don't have the time. When is this shipment coming? When does it have to be paid for?'

'Next week, Thursday.'

'So we have eight days to make this happen. That's a hell of a feat.'

'Can you do it?'

'I think so.'

'You have to *know* so. If that shipment arrives and there is no payment then there will be two cartels after our skins.'

'Wait here.' Della went into her room and opened the safe. She came back with a cloth bag containing the large uncut diamond that she'd brought with her from Spain.

Harold put his hand inside and lifted out the stone. He weighed it in his hand and turned it round, looking at its brilliance.

'Jesus Christ! That's a wonderful sight. Must be worth a million. Do you have lots more like this?'

'The rest are almost in my hands.'

Harold stood and reached across and kissed Della loudly and vigorously on both cheeks.

'Christ, Della. I never thought you was good for it. You've come good, girl. Tony will be jumping around when I tell him. When can you get the rest of them?'

'I'm working on it.'

'Well, I'm sold on you, girl. You tell me what you need and I'll get it. Fucking hell!' He held it aloft again and the light glanced across its facets. Marco walked in with a deep-blue suit on and a black shirt.

'Marco!' Harold called out to him. Marco walked across. He took the fist-sized diamond from Harold's hands and weighed in his own, then held it up to the light.

'Oh, yes. Now the fun begins.'

'You keep this one and show it to your Colombians,' said Della, 'but tell them to be very careful, tongues will start wagging when this kind of diamond, this big, this expensive, turns up in London.'

'Okay, no problem. A diamond expert is flying in from Johannesburg this evening.'

'What's his name?' asked Della.

Marco focused on her past the diamond. 'You don't need to know. Just get on with your job and I'll get on with mine.'

Chapter 51

'Follow me, please.'

Della cleared security and verification and she was escorted down in the lift to the vaults. The combinations and locks were passed and the clerk opened the massive door. He walked along the walls of boxes until he double-checked he had the right box, and took it out from its space.

He led Della into a small anteroom the size of a cupboard, where she could view the box privately.

She waited until she was alone and then opened the box with the key from Eddie's safe. She knew what she thought would be in there, but she was hoping there would be no surprise that left her feeling betrayed. The box was only small, but it was heavy. She knew that by the way the clerk had carried it. She steeled herself and flipped the lid right back as she stood over the box to take in the contents. At the top of the box, resting on a cloth bag, was a letter to Della. She smiled as she read it. Eddie was trying to take care of her in the only way he knew how. Under the letter was a Walther handgun and a box of ammunition.

Della pulled out the cloth bag and sat down to look inside; there was a rolling movement in the bag.

She tipped its contents gently onto a tray provided on the table. There was a collection of diamonds, some cut, some still in their original state; they were even better than the uncut one she had found in the safe at home. Della ran her fingertips over the diamonds and picked up a massive pink one that she recognised. She had seen pictures of it on the news. It was referred to as the Lost Rose. It had been an early find from the Argyle mine in Australia. It had been stolen when it was waiting to be exhibited in Dubai. The rough diamond had been cut into eight stones; the largest was in front of her now. She knew it was the same pink diamond in the ring that Eddie had given her for her thirtieth birthday. He had always said it would be the first of many and that the stones would be just as perfect and just as rosy pink as the first one: now she was looking at the reason he knew that.

At the bottom of the box, wrapped in plastic, was a wodge of fifty-pound notes. Della emptied the box.

Marco was waiting outside.

'I have people to see,' Marco said, as Della got into the car.

'What's the problem?' She watched him sweat on a cold day.

'Everything has changed. The shipment is only three days away now; it will arrive in a container at the docks. It needs to be moved fast. We need everything in place. Get the payment organised straight away.'

'Which dock?'

'Why do you want to know? You just get the diamonds all together in one place and make sure they are good. They will be examined by an expert. You have them now?' He looked at her bag.

'Not yet, but I will. I'll get them together in one place and they can stay there until the shipment arrives then I'll tell you where the diamonds are and I will have done my job.'

Marco turned to her and took her face in his hand and began squeezing. 'Your job ends when I say it does. When I have the cocaine in one hand and the diamonds in the other, then, only then, you can go.'

She wrenched her face away and instinctively put her hand inside her handbag to feel for the gun. They drove home in silence as Marco dropped Della and drove away at speed.

Della got inside, rang Carter and left him a message: 'We have to be prepared to step it up. Marco says the shipment is arriving early in three days' time. They're flying in a diamond expert from Johannesburg this evening. There's no way the diamonds I have add up to more than thirty million; he's going to know that. If I can get away later I will go to the flat, maybe see you there?'

Marco had the uncut diamond that Della had given him to be examined for quality on the seat next to him. It was wrapped in cloth. He pulled up to think. He looked at his phone again. He was tempted to smash it on the dashboard. Things had begun to really irritate him; he wasn't feeling in control. Tony was a liability. Marco had done everything he could to secure the finances. He had planned this. He'd spent years building his reputation up in the Colombian death squads and then moving to Spain to continue his work with the extermination cell in Marbella. He had ingratiated himself into Tony's inner circle, and now all his hard work had led him here, reliant on a woman! He must show his family that he could be the man to lead Europe's branch of the Zapata cartel. As soon as this deal was done he would kill Tony and take over the whole outfit. He was contemplating leaving Laurence alive as a figurehead. Laurence was rising in his esteem.

He sat back and watched the pedestrians scowling at him as they walked by. He'd pulled up on the pavement. He jammed the gear stick into reverse and just missed a woman with a pram who had started walking across the road behind him. She screamed at him through the back window; he swore at her and drove off, phone still in his hand.

Chapter 52

Carter listened to the message from Della. He checked the time – it was nearly five. He phoned Robbo.

'There's a diamond expert coming in on a plane from Johannesburg to London this evening. Check all the passenger lists and quick as you can. We need to know who it is.'

'Are you on your way back?'

'Yes. I'll be with you asap.'

Carter then phoned Maxi Seymour.

'How are you doing?'

'I'm doing okay. It's happening. I'm very discreetly sourcing diamonds that I can have on loan. Of course, if we don't get them back, my life is over.' He laughed nervously.

'I appreciate this, Maxi.'

Robbo had the flight details and passenger lists ready for Carter when he walked into the office forty minutes later.

'Here's the man. He's arriving at Heathrow in three hours.' He handed Carter a file as Carter sat down at the desk.

'Roland de Soir.'

'He's a forty-five-year-old South African diamond

expert, wealthy Swiss family, banking stock,' said Robbo. 'He worked for the Diamond Trading Company for fifteen years as one of their top guys before he was sacked three years ago for trading in blood diamonds on the side. He finds it hard to get legitimate work now – he's blacklisted.'

'Get hold of our pals in Border Control for me and tell them to pull him off the plane the second it lands. He's not to clear customs,' Carter said as he stood up and reached for his coat. 'We don't want to give him time to contact anyone. Tell them to make sure he doesn't use his phone on the plane; get the stewardess to lose it temporarily. I'm going to drive straight out to Heathrow now.'

Chapter 53

'Was that *the* Lineker's Bar, Willis?' asked Ross as they stood on the street outside a busy bar where a hen party were dancing their way inside, dressed in pink tutus and false breasts. She had been a long-suffering listener while Carter went on about teams and players and relegation and cup wins. They had spent an hour drinking in the bar and Willis had only just noticed its name.

'It's his brother,' Willis answered, looking away and down the cobbled street.

'Do you want to try somewhere less noisy?' asked Ramirez.

They stepped out of the way of a yellow Ferrari that was revving its engine inches from their legs.

'We'll take you to the best in town.'

'That's okay, but thanks, I'd rather get back. I'm not really dressed for it,' Willis said.

'Listen, all is relaxed here in Marbella; you will fit in fine,' assured Garcia. 'The richest people are the most simple dressers.'

'Somehow I don't believe that,' Willis said as she looked at the women passing her with stellar heels and tiny sparkly dresses. 'Look, do you mind if I don't come? I have a lot of things to write up. I haven't filed a report in two days.'

'It's totally up to you, Eb,' said Ross. 'I'll carry on, if you don't mind.'

'Of course not. It will make me feel less guilty.'

'Let us get you a taxi.'

'I can walk, no problem.'

'Nonsense.' Garcia made a call and a taxi pulled up. He told the driver the address and Ross gave the driver twenty euros.

'I'll see you back at the apartment, don't wait up.'

Ramirez passed in a bottle of water. 'You'll need to drink this. It's the sun and the sangria. Go to bed.'

Willis left Ross and the two Spanish detectives to it and headed home. She was feeling a bit worse for wear and very hungry as she tried to find more than the bottle of water she'd already drunk. Ross kept telling her to charge anything she wanted, within reason, to the room; after all, they had to eat, and so far the evening had consisted of a lot of drinking but no actual food and she had reached a point where she was about to start eating herself. She ordered a double burger with all the trimmings and the tray arrived.

She switched on her laptop and signed into Skype.

'Teen?'

'Ebbers! Where are you?'

'Oh, God, Teen. You'd love this place. It's so warm. I've already got a bit of a tan.'

'You've always got a tan. You okay? You seem knackered.'

'I mean, I'm darker, it's so lovely and warm here, and it's only December.'

'Jeezus, I'm coming out there. How long are you there for?'

'I'm coming back tomorrow, but you know what, Teen? It's made me realise I need to come away like this more often.'

'I'm always telling you that.'

'I know, that's why I'm saying it. You're so right. We need some more fun and sunshine and bars and all that in our lives, Teen.'

'You okay, Ebbers? You suddenly seem really pissed, Eb. I've never seen you this drunk. Are you still drinking?'

'No, look, I'm on water.' She held up the bottle. 'And look, Teen.' She turned the webcam on her stack of burgers and fries, onion rings and coleslaw. 'I'm in heaven.'

Chapter 54

'Evening, Mr de Soir. Sorry to delay your disembarkation.'

Carter walked into the Border Control interview room at Heathrow, carrying a tray with de Soir's briefcase in it as well as a new phone and an envelope containing SIM cards. He placed the tray on the desk and sat down opposite de Soir.

'Why have I been stopped from entering the UK?' De Soir had a mild South African hardness to his otherwise smooth well-spoken voice.

'Not stopped, just delayed. We need to ask you some questions. Why are you here in London?'

'I am visiting friends.'

Carter tipped the things from the tray onto the desk between him and de Soir.

'You plan on making lots of calls while you're here?'

'I never know how it works with the phone situation when I'm away. Better safe than sorry.'

'Who are the friends you want to call?'

'Just people I know by the bye. This trip is more about me seeing the sights, but I need to keep in touch with home. Is it illegal to buy several SIM cards?'

'Not at all. But it's something we usually only see

criminals do. For someone who is seeing the sights you bought mainly suits and shirts with you. I don't see many T-shirts and jeans in your case. I'd say you are here for business.'

'I'm always hoping to make an impression on the people I meet. I move in expensive circles, and maybe it will lead to work. But my work is international; it has nothing to do with being in the UK. I can be anywhere and work. I am not asking to be a resident here. Your tax laws would kill me.'

'I'm sure. You are a diamond expert, is that right?'

'Correct.'

'But you don't work for the Diamond Trading Company any more?'

'No we parted company some years ago. I am freelance.'

'Can you just explain to me the type of freelance work you are asked to do?'

He gave a one-shouldered shrug, sighed irritably. 'I assess a diamond's potential. I examine it to see what is the most we can extract from it.'

'Uncut diamonds?'

'Yes.'

'The ones that are so hard to trace?'

'Sometimes, but that is not my concern. I am brought in only to appraise them and give advice. I do not buy and sell.'

'Who are your clients mainly?'

'Collectors, wealthy people who have purchased a rough diamond and want advice.'

'Is that what you'll be doing here? Giving advice?'

'I told you, I am on holiday.'

'Must have been difficult for you when you and the

Diamond Trading Company parted ways. Your reputation took a bit of a knock, didn't it?' He shrugged. 'But I expect you have done your best to build it up again.'

'I'm doing okay.'

'That could all end here tonight, Mr de Soir. This could be the start of not just another sticky patch for you, but a lengthy spell in prison.'

'What for? For having a few SIM cards? Really? You didn't find anything else in my case because there isn't anything.'

'We know why you're here.'

'Really? Then you are better informed than me. I am here to see the sights, have a break, meet a few friends. There is no plan.'

'You're here to appraise the worth of some diamonds for a South American client.'

'I told you, I will often pick up work here and there.'

'And that's what you came here to do?'

He shrugged. 'I came here thinking I might pick up some work.'

'From a drugs cartel?'

'I only know about diamonds.'

'Maybe, but if we sit here long enough someone from the cartel will ring, won't they? To make sure you're settled into the hotel room they paid for? You came here to assist a drugs cartel in the purchase of a large amount of cocaine destined for the UK market.'

'I want a lawyer.'

'You don't get one. You are being held by the Border Control police, not me. We are just deciding whether to let you into the country or not.'

'I want to return home.'

'There are no flights back out tonight.'

'I want to talk to your superior.'

'I want to give you the chance to help us, Mr de Soir. As I said, the diamonds that you're here to look at are going to be exchanged for a large shipment of cocaine from South America. Now, I get the point that you make an honest living by doing what you do but, if we hadn't tipped you off, when the cocaine arrived and the cartel wanted payment you would have been shown the stones. You would have had to appraise them on the spot and you would probably have been shot. You know why?' He shook his head. 'Because you would have to tell them that the diamonds were no good and they would start killing one another. Even if the cartel let you go, you could easily get shot in the crossfire because we intend to be waiting.'

'I didn't know what the diamonds were for. I told you, that's not my business.'

'No, I'm sure you didn't.' Carter smiled. 'But, you can agree to help us by lying about the diamonds. That way we will make sure you're out of the way, with your money, by the time the shooting starts. The cartel will never know the diamonds failed the test.'

'I can't lie to their faces. I'll crack. I told you, I want to go back to Johannesburg. I have changed my mind about entering the UK.'

'You can't leave now. It's not safe. They will come for you and you'll tell them everything, believe me. We can protect you here. We'll put you in a hotel, under guard, and then, when it's all finished, you can go home. Of course, you won't get your money but they will buy your story about being held by us, because it will be true. Someone will take your place, pretend to be you.'

'Who would you get to be me?'

'Have you ever met your customers before?'

'No.'

'Do they know what you look like?'

'Probably not. There are a few photos of me but not many and not clear. I prefer not to be recognised in my line of work.'

'We have someone in mind. Now, I need to know every detail of the plan. We need to get our man in your place before the delay is too noticeable. We need to get him to your hotel room.'

'How do I look?' Maxi put his case in the boot of the car and then he got in beside Robbo and waited for him to answer before putting on his seat belt.

'You look the part.' Maxi nodded. Robbo could see he was nervous.

'We're very grateful, Maxi. I'll explain what I know, on the way to meet Carter by the hotel.'

'Just be myself, you said, but with a South African accent.'

'That's pretty near all there is to it,' replied Robbo as he drove.

'Yeah, why am I beginning to regret this already?'

'Come on, Maxi, this will go down in history. They might give you a medal.'

'What? Posthumously? So basically you want me to be him, Roland de Soir?'

'That's right. Carter will get all the information we need from him and you'll take de Soir's place.'

'I have heard of him. He knows a hell of a lot more than me about diamonds.'

'Don't worry. All you've got to do is bullshit enough to make them believe the diamonds are worth a lot more than they are. We need them to think they're getting a great deal. Three hundred million's worth.'

'What are the diamonds for?'

'A cocaine deal.'

'And is de Soir working for the dealers?'

'He's an expert brought in by them to make sure we're not ripping them off.'

'Which we are.'

'Yes.'

'Shit.'

Robbo dropped him off when they got near the hotel and Carter was waiting for him in his car.

'You okay, Maxi?'

'Not really.'

'Of course you are. This is going to be easy for you. De Soir was told to check in to the hotel. He didn't need a card: all he needed to do was say his name.'

'But—'

'Yes, I know. And, just in case there's a problem, we have his cards here. We have his wallet. I will give you his PIN.' Maxi nodded.

Carter handed him a new phone.

'This phone is the one that they told him to use. I have his personal one. For obvious reasons he's not allowed contact with the outside world until you're safe and this operation is over.'

Maxi nodded slowly, his eyes getting bigger by the second.

'Maxi, they don't know what he looks like. They only know he's a disgraced but very talented expert. He was told to go to the room and wait until they contact. That's all he knew. That's all you know. Perfect. Go to your room, settle in, order dinner, stay off the booze and wait. When they call, don't accept any social invitations from them, say you're here for business only. Your fee is a million dollars, bank transfer. Say you are in a hurry to get out. Anything that you are not sure about you can ring me and I will ring de Soir.'

'Yeah. I've just remembered why I really left the force now: I'm basically a coward.'

Carter smiled and handed over de Soir's things.

'It'll be a piece of cake.'

Maxi got out and walked down the road, pulling his expensive case behind him. He was a good choice, thought Carter as he watched him. More than that, he was the only choice.

Carter stared at his phone. Should he text Della to see if she made it back to the Holloway flat? Why did he find it so hard to think of her as just someone he had to protect as he would anyone else he'd put up in that flat for his or her own protection? Why did he care if she was waiting for him? She had just lost her husband. He was in love with someone else. What the hell was the matter with him? He stared at the phone in his hand and then he shook his head, put the phone back in his pocket. If she needed him she would call. He had others to worry about now, Maxi for one. Carter went home to grab some sleep.

Chapter 55

13 December

Willis woke up with a feeling of panic. It was six the next morning. The sun was belting into her room; the curtains were open. She needed water badly. She was lying next to the dinner from the night before. She wrapped a towel around herself and avoided the tray of burger and chips, uneaten. She stopped in the lounge area. She'd left the balcony door open overnight, the curtains were gently blowing.

She was cross with herself – it was something she'd never have normally done. She went to stand by the open doors and feel the breeze coming off the sea. Standing in the sunshine only made the banging in her head worse. She went to look into Ross's open bedroom door. He wasn't in his bed. Willis rang him but the phone went dead. She went back in his room and looked around. All his things were gone. She looked in the wardrobe, everything was gone, his neatly hung shirts, his shiny shoes. All gone. She sat on his bed and tried to think. Why was it so hard to think? She looked at her phone again and rang Garcia.

'Morning, Ebony.'

'Morning. Is Ross with you?'

'Detective Inspector David Ross?'

'Yes. He's not here this morning.'

'Did he leave a note?'

'What do you mean?'

'Is there a note from him? He said he was going to leave it for you. He's decided to stay here.'

Willis looked around her. She stood and looked under the bed, on the bedside tables, and then she saw the corner of a piece of paper sticking out from beneath the lamp. She pulled on it and the note from Ross slid out.

'Detective Willis? You find the note?' Garcia repeated. She held it in her hands and read it.

'It just says he's staying.' Willis felt a flash of anger. 'Do you know how I can reach him?'

'Isn't he answering his phone?'

'No.'

'Let me try for you, too, and then get back to you. What time is your flight today?'

'At one. I have to check out of here at ten. I suppose he's left me the hire car. I need to return that.'

'I will send a car to pick you up at the hotel and take you to the airport. You don't have to worry about the hire car: my officers will return it. Ross is very bad to do this to you, his colleague. We'll pick you up in an hour.'

'I want to be kept informed of the progress looking for Francisco and his daughter. I saw evidence that she was there. What is your plan now with that?'

'I will pass on your concern.'

'I will bring a team back out myself if necessary. This needs cadaver dogs and helicopter searches of the wasteland behind the house. I will be submitting my report as soon as I get back and I will recommend all these courses of action be taken.'

'I hear what you are saying. Trust me, I will get on with it. I hope you have a pleasant flight.'

Willis walked numbly back into her room and she saw the hire-car keys on her bedside table. For a minute she wondered whether Ross had put them next to her while she slept, then she remembered that she had been the one to have them last. She looked around her room. There was a white carrier bag with the girls' flamenco dresses in it. She had carried it in with her blouse and the sunglasses from the market. She had forgotten to give it to Ross. She looked at her phone again. Was this Spanish time or UK time? Was she going at the right time to the airport? Her head banged. She felt drained of all capacity to think straight. All she knew was that Ross had left her in the middle of the night and he hadn't even bothered to wake her up to explain.

Chapter 56

Carter took an early call from Maxi while he was getting showered and ready for work.

'A man named Marco has just left my room.'

'What happened? What did he say?'

'He brought me a rough diamond to look at. It wasn't hard to be impressed with it: it's the biggest and the best diamond I've ever seen. Where did he get it? I thought about asking him, but I didn't dare. He looks like a member of a death squad: no taste in clothes but plenty of money to buy the designers, scars everywhere and a snappy way with a knife, which he demonstrated on the fruit. He carved his name into an apple.'

'Nice.'

'Shit, Carter, this isn't funny.'

'Don't worry, you're seen as the good guy in all this. He obviously bought your story.'

'How do you know that?'

'Because he didn't kill you.'

'Seriously?'

'I mean it. Great job. What does he want you to do next?'

'Nothing, until he calls again and that should be in a few days, he says. Meanwhile, I can rack up the bill here, enjoy the casino, get some girls, all his words of course, not mine, but he's left me close to half a million in cash for any extra expenses.'

'You see – not all bad. Enjoy.'

'It would be but I need to get back in the shop. People will be contacting me about the diamonds on loan. They will be bringing them to the shop. Now I feel a double responsibility to give myself a chance of pulling this off.'

'You go back, as long as you return to the hotel to sleep. Make sure no one follows you. They won't be looking for trouble. You should be fine.'

Carter headed into work. He went straight to a meeting about Manson and the possible locations for the cocaine laboratory.

'Robbo pinned a map up on the board; at its centre was Swanley and The Paddocks. It was circled in blue, and the red dots signified where the business parks and industrial estates were.

'We know Manson has a van, which we presume is either parked at The Paddocks or the fireplaces' destination.'

'It's a softly-softly approach right now,' said Carter. 'We just want to find it; we don't want it closed down. The deal relies on it.'

'If there is just one facility, which is both the storage for the fireplaces and the laboratory to extract the cocaine, usual choice would be close to a motorway, so I've high-lighted these parks first. There are an awful lot of them. We presume it would have strict security. No one is going to want that broken into. It would have to be fairly empty apart from the cocaine lab.'

'Unless it's a front for something legitimate.'

'Going on the laboratories found in Spain, they were not. They were large facilities. It takes a big laboratory to process a ton of cocaine, dissolve it and extract it.'

'An old chemical factory?' suggested Pam. 'A place that makes cleaning fluids? If you think about it, there is the opportunity to hide it behind something that sounds innocuous.'

'But you still wouldn't want someone knocking on the door and asking to buy some Jif?'

'No, so something that is necessary but no one wants to go near it.'

'Somewhere not very smart, not super-swish. You don't want people wanting to know your business.'

'We've got several officers working on this right now,' said Robbo. 'They're all posing as prospective manufacturers looking for premises. We're working our way through the list around the M25 first.'

'I take it you're not going to bring Manson in and ask him, then?'

Carter shook his head. 'There's so much at stake. How many other shipments from any of Manson's firms have there been, Pam?'

'So far I have found six in the last six months. They range from ceramics to bespoke art pieces. Some of them must be genuine, I suppose.'

'Which port? Do they always come in at the same place?'

'Mainly to Felixstowe, then they are picked up by a haulage company and delivered to The Paddocks. They used a different haulage company each time. The driver is not in the equation. Manson always met the driver there and helped unload the goods.'

'So, we can expect them to get delivered there again,' said Robbo.

'Different cartel, I don't know,' said Carter.

'We don't know which port or where it will be taken? It's not looking easy, Carter,' said Robbo.

'No, and all we have is the cheap diamonds to pay for it.'

'Why wouldn't they take them straight to the laboratory?' asked Pam.

'I don't know, perhaps they don't have the facility for storing much there? Maybe the batch is mixed, some boxes are genuine, like you said, Pam.'

'We need to get another twenty officers out driving to these sites then, Robbo. Make sure they know what they're supposed to be looking for. The van would be great to find. Meanwhile, any luck with working out who Manson is talking to in the café? Justino? Did you find any more images of him?'

'No, it's just not clear enough. We'll keep looking.'

Chapter 57

Carter was walking back to his office when he met Willis as she came out of the lift on the third floor in Fletcher House.

'Ah, back from sunny Spain. You okay? You look like you're about to throw up.'

She nodded.

'Come with me.'

He took her elbow and thrust her into the nearest bathroom and stood outside the cubicle until she'd finished retching. He talked to her while she washed her face.

'Jesus, what have you been doing out there, or have you got a bug?'

She stood over the sink and looked into the mirror as she shook her head.

'Ross is gone,' she said, shaking her dripping face, holding on to the sides of the sink for stability.

'What? What are you saying, Willis? Make sense.'

'Ross stayed out there. He disappeared on me.'

'When? How? What do you mean?'

'He didn't come back to the apartment last night, or I thought he hadn't. Turns out he came and took his things and left in the middle of the night.'

'Without a word?'

'He left a note. I don't know whether it was genuine.'

'Where is it?'

'I don't have it.'

'For Christ's sake, Willis, what the bloody hell has been going on?'

'I tell you, nothing untoward happened.' She focused on Carter in the mirror. 'Nothing that seemed unusual, until these last few hours when everything seems weird. I think I've made a massive mistake leaving Marbella.'

'When was the last time you saw him?'

'We were out for the evening with the two local detectives we'd been working with and I went home early. I left him to stay out with them. It was all fine. And that's it. I woke up, and all his things were gone.'

'Were you drugged?'

'I don't know. I came home earlier in the evening, a bit pissed. Teen said I seemed really pissed when I Skyped her but I was drinking loads of water. I've drunk way more than that and not been so legless. I woke up next to the tray of food.'

'With food still on it? Okay, okay, I'll take it from here. You go home and sleep it off. You're no good to me like this.'

'I'm so sorry, sir.'

'I know. Give me your phone.'

Willis handed it over; she was struggling to stay upright as she leaned back onto the basin and closed her eyes.

'You know what? I'm going to get you home by squad car. Where's Tina now?' Willis shook her head. 'Well, I'll find her. I've seen her this morning. She must be working in the canteen. I'll phone and get her the day off. She's going home with you now. She'll look after you. Something's happened here. I don't know what, but you need to get to bed.'

He copied the things he needed from her phone and then handed it back, zipped it up in her jacket pocket. He put her in a taxi with Tina.

'Teen, you ring me if Willis doesn't seem to be getting any better. Go via the Whittington. I want a blood test taken. Dr Harding will be waiting in pathology.'

Carter went to see Robbo.

'Did you manage to get hold of the Spanish detectives?'

'They'll be on Skype in a minute. How's Eb?' asked Robbo.

'I think she'll be okay later. She's working whatever it is out of her system. I've organised a blood test but I think it's unlikely we'll find a trace of anything this long after she remembers having anything to drink. Tina saw her on Skype, talked to her at just after eleven when she said Willis seemed very drunk.'

'Here we are; they're coming online,' said Robbo.

'Okay, I'll come over,' said Carter.

'Hello, Inspector Ramirez,' said Robbo as the webcam came to life and they were looking at the face of the world-weary detective. 'I'll pass you across to Detective Inspector Carter,' he said as he turned the screen towards Carter. Carter leaned on the desk as he talked. He was agitated, worried.

'Morning, Inspector. I hope Detective Sergeant Willis got home all right. The police car that gave her a lift said she seemed a bit ill. I was worried they might not let her on the plane. Very strange. Is she okay?'

'She made it back, at least, that's more than can be said

for Inspector Ross. Where is he? Can you explain to me, please? I want to understand how one of my detectives comes back apparently having been drugged, and the other doesn't come back at all.'

'I know nothing about why Detective Willis is ill. She is not used to drinking, perhaps. I am sure she was not drugged. She had a few drinks before she left us yesterday evening. As for Inspector Ross, I think he always had his own agenda when he came out here. I think he's working for a different boss, if you know what I mean.'

'No, I don't. Please explain where he is right now.'

'Right now? I have no idea. We spent the evening with him until two in the morning and then he told us he intended to stay in Marbella and continue his investigations alone. He didn't need our help, he said. It was a big shock to us too.'

'He's not answering his phone. Can you put out a search for him, please?'

'I wish I could help, Inspector, but, if Ross has decided he can do better on his own, what can we do about it?'

'You can find him. Has he got a hire car?'

'No. Detective Willis abandoned the hire car and left it here at the hotel. We will deal with that for you. I'm sorry there's not more we can help with.'

'What else did Ross say last night?'

'He didn't say a lot but we had intelligence reports that it wasn't the first time Ross has been to Spain, making investigations, and he is known to act against orders. We're thinking that maybe there is some other motive here. Perhaps he is better connected here than you think.'

'You better be able to back up what you're accusing him of.'

'Please, I'm not accusing. This is just a chat between two officers trying to look after their colleagues. The last I saw of Ross was at just after two in the morning. We dropped him back to his hotel and he said he was going to pack, to leave a note for Willis, then we saw him come out really quickly, maybe within fifteen minutes, and we saw a car pull up near the hotel and pick him up.'

'Did you trace the number plate?'

'We tried but it wasn't on the system. That is all I can tell you, I'm sorry. If you want, we can put out an alert for the patrol officers to look for Ross, but somehow I don't think they're going to find him, and maybe he doesn't want to be found. He already had plenty of friends here, I think.'

Carter's face had become stony as he listened to Ramirez. He thanked him curtly.

'We'll be in touch. Thank you for your time,' said Carter.

'No problem.'

He watched Robbo switch off Skype.

'Jeezus!' Carter shook his head, his eyes still fixed on the blank screen as if he couldn't believe it.

'We better get hold of Ross's superiors and find out how much of that is bullshit. We better hope that Ross had some masterplan, and he isn't lying in a ditch somewhere with his throat cut.'

'Can he just have disappeared?'

'I don't think so. It all sounded much too matter-of-fact from Ramirez. Run a check on him and his buddy, Garcia. Are they bent? Have they had Ross killed? Handed him over for interrogation? If they have, then we are done for. Everyone working on this investigation will be at risk. Plus, we'll walk away with nothing again.'

'I've already contacted Ross's boss at the OCC and

they're not willing to deny or confirm anything,' said Robbo. 'They won't even tell us whether Ross was given permission to remain in Spain or even if he is still in Spain.'

'So much for different departments cooperating.'

Chapter 58

Billy Manson was resting.

His wife Jo knocked gently on the bedroom door and came in with a cup of tea.

'Didn't you sleep?' She looked at her husband lying on the bed, his eyes wide. He looked like he was hanging on to the duvet for dear life.

'Billy, you have to rest.'

'I can't, Jo. I've been going over things. I know we can't fly out of here but you and the kids can go away; go and stay with your relatives in Plymouth.'

'What, two weeks before Christmas? Why would we do that?'

'Yes, two weeks before fucking Christmas.'

'Don't swear.'

'I am sorry.' Jo closed the door; she came to sit on the bed and hold his hand. 'It'll be okay, Billy. It will all blow over.'

He gave her hand a squeeze and then dropped it.

'Just get out with the kids while I try and sort it, please – just do it. I am sorry for everything. It's all a big mess.'

'What are you talking about, Billy? You don't need to be sorry about anything. Look at the lovely home we have. The kids go to good schools. We have a great life.'

'But it's going to have to change. I messed things up.'

'Are we still in danger? What did Laurence Butcher say when you talked to him?'

'He's coming in with lots of bullshit ideas, but he has no idea what he's walking into. It's not going to work out with Laurence. Everything is finished here. I can't do business with any of the Butchers. The business is effectively gone.'

'We can start again.'

'Not here, not now. You can't make this better, Jo. All you can do is help me by giving me less to worry about. I need to fix it, on my own. You're just giving me more stress by staying here.'

'Why don't you talk to the police if you're that worried?'

'Why? You're kidding me.' The panic trapped in his lungs came out in a wheezy sound as he tried to laugh. 'Just do as I ask, please.'

'I'll do whatever you want, Billy, you know I will. I'd face anything in the future with you. Just don't block me out.'

He looked at her. 'Please go so at least I don't have to worry about protecting you and the kids. Let me try to sort this out. Just take the kids and go. The police want me in Archway in an hour. Please, Jo, just do what I ask. Do it now.'

'Will you please talk to the police?'

He nodded.

An hour later Jo Manson had packed the suitcases in the boot and loaded the kids. She stood and hugged Manson.

'Remember, we love you.'

'I know. I'll make it all right, I promise,' he said and drew back from her. He smiled. She frowned.

'I don't think I should leave you.'

'Just go. I'll be able to think straight if I know you're safe.'

'But what about you?'

'I can make the right choices then. You're right, I'll talk to the police. We'll make a fresh start.'

'You'll call me later?'

'Yes. Now drive safely.' He waved at the children and turned back into the house. He went out to the garage and found himself a length of rope and a ladder and then he went into the drawing room and climbed the ladder to loop the rope around the beam and tie it around his neck. When he was ready he kicked the ladder away.

Chapter 59

Carter texted Della to see if she was there and then he walked to the flat. It took him twenty minutes and he took a tour of the back roads behind Holloway, to make sure he wasn't being followed. The whole thing with Melvin had made him feel irresponsible. It made him question whether he'd underestimated Marco. In the back of his mind, he was also wondering about Della. That diamond she had hanging around was worth a million, according to Maxi. She obviously still had full access to a world that she said had nothing to do with her. Was his judgement compromised? Was he putting others at risk? Why did he still get excited about seeing her?

Della was unpacking shopping. She'd bought coffee and cakes.

'You still have your sweet tooth, then?' Carter said as he watched her lay the coloured macaroons on a plate. She poured him a black coffee.

'Still the same, yes. You still love your expensive wines?'

'Absolutely.' He smiled mechanically. She frowned.

'What is it?'

'I have some sad news, I'm sorry. Billy Manson killed himself earlier today.'

'Billy? But why? Why would he do that?' She looked at Carter with horror. Her eyes filled. 'Christ Almighty! What has been going on here, Dan? Is this all about Eddie?'

He shook his head. 'We don't have answers yet, but we're getting there. Manson had secrets.'

'I don't understand. You're saying that Eddie could have been killed because of something Manson was involved in?'

'I'm coming to that way of thinking.' Carter hesitated. He shook his head, as if he'd changed his mind.

'Tell me, Dan, tell me what's on your mind.'

'Della, every time I open my mouth I put you more at risk. People are dying because of loose talk. I don't want to give you any information that hasn't come from the right source. If you accidentally blurt it out in conversation . . .'

'What conversation? Do you think I'm bonding with Harold and Marco? Or even weirdo Laurence, who picks now to tell me he's always had the hots for me?' She laughed.

Carter smiled. 'You've almost got to admire his spirit of opportunism, hit 'em straight out of mourning.'

'It's not funny.' She smiled. 'It's not even flattering. Do you remember what a little oddball he used to be? I think it's been suppressed by Sandra over the years but he's a mini-Tony in the making. The way he talks to me, it's like he thinks of me as the Butcher family property.'

'It's nice to see you smiling, Della.' She looked at Carter, whose eyes were melting a little as he listened to her talking.

'How is life with you, Dan? I can see you've achieved the rank you always wanted. You're an inspector in the Met, that's impressive. Are you happy?'

He nodded. 'Yeah, I wonder sometimes. I'm getting old fast with the stress of the job. I'm getting jaded.'

'But you have a partner, a child. That must be enough to keep you young.'

'My son Archie is great. He's a real character.'

'And you love her.'

'I love her, yes. She's not easy, she's feisty and opinionated and so messy, it's a nightmare, and funny. She's very funny.'

'She sounds perfect for you. Much better than I would ever have been.'

He nodded, stared at his coffee.

'It took me five years to get over you and, even then, maybe, I never really did.'

'Don't say it, Dan.' Della took a step closer to him. 'I hold my hands up, Dan. I loved you more than I'll ever love anyone else. But I saw something else in Eddie that I hungered after just as much. The ordinary life of a hard-up copper, hardly seeing one another, always knackered, wasn't for me. I wanted more, and Eddie could deliver. I wanted the luxury home, the nice cars. I wanted it all. I was just twenty-six at the time. I didn't understand the value of real love.'

Carter's eyes stayed on Della as she said, 'I know you're not going to, Dan, but if you asked me if there'd been times when I regretted it, if I missed you, I'd have said truthfully there were many. I never felt the passion with Eddie that we had. When I left you I knew I'd lost my soulmate. But that's life. You make choices . . .'

'You threw it all away.'

'Yes, I did. It was just in me, that hunger for *things* over people, and it still is. It was wonderful, what we felt for one another, but I chose something else. We were like two kids in the flush of love. It wouldn't have lasted and we'd have worn each other down by now.'

Carter was nodding silently and looking out of the window. The brightness outside hurt his eyes, making them water.

He put his cup down. 'You're right. I must go, I have a ton of work to get through. We're thinking of bringing Marco in. I need you to get some DNA from him for me, a cup, cigarette, you know the kind of thing, and a fingerprint, on a glass would be ideal.'

'Should be easy, if he comes back tonight. What's it for?'

'I want to try and link him to the murder of an informant of mine. I think Marco killed him. I don't know why, maybe just because he's trying to warn me off. He knows that I'm a detective asking questions about him. Whoever did it wanted me to find him.'

'Was he killed like Eddie?'

Carter nodded. 'We have also had an inspector go missing after going across to Spain to talk to Tony. I'm interested in two detectives out there: Ramirez and Garcia. Do you know the names?'

'Yes, very much so. They are like Tony's private personnel.'

'Are you positive?'

'Yes, I've seen them a few times over the years. I'm sure if they wanted to have got Tony they could have by now.'

Chapter 60

Harold was standing in the Shoreditch flat and looking at the screen, at Tony's face.

'I think Marco put pressure on him, Manson cracked.'

Tony was clenching and unclenching his fists as he stood before the screen.

'You shouldn't have let him do that. We needed Manson, for fuck's sake. He knows how it all fits together. It's coming in under his company.'

'It had nothing to do with me. I'm not Marco's keeper. You chose him, Tony. I can't help it if he turns out to be a loose cannon, fucking nutcase. I can't be responsible if this plan doesn't come off. Now the East End is jittery with all the talk of death squads and mad Colombians who torture for the fun of it.'

'Man up, Harold. This is your last job. We're going to build you a palace when this job comes off.'

'If.'

'When, Harold. When. Now, what's this you're telling me that it's coming to Spain first and then on to the UK? Why? Why are these things altered without my consent?'

'Because we are here dealing with it and you are not. This is not about your consent. This is the cartel's call.

The Zapata call the shots. They wanted it unloaded at Valencia and reloaded on a smaller container ship to the UK,' answered Harold.

'What reason did they give?'

'They think it will be safer,' replied Harold. 'They are already using Manson's company to bring it across, which they weren't keen on. We need to give them what they want.'

'Okay, well as long as there is a reason. Will it delay it?'

'We have six days now, till the 19th, for Della to make sure the diamonds are ready.'

'Have you seen any of the diamonds?'

'I've seen one, it's a beautiful thing. The biggest stone I've ever seen. Eddie had it in the safe, she said.'

'I'd love to see it, Harold. Go get it now, I want to see it.'

'Marco took it to show the Zapata.'

'You make sure he brings it back.'

'It's one diamond.'

'I don't care. I want to see it. I'm taking all the risk here.'

'What, in your bombproof villa? It doesn't feel like that sitting where I am, Tony.'

Sandra walked into view. She was having an off day: no make-up, her hair in a scarf. She had on a tracksuit.

'Mum, you feeling okay?'

She stepped close to the camera. Her face loomed large on Harold's screen. 'Tony is wearing me out. He paces around the place. He's worried sick about you all. Don't fuck up now, Harold. Eddie died for this.'

'Eddie died *because* of this. It's not the same thing.'

Sandra gave a dismissive wave of the hand and walked away. Then changed her mind and came back and looked into the webcam.

'Where's Della right now?'

'She's out.'

'Yes, but where? Where? That is exactly my point, Harold. You make sure you know where Della is night and day or else I'm coming over to deal with things myself.'

'You're safer where you are, Mum.'

'I don't care about safe. I care about getting the right results. We never lived our lives worrying about safe and it's worked out fine so far.'

'Mum, okay, I get it. I need to talk to Tony again, I don't have long.'

Sandra went away muttering under her breath. She went to find Debbie, who was resting by the pool, a cold cloth over her eyes.

'You shouldn't lie in the sun so much. You're wrinkled enough.'

Debbie sat up wearily and took the cloth from her eyes. She put her sunglasses back on and picked up her iced water.

'I'm just trying to stay out of Tony's way for ten minutes. The sound of him pacing around is driving me nuts. It's like being in the zoo and watching the tiger going back and forth.'

'He has a lot on his mind. You should be more supportive.'

Debbie shook her head and smiled to herself.

'What can I help you with, Sandra, or have you just come over to brighten my day?'

'No need to get sarky. I just talked to Harold. It doesn't look to me as if anything's getting done properly over there. I'm thinking of going over there, to the UK. I need to, to see what's going on.'

'With the new deal, you mean? With the cocaine?'

'Shush, for Christ's sake. Don't you care who can hear? The police will be listening to every word we say in the grounds.'

'Whatever.' Debbie sat back and tilted her face up to the sun. 'You enjoy yourself, Sandra. I wish I could leave here, just for one day. It would be nice. The Christmas lights will be up on Oxford Street when you do your shopping. You'll be able to pick up chocolates from Harrods in person. You'll have a lovely time.'

Sandra sat down next to Debbie and leaned in to whisper.

'You're going the right way to a hiding.'

Debbie turned her head slowly to look at Sandra and she raised her sunglasses.

'Sorry? Repeat that, please.'

'You heard.'

Debbie smiled, unimpressed, and turned away as she sighed.

'Don't you forget who you are, Debbie.'

Sandra jabbed Debbie hard in the arm with her silicone nail. It cut into Debbie's skin. It began to fill with blood beneath the surface. Debbie flinched for a second only before she pushed Sandra hard. Sandra fell back onto the flagstones and took her time getting up, brushing herself off.

'You'll pay for that, Debbie. One way or another.'

'That's right, Sandra. You go to London and you try to justify the deals, the deaths. Your own son Eddie, the only decent one among you, he was killed because of Tony.'

'Tony's under house arrest, for fuck's sake. How do you think he could have done it, eh? Spit it out.'

Debbie stared hard at Sandra. 'We both know how Tony

makes his money; we also know what he's capable of. I've seen him snap someone's neck for nothing. I've seen his stuff on the Internet. He's worse than a child molester: he's a *sick* child murderer. You've bred a monster.'

'Shut your mouth, you piece of shit. Get out of here if you don't like it.'

Debbie laughed drily. 'I've had enough of listening to you. I'm past caring now. Tony is going over the edge. I wouldn't be surprised if this is the beginning of the end for us here. I can see what would happen to me if Tony died. You'd all turn on me, too, just like you are on Della. But I've decided that's not the way it's going to go, Sandra. Do you understand? I really hope you do. I am mistress of this house. I will call the shots if anything happens to Tony. I am his wife. You better start being nice.'

Sandra walked away muttering to herself, 'No way am I going to fucking London, when I've got enemies right here in my own house.'

Chapter 61

'The officers said they went in to find him hanging.' Carter stood before Bowie's desk shaking his head sadly. 'Bloody hell, did you apply too much pressure on him? Did you have any inkling he was suicidal?'

'No. We hadn't even begun to put pressure on. We were relying on us finding out where he transported the shipment. This is bad news. We hadn't even told him we knew that he must be involved.'

'How is his wife?'

'She's got family liaison with her. She had just arrived in Plymouth when he was found.'

'Why Plymouth?'

'Apparently, Manson wanted her and the kids to go away for a few days.'

'Can she tell us any more than that? Does she know about Manson's business?'

'I've briefed the family liaison. It means we have access to the property here. We can have a good look. I've got an officer in there discreetly going through all Manson's paperwork. I've had news from Della that we only have three days left to try and pull this deal together.'

'You got it in hand?'

'Yes, I think so.'

'Do we have word about which docks the shipment's coming in at?'

'This is a different cartel and it's up to them to get loaded their end in Mexico, probably, so I don't know. But we hope to when it arrives on UK soil. They must tell Della that.'

There was a knock on Bowie's door.

'Sir?'

'Willis? How are you feeling?' Bowie frowned. 'You look like you need to sit down or fall down. Take a chair.'

Carter pulled one up beside him for her to sit down.

'I thought you were staying in bed for the rest of the day,' he said.

'I feel much better; I wanted to come in and see what I can do about Inspector Ross. I can't forgive myself for just leaving him out there.'

'You didn't just leave him, Eb. You appraised the situation and you made a decision based on that.'

'Yes, sir.'

Bowie turned to Carter.

'What's the latest from the National Crime Agency?'

'They're not telling us anything.'

'Then we have to accept that Ross is safe, he is working.'

'What about Francisco?' Bowie asked Willis as she sat down. 'Did you discover anything?'

'We found plenty that needed to be taken further. I've already submitted my report on it and have made sure that my findings have been sent to the attention of the top man out there. He's got back to me to say they're upping their search and they will keep me informed. I heard about Manson,' said Willis, looking at Carter.

'Yes, we are going to have to rely heavily on Della. She may have to actually deliver the diamonds in person.'

'What about your informant?' Bowie asked Carter.

'Melvin's death was brutal. It was meant to be laid at my feet. They wanted me to see it first. I think this was Marco. He knows I'm a copper. He knew about Melvin. He knows what I look like. This is meant as a warning to me and to all those who might think about talking to me. It's working down there, people have clammed up.'

'This was the very situation we said we'd try to avoid,' said Bowie. 'You better stay away from Bethnal Green. Let someone else handle Melvin's murder. Willis, you can take it on.'

'Thank you, sir.' Willis stood and left.

After she left, Carter asked: 'You sure? This is her first case as an SIO.'

'I'm sure. She's methodical, she's dispassionate. She's perfect for this. Plus, it will make her feel better for the disappearance of Ross. Will you pick up Marco?'

'I've asked Della to get us some DNA of his for us to match to the murder scene. We need him on the outside for the deal to go through. He is the nearest thing we have to Tony himself. If we close Marco down too soon, we'll never flush Tony out.'

'I can't see how we will get him to leave his villa. It will have to be something massive to force him out of there,' said Bowie. 'Plus, the Spanish police will have to look the other way.'

'I think that's the only part of the plan that's a given for me,' answered Carter. 'I've been hearing a lot about corruption among the officers.'

'If there is going to be a war between the Mendez and

the Zapata cartels, should we try to round them up first?' asked Bowie.

'We daren't risk this deal not happening. If we want Tony we have to wait.'

'How is Maxi Seymour?'

'I think Maxi is okay. He's gone back into detective mode. Marco has only been to see him the once. He's going to be told when he's needed. He's gone back to the day job for now.'

'And what about Roland de Soir?'

'He's complaining like hell about staying in a three-star hotel with no gym and no room service.'

Chapter 62

'I got you some sunglasses,' Willis said as she handed them over. She had the look of someone racked with guilt.

'Hey, these are great. I asked Cabrina to get me some, but she's bound to forget.'

'How is she doing?' Willis asked Carter as he caught up with her, and they walked down to Robbo's office together.

'Finally having a nice time. She's found a group of other London girls and she's fitted in fine. I knew she'd be okay.'

'When does she come home?'

'She has another week yet.'

Carter put his new sunglasses on. 'How do I look?'

'Like you're wearing knock-off Ray-Bans. Better not wear them in the sunshine: they'll probably burn your eyes.'

'Thanks for the gift. Got anything else, like poisonous confectionery?'

'All out of that, I'm sorry.'

'Willis, stop a minute. Look at me, tell me how you're feeling.'

'I feel like shit.'

'Physically or spiritually?'

'Both.'

'You actually still look rough. I think you should—'

'Don't tell me to go home. I don't want to be there. I feel like I let Ross down in a way that I would never have let you down. Would I have just got back on a plane and left you? No way.'

'Stop going over it, Eb.'

'I worry that he's been kidnapped. We met a lot of hostility from the locals out there. A timeshare conman, Peter Tully, who had one of Eddie's villas, he had a go at Ross. He has influential friends, they all do. Money buys anything, it seems. There are a lot of powerful villains with police in their pockets. How do we know that he just didn't get taken and murdered for daring to cross Tony Butcher?'

'Give yourself a day or two to work this out, Willis. You'll get there; you always do. But, right now, you're still in panic mode. There were inconclusive results back from your blood test, so we don't know whether you were drugged or not. Now, it probably doesn't matter a whole lot.'

'There were opportunities to slip something in my drink, but I don't know why anyone would. It's not as if I was on a date.'

'Which makes it even more likely it was Ross himself.'

'Why?'

'To stop you asking questions. To make sure you wouldn't know anything. Perhaps he was thinking, I'll be kind, I'll give her a way out of this situation and get her on the plane home. She won't be able to endlessly go over it with her colleague and endlessly blame herself.'

'Perhaps that's it. He left me with his daughters' presents from Spain. If I took them around to his ex-wife's and gave them to her, she might tell me if he's been in touch.'

'You want to do it, you go ahead, but don't expect too much. Concentrate on the here and now. You now have to head up the investigation into Melvin's death as well as the workload you have already. I need you to let this go. You want my opinion? Ross is a clever guy. This is some plan he has going.

Chapter 63

Willis knocked at the terraced house in Clapham.

A pretty woman answered, tall with curly hair pinned up on top of her head. She had on a hippy, tie-dyed top and leggings. She was barefoot and very pregnant.

'Sorry to bother you. Is it Belinda?' Willis said. The woman nodded. 'I'm a colleague of David's, your ex-husband.'

'I know who David is.' She smiled. 'Please come in. I'm having tea and cake, come and join me. Has he sent you?'

'No, no, he hasn't. I hope I'm not disturbing you. I'd love some tea.'

'You're not disturbing me at all.' She led Willis into the kitchen. Its walls were plastered in kids' drawings. It was cluttered and messy. It had the smell of freshly baked cake.

'Please sit; I'll get you some tea. Milk and sugar?'

'Yes to both, please.'

'Here.' She cut Willis a slice of banana loaf fresh from the oven.

'When are you due?' asked Willis eating the cake straight away.

'I'm not for a month but I'm enormous, aren't I? Must be a whopper. Best not to think about it.' She grimaced. 'It's a bit late to back out now, isn't it?' She smiled as she manoeuvred herself into a chair to sit at the table opposite Willis. The wooden table had scribbles from pens and marks from hot plates. It was the kind of kitchen that Willis felt at home in. It was a million miles away from any kitchen she'd ever been in before but it made her instantly feel like moving in. Her mind was already trying to work out why Ross threw all of this away. Was it just too perfectly laid-back for Mr Immaculate? Or did Ross actually have a self-destructive button that was bigger than his brain?

'Has he sent you over to give his excuses? Is it work?' She rolled her eyes. 'Held up? Holding on? Holed up?'

'Sorry?'

'He comes up with some remarkable excuses sometimes. He's supposed to pick up the girls after their ballet class this afternoon. I thought he was coming back from Spain in plenty of time. It doesn't matter, I suppose. I was going along, anyway, to watch them; but he usually lets me know.'

'When did you speak to him last?'

'Yesterday afternoon. Is there something the matter?'

Willis shook her head. 'I was in Spain with him. I came back but he stayed out there. He's just hard to get hold of, that's all, and he left me with a present he'd bought for his daughters.' Willis handed over the carrier bag and Belinda pulled out the dresses.

'Oh, they're going to be so happy with these. That's typical of Dave: he remembers the small things and forgets the big.' She looked to Willis for empathy. Willis shrugged.

'Sorry, I don't know David well. We've only just started working together.'

'How long will he be in Spain for?'

'I have no idea, I'm sorry.'

'I tried to get hold of him,' said Belinda, her forehead creased as she tried to read Willis's expression and struggled to decipher it. 'His phone keeps going to voicemail,' she added.

'Yes, I know. I've been trying too.'

'Is it something to worry about?' asked Belinda, smoothing the round of her tight tummy as the baby shifted. 'I mean, have you come to tell me something awful has happened to him? Is this baby going to have a dad when it comes out?'

'No, we don't really know what happened at the moment but I am sure it's nothing to worry about.'

'He does quite a lot of secretive investigations. He speaks God knows how many languages. He's a genius, really. We could have made a fortune if he'd decided not to take such a moral-minded career.' She smiled at Willis's worried expression. 'Only joking.'

'I'm sure we will find out what has been going on soon. I just wanted to come and give you these dresses. Sorry, did you say Ross is the father?'

'Yes, a bit of a relapse night and we always were fertile.'

'But you're with a new partner?'

'Oh yes, don't worry.'

Willis shook her head. 'Sorry, I didn't mean to sound like it was personal to me. I'm not in any way involved with David. It's just he mentioned how supportive your new partner was. I thought this must be his.'

'My new partner is a woman – Adele – and, yes, she took a bit of talking round, when she found out that David is going to continue to be in our lives, but it's all settled down now. We'll be okay.'

'That sounds very ... adult,' Willis said, although she was not sure what she was supposed to say. It actually seemed a mess, to her.

'Does it? Can't think why. David is such a child. He loves his intrigue and his secrets. Like right now? He doesn't realise how bloody annoying it is, just to disappear. Thank you for bringing these over. The girls will be thrilled. Please, Ebony, can I have your number? Will you ring me when you hear from him and tell him to get in touch straight away.'

'I will. Thanks for the cake.'

'It was nice to meet you.'

'Good luck with everything, Belinda.'

Chapter 64

Robbo was waiting for Willis when she got back to the station.

'You feeling any better? You've got some colour back.'

'A little, yes.'

'Maybe it was sunstroke you had.'

'Could have been, I suppose. What's it like?'

'Cold and yet burning up, vomiting, sweats. Stomach pains.'

'Robbo, that's enough,' said Pam as she came round to see Willis. 'Main thing is you're on the mend.' She felt Willis's forehead.

'Sit down to be on the safe side,' Pam said. 'I'll get you a glass of water.'

'Okay,' said Robbo, 'let's crack on with the investigation into Melvin Pratt's murder. The post-mortem is in. Bet you're sorry you missed that.' He smiled. Willis nodded absent-mindedly. She didn't get the joke and she never minded the dissection side of things.

She opened the file and looked at the body diagrams. There were five in all. Normally, one would suffice.

'Dr Harding couldn't fit all his injuries on one page, so she apologises, but, to make it clear, she's split them into burns, blunt traumas, superficial wounds and deep wounds. You want a few minutes to look at those?'

'Yes, I think I will need it.'

'Good, I'll get a brew on. Pam?'

'Skinny latte, please.'

'Don't take the piss, Pam, white or black?'

'White.'

'That's a terrible way to die,' Willis said when Robbo came back with the coffee. 'The person who inflicted this kind of pain is the type of killer I've never met before. He laid out tools, like a tradesman. According to Sandford, he went through Melvin's kitchen, looking for what he needed. There were several empty aerosol canisters. He seems to have used anything volatile, any alcohol he could find, to set Melvin alight, like making a home-made blowtorch.

'Yes, this was brutal and forensic. This man saw how far he could damage the human body and then took it further. Harding estimates the injuries were inflicted over a period of five hours.'

Willis was crouched over Robbo's desk as she went through the details. 'God, I wouldn't want to be reading reports like this every week.'

'Could happen if we don't close the cartels down.'

'Yes, it's happening in Spain.' Willis's eyes met Robbo's and both knew what the other was thinking.

'Ross will be okay, I'm sure.'

She nodded, even though she knew she didn't agree.

'No signs of a break-in but it looks like Melvin often left the door open.' Willis continued going through the report. 'So it wasn't necessarily someone he knew. But it doesn't look like he was followed home from the pub. Someone waited. This happened an hour after the man upstairs heard him coming home drunk. Then he said he heard loud noises at just before twelve.'

'Looking at these statements, we're not short of people who saw Melvin that night,' said Robbo.

'It's a lot like Eddie Butcher's. It's from the same school of torture. Someone likes his blowtorch.'

'CCTV from opposite the pub picks out Harold Butcher talking to him outside and it looks like he gives him something. Melvin was found with a rolled-up bunch of twenties – I'm guessing that's what Harold gave him. I think we can count Harold out of the equation for this murder. We know this isn't his style.'

'For me, the man who jumps out as capable is Marco,' said Willis.

'Della's managed to get us a sample of Marco's DNA and his fingerprint. We already have Harold's and a few other villains' from the pub that night on file. We will see if the DNA from the murder scene matches Marco's from the sample Della got us.'

'Have you met Della yet?'

Robbo shook his head. 'She's staying in one of our flats down the road. Carter sees her. He's the only person she has daily contact with.'

'Is she being followed?'

'Not directly. She insisted she can't be. The surveillance on the flat in Shoreditch shows her comings and goings there. We have to leave her to do things the way she sees fit. An awful lot is resting on her.'

'I'll head down to see the site now,' said Willis. 'And I'll talk to the locals, get a feel for things.'

Chapter 65

Della was adding a backpack and a woolly hat to her outfit locked in the wardrobe. She had picked up her passport now and that was stowed in the cupboard as well. She had decided to move it from Shoreditch. She would keep it locked in the car from now on. She could always abandon the car at the airport. The main thing was that she was ready to run. She looked at the passport and was impressed. It was an older-style one, easier to copy. Eddie had been right: the contacts he'd given her all knew what she needed.

She got a text from Carter.

'You free?'

She called him.

'Sorry,' he said, 'didn't need you to call. Just thought you might want to meet for a catch-up.'

'It's okay. I'm on my own here. I'm free. I've decided to move into the other place now. It's getting a little tense here. I'm on my way over now.'

'Okay, I'll see you there.'

Della picked up her bag with her new identity in it and listened for any sound before she opened her bedroom door, looking back to see if she'd remembered everything. She walked straight into Harold.

'You packed up, ready to leave us so soon?' He looked down at the bag.

'I wish.' She tried to get past him but he stepped back into her way.

'What's in the bag?'

'What's it got to do with you? We're too far down this road not to trust one another, Harold. I'm going off to track down the diamonds.'

'I'll come with you.'

'No, you won't.'

'That wasn't a request. Who was that on the phone?'

'None of your business.'

'Give me your phone.' He held out his hand.

She gave it to him and he looked at the call list on it.

'Who's Danielle?'

'Hairdresser.'

'Now open the bag.'

She sighed, took the phone back and put it into her hand-bag and then pulled out the loaded handgun.

'Now, you know I can use this, Harold. Eddie always said I was a better shot than him. I don't want to use it. It's going to make a mess on the carpet and I will have to clean it and I don't want to miss my hairdresser's appointment. This is just a friendly little reminder to you, Harold, to stay out of my face. Don't expect me to come back here. I'll contact you when everything is ready to go. You stay in touch with me and let me know where and when you want the diamonds delivered. Give my love to Sandra if she comes over. I hope her plane gets blown up. I'd love to feel the soft rain of Sandra's brain falling from the sky.'

Harold's face registered his anger and she could see he

contemplated going for it. She lifted the gun and smiled.

'Don't be stupid, Harold.'

'I only want to help you get this right, Della. I want all of us to come out of this alive. We're on the same side. Let me help you.'

'No. I do this alone or I don't do it.'

'Okay.' He stepped back. 'Of course, your way, but just remember that I can help you.'

'Like you helped Eddie? You set him up.'

'No, I swear.'

'You can swear all you like but you must have seen Marco's rise to Tony's right hand. Why did you let it happen? You just watched while Eddie was set up. I know that he was. I know that you were the last person to see him before they came to get him and torture him to death. That means you, Harold, could have prevented it. That means you're as fucking guilty as the rest of them. Trust you? I'd sooner trust Sandra.'

Chapter 66

Willis went straight to Melvin Pratt's home. It was still cordoned off and Sandford was working inside. He stopped to come to the door to talk to her.

'You're senior investigating officer on this one?'

'I am.'

'Congratulations.' He smiled. 'We've done the main work here now, if you want to come in. You'll find a suit in my car.'

Willis got suited up.

'I'll take you through things from the front door,' said Sandford.

'Melvin arrived back from the pub and seems to have gone straight to bed.' Sandford opened the door to Melvin's bedroom and showed Willis.

'You can still smell it,' said Willis. 'The alcohol.'

'It's not just from the pub,' answered Sandford.

'No, I understand, I read the report.'

'He was dragged off the bed,' said Sandford, pointing to markers on the floor and on his plan where samples had been taken. 'There are fibres from his clothes. He was wearing boxers and a T-shirt. His skin was left on a nail sticking up from a board by the door. He was dragged

from his bed and through to the sitting room, to this chair.'
Sandford stepped across the hallway. 'The chair appears to
have been dragged with weight in it, across to the edge of
the rug. Maybe to give his assailant more room.'

The chair, with the remnants of Melvin's body fluids,
his skin, the scorch marks that blackened its bright-blue
material, could be seen from the hallway. It could be seen
from the front door, so an extended tent across the door
was more to hide the facts from public view than preserve
evidence.

'Was he keeping an eye on the door? Was he waiting for
someone?'

Sandford shook his head.

'Can't answer that one. Victim's legs were tied together.
His arms were tied behind his back and the wrists pulled
upwards, not secured but definitely with force. He was
periodically lifted, like this . . .' Sandford went behind the
chair to show Willis what he meant. 'One of his shoulders
had dislocated.'

'It's what we saw with Eddie Butcher: strappado torture.'

'The killer went through the kitchen. I expect you saw
the notes re his arsenal of home-made killing tools, torture
from the kitchen. He even took time to sharpen the knives
he found. He concentrated on four key areas of the body
to burn: the head and face, the genitals, the feet and the
hands. In between doing that he made himself something
to eat: cheese on toast.' Sandford held up a crime-scene
brown paper bag and showed Willis the remnants of a slice
of toast. 'Here's our DNA, I hope.'

'Plenty of the victim's DNA on this chair,' said Willis.

'Are you all right? You look a bit more shaken than
usual. I thought forensics was just up your street.'

'Oh, yes, sorry. I haven't been well. I'm just getting over some kind of a bug I picked up yesterday in Spain.'

'Yesterday? You need to go back to bed for the day. You're looking ill.'

'I'll be okay. Thanks.' She smiled. 'I just need some fresh air.'

'You're going to puke. You can be sick in the front garden. Mind the public doesn't see you. It'll be all over *News at Ten*. Here, have a bag.' He handed her a crime-scene bag and she went outside, hid behind a bin and was sick.

She emerged to the sound of an officer telling Harold Butcher he couldn't go any further into the crime scene.

'Okay, I'm standing here, all right?'

Willis walked across to him.

'Mr Butcher?'

Harold Butcher stood in his expensive cashmere coat and wearing his black leather gloves and his face was maroon-coloured, he had five o'clock shadow. He was sad and angry, and he didn't care who knew it.

'Is it Melvin?'

Willis nodded. It struck Willis as either arrogant or touching that Harold had come to make sure the rumours were true.

'How?'

Willis glanced behind her. 'As you can see, this is a murder scene.'

'I know that; I'm asking you how. Like Eddie?'

Willis nodded. 'But magnify his suffering tenfold.'

'Shit.' He dropped his head on his chest and breathed in deeply through his nose.

'Can you help us with this, Mr Butcher? You saw Melvin last night, I believe.'

'Yeah, he was drunk, shouting his mouth off; I gave him some money and I told him to go home. Was this definitely the same person as did Eddie?'

'No, but it was the same type of torture. With Eddie, someone ran out of time. His heart gave out.'

Willis watched him walk away.

Willis left Sandford to complete his job as she took off the forensic suit and bagged it up. She walked back along the street towards the church. Lev was serving customers. He had the demeanour of a man in deep thought, and the thoughts weren't nice ones.

'Coffee, please, milky.'

Willis paid and thanked him and went to sit at the window seat beneath the poster of Lev's grandfather. Her eyes settled beyond the window and on the road outside. It was a good winter's day: the blue sky was dotted with clouds, the wind had dropped. The streets were dry. It felt more as if Christmas was coming. But it didn't feel like that by the look on people's faces outside. Willis listened to the conversations as people came in to get their bagels. The talk was all about Melvin and 'What's it all coming to?'; 'How can this happen?'; 'This place isn't safe any more.' She watched Lev having to engage each customer with a fitting response. She watched him struggle with the constant flow of sorrow in and out of his shop. He was the centre of mourning, it seemed.

She waited until the shop was empty. She'd already eaten her bagel and had a second cup of coffee.

'Tough times today.'

He nodded. He eyed her with mistrust.

'You investigating it?'

She nodded and took out her badge to show him.

Willis picked up her plate and coffee mug and put them on the counter in front of Lev. She took a card from her pocket and paused as she passed it across.

'Do you still have the card Inspector Carter gave you?'

'Somewhere.'

'I need you to find it.' She smiled. 'I'm in charge of the investigation into Melvin's death. You knew him well?'

'Yes. I'd known him for many years. He started his tours in the last few years and he was doing well. Maybe too well, I don't know. I mean he gave talks about the villains in the East End; he overstepped the mark sometimes. A lot of these villains are still living here. Maybe he saw things he shouldn't have, and then he made the mistake of talking about it.'

Willis was thinking how Lev seemed as if he'd been working on what he was going to say. It sounded rehearsed, right down to the pauses.

'It was mentioned about him being warned off working. Did you hear that he'd been threatened?'

'He said he had, but Melvin had mental problems sometimes. He said things that weren't true. He imagined things. He said someone stole his dog, someone didn't want him to give his tours any more.'

'Is he the only one who gives these tours?'

'No, there's a woman. I haven't seen her either. They usually bring the people on the tour in for a bagel and I tell them a story about how my grandfather came over here and how the bakery began, just to bring local colour. But I haven't seen her either.'

'Do you know her name?'

'Janice. That's all I know her as. Janice from the tour, that's it. Wait, I have her card here.' Lev produced a stack of cards and dealt them until he found the one he was looking for. 'Janice Lander from East End Lives. Here, you take it.'

'How was he killed?' Lev asked her as she was walking out of the door. She stopped, stepped back inside.

'Tortured. Too many injuries to count. Finally killed with a Colombian necktie. Do you know what that is?' Lev responded with the slightest lift of his chin. 'Before that moment he was burned so badly that it was down to the bone. He had his face burned off. He was still alive when that happened. It took him a long time to die. It took someone a very long time to kill him – I hope I never have to see another murder scene like it but, somehow, I think I will. Colombian death squad members are moving in here. They come when there's work for them. They are the most ruthless, sadistic of all killers. You might know one already, Marco Zapata. He's been one in the past. This is his kind of work, Lev. We can stop him if we act now. We can stop any others getting a hold on this place. You feel like talking to me, you call.'

Willis walked down towards the church and made a call to the number on the card. A woman answered after a few rings.

'Janice from East End Lives?'

'Yes?' Her voice was nervous, tentative.

'Janice, I'm Detective Sergeant Willis. I'm investigating an incident. Can I just ask you if you're still giving the tours?'

'No. I'm not.'

'Can I ask why?'

'I decided to stop, that's all.'

'Any particular reason? I heard they were popular.'

'I was told that I shouldn't give the tours any more.'

'Told by who?'

'Look, I don't know what he was called. He was a big man with blond hair and he spoke with a foreign accent. He'd booked on to one of my tours and he just intimidated me for the two hours as I took my clients around. When he left he told me all about myself, he knew my address, my child's school, her name. He knew what time I dropped her every day. He knew everything about me – he told me to stop giving the tours. So I did. I noticed Melvin had taken his website down too. He must have been told the same as me.'

'Would you know this man again?'

'Of course, but there's no way I'm ever testifying against him. I can see in his face that he would kill me without a second thought. Me, my daughter and anyone else with us. I'm going to do exactly as he says, so please don't bother me again.'

'I may have to, I'm afraid, but no one can make you testify. Further down the line I may ask you to make a statement about what you just told me.'

'Why? Why should I?'

'Because Melvin has been murdered.'

Willis came off the phone, stopped and looked up. The gardens around the church were quiet. Only a couple sat on one of the benches. There was a mix of beautiful old housing and cobbled old streets. There was the Albert, an old empty pub on the corner of the road past the church.

Across from it was another derelict building. Willis wondered if the exit from Bethnal Green was already unstoppable. But was the place being bought up by cartels and not middle-class folk?

Chapter 67

Carter was waiting for Della when she got to the Holloway flat. She'd stashed her bag in the concealed luggage shelf in the car boot.

'Did you manage to find any more gems since you've been here?' he asked her as she came inside the flat.

'Hello to you, too.'

'Sorry, forgive me, I'm a bit wired. It's getting tense, juggling all these balls in the air.'

'I'm a ball now?' she teased. She walked towards him and smiled reassuringly.

'I found a good few, we can definitely use them. I estimate I have ten million pounds' worth.'

'Great, that will help a lot.'

'I'm willing to put them in the pot. How are you going with sourcing the rest?'

'We intercepted the expert at Heathrow, the man you told us about. We replaced him with one of us. He's pretty confident that he can get hold of enough to make it look real.'

'He has to know something of the trade. They'll know he's a fake otherwise.'

'He does. Marco's been to see him. He was shown a

rough diamond. I presume it was yours.' She didn't comment. 'He told our man to sit tight and expect to wait a few more days; Marco hasn't been in contact since. Is there a hold-up?'

'I overheard a conversation about it. The shipment is coming via Spain, being unloaded and then repackaged to come here. It's delayed it slightly. Pretty sure that it's still close.'

'Okay, good, that buys us a few hours at least and makes the shipment a bit more traceable if it's unloading in Spain. We were hoping we'd have found the cocaine laboratory that Tony uses. We keep looking. I thought it would be easy. I suppose I thought it would be a big outfit, chemical plant, that kind of thing. But it turns out it could be in somewhere as small as someone's flat. Still, I know Manson made regular trips to it. He would have wanted privacy unloading. He used a truck with a machine to help unload. Surely, he has to have been taking it into somewhere at ground level.'

'What about Manson's paperwork?' Della asked, staring out of the window.

'There isn't any. Has Marco or Harold mentioned what form it will come in? We are presuming it's coming like the other shipments, disguised in boxes that contain things Manson was importing for Paradise Villas.'

'No one's mentioned any of that side of things to me.'

Carter glanced across at Della a couple of times; she was deep in thought.

'You okay?' he asked.

'Yes. I'll be glad when it's all over. I bet you will, too.' She smiled. He nodded. 'What about Cabrina and Archie? Are they coming home soon?'

'One more week. They're fine. I'm glad they're out of the way. One less thing to worry about.'

'Who'd be a detective's other half, eh, Dan?'

'Pretty tough.' He grimaced. 'Worth it, though. What are your plans for the future, Della? What happens for you after this is over?'

'I hope to still be alive and I hope to live happily ever after.'

'Come on, bit more than that. Okay, here's the scenario: we take Tony, Harold and Marco out of the equation.'

'Can you add Sandra to that list, please.'

'Yes, okay, Debbie?'

'Debbie can stay.'

'So, what then?' asked Carter.

'We forgot Laurence,' Della said.

'Oh, yes, lovesick Laurence. What will you do? How do you see the rest of your life?'

'For Christ's sake, Dan. I've only just lost my husband. I don't know what I'm going to do.'

'Sorry.'

'No, I know you didn't mean it like that. But I seriously don't have a masterplan right now. I will go home and sit down and think. I will probably knock my villa down and start again.'

'Wow, that's quite a project. So money isn't a problem for you?'

'Eddie had a fair bit put away for a rainy day. He wasn't a great one to put his trust in banks.' She paused to allow for a smile from Carter. 'So he left it to me in various places and in various ways.' She turned and smiled at Carter.

'So you'll rebuild the villa; maybe you can take over Paradise Villas.'

'Perhaps. I'm not sure I want to work. I might get the villa done and bugger off. I might travel. I could let you know where I am in the world and you could fly out and join me.'

'Between taking Archie on the school run and being an overworked, underpaid homicide detective, you mean?'

'Exactly. I could be your secret life.'

'I can't deal with secrets that big.'

'So, if you had an affair, you'd tell Cabrina, would you?'

'Probably not, but if I had an affair I would know Cabrina wasn't the right one for me and I would tell her that.'

'Will I see you here later?' she asked Carter as he was going.

'Are you sure about staying here now?'

'Yes, I just have to go back to the Shoreditch flat. I've forgotten a couple of things.'

'You be careful. I'll text you later. Maybe I'll come by.'

'That would be nice. I don't want to be on my own.'

'I know. I understand.'

As Carter walked down the stairs to the car park he shook his head, disappointed in himself. *Stay focused, Carter, for Christ's sake. Stay focused.*

Chapter 68

18 December

Carter was called in to see Bowie.

'Maxi says he wants out.' Bowie closed the door as Carter entered his office. 'He got in touch with me direct.'

'What? He can't.'

'He can, unfortunately.'

'Shit.' Carter plonked himself down. 'That's the trouble with having to wait a few days. It's made us all jittery. He's done really well sourcing enough diamonds, fake and real.'

'He told me he's pretty confident they can pass muster,' said Bowie. 'He reckons they might just pass for a couple of hundred's worth with the big uncut diamonds that Della's handed over.'

'She has another couple to give him,' said Carter. 'Marco has one that's worth a lot.'

'Maxi says he can just about make it look like we have over two hundred million's worth of diamonds there but he doesn't want to be the one who faces the cartels. Can't think why that is!'

'He can't mean it. Marco has seen Maxi. We can't just

change experts. I need to talk to Maxi. It can still work. It has to.'

'I didn't push him on it,' said Bowie. 'He's stressed enough. He's got a bulging safe full of diamonds, too. They will all have to be moved somewhere that Della is able to access for when the time comes. Do we have any more intelligence on Tony? Do have an inkling of how Della intends to lure him over?'

'No, I'm afraid I don't. She won't share that with me. But I think I should stay with her now, till the end. It can't be long. She needs a lot of support to get through this. I can help her with the plan she has.'

'I agree.'

'We have had a lot more contact with the OCC in the last five days,' said Carter. 'They're tracking various container ships, hoping that the stop in Valencia will narrow it down for us. The new cartel may have a completely different way of bringing in the cocaine than we've been looking at. I think we still have to go with one of Manson's companies. Something made Manson top himself.'

'Do we know what his last twenty-four hours were like?'

'We have confirmation that Laurence Butcher went to him at his house.'

'Do we know what they discussed?'

'I presume he must have told him he was taking over. Maybe Manson realised he wasn't going to be able to continue importing the cocaine if Laurence was going to be taking on Paradise Villas full time, living here as well. No way Manson would be able to continue helping out the cartels or Tony.'

'But we won't truly be able to investigate any of the Butchers or the movement of the cocaine in previous shipments while we still hope to catch Tony red-handed. We just have to sit on it for a few more days. The minute it's done we can expose all we know about Manson's dealings.'

'Has family liaison got anywhere with Jo Manson yet?' asked Bowie.

'Nothing so far,' answered Carter. 'She's staying in Plymouth. She has family there, so we are still examining the contents of Manson's computer hard drive and all the paperwork in his office.'

'How is DS Willis?'

'I think she's okay. She seems to be fighting through whatever it was. She's interviewing witnesses in the Melvin Pratt case. Which, I'm glad I don't have to handle. I feel completely to blame for putting Melvin in harm's way.'

'Why was he killed do you think?'

'Has to be because they knew he was a snitch.'

'But he took a few photos, you said. Why did it warrant that and not just a beating at best?'

'I don't know. I'm hoping Willis will find out something different, but I feel responsible. The community know more than they are saying. Chrissie, from the Blind Beggar, was given one of my cards to contact me and send me round to find Melvin. I've only handed them out to a few people round there. But I'll lie low. I don't want any connection to Della made.'

'How is Della holding up?' asked Bowie.

'She's getting progressively more terrified. But she's still in this till the end. She doesn't see any other way forward for herself.'

'If nothing else comes out of this, we should still be able to seize a massive shipment of cocaine and we will definitely close down one way of them importing it.'

'I'm still hoping for more. I'm still hoping for Tony and the end to murders like Melvin's. I want this to be the end and not the beginning of cartels and Colombian death squads on our streets.'

Bowie nodded. 'Have we heard anything about Inspector Ross?'

'Nothing. Willis went round to see his ex-wife. Apparently, she was expecting to see him. She's heard nothing, either. But I am sure we will hear when the OCC want us to. Something tells me he's always got his own agenda going on. The OCC are not declaring him missing. They must have their reasons. I'm going to see Maxi now,' said Carter as he stood and grabbed his coat. 'I'll keep you informed.'

Chapter 69

Della hadn't seen anyone for three days. She'd been staring out at the cold sleet that slashed across the windows and she'd watched the seagulls that had made their home in the city, and she missed the warm sunshine and the smell of the sea.

She left a message for Carter that she needed to see him, but heard nothing back. Carter was busy, she understood, but now all her anxieties had come to the surface. Della had handed over most of the diamonds, at least the ones she was prepared to lose. The last ones were in Shoreditch. She needed to go back there but she was dreading it; she'd been ignoring angry messages left on her phone for days. Marco had the big rough diamond still and she had stashed another few smaller-cut, high-carat ones in the kitchen cupboard. She got herself ready to go, put on her make-up, told herself she had started the job and she would finish it.

She messaged Marco that she wanted to come to the flat and that she needed the stone back now.

As she walked up the stairs she smelled him. He had a pungent aftershave, a mix of fresh sweat on stale.

She felt her stomach churn.

'Della! Princessa!'

She walked into the sitting room.

'Yes, why shouldn't I be?'

'You got our diamonds?'

'You need to go and have a shower, Marco. You stink,' Della said, and waited until he'd gone away before she walked into the kitchen and opened the cupboard. She reached into the back to the packet of cereal she'd put the diamonds in. She pulled the bag quickly from the box.

Della froze. She closed the cupboard as she heard Marco come into the kitchen.

'Laurence and I had a little chat this afternoon.'

'Nice. Now get out of my way.' She turned and went to go past him. 'Go and get the diamond I gave you. I need everything together now. I want to make sure everything is right for your family.'

'Ha-ha, you're a funny woman. But I don't think you're a very honest one.'

'That's rich, coming from you.' Della had her hand just settled on the zip of her bag. The gun was tucked inside the inner pocket.

'Let me show you something,' Marco said.

'I want to go, let me pass!' Marco knocked the bag out of her hand.

'You . . .' He pushed her back against the cupboard. 'You haven't been honest, have you?

'Who is this?' He turned his phone round and showed her the photo that Laurence had taken of her and Carter at the window in the flat in Holloway.

'No idea.' She tried to dismiss it and move away from the wall.

He held her against the wall, by the throat.

She stared at him and her fear turned to mockery as she smiled.

'Do it, loser,' she said with small, shallow breaths. 'You kill me, there's no deal and you look like the prick you are.'

He contemplated snapping her neck but then drew back slightly.

'This man is a police officer.'

'He was my boyfriend once, a long time ago, before I knew Eddie.'

'Is that his flat you are in?'

'Yes.'

'You're a dirty little slut.'

'Eddie always provided for me. I felt empty,' she said, trying to smile. Marco grinned, his eyes still hard-boiled, as he didn't release her. 'I missed it, okay?' she added, feeling his grip lessen.

'You're working with this policeman?'

'I'm handling stolen diamonds, what do you think? He's just an old boyfriend. Do you still want the diamonds?'

'Oh, yes, princess, I want them, but that's not all I want.' Della started to fight the hand that forced itself up between her thighs. 'I want you to understand.' Marco leaned back slightly and smiled at her. 'You wet, princess?' He squashed her further into the wall and she cried out in pain as she squirmed and fought him as he forced his fingers inside her.

'Now you just remember, princess, as fine as you think you are, you are nothing.' Marco slowly withdrew his fingers at the sound of the door being opened.

Della pushed him back as she pulled down her dress. He kept her pinned to the wall. He blocked her movements.

'But you have the diamonds, right?'

'I've shown you a diamond, haven't I? You can see it's genuine. Now fuck off.'

He grabbed her arm. Laurence came up the stairs and shouted at Marco.

'Let her go. I want to talk to her,' said Laurence.

Marco did as he was told and pulled her across to sit at the dining table. Laurence sat down very close. Della was looking around for her bag. Marco had it in his hand and he was playing with the gun.

'Where did you get this?' asked Laurence.

'Eddie left it to me. He left it with some diamonds in a security box.'

'What's the deal with the policeman?'

'No deal. He's an old friend.'

'You're lying, Della,' said Laurence. 'He's a colleague. Eddie told me who you were, he was proud of it. He was proud to have an ex-cop as his wife. He thought it was funny. Have you all of the diamonds now? They must add up to more than a hundred million.'

'I'm still looking for some of it. I think Tony needs to come over and help me. He understands things like Eddie did. Some of these numbers and places Eddie left me don't make any sense to me.'

Laurence was smiling at Marco, and Della turned to see why.

'We think you're lying. We're pretty sure you've got the diamonds; you're just stalling. Does your boyfriend know where they are? Did you tell him?'

Marco was poised with a can of hairspray and a lighter.

A flame shot into the room as he pressed the nozzle and sparked the lighter.

'Not here,' said Laurence. 'Harold will be back. Not sure what he'd say to this method. We'll move her to the Albert.'

Chapter 70

Carter met Maxi in the same bar as last time. Maxi couldn't see him till after eight. Carter looked at the time on his phone: it was nearly nine. Maxi still hadn't appeared. It was getting late. He'd heard nothing more from Della; he'd go over there later. Willis wanted to see him, too. He had a million things to do and people to see. He texted Della under the code name Danielle.

'It will have to be a late takeaway, I'm sorry. I'll see you at about eleven.'

As he sent it he wished he hadn't.

Maxi walked in looking a lot less happy than the last time they'd met in the bar.

'I can only spare you ten minutes. I need to meet up with a man about some more stones.'

'Okay. Well, I appreciate it, Maxi. Have a drink at least.'

He sat down, still keeping his eyes on the door.

'It's not been a barrel of laughs, you know. Waiting, all the waiting.'

'In a five-star luxury hotel?' said Carter.

'Yeah, you can ponce it up all you like but it still feels like any minute the Mafia could burst in and shoot me to buggery. I haven't been able to enjoy the hotel; I've been back and forth like a bloody yo-yo. I still have a business to run, you know.'

'So you didn't use any of the cash he left you?'

'I ordered room service a couple of times.'

'Maxi, we need you to see this through. I'll see about you keeping that cash.'

'Huh, don't think that's going to do it for me. I left the force because I couldn't handle the stress; I still can't handle it. I thought this would be fun; it isn't.'

'Have you got all the stones together now? How's it all looking?'

'I'm waiting for the last few to be delivered from Contact X; they're the big ones. I haven't heard when that's happening. I've got a bucketload of ones that look worth more than they are already. I need the extra uncut ones to make it look convincing.'

'So you're still in this?'

'Look, I can't promise I won't bottle it. I've been getting panic attacks. I can't face any drugs cartel.'

'So, I'll make it that you don't have to. I'll make sure this is all done and dusted in private, just you and the diamonds. Would that be okay?'

Maxi nodded reluctantly. 'When will it happen, then?'

'The shipment will come in and Contact X will collect them and take them to Marco. Marco will bring them to you here. You'll okay them. I'll make sure you're safe. I'll have officers standing by.'

Willis was in Robbo's office. They were going over the statements they had collected so far about Melvin's last hours. Pam had gone home.

'Did Melvin elaborate about who had scared him off working?' asked Willis.

'No, he didn't say who it was.'

Robbo had loaded all the photos that came from Melvin's phone and they were studying them.

'Maybe he didn't, but the other tour guide, Janice from East End Lives, she described Marco to a T,' said Willis.

'Did he threaten her?' asked Robbo.

'He said he'd kill her daughter. He knew all about her and her daily routines.'

'Why go to so much trouble to scare off the tour guides?'

'I've emailed Janice and asked her for an exact break-down of all the places she went on her tour and all the people she regularly spoke to. She's absolutely terrified; she doesn't want to lodge any police complaint against Marco.'

'I can understand.'

'Harold Butcher came by the crime scene.'

'Guilty conscience, do you think?' asked Robbo.

'Not something you would normally associate with a Butcher,' Willis replied, 'but, yes, maybe guilty because he knew it was unnecessary and he might have prevented it.'

'I still don't think this had anything to do with him. This was committed by one man and we'll have the first set of DNA results back tomorrow.'

Harold got in and walked upstairs; the television had been left on. He was expecting to find someone watching it but there was no one. He knocked on Della's door. He could smell her perfume in the air. There was no reply. He went to the drinks cabinet and took out the bottle of thirty-year-old Famous Grouse and a glass and came to sit. He poured himself a generous drink and sat down to wait for the others to return. An hour later he phoned Marco.

'Where are you? Have you seen Della? Was she here?'

'Della is with us.'

'Who is us?'

'Laurence and me. She's been lying to us. She's been fucking an old boyfriend, a policeman.'

'Does she have all the diamonds?'

'She says not. She says she wants Tony over here to help her look for them.' Harold could hear the sound of someone in pain, a woman's voice.

'Don't kill her, then, you stupid bastard. Where are you? It sounds like you're in a warehouse.'

Marco didn't choose to understand what Harold was saying.

'Bring Della to me. I need to talk with her.'

'That's not possible. She can't come. We are looking after her from now on. Every move she makes we can see it.'

Harold sent a text to Tony. He wanted to Skype. Harold picked up his glass and walked across nearer to the webcam on top of the television monitor.

'Where is everyone? What is happening with the deal?' Tony screeched. Harold turned the volume down.

'Tony, did you order Marco to kill Eddie?'

'Absolutely not. One of the death squad did it.'

'Not Marco?'

'How do I know? What's got into you, Harold? You've been thinking too much, you know that's not your forte.'

'But did you order it? Did Eddie find out about Manson's sideline? Was that the problem, Tony? Did he say he wasn't going to allow it to happen and just as this new big shipment was coming in?'

'What are you saying all this for, Harold?'

'Because I am feeling pretty sure that Marco is out of control, and now he's got Della.'

'What? Why? How did you allow it?'

'He has her and Laurence, apparently.'

'Laurence is being held by Marco?'

'How do I know? I get home here, I look for Della and get told Della is being held somewhere by Marco and I can hear she's being tortured. I've seen the results of Marco's handiwork. There will be nothing left of her by the morning. The deal will be off. No diamonds, no Della, no deal.'

'Well stop him, for Christ's sake, you idiot.'

'Me, an idiot? You wound him up, Tony, now you have to watch him go. He's going to bring this whole thing crashing down around our heads. There will be no deal because he'll kill Della and there will be none of us left by the end of it.'

'No. I won't stand for it! Are you hearing me, Harold?'

'Really? Then you deal with it. Who was next on his list, Tony? Mum? Me? Della says she needs you over here. She needs help finding the diamonds.'

'I can't come, you know that.'

'You could if you wanted. Is it worth it, Tony? You decide.'

Harold terminated the call.

Carter checked his phone. He was just finishing up when he got a text from Della: 'Don't bother with a takeaway, come asap. I'm cooking.'

Chapter 71

Carter drove to the Holloway flat and parked up. He was feeling more sane since he spoke with Cabrina and Archie earlier that evening. He was back to normality. He heard all the things Archie had got up to. He heard the love in Cabrina's voice and he felt calm. Now he was back in work mode and Della was part of that. He wasn't going to let her be any more than that or any less. He pressed the entry button and he was buzzed up and took the stairs two at a time. He had a problem with lifts. It was a touch of claustrophobia that he didn't admit to; plus, he hated waiting for them, it seemed lazy – it made more sense to run up the stairs. The flat door was ajar when he reached it. He heard the sound of music. He heard someone in the kitchen. He couldn't smell anything cooking but there was definitely a smell of aftershave and sweat.

Carter crept silently across to the French windows; he picked up an orange from the bowl on the dining table, and walked around level with the kitchen wall and rolled it towards the front door.

Marco stepped out, gun drawn. Carter barged forward, pushing Marco back and then crashing from the wall onto the floor. For a few minutes they fought on the floor.

Marco's gun was knocked across the room. Carter thought he was doing really well. He had a chance. He was beating the bigger man, until Laurence stepped up behind and pushed a gun into his back.

'First shot will sever your spinal cord. Ready to smell your own shit?'

Carter rolled away.

'Stand up,' ordered Laurence. Carter did as he was told. He checked Carter's pockets, took out his keys. 'Phone?' Carter shook his head. He had left it in the car.

Marco got to his feet and picked up his gun. He stepped across and punched Carter in the face with it. Carter's nose cracked at the bridge and a cut opened up between his eyes.

'Where are the diamonds?' Marco said into Carter's face. Blood started to drip.

Carter shook his head.

'Move.' They pushed him out of the flat and down the back stairs towards the car park.

Marco tied him up in the back seat of Laurence's car and pushed him so that he lay flat, then Laurence drove for twenty minutes until Carter felt the wheels drive over cobbles and come to a stop. Marco got out and opened what sounded like a door. Carter raised his head to see the pub sign 'The Albert', and the back door was opened. Marco pulled Carter forward along the seat and dragged him out onto his knees and then pushed him head first though the trapdoor in the pavement. Carter's head hit the concrete below and he passed out.

'Do you know how it is done?'

He heard the voice of a man coming to him from the

middle of a dream full of pain and struggle, a dream where you can't move, where you fight to free yourself from something that's twisted around your body and the pain just keeps increasing.

Carter's hands were tied behind his back. The blood in his eyes blurred his vision. He tried to open them but he couldn't. He heard the man talking. He knew he was talking to him; he was sure he recognised the voice; but he couldn't quite get to consciousness out of the pain dream to make sense of it.

What was it the man was asking him? Carter managed to open one eye; the other was stuck fast with blood. He tried to see through the blur. His head was ringing with echoes. He saw shadows moving. He heard a woman's screams.

'Do you know how it is done?' The man repeated the question. Carter heard it that time and fought hard to open both eyes.

'Many people believe the right way is to slit across horizontally before dragging the tongue through, but this is not correct.' Carter began to focus. Now he could see the man was Marco. Marco was standing behind a chair, tilting it back, and he had a knife to the base of a woman's throat. It was Della.

'*No!*' Carter screamed into his gag.

'Here, this is where you begin your cut, at the base of the throat, insert here and then cut upwards.' He turned the knife over and pressed the point into her throat. His eyes stayed on Carter. Marco paused and looked up. 'Say goodbye to your colleague, Inspector Carter.'

'Enough,' said Laurence. 'There'll be plenty of time for that later. Hang him up.'

Marco hoisted Carter up on to a hook on the cellar wall. He felt pain as his shoulders twisted back and pulled upwards.

'What are these for?' Laurence jangled the keys from the self-storage in Carter's face. 'This set is for home, isn't it?' Laurence held another set with Carter's car key attached. 'This is a set of keys for a lockup somewhere, isn't it?'

'Allotment.' Carter was thankful that Cabrina and Archie weren't at home. He shook his head to try to stay conscious. He looked around the small cellar. There were a few empty kegs on their sides. There were smashed bottles swept to one end. A strip light dangled from the ceiling. Marco was watching him. Another man was in the shadows.

Carter looked across at Della. Her head hung down.

'Hope your allotment is big enough to bury two bodies,' said Laurence. 'You're going to watch Della die unless you tell us where the diamonds are.'

'I don't know anything about any diamonds.'

Laurence had a new message on his phone.

'We need to get Tony,' he said. 'His plane lands at two. It will take a good hour to get there. Leave Jo here to guard. We'll pick up Harold on the way.'

Marco addressed the other man in the room in Spanish. Carter understood some of it. His name was Jo and he had the job of guarding them while the others were gone. After Marco and Laurence had gone Jo walked around the cellar, he nudged the broken bottles with his foot and he sighed a lot. After an hour or so he came to stand in front of Carter and stare at him. Jo was chain-smoking cigarettes. Carter lifted his head and nodded towards the cigarette. He thought he might even try out his Spanish if he could get Jo to remove the gag.

'Your girlfriend?' Jo gestured towards Della. Jo's voice was thick with a Colombian accent.

Carter shook his head and said something into the gag.

'You relax.' Jo went around to the front of Della and stood looking at her. His eyes flicked up towards Carter. 'No girlfriend?'

Carter didn't respond. He saw Della lift her head and he saw her shoulders stiffen.

'Pretty woman,' he said, unzipping his fly. 'Pretty mouth.'

Harold was halfway through the bottle of Scotch when Marco came back in with Laurence.

'Where is she?'

'Who?'

'Don't fuck with me, Laurence, or you'll regret it. What do you think you're doing? Where's Della?' Marco was watching Laurence to see how he was handling it.

'What I'm doing is stepping up to the family plate. I reckon with a lot better management I can do it better.'

Marco smiled. 'Exactly.'

'Where's Della?' repeated Harold. 'Where are the diamonds?'

'Ah, we hit a slight snag. It turns out that Della has an old boyfriend back on the scene and we think he's been helping her. They intended to disappear with the diamonds.'

'Who is he?'

'Detective Inspector Dan Carter' – Marco laughed, as he exaggerated Carter's title – 'is going to be talking by the morning when his shoulders will be hanging by only skin.'

His face was grey, thin-lipped. Harold swung his head back and forth, dumbfounded.

'What do you think this is, a fucking game? The policeman will bring every copper down here looking for him.'

'We'll be done and dusted by then. One of them will talk. Della's not proving as strong as we had thought. She won't take much more. Marco has had a small accident with a blowtorch.' Laurence laughed.

'You fucking sick bastard.' Harold got up and went to lunge at Marco but stumbled.

'Drunk, Harold?' said Laurence. 'That makes a change, doesn't it?'

'Maybe she actually doesn't have all of the stones yet. Did you even consider that?' said Harold.

'She has to. She's had long enough. She's lying to us. Anyway, it doesn't matter: Tony is on his way now, he will sort it. We're going to pick him up. You coming?'

'No. Tell me where Della is and I'll meet you there.'

'No, because you know what, Harold? I don't think I trust you any more. I don't think Tony does, either. You know what he said to me the other day? Harold can disappear when this is done.'

'He said retire,' corrected Marco, laughing.

'Yeah, and we all know what he meant.'

'You going to be the one to do it, Laurie? You're Mister Little Big Man all of a sudden? You think you're clever, you think you're the new boy on the block, but you don't know who you're dealing with. You're wet behind the ears. You better learn respect.' Harold took a few steps towards Laurence and his eyes shifted to see Marco hovering.

'We're going.' Laurence turned and walked back towards

the stairs. We'll phone you later when we've got Tony. Try not to drink yourself stupid by then.'

Carter's rage settled in his gut as he stared at Jo for two hours and tried not to think of the pain, just of revenge. It helped him stay conscious.

He looked across at Della. He was worried about her. If anyone tried to touch her again he would firstly tell them where the diamonds were and secondly kill them very slowly. His mind went back to Cabrina and Archie. He hoped that, if he didn't make it through this, Archie would remember him and know how much he loved him.

Chapter 72

Willis was in Fletcher House early. It was just after six a.m. when she got to her desk. She had spent most of the night going through all the details of Melvin's death and something was still bugging her about the photos. She still hadn't heard back from Janice of East End Lives. She would spend the morning walking Melvin's route, the way Carter had done, in the hope of finding something to explain the motives behind Melvin's murder. Lev could tell her more, she was sure. He'd have had a few days to think about it now.

She called Carter and got no reply. She got to her desk in the inquiry team office and checked her emails: some forensic results were back from the crime scene at Melvin's. There was a match for Marco's DNA, that Della had provided. There was also a cross-reference to the Eddie Butcher murder, a blond hair that belonged to Marco Zapata was found on both bodies. She spent an hour studying the photos from Melvin's tour again. She kept going back to the photos of the old pub by the church.

She went down the corridor to talk to Robbo. He was

always at his desk by seven thirty. On the way she got a call. Willis looked at the number and didn't recognise it, almost didn't take it, but accepted on the last ring.

'Ebony?'

'Yes?'

'It's me, David Ross.'

She stopped in her tracks.

'Are you okay?'

'Yes. Sorry about having to leave you like that. I just knew I had to stay. We found Francisco's body. There's nothing to pin it on the Butchers yet.'

'What about his daughter?'

'She was found alive. Someone left her at the police station, the day after you left, but they kept it quiet. She's been in hospital all this time.'

'Do they know who brought her in?' asked Willis.

'The rumours are one of the Butcher household. But, Eb, I really stayed here to make sure of this side of the Butcher operation. We are getting close now, Eb. I can't stay on the phone. I've rung up with some information for you. We've been following a South American container ship and we're pretty sure that the shipment has left Valencia on its way to Felixstowe in the next eight hours, then it has to be unloaded. So expect it in the next twelve. Did you find out where the laboratory is yet?'

'No. Manson committed suicide and we haven't found any reference to it.'

'We'll have to hope we can follow the shipment or the Butchers to the laboratory. If not we're screwed. One good bit of news for you: Tony Butcher's left his villa and is headed for a private airstrip in the UK. Be ready.'

'Is it a hundred per cent?'

'Yes. Apparently, he's got his doubts about the deal happening unless he comes across. Are the diamonds ready for the exchange?'

'Carter's dealing with it. They're in a safe place, ready. Ross, are you okay? Where are you?'

The line went dead.

Willis called Carter again but his phone went straight to voicemail. She went down the corridor to Robbo's office. He was just switching on the kettle and starting up his computers. It was seven thirty.

'Robbo, is there a landline at the apartment where Della is?'

'Not as far as I know. What's the matter?'

'I need to get hold of Carter. His phone's dead. Ross is back in touch. The shipment is about to leave Valencia and Tony Butcher's coming over. He could, potentially already be here.'

Robbo clapped his hands together and looked skywards. 'For what we are about to receive may the Lord make us truly thankful.'

'We need to finalise arrangements. Carter had the diamonds moved yesterday. Where are they? Did he tell you?' asked Willis.

Robbo shook his head. 'He chose one of the self-storage places around the M25, but I don't know which one.'

'I'm going to go and find him,' said Willis. 'He needs to know this right away.'

Willis left Robbo and went down to use the detectives' pool car. She drove down Holloway Road, turned off onto a side road and parked up. She rang the entry button for the flat and waited. She rang it several times, then she rang Robbo.

'There's no answer at the flat,' she said.

'I'll text Della. We have code names. It should be safe.'

While she was waiting, someone came out of the block. She slipped inside and walked up the stairs. As she reached the flat door she saw bloodspots leading away towards the back stairs to the car park. She tried the door handle of the flat and it turned; the door opened.

Willis did a quick sweep of the flat and then took out her phone.

'Robbo? I'm inside. The flat door was unlocked. There's blood, and there's signs of a fight. There's no sign of Carter or Della. The beds are stone cold. No one slept here last night.' She bent down to examine the bloodspots. 'The blood's dried but there's a steady amount of it, large drips from sites close together. It's fallen from high up, possible head wound. I'm following it down the back stairs to the car park as we speak.' Willis walked down the back stairs and opened the heavy fire door leading to the underground car park.

'The blood pools. I would say the wounded person got into a car.'

'I've just got a text back from Della,' said Robbo. 'It was sent from the Shoreditch apartment. It says, "Yes, I saw Danielle yesterday. At home now."'

'Carter's BMW's here. Do we know what Della was driving?'

'A white Volkswagen Up,' answered Robbo.

'It's not here. I'm going to drive to Carter's flat.' Willis heard the ting of a message received and she saw a light come on in Carter's car. She walked over to it and saw the glow of a phone screen. 'Carter's phone is here in his car.'

*

An hour later Willis phoned Robbo again from outside Carter's flat. She'd been trying to get in for the last ten minutes.

'No, he's not here, either. This is feeling very wrong, Robbo. We have to know if that was really Della answering from the Shoreditch flat or if someone has got hold of her phone.'

'I've just talked to the surveillance officers. They said that they saw Laurence driving her car. Only Harold is in the flat right now. No sign of Della.'

'Okay. I'm coming back. I need to talk to Chief Inspector Bowie.'

Bowie was waiting for her when Willis got back to Fletcher House.

'Have you exhausted every possibility?' he asked. 'If we go in to the Shoreditch flat looking for Carter we blow this whole operation and we may still not find him.'

'He's not in the Shoreditch apartment; neither is Della. Chances are they are together, sir,' said Willis.

'With Tony Butcher here, David Ross back in touch, we are so close now to our objective, Sergeant. Both Della and Carter will want us to stick to our objective until we have proof otherwise. They know what they're doing. Keep looking for Carter but don't make it too obvious. Don't panic until we have good reason to.'

'Yes, sir. We think we know where the shipment will be coming in. Ross said he'd be in touch again when he had details.'

'That's good. That's all we can ask for. See if Robbo has come up with possible locations for the self-storage. Carter might still have his phone. We need to hack into it.'

'I left it in his car, sir. The car's being brought back to the station. We'll access it then.'

'Meanwhile, we act like we're not missing Carter, like we don't know he's gone missing. We hang tight, yes?'

'Yes, sir.'

Willis went back down the corridor to Robbo. He was working with Pam to try to locate where Carter had moved the diamonds.

'What's your brief?' asked Robbo when Willis walked in.

'The chief inspector is calling this one; I have to go about my business as if Carter isn't missing,' said Willis, obviously troubled. 'We can't afford to raise suspicions,' she said. Robbo nodded.

'Carter will be okay.' Robbo laid a comforting hand on her shoulder.

'I know but he's hurt already.'

'We don't know that it's his blood, not for sure,' said Pam.

Willis nodded, but she didn't look comforted.

'I think the chief inspector's right, Eb,' said Robbo.

'And if they kill him?' said Willis. She sat down at the spare desk and logged on. 'We have to try and find him. If Della is with him he will be under so much pressure to protect her. He will sacrifice himself.'

'What if Della managed to get a message out to someone?' asked Pam. 'Who would it be, do you think? Who might she have called?'

'She'd call her parents. Fredo's Ristorante in Ramsgate,' answered Willis.

'Here's the number,' said Pam, looking on the Internet. 'Do you want to ring?'

Willis took out her phone. Pam read off the number. Connie answered.

'Connie, it's Dan Carter's colleague, Ebony. I was wondering if you've heard from Della in the last few days.'

'No, I haven't heard from her at all. Is she okay?'

'Yes, I'm sure she is. It's just I can't locate her or Carter at the moment. If she calls you can you ring me on this number straight away?'

'Of course. I was so sad about Billy Manson. Was it suicide?'

'Yes, we're treating it as suicide.'

'He only came to see me recently. He brought a box of things from the office. He said they were papers to give to Della. They were Eddie's things.'

'Thanks. Please stay there. I'll come and collect the box from you now.'

She came off the phone. 'I'm driving down to Ramsgate, Robbo. Billy Manson left a box there just when the fireplaces were moved a week ago. Della's mother Connie doesn't know what's in it. Billy told her there were things that belonged to Eddie but there could be something else he was hiding.'

'Okay, well get back as fast as you can. We need to be on standby.'

Willis arrived an hour later and parked as near as she could get to Fredo's. She rounded the corner and was buffeted by the gusting wind straight off the harbour.

'Ebony, come in out of the cold. Have a coffee. We are just getting set up for lunch. What's this all about? Where is Dan? Is he with Della?'

'I think Dan is with her, yes. I can't stop, sorry.'

'Should we be worried? I don't know why Della has not been in touch. What's she doing over here?'

'I can't tell you anything, I'm afraid. I'm sure Della will tell you when you see her.' Willis was desperate to go.

'Okay, well I will wait to hear then.' Connie hugged her. 'Here.' Connie handed over the box to Willis.

'I can see you are worried. You keep in touch, please, Ebony.'

Willis nodded. She carried the box back to the car and opened it up as she sat in the driver's seat. She phoned Robbo.

'It looks interesting. There are mentions of his other companies. I'll be back within the hour.'

As she was about to set off she got a text from Ross: 'We lost shipment.'

Chapter 73

Carter looked up at the sound of voices. Jo jumped to his feet from his seat on the barrels; Della stirred. As they opened the door to the pub upstairs, daylight seeped inside the cellar.

Tony Butcher stood looking at Carter and shaking his head.

Tony was feeling the cold. He had borrowed a coat from Harold. The coat was too small and short on the arms. He had sandals on his feet, bare toes. He had found a red fleece blanket in the Transit van they'd hired, and wrapped it around himself and over his head, like an old Indian.

'You better start talking, son. I can see you're in a lot of pain.' Tony signalled for Jo to remove Carter's gag.

Carter tried to speak, his mouth was chalky dry. Tony gave him a drink of water.

'Let Della go,' said Carter. 'She doesn't know where the diamonds are, she told you. I took them off her, I hid them. I'll tell you, if you let her go.'

'You'll tell us anyway, won't he, Marco?'

Marco stepped forward with his cigarette and stubbed it out on Carter's cheek. The sound and smell of his own flesh burning hit his nose with the pain. He flinched.

'Marco knows how to get the best out of people,' said Tony. 'I admire your balls. What were you thinking? Get the girl, get the diamonds? You almost had it all. You were almost halfway to paradise.' Tony laughed. 'Eh, son? Eh? Eh?'

Marco stepped forward, made a flat hand and jabbed his fingers hard into Carter's lower abdominals. Carter instinctively raised his knees as the pain hit, his shoulders jolted and he yelled in agony. He saw Della react out of the corner of his eyes. He saw her shoulders move as if she were crying. Marco jabbed again, repeatedly, as Carter's shoulder joints began to strain at their sockets. Carter vomited bile. Marco went across to get his blowtorch.

Above the sound of Carter retching a phone rang.

Marco answered it.

'The shipment is here. I'm not fucking around any more with this guy.' Marco lit the blowtorch and walked across to Della. 'We'll make him talk.'

'He doesn't care if she isn't left with a face. You better talk, Inspector,' said Tony. 'Tell me.'

'The keys – they belong to a self-storage unit off junction twenty-six,' said Carter. 'You'll see the signs then for Cotters self-storage units. The code you need to get in the gate is 1066. The storage unit is number thirty-nine.'

'Untie her,' said Laurence. 'We'll take her with us as insurance.'

'No. They're no use to us any more.' Marco looked at Laurence and then at Tony.

'You're wrong, Marco. You are much too hasty. You rush head long in with that big fat head of yours and you don't stop to think of the consequences. Cut him down,' said Tony. 'This one . . .' He looked at Carter as he landed on the floor with a yell of pain as he was released from strappado. 'This one is a fantastic bargaining tool for us.'

'Exactly,' Harold joined in. 'You could be looking at your ticket out of here. Gag him again and leave him tied as he is. We'll come back for him if we need him. I'm not taking him with us. He'll be trouble.'

'What about her?' asked Marco.

'She comes with us. I haven't done with her,' said Laurence. Tony looked at him curiously and grinned.

'Now we pick up the diamond expert, Roland de Soir,' said Marco as he took out his phone.

Maxi had been about to get showered and leave the hotel to go to his shop when the phone beside the bed rang.

'We pick you up in twenty minutes from the outside of the hotel.'

'Where will we be going?'

'Don't worry. You'll be taken care of.'

'I need to know where it is.'

'Twenty minutes. Be outside.' The phone went dead.

Maxi tried ringing Carter but couldn't get through. He phoned Bowie.

'What do you want me to do?'

'Go with them and we'll follow you.'

'But—'

'Maxi, Carter is missing. A lot depends on this.'

'I'll do my best. He'd do the same for me.'

'Do you know what you have to do?'

'I know what Carter told me. It's a Colombian drug cartel called the Zapata family. I'm working for them to make sure that the diamonds add up to more than a hundred million pounds.'

Maxi showered and got ready to leave.

Bowie called Willis.

'Marco phoned. They're picking Maxi up to examine the diamonds. It means the shipment has arrived. We need them followed. We must not lose them.'

'Carter's told them where the diamonds are,' said Willis. 'He waited for the shipment to arrive. He must have.'

Willis felt a glimmer of hope.

Undercover officers sat in their cars across from the hotel, waiting for Maxi's pick-up.

Maxi came out looking anxious. His phone rang and he stopped to answer it. Just as he did so, a motorbike drove past the front of the hotel and slowed, and the driver handed Maxi a helmet. In a second Maxi was gone, and the bike was weaving through the London traffic. His phone was thrown beneath tyres as they sped away.

Chapter 74

'Who do you keep texting?' Tony asked Marco. Harold was driving. Maxi was sitting in the second row of seats. Laurence and Della were travelling separately in Della's car. The motorbike was in the back of the van. They were driving on the back roads towards Kent.

'I'm telling them where to deliver the shipment.'

'Ring instead, for fuck's sake.'

'Who knows about the laboratory, Marco?' asked Harold.

'Just me and Manson and the cooks we kept here. They stay for six months and then new come. We have it working sweetly.'

'Will the cooks work for the new cartel?' asked Harold.

'Sure. They work for us.'

'Why didn't Manson want to carry on?' asked Harold. 'He must have been making good money from it?'

'He didn't want to expand, go global. He was thinking too small. He was a small man,' answered Marco.

'And Eddie?'

'He was too scared.'

'Eddie didn't want anything to do with drug money,' said Harold. 'Never would have. He was against it.'

Tony kept quiet. Maxi stared out of the window, grateful to be ignored.

'Eddie must have suspected something. He was upset when I saw him,' said Harold. 'He must have suspected that his business was being used to import cocaine. I suppose he was bound to find out in the end. Manson couldn't keep it a secret, not if you were expanding.'

Tony glanced across at Harold and then at Marco.

Marco shrugged. 'Eddie was going to come in on the deal. I feel sure. Just others got to him first.'

'Others?'

'Yes, others. Now let's leave this,' said Tony, interrupting.

Marco was staring at Harold's profile now as Harold drove. Tony was sitting in between them.

'You were trying to force Eddie into taking on this deal,' Harold said, 'weren't you?' The van had become super-tense.

Marco shrugged. Tony remained silent but he had begun to fidget.

'Is that how it was, Tony?' asked Harold.

'It wasn't me who did it! I said to suggest it to him, not kill him.'

Harold drove in silence. He shook his head in disgust. Marco took his gun out and began cleaning it.

In the hire car, Laurence was in a happy mood. He was singing away to himself as he tapped his fingers on the steering wheel and periodically he looked across at Della. She pretended to be sleeping. It was getting difficult to cope with the pain. The sun was overhead, beating in through the car windows onto her face.

'Don't worry, Della, we'll fix that face. A bit of surgery. No problem. I'll pay for it. I'll look after you from now on.

You'll be all mine. Of course, it's going to take me a while
to forgive you for going back to your old boyfriend – I'm
going to have to be tough on you, I'm afraid. There will
be some punishment to be administered. There are always
consequences, after all.'

Della was grateful for the cool air when they stopped.
She opened her eyes a little to see gates opening to a self-
storage company and the Transit van in front of them.
Marco had got out to open the gates.

They drove inside and parked in front of a line of storage
units. The place was deserted. Laurence opened her door.

'Get out.'

Della opened her eyes a little more. Laurence reached in
and undid her belt. He brushed her face with his shoulder.
Della let out a muffled cry as the skin on her cheek folded
back.

'Well, move then and get out.'

Della watched Marco go inside a storage unit and then
return, grinning, to the van.

'Come.' He ordered someone outside.

Della watched as a face she hadn't seen for more than
fifteen years looked at her and almost lost his footing.

'Do you know her?' asked Marco, stopping in his tracks.

Maxi shook his head.

Marco looked at Tony and Harold. They turned to
Della. Laurence hissed into her burned face.

'Do you know one another?'

Della rolled her eyes, shook her head.

Maxi followed Marco into the lockup; Tony followed.
The others stood by the doors.

'I need to sit somewhere. I need a good light,' said Maxi.
'This is going to take some time.'

The suitcase of diamonds was compartmentalised; the uncut stones were wrapped individually and the rest were grouped in boxes according to their carat and worth.

Della turned her face from the sun.

'Can I sit in the shade, in the van?' she asked Laurence.

'No.'

'Yes, she can,' said Harold and he went into the boot of the van and brought out a first-aid kit.

'Do your face, Della.'

She took the kit and went to sit in the cool of the van, the door open. The darkness was comforting.

Marco came into the van and took the keys to the motorbike and picked up a sub-machine gun from the back of the van.

He looked at Della and grinned.

'No ideas.'

She used the mirror on the passenger seat and applied dots of antiseptic and pain-relieving cream. She swabbed her face with a dressing pad while keeping an eye on what was happening in the lockup. Della hadn't expected it to be someone she knew. Marco was watching every move as Maxi was jotting down his findings. After an hour Maxi got up to stretch his legs. He caught Della's eye and smiled.

The fact that he was a police officer gave her hope. She didn't know whether he still was, but he must have been planted. She thought maybe she was being monitored, watched.

'How much longer?' Marco asked Maxi. 'The shipment is being loaded at the docks right now. We need to hurry up.'

'It's a difficult process,' he replied. 'I have to grade every diamond. We could be here a long time. You were supposed to give me time to do this job.'

'You just have to tell the Zapata family that these diamonds are worth over a hundred million pounds.'

'I am not near that figure yet. You need to give me time.'

'We don't want to make the Crown Jewels out of them, for fuck's sake,' said Tony. Maxi nodded.

An hour later Tony was still pacing around the car park and Laurence called him back.

'Okay, we're there. We're done.'

'All good?' asked Tony. Maxi nodded.

'Okay. We have to go now.' Tony shut the suitcase and Marco carried it into the van. They relocked the storage and Della went back to sit in the car with Laurence.

Maxi stood waiting by the van.

'I can call a taxi,' he said. 'You don't need to worry.'

'Get in,' said Marco.

'My job is done. I can send them a written report.'

'Get in, or I'll shoot you.'

Before he got into the car Marco made a call to Jo. He made it discreetly so that he wouldn't be overheard. He didn't like loose ends. He didn't like plan Bs.

'Kill the policeman.'

Chapter 75

Carter slumped down against the wall of the cellar. He dozed in and out of consciousness. Now that he was no longer suspended by his wrists, the blood had returned to his shoulders and he felt the bond around his wrists had eased, stretched from the hanging. But the pain in his stomach came in sharp bursts with nausea, with breathlessness. The pain was growing all the time. He moaned out loud. He opened his eyes and saw Jo walking towards him pulling a length of wire, wrapping it around his fist.

'Time to say goodbye, my friend.'

Carter stayed slumped, groaning in pain. His eyes closed. He waited until Jo leaned across him with the wire and then Carter headbutted him. As Jo fell backwards Carter freed his hand from its bond. He'd been working it loose for hours. The strength in his shoulders wasn't there, so Carter used his body to push forwards on his knees and he headbutted Jo again, knocking him hard as he tried to scramble back and out of the way. Jo's forehead split open. Carter crawled after him. Jo picked up a piece of glass from the broken bottles piled in the corner and he lunged forward at Carter, jabbing at his face, missing and scraping the side of Carter's head. Carter swivelled his body round and kicked him hard, a double-footed punch kick. He sat back, waiting, watching. Jo's throat opened and blood began spurting. The shard of glass was poking out of his throat. Carter couldn't have helped him, even if he'd wanted to.

Chapter 76

'Must be our chemist friends,' said Laurence. Della opened her eyes enough to see the two men of South American origin. One wore glasses and was slim and slight; the other was taller and younger. They shook hands with Marco. Laurence was watching the proceedings. Tony got out of the van next and shook their hands also. The older man opened up the door to the barn and stepped inside, followed by Tony and Marco while the younger one went back inside the house. Harold was still in the van with Maxi. Della could sense the nervousness in Laurence. He was muttering to himself. Occasionally Della felt his breath on her as he stared at her. She heard someone approaching the car. The back door of the car opened and Harold got in.

'When is it arriving?' asked Laurence as Harold made himself comfortable.

'We're waiting for a guy named Justino to call. He's driving the lorry.'

'Who is he?'

'He's someone big in the cartel. He has to be satisfied with everything. They've already received half of it in cash.'

'I presume those were the chemists?'

'Yes. I thought you'd been out here before,' said Harold.

'No.'

'If you're going to be taking over this side of things with Marco, you better get out of the car and go and see how it works.'

'Why? What's it got to do with me?'

'You take over Eddie's business and your name will be on the company that they'll be using to bring the shipment in. Get in there, Laurence, and make sure you understand it.'

Laurence got out of the car reluctantly and Harold waited till he was out of earshot.

'You okay, Della?'

'Will you help me, Harold?'

'I'm going to have a hard job coming out of this day alive myself. You should have got away while you could. I suggested it, if you remember.'

'Yeah,' she sighed. 'Do you know what's happened to Inspector Carter?'

'I know Marco ordered him dead. That's all I know.'

Laurence walked back over to the car.

'Tony wants you inside, Harold. The shipment is an hour away.'

'Okay.'

Harold left. Laurence locked Della inside the car.

She watched them walk away. She had one thought now: if she didn't get away now, the shipment would be here and it would be too late. She had to seize her moment.

Carefully, she opened the glove compartment and felt inside: she had Sellotaped an object to the roof. She pulled at it and took it down, took it out of its cloth bag. It was the knife she'd been given by Johnny Mann, the Hong

Kong detective. She tied the silk string around her wrist and tucked it up beneath her sleeve.

Twenty minutes later Laurence came to check on her again. He unlocked and opened the door and leaned over. His breath stung her face. The heat on her burned face was rising.

'Hello, sleepyhead.' Laurence moved his hand up her leg to cradle her crotch. 'You make a good hand warmer. You're all warm and—'

Della stabbed him in the neck three times as she grabbed his head and held it locked in her lap. The warmth of his blood flooded over her thighs. When he stopped struggling she let him slip back down on the ground beside the car. She reached down and found the car keys and her phone in his pocket and then she slipped across to the driver's seat. Switching the engine on, she slammed it into reverse, and ran over Laurence in the process. Shouts from the barn went up. She saw Tony running towards her. She turned the steering wheel full lock and put her foot flat on the accelerator, spinning on the shingle. Behind her the air cracked with the sound of gunfire. She heard the metallic clunk as a bullet punctured the passenger door. She switched on her lights and drove at full speed.

Chapter 77

'Where's DS Willis?' asked Bowie as he came into the inquiry team office to find everyone busy sorting the contents of Manson's box. It was four thirty in the afternoon.

'She's searching for DI Carter, sir,' answered Robbo. 'She wanted to check out a couple of places that Melvin photographed. Marco left traces of Eddie Butcher at Melvin's murder scene, perhaps from the instruments he brought with him or from his shoes. We know Eddie wasn't moved far from where he was murdered because of the post-mortem results and the lividity settlement in his body. She still feels that somewhere on Melvin's East End Gangster tour is the answer to why Melvin was killed and where Eddie Butcher died.'

Bowie nodded. 'Inspector Ross has been in touch. He's up in one of the helicopters searching for the laboratory as they lost the shipment when it was switched. Did you find any possible sites?'

'Yes. We're tracing a few possibles, three of which are in Kent.' The contents of Manson's box were spread out across the three desks in the office. All other work had stopped in MIT 17. The papers had been divided into groups according to type.

'This is his Peruvian artefacts company,' said Pam, as she added to a pile on the desk.

'That makes at least twelve possible names that the shipment could be coming under.'

Robbo picked up the email.

'Here's our list of possible sites for the laboratory.' He opened a file on the desk for Bowie to look at.

'We are compiling as much information as possible on these last three. They are fifty miles apart, so I want to make sure we get the best chance of sending the helicopters to look at the most likely one and not waste their time.'

'Another delivery note to the farm in Sevenoaks,' said Pam as she handed a piece of paper to Robbo.

'Where's this one?' asked Robbo.

'Here.' She showed him a map of the area.

'The delivery address on this is a piece of land outside Sevenoaks and it was bought at auction by Manson two years ago. It's a detached bungalow set in sixteen acres. It was part of a farm that was cut up and sold.'

'The owner is a Mr Smithson,' said Pam. 'He's a single occupant. He's retired. There's a photo of it now from satellite. Mr Smithson got permission to build a large barn eighteen months ago but has largely left the bungalow unrestored.'

'Does this man exist in any polling register?' asked Bowie.

Pam shook her head. 'But Smithson was Manson's wife's maiden name. It's possible he got hold of those documents.'

'It's throwing off a lot of heat for a supposedly derelict barn,' said Bowie as he examined the satellite images of the farm.

*

It was nearly five and the lights were still on in Lev's bakery. The shop was still open. Willis parked by the church and started walking towards the Albert. She stood outside and tried to see into the boarded-up windows but couldn't. She stamped her feet on the delivery hatch in the pavement and squatted down to try to open it. It was locked. Willis got out her keys and slid the thinnest one she had around the edge of the hatch. She pulled it out and looked at the residue. There was none, the hatch had been recently opened.

She stamped again, jumped this time, landing hard on the hatch.

'If you stamp any harder you'll drop through,' a voice said behind her. She turned and saw Carter.

'Dan ... where did you come from?' She hurried across and stood looking him up and down.

'From under your feet.' He leaned on her as she helped him to her car.

'I'll drive you to the hospital.'

'It can wait, Eb. I need to help Della and Maxi.'

Willis called Robbo.

'I have Carter.'

'Is he okay?'

She looked him over. He nodded at her. 'He says he's all right but he hasn't seen himself in a mirror.'

'Tell him Della got away. She sent me a message describing where the laboratory is. It's a place we've been looking at,' said Robbo, 'a farm premises in Sevenoaks.'

Willis handed Carter her phone.

'What about Maxi?' asked Carter.

'We know nothing about Maxi, I'm sorry.'

'We'll head out there now, Robbo.'

'Okay, I'll let Ross know and you can liaise with him. I'll get a rendezvous point for you.'

'Thanks, Robbo. You need to get a forensic team and a body bag down to the cellar in the derelict pub by the church. I couldn't help him. A man bled to death down there. I'll write it in my report.'

Carter dozed in pain on the way to the rendezvous with Ross. His left shoulder was dislocated and made his arm useless. His right had some strength returning.

'What about Della?' Willis asked when Carter came to and sat up.

'She's incredibly brave, incredibly strong. I don't know many people who would be able to hold it together enough to escape from their captors who had burned her with a blowtorch and raped her.'

'Survival.'

'Yes. I just can't tell you how much I admire her.'

'She got away.'

'Yes, and, if Bowie asked me whether we should chase her, I would say no. She risked everything to deliver Tony to us and she came through with her promise. It's up to us to take it from here now.'

After thirty minutes of driving, Della reached Gatwick Airport. She got the bag out of the boot and changed into her outfit inside the car, then she kept her head down as she slipped inside the airport into the ladies' toilets. She looked at herself in the mirror. Her hands were shaking as she applied her mask. It didn't want to stick to the seeping wounds on her face, but it settled after a few attempts and then it felt good to have the burns protected. She looked at herself in the mirror and adjusted the wig so that it fell over her forehead a little, and pencilled her eyebrows to make them darker.

She texted Robbo and left a message for Carter, before removing the SIM, wrapping it in tissue paper and flushing it down the toilet. Then she dropped the phone into the sanitary disposal unit before going to buy her ticket.

Chapter 78

Ross set the helicopter down several miles away from the farm premises and waited in a Land Rover. He flashed the lights as he saw Willis's car in the lay-by. He pulled over for them to get in and looked at Carter.

'Jesus, are you okay? You need stitches.'

'Yes, I know. I'm okay. I have a mate in there, Maxi Seymour, he's pretending to be Roland de Soir, the diamonds expert.'

'Shit. I was hoping we could change tactics now Della was out and safe. We also have Tony and Harold to try and get out alive to prosecute.'

'Did he strike a deal?' asked Willis from the seat in the back.

'He's been in touch,' answered Ross with a smile.

'How far away are we from the farm?' asked Carter.

'Twenty minutes; the shipment's going to be there any minute now. They switched lorries on us before but we found it again after we knew where it was headed.'

'What's the latest?' asked Carter.

'We have thirty officers in the fields surrounding the bungalow. We know there are two men inside the bungalow and four men in and around the barn. We estimate there will be one more person accompanying the shipment when it arrives.'

'The snipers are in position on the neighbouring fields but they're not able to get the best view. They can't get on high ground. They are going to get onto the roof of the bungalow once the operation starts.'

'We know Marco and the Butchers will have automatic weapons. Harold has told us he won't arm himself and he'll try and duck out when the shooting starts.'

'Maxi has to come first,' said Carter. Ross nodded. 'And we need them to take acceptance of the shipment,' continued Carter. 'We need them to open the boxes and take receipt of the cocaine to test it; otherwise they will claim they had no idea what it was. Once the diamonds are handed over, we move in.'

'I know, and we need Tony alive,' added Ross.

They came to a stop in the gateway of a field. A unit of officers was waiting for them.

'Okay,' Ross whispered as they stopped the car and killed the lights, 'we're a mile away, on the other side of the barn. We'll cross over on foot now. You ready?' He looked questioningly at Carter.

'You can be more help to us if you stay here on standby.'

'Don't worry about me.'

'You all right, guv?' Willis asked as she watched Carter trying not to wince when he put his body armour on.

'Can you shoot?' Ross asked him.

Carter nodded. He was keeping an eye on Willis and smiled reassuringly at her.

He was handed a Glock .27 gun and two spare cartridges by one of the officers. Ross had already started walking.

Carter inserted a magazine, and then tucked the gun into his jacket pocket and followed.

Willis walked alongside Ross as they crossed the dew-laden field.

They reached the edge of the property, clipped the wire fencing and climbed through. Ross signalled to Willis to stay close to him as they crept towards the back of the barn.

Carter stayed back. He knew his limitations. He wanted to make sure he was there for Maxi.

Maxi had had his hands tied ever since they'd picked up the diamonds. He wasn't trusted not to run. He stayed shut inside the Transit van. He'd been in there all day. He was working through as many scenarios of escape as he could come up with. His eyes were drifting back to the motorbike all the time. He'd been a good rider in his time. He'd loved his old bike. It had all stopped when he got married. The bike had to go, to get a sensible car for the kids. The big snag in his plan was that he had to find some way of cutting the ties on his wrists and he had to get the keys for the bike out of Marco's pocket. He wished he'd had the guts to get in the car with Della when he'd had the chance. She'd seized her moment and now he must find his, but he had a feeling this wasn't going to happen, as the lights of a lorry came down the lane towards the farm.

'It's here,' said Tony, giggling, excited.

'Are you going to help me move him, then?' Harold called him again. 'Or are we going to leave him here?' Harold was standing over Laurence's body.

'Just drag him out of the way for now. He's not bothered, is he?'

Tony still had the blanket wrapped around his head
and shoulders but he had borrowed some shoes from the
younger of the cocaine cooks.

The lorry came to a standstill in front of the barn. Marco
went round to the driver's window and spoke to him in
Spanish.

'What's he saying?' asked Tony.

'He's telling me how he didn't bring the shipment from
the docks. It was switched along the way. He doesn't think
he was followed. This is Justino. He's a cousin.'

'Welcome. Welcome,' Tony said as he shuffled around to
stand beside Marco. Marco grinned and said something
about Tony.

Justino laughed. 'Hello, Mr Butcher.' Justino smiled,
flashing a gold tooth at the front of his mouth. He jumped
down from the cab. He was a better-looking side of the
family. He was taller and slimmer but with the same confident swagger and the same love of expensive clothes.

'Let's get a look at it and get the cooks out to test it,'
said Harold.

Marco went around the back of the lorry with Justino
to help him.

'What are you looking at?' asked Tony as he turned and
caught Harold staring off into the darkness and the trees.

Harold shook his head.

'Hey . . .' Tony hissed across at Marco. 'Harold has seen
something. Stop doing that and go and look.'

Ross's team froze. Willis didn't dare breathe. Carter
leaned against the back of a tree so as not to risk moving
or losing his balance.

Justino reached inside the passenger seat of the driver's cab
and took out an AK-47 automatic rifle and Marco got his.

'It's nothing, let's get on with this,' said Harold. 'Open up, let's get this done and we can all get out of here.'

Harold began unlocking the door. The metal ramp lowered. Marco started walking back. The cooks came out of the bungalow and walked over to the lorry ready to start testing.

Harold stepped inside the lorry with Tony. Justino and Marco followed and Marco proceeded to open one of the boxes. The older of the cooks stepped forward to take a scraping of the contents and then handed it out of the back of the lorry and down to his colleague.

'Five minutes,' he said, holding up his splayed hand in the air to emphasise the number.

'Okay. Let's start shifting this gear.' Harold began to slide one of the boxes out.

'It's pure.' The cook returned with his approval. Then he went back inside the barn.

'Get the diamonds and bring Roland,' said Tony.

Harold went to get the suitcase from inside the bungalow.

'All right to do it here?' asked Harold, walking up into the back of the lorry.

Justino shrugged. 'Marco says it's good, just need the expert to okay it too, then I'm happy.'

Maxi was led out of the Transit by Marco. Ross signalled for his team to start fanning out and to be ready. The deal was about to be done.

As Maxi walked towards Justino the talk in Spanish began and grew in volume as Justino kept his eyes on Maxi.

Ross whispered, 'He knows that's not Roland de Soir. He's met him once before. Stand by.'

'I told you he knew Della. He's a cop,' said Marco. 'It's a set-up.'

Maxi stopped in his tracks and then held up his tied hands as if he was about to remonstrate. Justino began firing. His body twisted as he was hit several times by marksmen and his gun carried on firing as he went down. The sound of shots cracked in the air and Maxi went down. Marco dragged him towards the barn entrance.

Tony scrabbled forward and picked up Justino's weapon. He carried on firing indiscriminately around him. A police officer tumbled off the roof of the bungalow. He hit another one in the fields beyond the Transit. Harold hid inside the van. Ross signalled to the main group of his snipers to stop firing. He singled out one officer. Everyone knew that Tony had to be taken alive. Tony stood in the lights of the farmyard and the residual light from the barn and he kept firing randomly into the dark beyond. A single shot stopped him. The officer hit him in his shoulder and he dropped the gun.

Officers ran in fast to arrest Tony and Harold. The cooks were handcuffed and then led to safety.

Marco called out from just inside the barn. 'I have your man and we're coming out. We will get in the van and leave. If you try and stop me I will kill him.' He walked out with one arm around Maxi's neck and another holding his sub-machine gun.

Maxi was limping; his right leg was bleeding badly. Marco had been shot in his side.

Carter crawled along the ground to get closer. He could see Maxi clearly now. Maxi was walking towards the Transit like a man on the way to his execution. His eyes locked onto Carter and Carter knew that there was just enough light for him to attempt a shot.

Maxi's eyes were fixed on the barrel of Carter's gun. He was just a few feet away now. Years ago they had been good friends and they had understood the way one another thought. A long time had passed since then.

Carter shouted, 'Now!' and Maxi dropped like a stone as Carter shot four bullets into Marco and he stumbled backwards with the impact. Two of the bullets went straight through him. Maxi picked up Marco's gun and made sure he stayed where he was.

'Just like old times, Maxi.' Carter smiled as he walked across.

Maxi shook his head, relieved.

'Christ, I need a drink.'

Chapter 79

20 December

Carter looked at his watch: it was half seven. He was in early for the debriefing which was starting at eight. He had to be at the airport at ten to pick up Cabrina and Archie. He hadn't seen them for two weeks. It seemed as if a lifetime had passed during that time. He'd told Cabrina not to be shocked when she saw his face. He had been stitched up; his broken nose was taped; the burn on his cheek was covered with a piece of gauze. His body was one big bruise and his left shoulder had been reset and taped up to keep it stable, but it was still in danger of dislocating again with any sharp movements or pulls.

Carter sat in the car park in his car. He wanted to listen to Della's message one more time. He called his voicemail and listened to her voice.

'I'm about to get on a plane, Dan. I hope and pray you made it too. I killed Laurence in self-defence' – he heard the pause in her voice – 'but I'm not coming back to make a statement, not now, maybe not ever. I loved being with you again. I just wanted to say that. If ever you need me, tell Connie and she'll pass the message on. I have to go now. Take care, Dan.'

Carter closed his eyes for a few seconds and smiled as he pressed the button to erase the message. He had loved being with her again, too, but now he understood why they broke up. They were chasing different forms of happiness. What brought Carter contentment would never be enough for Della, and her life wasn't real to him. It wasn't what mattered, the wealth, the trappings. It made him lonely thinking about it. He parked up and went into Fletcher House.

At eight, Carter stood and addressed the assembled team. The whole of MIT 17 were gathered to hear the outcome of the previous day's events. David Ross was also present. Bowie was hovering by the door with a big smile on his face.

Carter waited for the team to settle.

'Tony Butcher is now in custody.'

The room erupted into cheers.

'But, it came at a price, a high one. We have two officers dead, three more injured. So this success is tinged with great sadness for their families and colleagues. They died bringing a man in who was about to change the face of the UK drug market for ever, to flood this small island with enough cocaine to increase our addicts tenfold. They paid the price for the rest of us, and we are eternally grateful.'

The room fell silent as each officer remembered the dead.

'Now, we come to the celebration of what we achieved. Tony is right now shivering in a cell in King's Cross. He will be interviewed later on today. Harold is cooperating with us; he will also be interviewed later. Marco Zapata is in intensive care under heavy armed guard. We think he will live. When he comes to, he will be charged with the murder of Eddie Butcher and Melvin Pratt. Another of the

Colombians died at the scene, Justino Zapata. His death is going to cause a major upset in the Zapata cartel. We must expect there to be a period of bloodshed while the cartels lick their wounds. Both the Mendez cartel and the Zapata will be looking for revenge. Sandra Butcher was shot and killed this morning on her way to a hairdresser's appointment in Puerto Banús, a ride-by motorbike shooting. This will be the start of a tense time.

'Now we have the task of extracting information from Tony and Harold and making many more arrests around the country. We want to knock out the distribution networks, trace all the other laboratories and close them down. But we have that rare thing in custody – we have the man himself, Tony Butcher. Well done.'

A cheer rang around the room. Carter left Ross and Willis to finish the briefing as he headed out to get into his car and drive to the airport.

'Daddy!'

Archie ran full pelt into Carter's arms and Carter was so grateful that with stitches, with black eyes, with a hole in his cheek from a cigarette burn, his son still loved him and recognised him. He caught him one-handed and hoisted him up.

'I prepped him.' Cabrina kissed Carter on the good side of his face. She looked as if she were trying not to cry. 'I told him Daddy was trying out a look for Hallowe'en.'

'Take the mask off now, Daddy,' said Archie, frowning.

'I will do, son, in a while.'

Archie stared at his dad and smiled nervously as he hugged his neck.

*

Ross and Willis went for a coffee after the meeting.

'I hear you met my ex-wife,' said Ross as they sat down at a table with their drinks.

'Yes. I took the girls their dresses. You left them with me when you disappeared.' Willis locked eyes with him before he looked away.

'Yes, I'm sorry about that. I realised unless I stayed in Spain we would have no hope of catching Tony. The police were in his pay. I thought, if it looked like I was on the take too, I could watch them closely and monitor, and affect the outcome of the operation.'

'Was I drugged? I didn't hear you come back into the flat.'

He nodded. 'It was just meant to help you sleep – I couldn't risk having to include you in the deal. I didn't know how corrupt Garcia and Ramirez were until they offered me bribes that evening.'

'It's an odd thing to do to your partner.'

He shrugged. 'I did it with the best intentions. I did it because I cared about you. I had no idea it would make you ill.'

'I don't even take aspirin.'

'I'm sorry.' Willis sipped her coffee. 'Can I make it up to you? Can I buy you dinner? The girls would love to meet you.'

'Your ex-wife is expecting your baby?'

'Yes. Strange but true. We can be friends, can't we? I don't have many of those and I felt we bonded in Spain.'

'We bonded, until you slipped something in my drink.'

Ross went to speak and instead he shrugged.

'It was done to protect you at the time. You were going back to do a crucial part of the operation. I felt I could be more use in Spain doing what I do best. It would never have worked if I'd stayed to explain to you that night. Garcia and Ramirez would have known I was talking to you. It had to be convincing. I did it because I know you care about your job, you care about getting it right and you would have struggled with my way of doing things.'

She nodded, deep in thought.

'I care about you. I'm very fond of you.'

Willis stared into space as she thought things through, then she turned back to him.

'Italian. My choice this time.'

Epilogue

Christmas Eve

At seven in the evening Della sat in the Aqua Bar in Hong Kong. It had 360-degree views and floor-to-ceiling glass. Below her the skyscrapers clustered around the harbour mouth, lit up in brilliant colours, blazing like jewels in the dark. It made her feel alive. She'd forgotten how much she loved the bright lights of the city, and not just any city. Hong Kong was a place that felt as if it had no time zone, no sleep. It had its own set of rules. Only money mattered and she had plenty of it. She could reinvent herself here. She touched her face. It felt much better. The plastic surgeon had done wonders.

She ordered a second Bloody Mary and waited for the waitress to bring it, and then she raised her glass in a silent toast.

'To Eddie. To diamonds and memories and men I have loved. To you, Dan. To the future.'

A tall man, mixed race, beautifully dressed, appeared beside her.

'Is this seat taken?' he asked.

She smiled and nodded.

'It is now. Detective Inspector Johnny Mann. How lovely to see you again.'

Acknowledgements

Thanks for help with this book go to Dave Willis, invaluable as ever; and to John Jacobs, Frank Pearman, Katie Sarah Carew and Peter Selley for their expert knowledge. Thanks to Becky Long at Visage and Della from True Colors for being great listeners and sounding boards.

Big thank you, and one I never take for granted, to all my friends and family who make time to help me with every part of the creative process. I'm thinking especially of: Norma, Noreen, Traci and my sisters Clare and Sue, my Mum and my kids Ginny and Rob. Plus, there are so many others who show their support: fans and critics alike, both are much appreciated.

Marbella connections remain unnamed but much appreciated.

Big thanks to my agent Darley Anderson and everyone at the agency. Thank you to my editor Jo Dickinson and the team at Simon and Schuster.

Lastly, there are two special fans who helped me in naming this book *Cold Killers* and had characters named after them: Debbie Sturt and Sandra Church... I've had great fun with your names, but sorry I couldn't make Debbie and Sandra any nicer!